PRAISE FOR *THE CIRCLE OF THIRTEEN*

"*The Circle of Thirteen* is a remarkable tale, nothing less than visionary account of a new world order, fascinating and provocative."

—JOHN LESCROART, *NEW YORK TIMES* BESTSELLING AUTHOR OF *THE THIRTEENTH JUROR*

"A wonderful, uplifting thriller full of strong and unforgettable women, a book that will keep you turning the page."

—ABRAHAM VERGHESE, *NEW YORK TIMES* BESTSELLING AUTHOR OF *CUTTING FOR STONE*

"We open the door upon a world so near to our own—and yet so far. A fantastic, futuristic view of the reality that we may already have created."

—KATHERINE NEVILLE, INTERNATIONAL BESTSELLING AUTHOR OF *THE EIGHT*

"In *The Circle of Thirteen*, Bill Petrocelli has created a story that flashes forward and backward through time, creating a futuristic world that bears some striking similarities to today. *The Circle of Thirteen* is a true celebration of the power of women in the face of great odds."

—LISA SEE, #1 *NEW YORK TIMES* BESTSELLING AUTHOR OF *DREAMS OF JOY* AND *SNOW FLOWER AND THE SECRET FAN*

"A unique and thoughtful thriller."

—MARTIN CRUZ SMITH, *NEW YORK TIMES* BESTSELLING AUTHOR OF *GORKY PARK* AND *DECEMBER 6*

THE CIRCLE OF THIRTEEN

THE CIRCLE OF THIRTEEN

A NOVEL

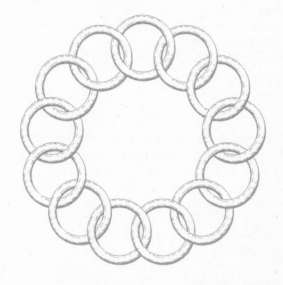

WILLIAM PETROCELLI

TURNER
PUBLISHING COMPANY

Turner Publishing Company
200 4th Avenue North • Suite 950 Nashville, TN 37219
445 Park Avenue • 9th Floor New York, NY 10022

www.turnerpublishing.com

The Circle of Thirteen

Cover design and book illustration: Maxwell Roth
Book design: Kym Whitley

Library of Congress Cataloging-in-Publication Data

Petrocelli, William.
    The circle of thirteen : a novel / William Petrocelli.
        pages cm
    ISBN 978-1-62045-414-5
    1. Women--Fiction. 2. Terrorism--Prevention--Fiction. 3. Suspense fiction.
    I. Title.
    PS3616.E8668C57 2013
    813'.6--dc23
                                          2013025154
Printed in the United States of America
13 14 15 16 17 18 0 9 8 7 6 5 4 3 2 1

For Elaine,
my first and biggest fan

PROLOGUE

LINDA SLIPPED the door open just a crack, but that was all he needed. Her ex-husband hit the door with his shoulder and slammed it hard against her, forcing her to stumble backward. She grasped the arm of the couch, fighting to recover her balance.

"Jack, don't start anything." She tried to stay calm, but her voice was cracking.

He glared at her and then looked quickly around the room.

"You got no right coming back here," she said. "I've got a restraining order that says you can't come in."

"Your restraining order doesn't mean shit. Where's Jesse? I want to see my boy."

"No. I'm not going to let you. You've been abusing him and pumping hatred into him—telling him lies about me and everything else." She watched him anxiously, waiting for his next move. "You'll see him only when the judge says you can."

"I want to see him now."

His eyes were bloodshot, and the smell from his body was acrid.

"I swear to God, if you lift that arm one more time to hit me or my son, I'll have the sheriff throw your ass in jail." She tried to stop shaking, but it wasn't much use.

"Where is he?" he hissed, stepping closer. "In his room?"

She found herself nodding yes, as she tried to hold back her sobs. "He's probably hiding from all the noise."

JESSE BURROWED DEEPER into the pile of laundry at the back of the closet. He was holding the medal so tightly that his fingers hurt, but he wasn't going to let it loose. His father said the medal had been given to him for bravery, so maybe it would make him brave too.

If he squeezed it hard enough, maybe it would make the voice in his head stop.

Are you going to hide there like a little pussy?

He closed his eyes, trying to make the voice go away. But it kept talking.

Stop whining. Don't be a little baby!

The voice kept talking and talking, like it had taken over his head. It sounded like his father, but it couldn't be him. He could hear his father yelling in the other room.

Did you flinch? Did you think I was going to hit you?

He knew the words. That was the worst part. He knew the words before the voice said them. But when the voice said them, they came out all twisted.

I don't hit you for no reason. I only do it to knock sense into you after you've been listening to the shit your mother's been feeding you. Are you going to cry?

He pushed himself further into the closet, trying to curl into a ball.

Maybe you're not good enough to hold that medal. It says your daddy helped protect the country from those fucking Iraqis. Now, you're holding it like a baby.

Stop it, Jesse wanted to scream. It made him mad when the voice started talking like that. He wanted to grab the voice and choke it until it stopped.

JACK STEPPED CLOSER, stopping just a breath away from Linda's face.

"Look, just go away." She lowered her voice, fearful that he was getting ready to strike. "Please. You know yourself that you haven't been right since you got back from Iraq. You wouldn't take your treatments, and—"

"What treatments? Those fucking Army programs? That was a joke."

"The probation department says you need a full psychological evaluation."

"Stop it!" he screamed. "I don't want to hear that!"

DON'T TELL YOUR mother I'm teaching you how to do this.

He remembered his father saying those exact same words. At the time, his father had a grip on his shoulder and was helping him hold his arm out straight.

Hold it tight. See that target? Now, line it up with both of the sights. Good. Now squeeze it slowly. . . . That's it! Did you feel it jump? Did you feel that inside you?

At the time, he'd felt the air around him exploding. And he remembered that his father had stopped yelling at him and was even smiling.

Do you feel that inside?

You shouldn't be saying that. You're just a voice. You shouldn't be talking.

Do you feel it?

He wanted the voice to stop.

Do you like that feeling?

The voice made everything sound spooky and dirty.

Do you?

If he could, he'd kill to stop that voice.

LINDA EYED HER ex-husband with growing panic. The last outburst seemed to drain his energy, but suddenly his anger was back.

"Jack? What's the matter?" She tried to see what he was staring at through the window.

"What's she doing here? I won't have her in my house!"

The back door slammed. Linda heard someone walking through the kitchen and was relieved to see her friend poking her head into the living room. "Linda, are you okay? I could hear the shouting outside."

Linda sighed. "Oh, Shirley, I'm so glad it's you. I didn't hear your car." As she said it, she saw the look in her husband's eyes. "Shirl, you'd better stay in the kitchen."

"I won't have it! Get that dyke out of my house!"

Linda stared at him, suddenly determined to guard her turf.

"This is not your house, and no amount of shouting is going to change that. You are not to come in here and start insulting my friends."

"She's not just your 'friend.' She's your goddamned dyke."

"You're so full of anger that you don't know what she is or what I am. I'm calling the Sheriff. Shirl, get the phone from the kitchen."

STOP! HIS HEAD was hurting badly.

If she was any kind of a mother, she'd stay home and take care of you. You'd be getting all the things you're not getting now.

Please stop.

Women make men weak. Your grandfather came home from Vietnam and found women getting all the jobs, leaving kids at home, and flashing their pussies everywhere.

He was having trouble breathing.

Your mother and that other woman are probably doing all kinds of stuff that's wrong. You know what the Reverend says: It's sinful. It brings the devil into the house.

The closet was closing in on him.

They think they don't need men. They think they don't need us.

Linda cringed as Jack's hand came out of his pocket, holding a pistol. "Oh, shit." Her knees started to buckle. "Jack, please calm down."

"I want to see him."

"Just put the gun down, and you can see him." She tried to stifle the fear racing through her. "We'll do this calmly; I mean it. But you have to put the gun down first."

He waivered but then set it on the table. He kept his eyes on it as he stepped away.

"Okay, let's go find him. He's probably in the closet, hiding from the noise."

As they turned to go to the bedroom, Shirley appeared from the kitchen. "Linda, I called 911, but they have me on hold and . . . " Shirley stopped in her tracks and let out a scream. "Oh, god, he's going for the gun. Let me—!"

"Don't!" barked Jack. "Back off or I—"

The noise slapped at Linda, hitting with such ferocity that she could do little more than whimper. Then there was silence, broken only by the sound of his feeble gasps.

"Oh, my god! Shirl, you . . . "

"I just . . . I don't know what happened. I thought he was going for the gun, and I tried to get there first. It just happened so fast."

Shirley looked down at the gun in her hand and dropped it to the floor like it was on fire. Reaching for a chair, she tried to steady herself.

"We have to call an ambulance!"

Linda held Shirley, while she tried to keep herself from collapsing.

"Okay. The phone's in the kitchen. Let me get it."

"My knees are a little weak, I think . . . Oh my god, Linda, watch out. It's Jes—"

One loud burst was followed by another.

"Oh no, dear god, please don't . . . "

JEWEL MURPHY WATCHED as her boss, the Chief Deputy Sheriff, lifted up the yellow tape blocking the front entrance of the house and walked through the door into the living room. She didn't know how he could manage to walk so slowly in these kinds of situations, but that was how he was.

"What have we got, Jewel?" he asked.

"We've got three bodies, two females and a male. One woman is named Shirley Gomez. Her driver's license was in a purse in the other room."

"The neighbors were slow in reporting the shots," she continued. "The paramedics got here when we did, but it was too late. We're just waiting for you to get here and wrap it up."

He looked around the room for a second. "Do we know who the other woman is?"

"Her name is Linda Mattock. She lived here. The guy is Jack Mattock, her ex-husband. She had a restraining order to keep him away from the house, but it didn't do much good. From all appearances, they all died of gunshot wounds."

He circled the room, pulling back the sheet over each body. "Is that about it?"

"No, there's more. We found a little kid in the closet in the back bedroom. We've got him in the car around the corner with an officer who's trying to take care of him."

"A little kid was here? Did he see anything? He must have been scared shitless."

"I guess. When we found him, he was just staring at the wall. I figure him to be about seven—maybe eight. He was in too much of a daze to talk. He had this thing in his hand that looked like an army medal that he wouldn't let loose of."

"What about this other woman? Was she living here?"

"It looks like it. We found enough personal stuff to indicate that the two of them seemed to be living together."

"Well, that's probably what set him off. He was already upset with his ex-wife for kicking him out, and now she takes up with a lezzie . . . " He seemed to realize that he'd gone too far. "No disrespect, but that's what it looks like."

"That may be what it looks like, but I'm not sure what the facts are. I knew the Mattock woman, the one who lived here."

"You did?"

"She worked at the big outlet store in the mall selling cosmetics. I used to see her all the time when I went in there, and we usually got to chatting."

"Did she tell you anything?"

"She said she was having a hell of a time making ends meet. Her pay was crappy, and she had no health insurance. The house is in foreclosure."

"Was she getting any money out of him?"

"Nothing. She said he never had a job after he came back from the war. The government put him in some psychiatric facility for a few months, but then they cut him loose. He just drifted after that. He used to come by the house and beat her and the kid."

"What did she say about . . ."—he looked at his notes—"Shirley Gomez?"

"Well, she said that she had a woman friend who was going to be living with her and sharing expenses. She said she was really fond of her."

"Can we assume that they were—"

"—You can assume all you want, but I think a lot of people have already gotten hurt by too much 'assumin'.'"

"What do you mean?"

"Linda told me her husband was spreading all kinds of rumors about her. He even got the preacher at their fundamentalist church involved, and that guy started making some pointed references about her in his sermons. That got the kid all upset."

He shook his head, as if to say that he'd heard enough. "Okay, it's pretty clear. Get it wrapped up." He shook his head in disgust. "Shit, another murder-suicide."

"I'm not so sure."

He looked at her sharply. "I don't see what you're driving at, Jewel. That's sure what it looks like." He started listing the points on his fingers. "The guy's in the house in violation of a restraining order. He's got a gun. He's got a record of wife-beating. Both of the women look like they were shot from about five to ten feet away, and the guy appears to have died from a close-in wound from the same weapon."

"I just don't think so." She paused, waiting for a reaction, and then kept going.

"First of all, the wound on his chest is in a spot that would be at an awkward angle if it were self-inflicted. Secondly, the Gomez woman appears to have blood spatter on her arms and torso that isn't from the shot that hit her. But it's in just the right spot, if it was his blood that hit her during a close-in shooting. We'll know more, of course, when we get the blood reports. There are also spots of blood leading from the living room back to the closet where we found Jesse, the little boy. He had some blood spatter on him as well."

"Well, that probably means that the kid ran into the living room after the gunshots and got blood on himself that he tracked back to the bedroom."

"Maybe."

"But you're thinking, maybe not?"

"Look, we need to run tests to see if I'm right. I don't see gunshot residue on the husband, but I think it's on the Gomez woman. There may even be some on the boy."

"So, what do you think happened?

"I think the Gomez woman shot him—"

"—And?"

"You're not going to like this." She hesitated for a moment. "I think the little boy shot the two women."

PART ONE

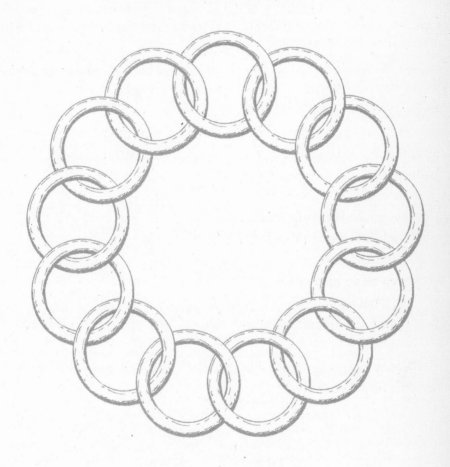

MAY 4, 2082

WHERE'S JULIA?

UNEASINESS HAD WORMED its way inside her, but Madeleine told herself to stay calm. She knew how to keep a lid on her emotions. And when she did so, she saw things that others might miss. That had been her edge throughout her career. It was that kind of self-control that allowed her to work her way to the top of the United Nations organization.

Now she was angry at herself for being so nervous. Quit pacing around like a bloody fool!

Her discussions with Julia Moro, her handpicked U.N. Security Director, had her rattled. The dedication ceremonies for the new U.N. headquarters were less than an hour away. And the closer those ceremonies got, the antsier she seemed to get. There was no reason for that, she kept telling herself. She looked around the big rotunda where all the dignitaries were gathering and saw that everything was calm. There'd been anonymous warnings of a possible attack, and there'd been incidents in New York City that *may* have been related to the United Nations. But that *may* was important. There was no real proof of anything. Those rumors and theories had taken on a life of their own, but Madeleine Boissart had to remind herself that none of them had checked out. There wasn't a single hard fact to suggest that the ceremony would be anything other than a great success. She could discount all of the worriers—all of them, except Julia.

"Madeleine, I have a bad feeling."

Two days earlier they'd been making another security review, going over every detail of their protection plan for the new U.N. headquarters. It was probably the hundredth time they'd done it. They'd been at it for hours, and they were both tired. But then Julia edged herself forward in her chair and repeated her warning.

"I know we haven't isolated a specific threat," Julia said, "but every instinct tells me something's wrong. It's too tempting. It's the gathering of world leaders, it's the dedication of the new building, it's the unveiling of the sculpture of the Women for Peace leaders—the whole thing is just a big, ripe target for anyone who wants to do us harm."

Madeleine didn't know how to deal with that. Even if Julia's warnings were true, what more could they do that they weren't already doing? If she got caught up in Julia's sense of danger, she risked being frozen with panic and indecision. And where was Julia at that moment? She said she was chasing after something important, but Madeleine would have felt more reassured if she were somewhere where she could see her. In the meantime, she knew they had to move ahead with the ceremony. The dedication was starting in a few minutes, and Madeleine had to trust that their security measures would keep things running smoothly.

MADELEINE STARED AT the Circle of Thirteen—the huge sculpture of the thirteen leaders of Women for Peace that stood in the middle of the rotunda. This large, bronze statue had been inspired by the scene from the final, tragic moments of that group of women. Now it dominated the main floor of the new U.N. building. Once it had finally been unveiled, Madeleine was startled by its power. She found herself choking back emotions that she hadn't felt in decades. She forgot her anxieties for a few moments and just tried to absorb it.

For the last several weeks Laria Kwon, the artist who had created it, had insisted that her large, bronze artwork be covered up to protect it from all the construction work in the building. Kwon's grandmother, Marta Kwon, was one of the thirteen women depicted in the sculpture, so she had a special reason for wanting everything done just right. The workers had unveiled it just before dawn. Now, Madeleine could see it in the way that was intended: bathed in morning sunlight from the large clerestory windows on Fifth Avenue and accented with multicolored beams streaming down from the huge chandelier that was hanging above. The dramatic lighting created a rhythmic pattern over the polished surface. At nearly four meters in height, the sculpture was the dramatic focal point of the building.

This was no ordinary statue. Everyone knew where they'd been at the moment depicted in this sculpture, when the captivity of The Thirteen had reached its tragic climax. In Madeleine's case, it was a café in Perugia where she and her fellow postdoctoral students watched in horror as the events unfolded on the vid-screen in front of them. Kwon's sculpture had captured the immediacy of that moment. The thirteen women were gripping each other in what would be the last seconds of their lives. The emotions in their faces were raw. Fear was mixed with hope; resignation was side by side with defiance. Aayan Yusuf was holding her head high in the way everyone seemed to remember. Wang-li Minh was still deep in meditation, while Magdalena Garcia was forever bowed in prayer. At the top of the circle, Deva Chandri was embracing the women by her side, her eyes staring straight ahead, looking somewhere beyond the agony of the moment. The rest of The Thirteen—the original leaders of Women for Peace—held expressions that became seared into the minds of millions on that day twenty-five years earlier. It was an unforgettable moment that had now been captured in bronze—the instant just before catastrophe.

THE DIGNITARIES FILING in for the New Charter Day ceremony were not the type to be easily impressed, but they all seemed moved by Kwon's statue. Many stopped to admire it, taking time to walk around and view it from different angles. Seen up close, the sculpture was a clear success. But Madeleine wanted to be sure the rest of the world would be getting the same view. She activated one of the flash-screens floating above her to get a quick video-image. The picture looked good, but it was only a pre-showing. The screen wasn't yet displaying the full depth of image that the omni-cameras would be transmitting. That test would come a few minutes later, when those self-propelled devices moved themselves into position to transmit images from multiple angles. Once Madeleine gave the signal, the cameras would send out pictures in full, three-dimensional holography. When that happened, more than five billion people worldwide would have an intimate view of the sculpture and the gathering of world leaders. For many viewers, the event would seem to be happening in their own living rooms.

Madeleine wanted everyone in the rotunda to quickly sit down in their reserved seats circling the sculpture, but hardly any of the guests were cooperating. That made her uneasy. The entire history of the United Nations seemed suddenly piled on her shoulders. The last two decades of that history were the heaviest. For the last twenty-four years, since its re-founding in 2058, the U.N. had functioned as the nerve center of a world that had been on the verge of collapse. Any breakdown now, any security breach—any disruption of this anniversary celebration—could have catastrophic consequences.

Few of the guests, however, seemed fazed by the importance of the occasion. The schedule called for the world leaders gathered in the rotunda to move to their seats, but Madeleine was dealing with people who couldn't resist an outstretched hand or an opportunity to schmooze. She'd have more luck, she thought, with a roomful of preening cats.

She tried urging the dignitaries to get to their chairs. Some leaders of the U.N. Legislative Assembly cooperated, but others paid little attention to her. The heads of the Social-Democratic bloc wandered off to the far end of the rotunda to peek into their new meeting chambers before sauntering back. Other members just wandered around as they pleased. The Archbishop of Canterbury was telling a long story to the President of the European Union about her days at the university with Bishop Maria Balewa. To make her point, she pointed up at the bronze figure of her friend, one of the Thirteen portrayed in the sculpture. Madeleine tried to interrupt the story, but they both ignored her. She turned her attention instead to the President of China, a balding, slightly overweight man with a brittle smile. He seemed ready to follow her to his seat, but then apparently decided he needed to say something to his presidential counterpart from the United States. To get her attention, he reached over a couple of people to tug at her sleeve. The security details from both countries moved in nervously around them.

This is hopeless, Madeleine thought. She looked around and found the President of the Russian Federation; he, at least, seemed happy to cooperate. He had his arm around the Prime Minister of the Caribbean Union, and the two of them headed for their seats, laughing as they walked. Madeleine knew there were rumors of a personal relationship between them, but that didn't bother her. She just wanted them to sit down.

MADELEINE TRIED TO calm her fears. Nothing was out of place, she kept telling herself. The guards were pacing slowly around the entrances, as they had been for the last few hours; none of them looked agitated. The electronic identification badges on the guests seemed to be flashing properly. The micro-signaling devices built into the walls and roof weren't showing any problem. The Mother Grid was monitoring computers around the world, and none of them was reporting any unusual military activity or anything out of the ordinary. None of the aerial or ground surveillance units outside the building had reported anything amiss. The national security teams were all moving calmly around the perimeter of the invited guests. Clearly, they hadn't seen anything that had them alarmed.

But her anxiety kept growing. There'd been warnings in the last few weeks—many of them. But none of the anonymous electronic messages could be pinned down to a source. Julia and her team had worked with the security services around the world and failed to find anything to verify that there was a real danger. More worrisome were the acts of vandalism and violence that had hit New York in the last few weeks. Two weeks earlier, a firebomb had exploded in Union Square at 3:00 A.M. after a timer had apparently malfunctioned. A few days later, an unexploded bomb had been found in a trash can across from Washington Square. After that, a bomb intended for the Grand Central Market exploded on a train. Nobody had been killed in any of the incidents, but that was more a function of luck than anything else. A wave of graffiti with an ugly, fascist theme had hit the city. Crude drawings of an arrow and circle, the mark of *Patria,* had been etched on several walls. Even though that terrorist organization had disappeared years earlier, their hateful symbol seemed to show up whenever right-wing gangs wanted to intimidate people. Julia seemed to think this was related to today's United Nations gathering, but Madeleine wasn't so sure.

Madeleine was born in France, but she'd lived in New York for almost thirty years. She knew how tough New Yorkers could be. The weather disasters and other environmental disruptions of the 2030s had hit their city with a greater ferocity than most places, but they had bounced back. And New Yorkers hadn't been spared any of the other problems that had followed in the wake of the storms and droughts, either. The cartel that had seized control of the world's food supply had squeezed the life out of New York's economy just like it had everywhere else. But when the power of that criminal enterprise was finally broken, New York had come back stronger than ever.

Still, as resilient as New Yorkers might be, Madeleine knew they could be as jumpy as anyone else. There'd been an undercurrent of anxiety in the city in the last couple of weeks. Every rumor of violent activity brought an outpouring of anguished messages on networking-screens on the walls of buildings throughout the city. In a couple of locations the postings were so voluminous that they filled up the message area, forcing some of the responses on to impromptu flash-screens. Passersby stopping to read the messages sometimes got into arguments with each other. One argument got so heated that it held up traffic on the transit grid for twenty minutes at Broadway and E. 34th.

Madeleine tried to keep this all in perspective, recognizing it for what it was: a generalized sense of fear that often accompanied any major event. Part of her job was to keep the lid on things, calming the concerns of her boss, the Secretary-General, and easing any anxiety among her subordinates. She'd been Military-Legal Director of the United Nations for almost a decade, and there'd been incidents almost every year that didn't amount to anything. Right-wing demagogues from around the world, who seemed continually angry at the U.N.'s social policies, would make some wild denunciations, and then other fringe groups would pick up on them. All of their ranting would work its way down to the lunatic fringe in different corners of the globe, but usually the threats ended right there. She'd seen this before, she told herself. This wasn't anything new.

But Julia thought differently. Madeleine remembered how she'd said it.

"We're dedicating a new building with all the world's leaders here. That's reason enough to be concerned. But there's more to it than that. It's the unveiling of the statue of the leaders of Women for Peace that has me the most uneasy."

Julia hadn't budged from the edge of her chair as she laid out her thoughts.

"It's been twenty-five years since the Thirteen were killed. Their story is all over the media. You can't walk down the street without some new commentary about them trailing along beside you on the news-screens. Most of the stories are upbeat—I'll grant you that. But you and I both know there's an undercurrent to all this. There's still a lot of anger and resentment hiding in dark corners."

"Twenty-five years is a nice round number. It's the kind of number that captures everyone's attention. It's just the right number of years for a lifetime of hate to bubble over in someone's mind."

Madeleine remembered Julia staring off at some inner thought as she spoke.

"If I were going to do something, this is when I would do it."

MADELEINE WATCHED THABO Nyrere, President of the South Africa Federation, shuffle over to his seat in the first row of dignitaries. He sat down, carefully placing his cane on the floor beside his chair. Nyrere was the only current world leader who had spoken at the original signing ceremony for the New Charter at the San Francisco Opera House in 2058. On that bright morning he had talked about his friends within the Women for Peace leadership and how their sacrifice had made the new United Nations possible. There were tears in his eyes that day. Now, twenty-four years later, he was getting ready to speak again, and the tears had returned.

Everyone was finally seated. It was time to activate the omni-cameras. Madeleine gave the signal to the Secretary-General. The dedication ceremony was about to begin.

She felt the buzz of a message on her vid-phone. Was it from Julia?

JULIA'S MIND WAS racing, far out in front of her feet.

As she cut across Madison Avenue, she spun to avoid a taxi that was honking madly at her. But that maneuver forced her into a near collision with a bicycle that sent the rider careening across the pavement. Julia yelled back an apology, but she couldn't stop. Right now, time was everything.

She reached the other side of the street near E. 84th and began weaving her way down the sidewalk, dodging baby carriages, people with walkers, and dogs on leashes. Every New Yorker who wasn't at home watching the U.N. ceremonies seemed to be out on the streets, determined to get in her way. She pushed through the crowd, mumbling excuses, poking furiously at her vid-phone as she tried to make emergency calls.

Her brain was flying in multiple directions. Dark alleyways from her past had suddenly been illuminated, and she wanted to explore them, to find answers to questions that had been gnawing at her for a lifetime. But all of that was for later.

For now, she allowed herself only one quick thought: the nightmares that had plagued her for years might not be the dead hand of the past trying to hold her back. Maybe they were the hand of the future pulling her towards this moment.

She had to find Jesse and stop him.

THE BLAST HIT with a roar.

The omni-cameras that had been focused on the dedication speeches were knocked out immediately. People around the world who had been watching the holo-cast of the U.N. ceremonies reacted in horror as a fireball seemed to spread across their living rooms. When that terrible image dissipated, there was a blank, eerie emptiness. Only a few cameras remained functioning. What they showed was a scene of chaos at the new United Nations headquarters. All that was visible were the bright tongues of flame that licked their way across the bronze surfaces of the thirteen Women for Peace leaders.

PART TWO

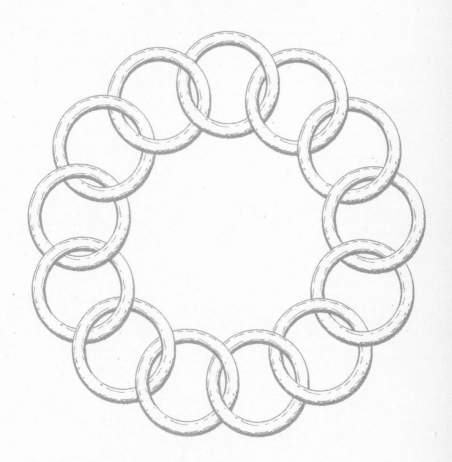

TWO WEEKS EARLIER

SUNDAY, APRIL 19, 2082

TARRYTOWN, NEW YORK

JULIA

IT WAS UNDER MY eyelids, daring me to open them.

It was a fear that hit me in that not-yet-awake moment when I was coming out of an uneasy sleep. That's when it usually happens. The images that seized me this time were those of a dying woman, a baby screaming in agony, and a fire that threatened to consume them both.

Sometimes I'd find Dhanye shaking me. "Julia, what is it? Wake up." But this time I crawled out of the nightmare on my own, wondering why it happened when it did.

What was behind it? My old fears were flexing their muscles at the worst possible time. Were they just taking advantage of the dread I felt about the upcoming dedication ceremony? Or was everything rushing together towards some awful resolution?

DHANYE'S SOUND SYSTEM was trying its best to calm me down, coddling a violin sonata, filtering it softly through the bedroom walls, creating the illusion that the music was coming from everywhere. The sunrise over our Hudson River home was beginning to thread its way through the matrix of windows and mirrors, turning itself into a warm glow that circled the room. Images of trees and plants from the community garden would be appearing next—more of Dhanye's doing—and with them would come a hint of the water that trickled through the trellises outside our walls. All of it formed a soft, green under-layer for whatever images might begin dancing above the wall's surface.

I've always been touched by the love that went into that project.

"Julia, we have to do something when you're jarred out of your sleep. There must be a way to soothe you. Maybe this will help."

Dhanye's idea was to ease me into the morning in a way that would put everything at my command. I just had to whisper to the room-controller, and the space above the wall's surface would be filled with murals in sinuous, pastel patterns. I could order one of my favorite scenes to appear, like the dancing dolphins or the kissing swallows from the walls of ancient Crete. Once I'd eased my mind with those images, I had only to edge over to my sleeping lover and find a place for my lips. Then I'd breathe out a kiss, and Dhanye would give a soft moan and roll over. Our mouths would meet, and we'd begin breathing lightly, tongues circling and probing, as we quietly searched for each other.

But some mornings, it didn't work out that way.

I awoke this time with a sickening fear that everything I loved could be swept away in an instant. This morning, I realized, I was pretty miserable company.

NIGHTMARES HAVE EATEN at me since I was a child. I'd awake with wet sheets twisted around me, convinced that the shadows were moving, frozen in fear that there was something that would swallow me up. Maya, my adoptive grandmother, would hear me and come racing into my room. Within seconds she'd be on my bed, holding me, whispering softly, trying to stop my screaming. Her words have vanished from my memory, but I can still feel the rhythm of them as we rocked together.

The basic plot of my nightmare didn't change much from night to night. Even softened by Maya's soothing words, I knew I had woken up screaming about my mother.

As I grew up, my terrors found a way to make hit-and-run raids, grabbing things out of the daylight and twisting them to their purposes, attacking me when I was least prepared. In my teenage years I'd wake up in the middle of the night, fearful of some nameless, formless thing, until my mind went racing after whatever anxieties it could find. It usually settled on something that would keep me awake for the rest of the night.

I have to admit it. I was a bit of a mess.

My friends noticed it. I'd be sitting in our favorite café in Larkspur, our little town north of San Francisco, and my mind would wander off, gripped by some inner shadow or just lost in a fog of sleeplessness. When I snapped out of it, they'd be staring at me.

My best friend, Chloe, would call me on it. "Julia, you scare me when you act weird like that."

They all had ideas for dealing with my problems, but none of them made much sense. One thought I needed hypno-transference therapy. Another argued for a nano-probe treatment. Chloe had a simpler idea: she offered to share an inhaler of distilled cannabinoid, which, she claimed, would help me blot out any unpleasant thoughts.

Maya put her foot down on all of that, but she didn't really have to. I'd already said no to them: I had to deal with my problems alone. It's a stubborn streak, I suppose, but it's one that's kept me going. Sometimes even now when I'm lying in bed, wrestling with worries, trying to read the shadow patterns on the ceiling, I'd happily blot them all out with a pill or some simple therapy. But that's not going to happen. There isn't any shortcut. Either I'm chasing my fears, or they're chasing me.

MY MOTHER IS still in my nightmares. Sometimes I see her as she looked when she first tried to escape from her life. On other nights, I see her as she appeared that last, sad time I visited her. As I've grown older, she's somehow become younger in my dreams. Often she has the face of a lonely waif, looking as she must have appeared on that day when Maya first found her on a street in San Francisco. And in a sad reversal of roles, I sometimes see her as a toddler. In that strange image—the one that woke me up this morning—she's lying in her crib whimpering and reaching out to a woman who is lying deathly still. Her cries and screams could go on for days, if I let them. The only way to stop them is to jar myself out of my sleep.

And Jesse is there too.

He disappeared years ago, and for all I know he may be dead. But that hasn't kept him from appearing in my dreams as a hooded, menacing presence.

IT WAS JESSE who killed my grandmother and left my infant mother in her crib near death. And many years before that—when Jesse was still a young child—he killed his own mother and another woman. After I learned all that he had done, I spent years chasing after him, following every lead, trying to track him down.

When I was growing up, Maya warned me not to obsess about him or dwell on what had happened. Violence of men against women is an old story, she said. Fight against it, yes, but don't let it take over your life. Maybe so. It was Maya who raised me, and she was generally right about such things.

But I chased after him anyway. I learned what I could from Detective Jewel Murphy, someone who knew Jesse from the beginning. She witnessed his first crime, and she told me that she had had a foreboding of what might happen later on. I did all I could to find him. I tried without success to learn his movements. And as I searched for him, I was searching also for anything that would explain his mindless violence on that day in 2030 when he killed my grandmother and left my infant mother clinging to life. I played and replayed the video of that event, but I never came up with an answer.

I finally ended my chase two years ago, realizing that it was futile. It became clear that this hopeless effort was cutting me off from my work, my friends, and my family. Worst of all, it was cutting me off from my own feelings. I knew I had to stop.

Although my search for Jesse was over, that hasn't stopped him from coming back to haunt my dreams. He appears even now as a phantom actor in an endless loop in which nothing changes very much. Each time, there is a woman lying on the floor with a man pressed against her, squeezing the life out of her. And each time, I can see my infant mother, huddled helplessly in her crib as her chances for sanity drip slowly away.

2030

NEW YORK CITY

THE TWO passengers across from him had pushed themselves to the end of the row of seats, trying to trap some heat in the corner. They seemed nervous—probably worried about the hurricane warnings. The last hurricane was only a week behind them, and the next was on track to hit New York within a couple of days. The girl squirmed against her boyfriend, wiggling her way inside his frayed overcoat. Jesse caught her glancing across the aisle at him. At first, it was a blank stare. Then she smiled.

You know what that smile means, don't you, Jesse?

Her face was changing; he was sure of it. Was he the only one to see it? It was mutating from soft to hard and then to something grotesque. He started to scream, but the sounds died in his throat. The subway car seemed to be closing in on him; the light in the car was getting darker and shedding its texture. Where did that face come from? Had she been foully conceived like the others, or was she just some post-op, hormonal creature out of a nightmare? The face pulsated in front of him, throwing off a sickening glow.

Don't be a little pussy.

He started to sweat; his legs were getting weak. He panicked for a moment.

Don't be a little baby, Jesse.

Then it stopped.

The voice had gotten the best of him, and he'd been consumed by fear for a few seconds. But now his rage had come roaring back. His brain-on-fire—that heated inner force that sprang up in these kinds of moments—was now in charge of things, shoving images out of the way, burying haunted memories. His nerves were under control, and his disgust was rising. He remembered what he'd felt earlier. He'd seen the two of them getting on the subway, and he'd immediately disliked them both. She'd been chiding her boyfriend about something. She was a bitch, and he was letting her belittle him. He was being humiliated, and he was too weak and stupid to realize it.

You could do it—or are you afraid?

The voice kept trying to goad him, but his brain-on-fire was now pushing its own ideas. He had the power now to take these two out. The smile on the girl's face was gone. What she saw in him now had put fear in her eyes. He could do it, and she knew it. The camera at the end of the car was using out-of-date technology, and it only had a side-shot of him. If he did it right, he could stifle their cries. If the other people in the car saw anything, they couldn't identify him. The speed of the trains had been lowered during the latest energy crisis, and the lights were about one-third of their normal brightness. By the time anyone saw anything—or realized what they were seeing—or got up the nerve to act on what they'd seen—he'd be gone.

Do it! You've done it before.

—Stop it! These two aren't worth it. Get out of here!

He was expecting to hear that.

The last command came from inside his head—from the brain-in-charge that he counted on at times like this to step in and take control. He shared a skull with this brain-in-charge, and the gap between them oozed with his admiration of its withering intelligence and utter lack of sentimentality.

He and his brain-in-charge took control. They now had the situation well in hand. You know why you're in New York. Do it, and get out of here! His brain-on-fire tried resisting them, wanting to scream some more about the two losers across the aisle. But Jesse and his brain-in-charge forced that fiery brain to shut up, sharing a secret smirk as they did so. But as they stuffed that restless brain-on-fire into some inner cave, they knew it would be ready for them when they needed it.

The train suddenly ground to a halt. He'd gotten on at West 4th, and the train had lumbered past three dark, abandoned stations. Now that it had stopped completely, the lights sputtered, leaving only a faint emergency bulb at the end of the car. Something was moving outside, but the graffiti on the windows made it hard to see.

THE NEWS COMING in on his data-sleeve confirmed what he'd seen on the vid-screens in the subway station: there'd been a small nuclear explosion near the Straits of Malacca that had blocked the channel and destroyed several ships from the food mega-company, Uniworld Commodities. The news outlets were calling it a major crisis. But as far as he could see, the pundits were just spouting their usual gibberish, trying to guess what it really meant.

There were hints that the Cartel was responsible. Uniworld had been moving in on the Cartel's drug-growing areas, and now it seemed the Cartel was hitting back. The fight between the two of them had been brewing for years, ever since Uniworld had taken advantage of the big heat storms and the crop failures to swallow up the major food distributors. That move had given Uniworld a stranglehold on the economy in several countries. More than that, it gave them the money to wean away the politicians that used to belong to the Cartel.

But not so quick: was this really a turf war? He had to think the way they think. Both of these giants knew how to move into an area after a catastrophe and pick up the remnants of the economy. They could both make disasters work for themselves. According to the charts now flickering in front of him, the prices of food and everything else were shooting up across the board in the wake of the nuclear explosion.

His mind was racing. Could the Uniworld bosses have blown up their own ships to raise prices and get more control over the market? Yes, of course they could. That was exactly the kind of thing they'd do. But there was something more. If he was going to think like they did, he had to take it one step further. This wasn't a turf war at all. All of this was just a charade. The minute the thought crept into his head, he knew he was right. These two giants had gotten together to carve things up between themselves. This was a merger. This so-called conflict was just a way of throwing everyone off track.

He needed to move. If he was going to get in on what was being divided up, he had to get the documents he needed and get out. He'd spent years with a group of former military contractors—black-bag operators—and they had taught him how the system worked: if you find a place where no one can touch you, you can control things from there. He was close to nailing one down. He'd been nurturing a contact inside the corrupt Baluchistan government ever since the U.S. pried that province away from Iran. Once he was safely there, he could do anything he wanted.

The people with the money needed him, probably more than they knew. The situation in the streets was dangerous; there were lots of angry, unemployed men. The food riots were getting worse. The fat-cats didn't know how vulnerable they were until some angry ex-employees got past the security system of a wealthy hedge-fund operator on Long Island. The man they went after was a pig. He had stripped their company of its money, and he was spending it on cars and a bullshit art collection. The guys who got into his estate just wanted enough money to hold up their heads—and, maybe, pay the child support some bitch lawyer was squeezing out of them. The pictures of that scene were now being played over and over on the news-screens. They showed the big-name executive, dressed in his golf clothes, lying on his putting green with his throat slit.

He knew they needed him, because he knew how to deal with that kind of anger. He could work with it, get inside it, and stroke it to a fine point. His brain-on-fire could reach inside men like that and grab at the source of their pain. He could draw it out and rub it against their faces. See it? Can you smell it? Can you hear the high, whiney voices, the feminine whimperings that led you down this path? Can't you feel all those pretty little straps they use to tie you down? Listen to me, I know. You're weak, he'd tell them, but if you work together you'll be strong. Right now, you're nothing. But if you bring your anger to a righteous boil and set it moving in the right direction—if you aim at the right target—you'll be something again.

If they paid him enough, he could turn a mob of men into a weapon.

THE TRAIN STILL wasn't moving. He gave a couple of hard kicks against the window until the glass popped out. There was water outside the car; he crawled through the window, landing in it up to his ankles. He heard footsteps, and a man in a workman's uniform appeared out of the gloom.

"What's going on?" Jesse demanded.

"An emergency crew will be here shortly to give instructions." The repairman started to walk away. "Until then, everyone should get back in the car and stay calm."

He's making you into a pussy.

He grabbed the worker by the neck and spun him around. "I asked you a question. What's going on here?"

The workman gurgled, "My instructions are . . . "

Jesse squeezed tighter, and the conductor pointed to the front of the train. "About two hundred yards," he gasped. "The water caused a collapse on the side of the tunnel. There's an electrical fire—"

He let loose of the workman and began running back through the darkened tunnel that the train had just come through, looking for a way out. He backtracked until he reached the Delancey Street station, which had been closed for the last several years. The central room of the station was bathed in a faint bluish emergency light, which made the mawkish-looking mural of an orchard on the back wall look especially pathetic. The hardcore homeless were trying to reclaim some space—and some dignity—from the rats that were roaming freely throughout the tunnel.

He jumped over the rusted turnstile and bounded up the stairs, emerging into a darkened street. The wind howled at him from between the buildings, and the rain was coming down heavily. There were a few cars but no other people. He walked several blocks until he found the street and the address he wanted. A mound of rags and debris blocked the door. He kicked at it, and he heard a moan in response. He kicked again.

"Hey, man, what are you doing?" A pair of glassy eyes emerged from the filth. They were part of a face that was groaning from the kick in the ribs. Another man was sleeping next to him, too stoned to open his eyes. Between them lay their paraphernalia.

"Get out of the way."

"This is our doorway—me and Pete, here." The man tried to sound defiant, but he mustered only a blurry coherence.

He grabbed at him. "I told you to move."

"Look," the guy whined. "We don't mean no harm. We'll do what you want." The second man was awake now. He had a fearful look, as he eased himself backwards.

"Okay, everybody freeze."

The voice behind Jesse was high-pitched and nervous. "There's a curfew in effect here, and you gentlemen are violating it."

Jesse turned around slowly and saw the outline of a National Guardsman, water dripping from the jacket and helmet. But it wasn't a guardsman at all—it was a guardswoman. Nothing about her was right. She was too small for the job, and she had a nervous bounce as she talked. This was a travesty, he told himself. Nothing about this woman could command respect. She was trying to do a man's job, and sooner or later she was going to pay for it.

"I'm going to check IDs. I want you to hand them to me slowly, one at a time."

She turned to the two men on the ground. "This means you too." Neither of them moved. "Listen, this is not a game I'm playing here. I told you to get up."

Her tone brought him to a boil. *You bitch, how dare you talk to them that way?* His brain-on-fire was screaming. His hands were itching to move.

"Okay, then, we'll start with you. I'll have to see some identification."

That wasn't going to happen. The last thing he needed was for her to run his ID through the scanner on her belt. He couldn't let someone like her drag him down.

"Corporal, will it be okay if I reach into my pocket for my ID? I don't want to surprise you with any sudden movements."

She nodded her assent.

He reached slowly into the lapel pocket with his thumb and forefinger, keeping the other fingers extended in an exaggerated fashion, as if signaling his respect for her authority. But instead of an ID, he grabbed the end of a thin blade that he whipped out quickly across her face, drawing blood and causing her to shriek. The surprise of his attack was all he needed to knock the rifle out of her hand. She reached for her belt to give a distress signal, but he grabbed her arm before she could do it.

The two drug addicts appeared awake enough now to realize that this was trouble. They pushed their way down the street into the darkness.

She was under him now, pinned against the back of the doorway.

No! You try to weaken me like that, and you end up being nothing.

He felt a knee, and his balls howled in pain. His brain-on-fire was screaming. She wiggled a hand free and scratched at his face, drawing blood down his left cheek. Infuriated, he pushed down on her even harder. He kept squeezing. She should have known this would happen.

JESSE PUSHED HARD on the doorbell. When he didn't get an answer, he leaned on it again. It was just a matter of time before the National

Guard came looking for their missing soldier. Or maybe they'd grab the two addicts and squeeze the story out of them. He needed to get in and out quickly.

He heard someone fumbling with the peephole, followed by a loud, happy screech as the woman hurried to unlock the deadbolts. The door opened, and she jumped into his arms, wrapping her legs around him and forcing him back on his heels.

"Jesse," she screamed. "Oh, my god, it's you." She kissed him violently.

A child screamed from the other room. "Honey, I'll be there in a second. It's Daddy! Daddy's come home to us." She jumped up to kiss him again, but he stopped her.

"Oh, Jesse! I was so worried that I'd never see you again."

She took his hand and dragged him into the other room where the light was a little brighter. "Oh no, you're bleeding!" She poked gingerly at the scratch on his cheek.

"Cheryl," he said, "I've got it under control. I don't need anything."

"I'll get you a towel." She came back with a damp cloth, but he brushed it away before she could push back his hood and daub at his face. He'd almost forgotten how much he hated it when she pawed over him—or when any woman did.

Cheryl beamed. "God, you look good, scratch and all. Oh, you're still wearing that thing around your neck."

"It's not a thing, it's a medal."

She shrugged, seemingly anxious to change the subject. "I can't wait for you to meet your daughter." She dragged him over to the crib where a toddler with brown eyes looked up at him. "Amy, this is your daddy! And, Jesse, this beautiful child is your daughter."

Cheryl urged him to pick her up, but he brushed off the idea.

"She's been sick and whiney. She caught that nasty new virus that's been going around. Thank god I could get the right medicine. I have to give her some in a minute."

He ignored her, pointing to a video-camera on the wall behind the crib. "What's that?"

"Oh, that's just an old system that was built into the wall. I use it to watch Amy when she's in the crib and I'm in the kitchen. But come here! Let me look at you. It's good to see you."

He walked around the apartment, checking the windows and doors.

"How do you survive around here with the electricity going out all the time?"

"I have a portable generator that kicks in if the power goes out." She stared at him. "Jesse, why are you still walking around with your hood and your jacket and your gloves still on? Come sit here for a moment. We have so much to catch up on."

"It's not Jesse."

"What do you mean it's *not* Jesse?"

"I used that name back then, but I don't use it anymore."

"Well, what should I call you?"

"It doesn't matter. How come you moved without letting me know?"

"Jesse, I didn't know where to find you. I stayed in the old place for a couple of months, thinking you'd come back, but you never did."

"You went off without me knowing. You shouldn't have done that."

"What was I supposed to do?"

He walked around the apartment without answering her. The place disgusted him. He poked at a mess in the corner of the room and then pushed down on the Murphy bed.

"Is this the best you could do?"

"I don't have a lot of money, Jesse . . . or whatever your name is. I got this apartment cheap. This building may be condemned soon; the rising water in the East River is undermining a lot of foundations in this area. We've had five hurricanes in the last two years. Five! Can you believe that for New York?"

"That lease, does it have my name on it?"

"Of course not! You know I wouldn't do that. You asked me not to put your name on anything, and I didn't. I've respected your privacy. You're not even on Amy's birth certificate. Jesse, I love you. I wouldn't do anything to hurt you."

He walked around to the door and checked the lock. "Is this the only way in?"

"Yes!" Her exasperation seemed to be getting the better of her. "You haven't even hugged your daughter."

"You said you were having a son."

"I said I *thought* I was having a son. I hadn't taken the test or anything. I just thought . . . I guess I just wanted a son, because that's what you wanted."

"Where are my things?"

"What things?"

"The box I left with you for safe-keeping. You didn't lose it, did you?" The rising menace in his voice seemed to startle her a bit.

"I've got that old box of stuff that you left when you took off, if that's what you mean. It's in my closet. I wouldn't just leave it behind. Don't you trust me at all?"

He moved over to the closet and began poking through the shelves.

"Well, make yourself at home," she said sarcastically. "If you'd asked nicely, I would have gotten it for you."

He came back with the box in his hand. "You opened it."

"I didn't *open it,*" she said. "The box fell when I was moving into the apartment and some of the stuff fell out. I put it back the best I could."

"Did you look at it?"

"Not really. There were a couple of passports with your picture and someone else's name." She suddenly smiled. "Was that it? Was that your real name?"

He worked his way through the contents of the box without answering her.

Amy started crying, and Cheryl walked over to pick her up. She rocked back and forth with her daughter on her shoulder, whispering something in her ear before putting her back in the crib. He let mother and daughter go through their ritual.

"When are you going to pick up your daughter and give her a hug?"

"How do I know she's my daughter?"

Cheryl exploded in anger. "What are you saying?" She lowered her voice to a hiss. "What do you mean she's *not* your daughter?"

He ignored the question.

"Listen to me, Jesse, or whoever you are, you can do a lot of things to me. You can abandon me, like you did before. But I will not let you deny that you are my child's father. I owe her that much."

He gathered his things, trying not to leave anything that might identify him.

"Do you hear what I'm saying?"

He did—and it started to bother him.

"Cheryl, calm down."

She grabbed at him. He didn't like her touching him like that.

"Just calm down. If you want money, I'll send it."

"Don't tell me to calm down." She started pounding on him with her fists. "I may not have put anything in those papers, but I know plenty about you. I'll get a blood test and prove you're the father, if I have to. I'm not going to let you get away with this. I know all about the years you spent in the mental hospital, I know what you did to your mother. I could maybe forgive that, but I can't forgive this."

He felt a sudden surge of anger. How dare she challenge him! Her closeness was making him sick. Each second she defied him was a humiliation.

His brain-on-fire sprang loose from its restraints. He lifted her with all his strength and heaved her forward, pounding her head against the wall. He heard a snap. She slid down to the floor and lay there without moving.

He stood over her for a second, trying to think about what had happened. He was still breathing heavily, but now his brain-in-charge was back in control. He needed to think. He kneeled next to her and tried to listen. He thought he heard a whimper, but any sound was drowned out by the child screaming. Her neck had probably been snapped, but he couldn't be sure if it was fatal. He took a second to calculate. She was probably going to die, but she might live. Unfortunately, he reasoned, that would be worse.

This wasn't what he wanted, but now he had no choice. A dead guardswoman outside, a vengeful mother inside, the questions, the investigations—that can't be allowed. He couldn't take that chance. He put his hands around her throat and pushed down hard until he was sure that she had stopped breathing.

The child was screaming at the top of her lungs, a sound that turned to a fearful whimper as he walked towards her. He stared at her for a second.

You're nothing.

There was nothing there.

He reached up to grab at the camera, but he knew he couldn't pry it out of the wall without some tools and more time than he had to spare. With all of the screaming, someone might be there any minute.

He picked up the box and left.

SUNDAY, APRIL 19, 2082

TARRYTOWN, NEW YORK

JULIA

MADELEINE AND THE others had gradually disappeared from the room. The meeting was over. As the holographic images faded out, I heard Madeleine say, "Julia, we'll talk in the morning." I was left sitting alone in the familiar surroundings of my home office.

Sunday afternoon meetings were rare, and this one had been blessedly short. Toki, my house-bot—a stickler for efficiency—was back at work, tidying things up. Earlier, he had slipped around the room, organizing the desk, darkening the windows, arranging the equipment, and activating the cameras to let everyone appear in life-like form. He monitored the gaze-detection lines of the participants and checked the quality of the holographic images while the meeting was in progress. Now, he reversed the process, putting things away, adjusting the lamps, and lightening the tone of the window to let daylight filter in from the garden. I decided to push the button that coiled back the glass on the window, allowing it to open and bring the afternoon breeze into the room. Toki would have done that for me too, but sometimes I liked to show him I was still in control.

The meeting hadn't accomplished much; Madeleine just needed to talk. With the May 4th opening of the new headquarters just two weeks away, she was nervous but unwilling to admit it. The increasing number of *Patria* slogans on walls around the city was making everyone jumpy. There had been warnings in the last few days—all of them anonymous, none of them specific. In fact, our technical team had concluded that they were all replicant-generated from some untraceable source.

But it was the bomb the night before in Union Square that had everyone on edge. Vid-casts in the city and the rest of the world were now chasing that story. Avram Sharet, my deputy director, passed around a video-memorandum from the NYPD. According to the vid-mem, the bomb had been set to go off at 9:00 P.M., when it would have caused maximum damage, but for some reason had gone off in the middle of the night at 3:14 A.M. Avram thought it might have been the work of amateurs. I looked at Madeleine to see if that news made her any more comfortable. It didn't. Even the rounding-effect of holographic imagery couldn't hide the concern on her face.

THE BREEZE FROM the garden finally enticed me outside. Dhanye was already out in the community garden talking to Moise, the retired man who lived across from us. He'd been there all morning working on a job he had assigned to himself: adjusting the catch-basins for the community rainwater system. The Weather Authority was promising a moderate storm for the next day, and he didn't want to miss a drop of it. At the moment they were standing near the rows of vegetables outside our window, where Dhanye was helping him prop up a large trellis. They weren't having much success. Moise's partner, Selva, who had been working in the fruit garden across the pathway, came over to help. The three of them started laughing as they tried to get the trellis in position, only to have it collapse on top of them. The scene was oddly comforting.

I learned to appreciate plants from my grandmother Maya. She'd probably smile if she heard me say that, because we both knew I spent most of my childhood years trying to resist learning anything. I had my own worries as a kid, and I didn't want to listen to her or anyone else. But things change. In my case, they seem to have changed after I met Dhanye—maybe, *because* I met Dhanye. Now I find myself enjoying my time in the community garden, edging closer to the feeling that Maya probably had during the years when I was growing up in Northern California.

Age has slowed Maya down. She's too old now to take care of the garden in our old co-housing community. But in my fondest memories, she is still down on her knees, turning over the soil, scraping around the edges of the fruit and vegetable plants, treating them like old friends. Like millions of others in those years, she tried to help the plants sustain themselves with less water, fewer nutrients, and less of their natural soil support. She learned to divert, cajole—and sometimes just outsmart—the invading pests and creatures that had been forced north because of the mismanagement of the climate. She had a special shelf in our apartment where she saved the natural seeds that the plants produced, hiding them like they were jewels. Years earlier, she had convinced herself that the crime bosses who ran the agribusiness cartel were probably planning to seize all of those seeds so they could coerce everyone into using their own pale, anemic hybrids.

The debasement of the food supply was high on Maya's list of unforgivable sins. She wasn't going to let me or the other children in our co-housing community forget it. She'd walk me through the garden and grab some lettuce or carrots to put in my hands.

"Think about where these came from," she would say. "It takes sunlight, it takes seeds, and it takes insects. It takes water, and it takes uncontaminated land. But mostly it takes people like you and your friends to understand how precious this is."

It's easy to see why she felt so strongly about it: she grew up in a generation that almost lost everything. It's hard for someone like me, born in 2043, to feel the impact that the '20s and '30s had on Maya and her contemporaries. The concentration of wealth, which had been building for decades, had left record numbers of people unemployed and teetering on the edge of poverty. But it was the environmental disasters of those years that shaped their lives more than anything else. Everything came down to food. The climate change and the resulting crop failures caused a sharp drop in agricultural production worldwide. That food scarcity led to contamination and food-borne diseases that hit close to home.

But Maya saved her greatest anger for the predators—the human predators—unscrupulous men who tried to profit from the crisis. As the food situation got worse, a syndicate of criminal money and hidden, private wealth began to flex its muscles. The Uniworld Cartel moved in to take over most of the world's food distribution system. By then, Maya and the others in her generation knew they were in for a long fight.

I heard Selva screaming in delight from across the garden.

"You and Julia are having a baby? That's wonderful!"

Dhanye was standing next to her, all smiles, probably telling her that the baby was due in October. That was the only announcement we'd need to make. Now that Selva knew, everyone would know. Selva headed the Child Care Services Team for our co-housing community, a group she called the "Grandmas Committee." Even with the due date six months away, she'd be busy in no time scheduling babysitting shifts for most of the retired women in the community as well as some of the men.

I didn't walk over to join in the congratulations. I'm not sure why. I just kept busy clipping branches from some of the Willow Hybrid trees that were keeping the western light from reaching a nearby Red Haven peach tree. The peach tree would do better, I knew, if it got more late afternoon sun; it was a piece of gardening lore that I'd learned from Maya. The Red Haven was a few meters away from an Elberta peach tree, and my goal was to do everything I could to encourage a healthy cross-pollination between them. If the bees refused to cooperate, I might even have to carry the pollen back and forth between the trees.

It was, I suppose, a little bit like fertilizing an egg to produce a child.

It was Dhanye who first brought up the idea of having a baby, and I quickly agreed—maybe too quickly. "Julia, are you sure you don't want to think this over a little bit?" We both knew that the thought of a baby stirred up some painful childhood memories for me. I could usually whisk them out of my mind, but sometimes they drifted back before I knew what was happening. No, I said, I was sure. We were both in our late thirties; it was a good time for us to have a baby. I said I wanted us to do it.

And I was sure I wanted it. Maybe I just didn't want to think about it.

I still remember a day thirty years earlier in another grove of trees a continent away. Maya was sitting next to one of the peach trees and had peeled off a piece of loose bark. She began explaining to me the bacterial disease the tree was fighting; she called it *crown gall*.

"This is different from the fungal disease I showed you before."

I didn't know what she was talking about.

"You remember," she insisted. "You wanted to know what it was called, and I told you it was *alternaria rot*."

I had to shake my head again and tell her I didn't remember.

She stared at me for a few moments, and then I saw the moisture welling up in her eyes. She finally had to get up and walk away, trying to keep me from seeing her tears.

I realized then that it was another little girl that Maya had told that to. It was a little girl who looked a bit like me. That little girl probably listened quietly to what Maya had to say. And on those days when she was in control of herself, that little girl was probably less rebellious than me.

But all that had happened many years earlier—before my mother broke both of our hearts.

I'D BEEN SITTING by myself in the living room, and my face must have betrayed me.

Dhanye saw it immediately. "Is there something wrong with Maya?"

Toki rolled into the room, anticipating a need. But his sensors must have detected an emotional situation beyond his capabilities. He turned and slid back out.

"I don't really know. I had something I wanted to talk to her about. It's only 5:00 in California on a Sunday afternoon. I thought she'd still be awake."

Dhanye sat down next to me, grabbing my hand and giving it a squeeze. It was a gesture that held a special power for us. Light fingers, dark fingers; one supporting the other, each giving the other strength.

"Julia, Maya's ninety-five. Sometimes people that age just need to sleep for no apparent reason. You know the health problems she's had."

"I know. It's just . . . " I didn't know how to complete the thought. "I'm sorry," I finally said. "I'm just glad you're here with me."

We both sat there for a moment, fingers sliding softly against each other.

When I was growing up, Maya Flores was everything for me. She was my adoptive grandmother, but she did more than any parent could have done. I only began to understand that after my hopes for a normal life with my mother had been dashed. The age difference between us was more than fifty years. Maya's children, Lara and Antonio, were old enough to be my parents. But that hardly made a difference.

Maya's story was my story.

2032

SAN FRANCISCO

MAYA

THE IMAGE OF a thin, elderly man jumped without warning on to Maya's vid-screen. His face was contorted with fear. There were sounds of explosions and screams mixed with an unmistakable cry for help. Maya tried the controls, but the image froze. She tried shouting commands—anything to get the transmission open again. Nothing worked. She was left staring at the terrified face of her client etched into the screen.

Maya grabbed what she needed from her cubicle and fought her way through the maze of desks in the Social Services Agency. Everything seemed to be in her way. Did anyone know what was happening at the Verafoods warehouse? A woman's group had been picketing the building, and Maya wondered whether that demonstration was still going on. Another social worker across the room said she'd heard reports of a fire. That news left Maya feeling weak for a moment, but by the time she reached the door her determination was kicking in.

"If you can reach Eloni, tell her I'm headed towards the Verafoods warehouse."

She sensed she was going to need the help of Eloni Ubaka, her student intern, and anyone else she could find.

Maya raced down five flights of stairs, not bothering to try the elevator. It had only worked sporadically in recent weeks. Right now, it would just slow her down. She hit the street, half walking, half running. The air was a brownish gray, and it had a bite to it. The fires in the East Bay hills had caused the Air Quality Index to crawl up into the red zone. She could already feel the pollutants scraping at her throat. She thought about going back for the surgical mask in her desk drawer, but she didn't have time.

A lone taxi went by without stopping. Even the *illegals*—the old, creaking pickup trucks that had been retrofitted for passengers—were so stuffed with riders that they didn't bother to slow down. She kept looking over her shoulder for a bus. However, the intervals between buses had been getting longer in recent months. No one had officially announced a cut in service, but that's what it felt like.

She cursed her vid-phone as she ran. The outlaw network she was using was painfully slow. She finally started getting some information: the blaze was at one of the Verafoods' buildings, a block-long structure owned by Verafoods' parent company, Uniworld Commodities, down in the warehouse district. There was a food warehouse on the main floor and a rabbit-warren of apartments above it. The fire department was calling it a multi-alarm fire. As she was running, she got a message from Eloni, who was several blocks closer. "From what I can see, it looks pretty bad."

IT WAS GABE's aging, desperate face she had seen on her office screen. Gabe Polecki was a client, but he'd become more than that. He was a friend—one of the few close friends she had. When he'd first walked into her office in 2030, two years earlier, everyone was in a gloomy mood. She and her colleagues had been trying to digest the latest grim unemployment figures. How would this affect their own jobs as social workers? Would the company that held the contract for city workers start another round of layoffs? The news-screen had been showing frightening pictures of the nuclear explosion off the Straits of Malacca. Would that mean more food shortages? Would this weaken Uniworld's control over the food system, or would it just get tighter? The rumor was that the food giant and the drug lords had joined in a single cartel. Gloom hovered around their desks, as they wondered how much more bad news they could take.

But something about Gabe cheered her up that day. He walked slowly, a painful step-by-step passage along the frayed carpet leading to her cubicle. He settled into the metal chair, stretching out his weak leg until it came to rest against the waste can under her desk. Switching hands on his cane, he wiggled a bit to find a more comfortable position for his hip. When he was through with that maneuver, he tapped her desk lightly, as if to let her know that he was through being a bother. Then he gave her a big smile.

Maya's job involved learning things about her clients, but she ended up sharing a lot about herself with Gabe. She was new to San Francisco and hardly knew anyone outside of her office. She spent most of her waking hours working, fighting long lines in the markets, and taking care of her two kids. Gabe listened quietly to her problems.

Her relationship with Gabe was a two-way street. If he was ever desperate, he knew to call her first. She set it up that way. He had no idea how to program his vid-phone. *Look, doll, can you help me with this? I gave up trying to work these things about twenty years ago.* Maya could never resist an old man with a twinkle in this eye—and Gabe, at eighty-seven, had eyes that were always alive. She set up his vid-phone with a one-stop, emergency voice command. Just call out my name, she told him, and the vid-phone will know how to reach me. *Really? Maybe I'll call you for a date.* He was a complete flirt, but Maya, at age forty-four, had to admit she loved it. *If I were thirty years younger, believe me I'd be making my move right about now.*

Gabe took an immediate interest in her children. He picked up the pictures of Lara and Antonio from Maya's desk and studied them. "I can see how precious they are to you." Maya didn't know how poignant those words would become.

"So it's just you and the children. Is there anybody else in your life?"

If another client had asked her that, Maya would have cut him off. But she didn't mind it from Gabe. She told him about the divorce she went through in Los Angeles. "There's no one at the moment," she added. There must have been an edge to her voice.

"Ah, don't worry about it. You're so . . . " He seemed to grope for the right words, not quite finding them. Finally, he just blurted it out. "I know you'll find someone."

Gabe had a regular appointment each month, but he came by much more often. Sometimes he brought her flowers and put them in a little cup on her desk. Where he found them, God only knows. Once in a while he had a question he needed answered, but usually it wasn't much of anything. They both knew it was a pretext. *I come here because I love your plush office.* That got them both laughing, as they squeezed into her cubicle.

After a while, Maya realized that Gabe's cheerfulness was often an act. His pain was evident every time he lowered himself into the chair. He tried to laugh off his leg injury and his limp. *I picked it up in Vietnam. I got it from one of our own fucking land mines, if you'll pardon my French.* When he was younger, he said, the injury didn't hurt as much as it did now. He'd had a couple of operations that patched him up to the point where he could hold down a job. *I wrangled one of the cushier jobs in Detroit, testing seats on the assembly line. I used to spend a lot of time just sitting on my ass.*

But a lot of things had gotten worse as he got older. There was a sadness wearing at him that was only visible when you knew him. Sometimes Maya caught him just staring at nothing, lost somewhere in the past. He finally told her what it was. There were times, he said, when his mind circled around until he found his way back to his daughter, Addy. She was his only child. His sadness—all of his hidden pain—began with her.

Captain Adrienne Polecki was a U.S. Army nurse. He showed Maya a picture of her. She was a tall, striking redhead, just a few years older than Maya would have been at the time the picture was taken. She had

Gabe's smile. She graduated first in her class. According to Gabe, she was always first in everything.

She was also the first in her unit to be killed by a roadside bomb in Iraq.

Gabe told the story almost without emotion, but Maya couldn't control her own tears as she listened. When he mentioned the year Addy had died—2006—Maya's insides twisted into knots. Her mother had died of cancer that same year. As she listened to Gabe, she felt a connection that was almost more than she could bear. She'd lost the only parent she'd ever known within weeks of his loss of his only child.

A few months after Addy's death, Gabe was laid off. He and his wife, Estelle, didn't know what to do with themselves. They finally put together what little money they had and moved into a senior housing unit in Arizona. But he didn't really like that part of the country. Then, when the firestorms had hit that area six years ago, they lost even that. Like a lot of refugees from the weather disasters, they'd come to Northern California. But within a year, his wife had developed uterine cancer and died. Gabe was on his own.

He'd reconciled himself to how he was living now, and he didn't like to discuss it. The last thing he wanted was to be a bother to anyone. But Maya pushed him on it.

"You have to get out of that place you're in. The Verafoods building is a health hazard and a firetrap."

Gabe shrugged. "I don't get it. There are all these people living upstairs in cramped little places, with most of them working downstairs for crappy pay. It's like something out of the nineteenth century."

"That's how they operate, Gabe. There's a lot of criminal money behind Verafoods. They get themselves exemptions, and then they pay off the inspectors on top of that. You mention workers' rights or tenants' rights to them, and they just laugh it off—or they'll send somebody out to rough you up."

He shrugged. "So, where am I supposed to go? You've been looking for something for me, but you said yourself there's nothing I could afford."

"I know." Maya couldn't get the irritation out of her voice. Her frustration was more with herself than with him. "Maybe you could stay with me for a while."

Gabe shook his head. "That's nice of you to offer. But remember, I saw your little apartment when you had me over for dinner. You don't even have room to turn around in there. Whose bed would I take—Antonio's or Lara's?"

"We'd figure out a way."

"I appreciate that, but there are lots of people in the same boat as me. There're maybe three or four hundred people living above that warehouse. Lots of them have little children. Are you going to find something for them too?"

His comment stung a little. "I'm doing the best I can, Gabe."

Gabe was suddenly contrite. "I didn't mean that the way it sounded. You're working in an impossible situation." He smiled a little, teasing a small grin from her. "You're a better friend than any old guy like me deserves."

MAYA COULD HEAR the blaze roaring its way through the huge structure, coughing up pieces of the building in loud, cackling bursts. A block away, she was forced to slow down. People in the street were blocking everything, and their numbers seemed to be growing. In front of the crowd was a set of hastily erected barricades. Behind them were men wearing armbands that said "SFPD Auxiliary Police." They looked edgy and nervous, unsure of what they'd do if pushed. Maya recognized them immediately as contract-cops—hired guards from SecureCorps, a company that mostly did enforcement work for the big corporations. They were widely hated by her clientele. But when the police were shorthanded—like now—they brought the SecureCorps cops in to help.

People pleaded with the guards to let them past the barricades to look for relatives or friends caught in the fire. The younger men were stripped down and shirtless in the oppressive heat. Everyone looked restless. One group lunged forward, but a burly guard met the man in front with a rifle-butt to the head. A woman screamed that these were the same men that had brutalized the family next door to her a week ago, dragging a child out of the house headfirst during an eviction. How come they have jobs when we can't find any? one man shouted. Two other men yelled out a story they'd heard about a SecureCorps driver—one who'd run over a child in a picket line a month earlier, killing him. Those pickets had been protesting the same conditions that had now led to this fire. "Murderers," the chant began. "Child-killers!"

Maya told herself to keep moving. She eased towards the edge of the last barricade and slipped around it just as the crowd made another surge forward. She kept close to the side of the building, until she reached the corner. There, the full scale of the catastrophe hit her. The Verafoods building was totally ablaze; large parts of it had already crashed to the ground, and the smoke and heat were so intense that she found it hard to breathe. Water and debris were everywhere, turning the street into a slick, sinister obstacle course. The fire had spread to adjacent buildings. Maya found herself pushed against the wall as a crew of firefighters raced past her.

She suddenly realized the futility of her situation. She couldn't think of anything to do to help. She heard shouts from across the intersection, where the police were holding people back from a side street. A group of women were pleading with the cops to let them by, and Maya recognized them as part of the group that had been picketing the building. "The medics need our help," the women were shouting. One of them, a woman in a saffron scarf, had eased her way forward and was passionately pleading her case to the officer in charge. Maya wondered if she should try to join up with them.

Then she heard a familiar voice. "Maya!"

Eloni Ubaka was running towards her from the direction of the fire. Her jeans were covered with soot, and her sweatshirt was ripped in a couple of places. She had streaks of ash on her face where she'd probably used her hands to wipe off the sweat. Maya thought her young student intern might be on the edge of collapse.

"I'm okay," Eloni assured her. "I just need to rest for a second."

Maya started besieging her with questions. Are there any survivors? Is there an emergency area? Can we go back there? Can we—

"Maya," Eloni stopped her.

"I have to tell you . . . " she hesitated for a second, and then she blurted it out. "Maya, Gabe didn't make it. I know how close you were to him. I'm really sorry."

Maya felt the energy draining out of her as she protested against the news. "How can you be sure? Did you . . . did you see his body?"

Eloni nodded that she had; there was a temporary morgue on the other side of the building. Maya couldn't accept the news. There's all this confusion, she said. It would be hard to recognize anybody. She reeled out objections, not really believing any of them.

Eloni nodded. Then she pulled something out of her sweatshirt and held it out to her. It was Gabe's vid-phone. For a second, Maya just stared at it, holding back from taking it. If she didn't touch it, maybe this wouldn't be true. When she finally had it in her hands, she rubbed it absently. What should she do with it? It was just a piece of machinery, but it was the last remembrance she'd ever have of her friend. She looked for something to lean against. Eloni asked if she could help. Maya shook her head no.

She stayed that way for a few minutes, fiddling with the controls of the phone, not expecting anything. Given Gabe's ineptitude with the device, there wouldn't be much to see. Unexpectedly, his auto-image popped up on the screen. Maya had set it up for him, but she didn't think he knew how to use it. From the looks of it, he'd been trying to tie that image to a message that was in his drafts folder. She clicked to see what it was.

"Maya, I just want to tell you how much our friendship has meant to me." It was the image of Gabe speaking to her. "I've been working up the nerve to send this to you."

Tears came to her eyes, as she found herself sinking to the ground and bawling uncontrollably. But her fingers kept going until she got to the end of it.

"There's always someone out there who will love you. I know that now. I think maybe it happens when you least expect it. That's how it happened to me."

"I guess you just have to be ready for it."

TUESDAY, APRIL 21, 2082

TARRYTOWN, NEW YORK

JULIA

I LEANED MY head back against the tile, breathing in wisps of steam from the heated pool. The soothing feeling crept up my spine and spread to my limbs.

I'd been poring over reports all day, but I'd gotten nowhere. Madeleine and I had talked several times, but we were still going over the same old questions. I had to stop for a while. I felt a little guilty about it, but at that moment I was greedily sharing a wonderful feeling. An outstretched leg rose out of the water like a sleek, elegant waterfowl, hovering for a second, before it landed lightly on my shoulder. I kissed each of the toes, drawing the foot closer until it was warm against my cheek. I stretched out my own leg until it touched the tile on the other side. My foot came to rest on Dhanye's shoulder. It was just a hint. Ahhh—the hint was taken.

The baby, of course, floated between us, confined at the moment to its own pool of amniotic fluid. Was she—or maybe he—enjoying this moment as much as we were?

"Are you sorry we didn't choose the baby's sex in advance?"

"No. I'm fine with the way we did it," Dhanye said.

"I thought because of what happened to Raji you would—"

"No, really, I just want a healthy child." Dhanye's smile turned into a slight laugh. "Julia, we've talked about this a lot. I know how you feel. You don't even want to know the baby's sex before it's born, let alone choose it. That's fine."

"I just think . . . well, maybe it's better to leave that one thing alone."

The pool was my favorite place, nestled, as it was, in a room on the lower floor. The house was Dhanye's when we met, but it was my home now as well. The wall at one end was dominated by the softly lit image of the Woman of Thera—a figure of delightful, insouciant charm. She shimmered over the tiles, reaching out to harvest the ancient plants in front of her. Her long hair, striped pants, and open bodice set the tone for her pose. She looked as supremely confident as she must have felt when some unknown Minoan artist painted her 4,500 years earlier. At the other end of the pool, water flowed from an opening in the ceiling; it was a soft drop that seemed more like a mist than a waterfall. The pool itself was one stop in a continuous, solar-powered flow of water. It was part of a loop that pumped and filtered the water up to the vegetable trellises on the side of the house before allowing it to flow back down. The light in the room responded to our moods, increasing in brightness if we were swimming and lowering itself to a soft glow when we just wanted to be close to each other. This was the pool where we fell in love.

I waded the brief distance between us and held Dhanye in an embrace.

"Darling, it's morning in Mumbai," I finally whispered, easing away slightly. I got a nod of understanding. "We better head upstairs and get ready."

IT WAS THE anniversary of Deva Chandri's birth. If she were alive, Dhanye's grandmother would have been ninety-six years old.

When I married Dhanye Chandri, I knew I was marrying into the legend to Deva Chandri and the thirteen leaders of Women for Peace. It was a strange sensation. The story of the Thirteen was known to one degree or another by almost everyone on the planet, but feeling it up close gave it an added poignancy. I felt their triumphs and their agony a little more intensely. And there are obligations that went along with the legacy. When Madeleine informed me that the U.N. Events Committee had chosen Dhanye to give the response on behalf of the thirteen families at the dedication ceremonies, she seemed surprised at my subdued response. I knew that it was an honor—I even said so. But Dhanye would be seated there in the front row of the dignitaries, right in the center of the rotunda. It was just one more thing to worry about.

As the unofficial leader of Women for Peace, Deva Chandri has always evoked an outpouring of emotion on her birthday. The other twelve leaders inspired the same kinds of reaction. Melinda O'Connor's birthday is now a national holiday in Australia. Rebecca Meyer has been the focus of ceremonies each year in Jewish congregations across America. Maria Balewa and Aayan Yusuf both have annual pageants in their honor in Africa. And because the Thirteen were killed on a mission to protect the lives of other women who were threatened with death, it's no surprise that these occasions have always had a particular significance for women.

The flood of good feelings on Deva Chandri's birthday, however, threatened to overwhelm the memory of the woman herself. Dhanye's sister, Indira, was worried by the cult-like aspects of some of the celebrations. Last year she insisted that the annual ceremony be brought under control with a more family-centered event in Mumbai, the city where Deva was born. It should be brief and dignified. The most appropriate place, Indira suggested, would be the Deva Chandri Spiritual Center, which had been opened in her honor fifteen years earlier. Dhanye readily agreed to the idea.

We made ourselves comfortable on the couch while Toki activated the holo-transmission system that connected us to Mumbai. Within moments the area around us had darkened, and the scene from India opened up at the other end of the room. Indira and her husband were there, surrounded by friends. Her three children sat on a bench near the front. The youngest was trying to squeeze a little more space for herself between her brother and her older sister. Indira must have already activated the holo-transmission that was emanating from our living room, because the children were staring straight at us. I could see what they were thinking: are Dhanye and Julia really right there?

The youngest waved, giving kind of a shy, half-wiggle of her fingers. I waved back. The children seemed astonished. I knew the feeling. I felt the same way when I took part in my first holo-transmission. It had happened many years earlier, when I was just a little older than they were now.

The birthday ceremony was taking place in an unadorned room. The dominant feature was the sculpture on the center wall: an inter-locking circle of thirteen rings that had come to symbolize the Circle of Thirteen. It was a familiar symbol that had been adopted by most of the affiliated Spiritual Circles around the world. Beneath the metal ring—written in five languages—were the last words of Deva Chandri: "We have seen the face of God, and she is beautiful."

Indira was proud of the diversity of their local Spiritual Circle, which included many Hindus, Buddhists, Muslims, and Christians. They were all invited to share their traditions within the meetings. But the largest group consisted of women with no outside affiliation at all. "We pretty well run things," Indira once told us, laughing as she said it. "We spend so much time talking about our families that we don't leave the others any time to quarrel."

For this ceremony, Indira had limited the incoming transmissions to just a few people. We'd done the same thing on our end, inviting only two of Dhanye's closest colleagues from the NYU history depart-ment. Toki wheeled back into the room with the small plate of food that Dhanye and I had prepared earlier from the garden. It was more of a symbolic centerpiece than anything else. He stood there for a mo-ment, not realizing the emotional nature of the occasion. I finally had to tell him to move. Toki, like most bots, is sometimes a little slow at taking a hint.

The ceremony was being sent out to the rest of the world in open-transmission. Anyone could view it in non-holographic form. There were probably several million watching it. The screen at the far end of our living room showed a candlelight vigil on the Champs-Élysées in Paris. The crowd was watching a huge vid-screen, which showed the ceremony from Mumbai along with the scene from our living room. For us, it was like looking into a mirror that was flashing back our reflection from another mirror.

Interest was higher than normal this year, probably because of the tie-in with the memorial for the Thirteen at the U.N. dedication ceremony in a few weeks. The huge crowd in Paris seemed to be in a warm and respectful mood. I kept telling myself that this sentiment—and not the bombs and the graffiti and the threats—represented the true feelings of people worldwide. But even as I said it, the cop within me remained on alert.

DEVA CHANDRI'S BIRTHDAY celebration had gotten sadder for the family over the years. For Dhanye and Indira, the occasion brought all their other losses up to the surface. The memory of their mother and father, who had died fifteen years earlier, pushed its way into their thoughts. Their mother, Dhriti, who was Deva's daughter, and her husband, Henri Rameau, were killed in a plane crash while on a peace mission.

But that loss was overshadowed by a more recent tragedy that hurt the family deeply. The fingers that had been stroking my hand suddenly tightened their grip. I glanced to my right, and I saw Dhanye's moistened eyes.

"You were thinking about Raji, weren't you?" I didn't need an answer.

Dhanye's brother had been killed about two years ago, and the memory of his death had the capacity to bring Dhanye and Indira—and me—to tears.

THE LAST ONE to appear was Maya. It was still light in California. So when her holographic image appeared, it was in a slight silhouette. She was sitting comfortably on a couch. Lara sat next to her, holding her mother's hand. She'd been doing that more and more since the death of Carlos, who had been Maya's companion for many years. Maya was okay, as far as I could see. She seemed a little frightened, but she was fighting her way through it. I wanted to talk to her, but that would have to come later.

Maya sat quietly, listening to the other speakers, seemingly resigned to her memories. But as I had come to find out, those memories were still very intense. As she grew older, she had begun to confide in me more and more. I had a good idea of what she was going through at moments like this. Her thoughts would wander all the way back to a moment that she always thought of as one of the most important in her life. It was what happened right after the Verafoods fire.

2032

SAN FRANCISCO

"ARE YOU OKAY?"

The voice came from the woman who was squatting down in front of her; Maya could feel the woman's dark eyes probing her. She blinked, trying to focus. She had to cough before getting her breath, the fumes from the nearby blaze making it difficult to breathe.

Maya had seen this woman earlier, near the barricade at the Verifoods warehouse. She'd been pleading with the policeman to let her and the others through to help the victims. Her head scarf was now down around her neck; strands of her graying hair had sprung loose from their pins and were falling over her ears. Her light brown skin seemed to accentuate the urgent look in her eyes. Those eyes were telling Maya something she couldn't yet understand.

She repeated the question: "Are you okay?"

Maya wasn't sure, but she wasn't going to admit it. "Yes, I'm fine."

She didn't know if the woman believed her. Was she making any sense?

"There was a young woman who left you a few minutes ago."

"You must mean Eloni, my student intern."

Finally, there was a smile.

"Yes, it was your friend, Eloni. She went to help with the rescue teams. She said you told her to go. You were on the vid-phone with your children when she left."

Maya didn't answer. How could she? She didn't remember it. The last thing she recalled was the message on Gabe's vid-phone. After that she must have blacked out.

"It could happen to anyone." The woman gave Maya a sympathetic smile, as she helped her to her feet. "Come on. We have to get out of here."

Maya was still a little unsteady. The noise behind her was getting louder. The crowd must have pushed past the barricades. She looked back and saw the police trying to hold people back, but they'd broken through at several points. She heard muffled gunshots and a couple of thuds. Seconds later, the foul air had a new bite to it: tear gas.

"Stay near me."

They ran down the block, with Maya tagging close behind. They turned at the intersection, and Maya was shocked by what she saw. Emergency Services was using the side street as a holding area, but the emergency workers had been overwhelmed. The injured were everywhere, lying on concrete slabs or improvised cots. Many were just propped up against chain-link fences. They were covered with blankets, tarps, cardboard, or anything else the overworked emergency workers could find. The moans were coming in loud, wrenching wails that seemed to overlap each other, competing for attention. The outnumbered nurses and medical workers were running from patient to patient. In many cases, they were just trying to keep them comfortable. Maya knew what they were thinking: Which one should we try to help first? Is this one likely to survive, or not?

Then something caught her eye: a little girl, no more than four, was walking alone up one of the darkening side streets. She was carrying a doll in one arm and dragging her backpack along the pavement with the other. Maya knew immediately she must have wandered away from the holding area. She was lost, but no one seemed to have noticed.

Maya's companion—she didn't know her name—grabbed Maya's sleeve and pointed to the child. Without a word, they both started running after her. She was still a half-block in front of them when Maya heard shouting and an explosion further down the street. Good god, she thought, the girl is walking right into the riot. Seconds later, a group of teenagers appeared on the cross street, heaving rocks and loose building material at their pursuers. Others were overturning trash cans and setting them on fire.

When Maya yelled for her to stop, the little girl looked back, but she must have been frightened by the sight of two women racing towards her. She took off running in the opposite direction, towards the fighting. Maya's fear escalated. She wasn't sure they'd reach her before she got caught up in the riot. Suddenly, there was a loud burst at the end of the street, and the intersection was filled with retreating rioters and police flailing at them with night sticks. There were thuds of tear gas canisters, followed by the sharper sounds of gunfire.

The little girl screamed and stopped in her tracks. Maya realized that she and her friend must have seemed less frightening to the little girl at that point than what was in front of her, because she turned and started running back towards them, crying loudly. She dropped her backpack in the gutter but held her doll tightly. Maya's companion got to her first, and the little girl leapt into her arms, burying her face in her rescuer's hair.

Maya reached the two of them and began rubbing the child's back. "It's all right," she kept repeating. "It's going to be okay; we're going to take care of you."

The words seemed to have a soothing effect, but the child was still hysterical and unable to answer their questions. Maya and her companion nodded to each other, mouthing questions about what to do next. Do we know who she is? Maya formed the word "no" and shook her head. We'd better take her back and find out who she's with. "Go ahead," Maya whispered. "I'll get her backpack."

It was still sitting in the gutter, surrounded by wet debris that was beginning to soak through it. As Maya reached down for the backpack, she heard the roar of an engine go past her and a squeal of brakes. She looked up and came face to face with a motorcycle cop who was blocking the direction from which she had just come. Within seconds, another motorcycle cop swung in next to him. Reinforcements arrived, as a pair of squad cars moved into position behind them. She realized immediately that the police were setting up a barricade against the rioters. She was on the wrong side of it.

"Let me past," she pleaded. "I need to get back." She told them she was trying to save a lost little girl. She tried every argument she could think of, but nothing worked.

"My orders are that no one goes past. No exceptions." The cop revved up his engine, as if to make his point. "Now get out of my way, lady, before you get hurt."

But it was too late for that. As Maya turned, the rioters forced their way through the intersection, moving straight towards her. Two of them threw pieces of pipe at the police, and a policeman shot a tear gas canister between them. One of the rioters, who had his shirt wrapped around his hand, picked up the canister and threw it back. They shoved their way past Maya, knocking her to the ground. Three men then tripped over her, the last one stepping on her leg. But there was no one to yell at, no one to argue with. There was nothing to do but wait for it to end.

MAYA COULDN'T SLEEP. The bruises on her leg bothered her, but that wasn't the only thing keeping her awake. She had a deeper worry that gnawed at her through most of the night, a worry that was intensified after the day's nightmarish events: how could she raise her children in a world like this?

Lara was upset with her the minute she got back to the apartment. "You were talking weirdly when you called earlier."

Lara looked to her ten-year-old brother to back her up, but Antonio was just staring at Maya's torn clothes and bruises. Things got worse during dinner. The bread Maya had been saving all week was starting to get stale. It would be two days before the bakery had any more. The refrigerator was on a low setting to save power, and the vegetables looked wilted and limp. She threw it all together as best she could, and they ate quietly.

As she was clearing the table, she realized that she finally had to tell them Gabe had been killed in the big fire. It was like the air had been sucked out of the room. Lara reacted in disbelief, walking into the bedroom and shutting the door. Antonio looked up from his homework. Maya could see tears in his eyes.

SHE ROLLED OVER and dozed a little as she lay in her bed, but sleep seemed less restful than being awake. When she awoke for good about 2:30 A.M., she was sweating and her heart was pounding. The windows were open because of the heat, but that brought in the sirens, gunshots, and explosions—the sounds of a city in convulsions. About 3:00 A.M., Antonio woke up crying and crawled into bed next to her.

She lay there until she was sure Antonio was asleep, and then she eased herself out of bed. There was no sense pretending she was going to get any rest. She tiptoed into their small kitchen and started heating water for a cup of tea. She measured it carefully, not wanting to get any closer to the potable water limit for their family than they already were. She remembered how she used to brew a big pot of tea and sip it at her leisure during the course of a morning. Those days seemed impossibly distant.

Maya turned on her vid-screen in the kitchen and set it for night illumination. She wanted it as low as her eye-calibration would allow so it wouldn't wake up Antonio. She'd avoided the news reports since she'd gotten home, but now she was desperate to find out what was going on. She touched the screen until she found an independent news source and then activated the rolling news feed. When she read it, she almost wished she hadn't.

184 confirmed dead in Verafoods fire, the news-screen reported. *Another 213 hospitalized, at least 50 in critical condition.*

It was as bad as she had feared. Maya touched the screen next to the death statistics, and a list of the victims appeared. Scrolling down, she found the name "Polecki." She touched the link, and Gabe's picture came on to the screen. It was hard to tell how old the picture was, but, as always, he was smiling. As she nursed a tear, she reached across the desk to give a little pat to his vid-phone.

There were more statistics. *Seven confirmed dead in city-wide rioting. 117 were hospitalized, including 6 police officers and 25 others.* Maya guessed that some of the "others" were SecureCorps guards who had probably borne the brunt of the rioters' wrath. The police confirmed that rioting was still going on in several parts of the city. Roving bands had been spotted in the Bayview and Ingleside districts. The rioting had also spread outside of the city: there had been battles with police in both Oakland and San Jose, as well as a firebombing of a Verafoods office in Menlo Park.

Demonstrations outside of the Bay Area had been mostly peaceful. Large crowds had gathered in cities along the West Coast in the afternoon as word of the fire spread. Demonstrators in Seattle and Vancouver had confined themselves to picketing and shouting outside the Verafoods offices, but riot police had been called in to control the crowd in Los Angeles. It was already daytime in Europe and Asia, and there were reports of demonstrations in London, Berlin, Barcelona, and Cairo. If you're a worldwide company like Uniworld, Maya realized, you can anger people in lots of places.

The women's group that had been picketing the Verafoods warehouse was now urging everyone to march on the regional headquarters of Uniworld/Verafoods in downtown San Francisco. The demonstration was set for that morning—to begin in a few hours. Maya found a video of an impromptu press conference from the night before. She hoped to see the woman who had helped her, but another woman from the group was speaking. The trailer across the bottom of the screen identified her as Marta Kwon. She was pleading with people to stop the rioting. "Violence only breeds violence," Kwon said. "Real change can only come from sustained, non-violent protest." She urged everyone to be on Mission Street at 10:00 A.M. in front of the Verafoods' downtown headquarters. "Don't be intimidated," she said. "Some will try to scare you into submission, but don't let them."

The intimidation had already begun. The next news bulletin was from the Governor—a weak, nervous statement in which he said that protests against Uniworld and its Verafoods affiliates could put the state's food supply in jeopardy. Maya was appalled. It was more of a naked threat than anything she'd ever seen. Push these companies too hard, the message was saying, and they could retaliate by cutting off the food distribution system entirely. Will they shut down their other warehouses? Cut back their shipments to local markets? Send California-grown food to another country? All of those things had happened a year ago when the California Legislature had tried to stand up to them: food grown in California fields was suddenly shipped out of the region, leaving local grocery shelves empty. Do you want that again? the political leaders seemed to be saying. They have the clout and the money, so don't expect us to protect you.

How had it happened? How had everything deteriorated to the point where she was now just sitting in a dark room, watching the world go to hell?

Maya thought about Gabe, the friend she'd lost, even when she'd tried to help him. She thought about the woman who'd tried to help her that afternoon, and she thought about the lost little girl they had both tried to help. She didn't know where they were. She didn't even know *who* they were. The more she thought about it, the more she realized she didn't really know what was happening to anyone, anywhere in the world. The only thing she knew was this tiny apartment and her two sleeping children.

It seemed that most of her adult life she'd just been watching things slip away. There were moments of resurgence: a few years after her mother had died, she'd met her future husband and convinced herself that she was in love. But each year after they were married, their relationship had deteriorated a little bit more. It would rebound for a while, but then it would slip into an even deeper trough. They finally reached the point where the whole thing had collapsed. Was that what had happened to the world around her? There had been a few times when it had seemed that things might get better, but then the problems had come roaring back. Each time they seemed even worse. Each recession got deeper. Each war was more brutal. Finally, the climate crisis and the crop failures left them with no simple way to rebound. Everything had gone askew. The money all seemed to go elsewhere. Maya found it hard to come to grips with what had happened. Sometimes it seemed like the world had tilted and all the wealth had rolled off the table into just a few pockets.

THE LITTLE GIRL's backpack was still sitting in the corner near the refrigerator where she'd left it. She picked it up and stared at it. There must be some connection in there to someone. Inside, there was the usual child's stuff: a stale piece of candy, a couple of crayons, an old sweater, a pair of princess cards from some old board game. There was nothing with a name on it. Then she squeezed the bag and realized that there was something else in there. She felt around for a flap, but there wasn't one: the package, whatever it was, was sewn into the lining. She grabbed some scissors and ripped out the stitching, pulling out a package with a warning notice: *for emergency use only—keep away from children.* The label identified the contents as *Tormaxin—50 mg dosage.* The capsules were designed to squirt the medicine into the mouth, the way you'd give it to a young child.

What illness did Tormaxin treat? A few touches of the vid-screen, and she had her answer: Lynn-Taksin disease. Oh my god, Maya thought, does the poor child have that? She knew it was a disease that affected the central nervous system and was linked to a form of depression. She'd seen too many people sicken and die of that in the last five years. Maya fought a sudden feeling of panic.

She checked the power grid on her vid-screen to see how many minutes she had left on her service. She had to move fast if she was going to find the child. Maybe the little girl or her parents were in the Social Services database. She found several client files that contained

Lynn-Taksin references for one reason or another. Then she found the one she was looking for: Deborah Moro, age thirty-six—the adoptive mother of a girl named Amy Moro, age four, who had been diagnosed with the disease. She touched the screen under Deborah's name and saw a picture of a plump, dark-haired woman. One more touch, and she had a picture of her adopted daughter, Amy. It was the same girl they'd found yesterday.

Maya scanned the case history with concern. Amy had been found almost two years earlier in an apartment in New York City. Her birth-mother was lying dead in the same room, an apparent murder victim. The authorities estimated that Amy had been there alone for almost sixty hours without food, water, or the medication she needed for her condition. If she had gone much longer without being found, she would have died.

Maya skipped the part about the NYPD's efforts to locate the killer, as she tried to find more information about the child. But the news didn't get any better. Her doctors determined that Amy's failure to receive her medication, the Tormaxin, during that sixty-hour period had probably caused some permanent damage. She was already showing strong signs of being withdrawn and non-communicative. One line struck Maya as particularly ominous: "Although she is too young for us to make a definitive diagnosis, the child seems to be suffering from a form of autism and mental deficiency, with a tendency to black out or lose her memory in certain instances."

The only good news was the willingness of her foster mother, Deborah Moro, to take care of her. The case worker noted that Deborah had formed a strong bond with Amy. She had arranged to adopt her and have her last name changed. All the papers had been signed before the two of them left New York and moved to San Francisco.

But the more Maya read, the greater her apprehension grew. It was a feeling so awful that she didn't want to take the next step. But she had to do it. She might be racing against the clock with the child's health. She checked the list of confirmed deaths in the fire and found the name she didn't want to see: Deborah Moro.

Maya got out of her chair and walked to the window. Was there a breeze out there—anything resembling a breath of life? She gripped herself tightly, trying to hold back the tears. But she found herself weeping in short bursts. She tried to visualize her own children in that situation, but the images were too awful to hold in her mind for long. They were finally replaced by a simple, deep sadness, as she tried to comprehend the terror of a little girl who had lost two mothers in just two years.

PEOPLE WERE OUT early. Some of them, Maya thought, had probably never gone to bed. A thin layer of smoke was still fouling the air, but it didn't seem to deter anyone. These weren't the rioters from yesterday, Maya realized. The people on the street this morning seemed more sober, more focused. The crowds grew larger as she got closer to downtown. Everyone seemed headed to the demonstration at the Verafoods headquarters in response to last night's plea from the women's group.

Had something begun to change since yesterday? In the middle of the night, her despair seemed bottomless. Now, there was a sense of purpose in the air. Maya's vid-phone lit up with Eloni's picture. Her intern was speaking through her auto-image, sending a message to her student friends and everyone else she knew: *Be there for the demonstration,* she was urging. *Now is the time to show your outrage. Support the women's group that organized this protest!* Maya watched as messages began coming in from all over, echoing what Eloni was saying. *Our grandparents and parents took to the street when things got bad, and now it's our turn.* The Verafoods fire had seemingly touched off a sense of outrage. *The unfairness in our society has been building for decades,* one message pleaded. *We're tired of them manipulating our food supply and corrupting our politicians. We can't sit still any longer!* The messages seemed to come down to a common theme: *Now is the time to take back our democracy!*

By the time they reached Eighth Street, the group had merged into a crowd of tens of thousands. The marchers were about twenty rows deep, encircling the monolithic Uniworld offices on the block between Mission and Howard Streets. The marchers seemed to be of every age, and they were heeding the pleas from the organizers to keep it peaceful and orderly. As Maya got closer, she could see the crowd growing, as thousands more turned on to Eighth Street from Folsom and Harrison Streets.

The sidewalks were a sea of homemade placards. The anger of the crowd showed in the signs. *Arrest the criminal food monopoly! The Uniworld Cartel: Wanted for Murder.* In the front were several labor unions, leading chants that demanded that the Verafoods management come out and meet with the protestors. Behind them was a group of hospital workers with a banner that read, *Our hospital beds are filled with your mistreated workers.* The largest sign of all was an electronic billboard that morphed from a photo of the earth, to a death's head, to the Uniworld logo.

Maya was astonished that the women's group had put together a protest of this size so quickly. Overnight they had erected a podium at the corner of Seventh and Mission Streets and put several improvised vid-screens along the route of the march. The screens carried a steady stream of messages to the people circling the building.

"My thanks to you all!" The speaker at the podium shouted through a bullhorn.

"My name is Rasa Malik, and I'm Northern California Director of the Service Workers Union. These shadowy companies with their secret owners have been exploiting people for years, forcing them to work in dangerous conditions, reducing their wages to near-slave labor, and then sending their goons after anyone who tries to compete with them. What happened yesterday, right here in San Francisco, was heard around the world. Today is the day when we start to fight back."

A roar went up from the crowd.

As Malik stopped talking, a woman who identified herself as Annette Dubois appeared on the vid-screen. She said she was speaking from Los Angeles.

"Look behind where I am standing and you can see the thousands of people marching at this moment on Figueroa Street and Olympic Boulevard. This protest is growing."

Faces from other protests around the world began appearing on the screen. A tall, striking woman who identified herself as Aayan Yusuf spoke from in front of a noisy crowd of several thousand on a Parisian street outside of Uniworld's European headquarters. A rabbi named Rebecca Meyer took the screen after that, speaking from a march that was gathering on Seventh Avenue in New York City. A woman named Yoko Nakamura, speaking from Tokyo, pointed to a hundred or so colleagues from an International Conference of Jurists, who were standing behind her as she spoke. Like everyone else, they were chanting and urging people to take to the streets in protest.

Other women with monitor badges were walking along the street next to the marchers, talking through bullhorns and exhorting them to action. They kept up a running message about Verafoods and its Uniworld parent corporation.

"Yesterday's fire was caused by Uniworld's manipulation of the world's food system," Franca Peres said. "It's owned by some of the dirtiest money in the world, and the other big-money interests are allied with them. This is the same money that has corrupted most of our politicians. Are we going to put a stop to that?"

The crowd roared back "yes!"

Maya found herself immersed in the crowd with the mood of it rubbing off on her. But she had to keep her anger in check, because she was on a mission of her own that morning. She elbowed her way past the marchers, scanning the crowd as she did so, trying to find the woman from yesterday.

Then she saw her.

Maya had just turned the corner on to Mission Street after circling the building, when the woman she was looking for stepped down from the podium. She saw Maya at the same moment and rushed towards her, grabbing her in a tearful embrace.

"I was so worried about you," she said. "After the police shoved you back yesterday, we weren't able to find you. I'm glad you're okay."

Maya was momentarily at a loss for words, finally fumbling out an explanation of what she knew about Amy's condition.

"Do you know where she is?" Maya asked.

"She's with me. I didn't know where she belonged, so I just took her home last night. Some teenage girls are watching her for me at our makeshift emergency center. Come on. I'll show you." She started trotting south down Beale Street, running against the grain of the marchers.

Maya caught up with her. "The organizers must need you here. Just let me go."

"No, no. The others can handle it," she insisted. "If you're right about the medicine, then we need to get it to her as soon as possible."

AMY WAS SITTING quietly on a box, paying little attention to the girls who were taking care of her. She was holding a book, which she held up as they approached.

"I read her a story last night, and I'm afraid she wants me to read it again."

Maya told her to go ahead and read the book. She thought it might be a good distraction, as she gave Amy the medicine. But Maya was surprised that Amy hardly put up any resistance at all. She seemed almost transfixed by the attention of the two women, glancing up from the page every few seconds, staring back and forth into their eyes.

Maya felt a string being plucked somewhere deep in her heart. She realized in that moment that the three of them had been drawn together in a way she didn't quite understand. Although she couldn't describe the bond between them, she had a feeling that it was unbreakable. She sensed that the woman standing next to her knew it as well.

"I'm Maya Flores," she finally said. "And I don't even know your name."

The woman grasped her hand softly. "I'm Deva Chandri."

WEDNESDAY, APRIL 22, 2082

TARRYTOWN, NEW YORK

JULIA

I WAS AWOKEN at 3:47 A.M. I tried going back to sleep, but it didn't work. I thought about staying in bed a little longer, just staring at the ceiling with my eyes closed, but I gave in to the inevitable and got up. I tried not to wake Dhanye. In the mood I was in, it was probably best that I mope around the house in the dark alone. In my late-night wanderings I usually gravitate towards the kitchen. There, I can sit in the dark and look out the window down the hill towards the Hudson River. I was surprised to find that a soft glow had settled over the river and spread to Nyack on the opposite shore.

The room suddenly got brighter. Toki had glided into the kitchen and adjusted the lights, probably thinking I needed more illumination. I shooed him out of the kitchen and told him to turn off the lights behind him.

MAYA WAS IN a pensive mood when I'd talked to her the night before, after Deva's birthday ceremony. The whole occasion had left her a little weepy, so I sat as close to her holographic image as I could without making her uncomfortable. It had been a while since we'd just sat and talked. As she thought about Deva, she said she'd been thinking about the other women as well. She'd been reflecting on the legacy of their last words. The things the Women for Peace said on that last day carried a special meaning. It was something that Maya dipped into like a form of nourishment. She wanted to know if I remembered the words of Gabriella Rodriques.

The movement from life to death and then to life again is something we do together. We share it with those who've gone before us and those yet to be born.

Did I agree with that? she wanted to know. I probably did, but I didn't know how I should answer her at that moment. Where was she going with all this?

Maya was getting philosophical, and that had me worried. She said she couldn't believe how time had slipped by. The sense of lost time had become a recurring theme with her. When she was a child, she said, each year had seemed like an eternity—the wait from one Christmas to the next was almost endless. But as she had gotten older, each added year was such a small piece of her accumulated memory that it became proportionately briefer. It was one of life's little tricks, she said. The less life you have in front of you, the faster it seems to go.

I wanted to stop the conversation right there. If she kept going like that, I was afraid she might convince herself that it had all telescoped down to nothing.

It wasn't a nightmare that woke me up that morning but rather a call from the NYPD. Ever since the bombing in Union Square, I had arranged for them to call me at any hour if there was another incident. When the alarm light flashed next to my pillow, there was an apologetic cop on my night-screen telling me that a powerful bomb had been found in a trash dump near NYU. It had been set to go off at 8:30 A.M. There were new, hateful *Patria* graffiti scattered in the area and some anti-U.N. scrawlings on the buildings around the park.

Someone had also slashed through a poster-size image of Deva Chandri and left it on a park bench about ten meters away.

How far was I going to let my imagination run with this? The bomb was on a major walkway between the Astor Place subway stop and the NYU History Department. Dhanye walked that route three mornings a week. Was that just a coincidence? The program for the U.N. ceremony had been announced yesterday, and Dhanye's name had appeared as one of the speakers. Could that have had anything to do with the bomb? Millions of people had watched Deva Chandri's birthday celebration last night, and they must have seen the vid-cast from our living room with the two of us sitting on the couch. Everyone watching would know that Deva was Dhanye's grandmother. Don't the odds say that at least one person out of all those millions would have enough anger in his heart to want to destroy our family and everything it stands for?

I had to control my paranoia. Ever since I was a little girl I've had to fight the feeling that everything I loved could be wiped away in an instant.

I BECAME PART of this story in 2047. That's the earliest date when I can really remember anything. I was four years old at the time, and some of my memories from then are vivid—maybe too vivid.

My first recollection is of my mother. I've always thought of that first memory with her as a happy one. It was a warm evening in our co-housing apartment in the Mt. Tamalpais foothills, just north of San Francisco. The window must have been open, because I remember the noise of our neighbors outside working in the community garden. My mother and I were snuggled on a daybed with the pillows propped up on one side. I was leaning against her, cuddled up under her arm. My favorite blanket was on my lap, but it was spread out so we could share it.

I remember my mother looking beautiful to me, although my memory of how she looked at that moment was probably affected by everything that came later. She had light brown skin that seemed to change throughout the day, giving her a slight glow that was irresistible. I remember her scent, thinking at the time it was an exotic perfume from some faraway land. She had long, auburn hair, but she rarely wore it straight down; it was always in swirls and swoops, held up by barrettes, pins, and other fasteners that were endlessly fascinating to a young child. I liked to dive into her mass of hair and find the hidden clasps. That wasn't the only thing hidden about her: she had a mysterious quality that even a young child could sense. It's hard for me to believe—even now—that at the time she was only a teenager.

In this, my happiest memory, we were reading my favorite picture book. It must have been near bedtime, because the storyline was written with an eye to getting children in the mood for sleep. It usually worked on me, but sometimes we had to go through it twice.

By the time the lights had dimmed and everyone in the story was asleep—when the little mouse was seated on the windowsill, looking at the moon and the stars in the nighttime sky—I was almost asleep as well. It was a quiet, magical moment when I felt as safe and happy as all the characters in the book. I remember my mother carrying me into the bedroom and whispering something that I still can't quite recall.

But it's painful to go back to that moment—even now. This happiest of memories always brings back tearful reminders of some of the worst moments.

When I discovered my mother unconscious for the first time, all of the elements of that happy memory were repeated but in a frightening, distorted form. I remember holding the book under my arm, dragging my blanket through the apartment, looking for her, hoping we could read the story together. I found her lying on the bed, stretched out between some of her favorite pillows. She wasn't moving. Her skin looked pale. I didn't know she was near death, but even as young as I was I knew something was wrong. Her hair was splayed in all directions, with the barrettes, pins, and clasps all hanging uselessly from the strands. I tried to wake her up, but I got no response. I shook her a little harder—nothing. I left the room for a few moments, not knowing whether to cry or not. Then I came back and tried again. When my mother still didn't move, I went next door and rang the doorbell. Our neighbor, Fiona Chiang, gave me a big smile, but that faded quickly when she saw the look on my face.

I told her my mother was sleeping and wouldn't wake up. I could see the fear in her eyes, even as she tried to hide it. I realized when I got older how hard it must have been for her to do what she had to do without alarming her little neighbor. She told me to sit down and have a cookie. She didn't get the cookie jar and offer me one like she usually did; she simply waved in the direction where the cookies were kept. I sensed that she was in such a big hurry that she didn't care how many I ate.

She told me to stay there and not go out. She said everything would be all right. She quickly slipped out the door and closed it behind her. I sat there for what seemed like a long time. I remembered looking at the door. I could hardly take my eyes off of it. Everything was happening beyond that door, across the hall, in our own apartment where my mother was . . . where my mother was what? At the time, I couldn't even articulate what awful thing might be happening. I remember flashes of light under the door and the noise of people on the stairs and the squawking of their vid-phones.

Ms. Chiang came back into the apartment just as I was looking out the window. Men and women in uniforms were rolling a cart into the back of a big vehicle. That's an ambulance, she told me gently. It's going to take your mom to the hospital where they can take care of her. There was something wrapped in white sheets on top of the cart. It didn't look like my mother. It was too small and lonely.

WHEN THE DOORBELL rang later that night, it was Maya.

When I think about that moment now, I realize this was my first clear memory of her, though I must have known her before that. I realize now that she was around our apartment all the time while I was a baby, but this is my first memory in which she comes into focus.

Maya had a quiet, solemn look on her face. At age four, I couldn't comprehend what she was going through. Even now I have a hard time understanding the emotions that must have been tearing at her.

"How's Amy?" The words came spilling out of Fiona Chiang's mouth as soon as Maya walked in the door. She tried to keep it to a whisper, but I heard her anyway. "Is she going to make it?"

Maya nodded her head. I latched on to that gesture, making of it what I wanted it to be: Maya was telling her that Amy—my mother—was going to be all right.

She may have wanted to say something more, but she probably saw the look on my face and realized I would be hanging on every word. She walked over and put her arm around me. She gave me a hug that lasted a long time.

"Julia's coming home with me," Maya said quietly.

PART THREE

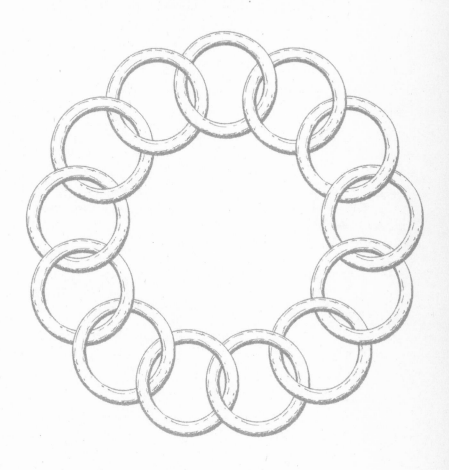

THURSDAY, APRIL 23, 2082

TARRYTOWN, NEW YORK

JULIA

THERE WAS A signal on my emergency line. I put down my break-fast roll and grabbed my vid-phone. A young officer from the NYPD was on the screen, reporting an anonymous bomb threat they'd just received. It was apparently aimed at the Food Market in Grand Central Terminal. She said the alert was confidential, because there hadn't yet been any public announcement. Their electronic surveillance team was trying to track the source of the message, but so far they'd had no luck.

I switched off my vid-phone and stared out towards the river. The remains of my breakfast looked suddenly inedible. My mind was full of questions, but there was one in particular that I knew I had to pursue immediately. I called back and got the same officer.

"Can you read me the text of the message?"

She looked at her notes and came up with the answer. "It says, 'Someone's planning to put a bomb in that big market—the one that's named for those women.'"

That drew a harsh line under everything that had been worrying me. The target hadn't been chosen at random. They were aiming their anger at the building named for "those women." The Rebecca Meyer Food Market was closely identified with the thirteen Women for Peace leaders. It was even hosting a reception in a few days to celebrate the upcoming dedication of the U.N. building. Someone was sending us a message.

THE REBECCA MEYER Food Market is huge—a major shopping hub for the city. Visitors to New York are sometimes surprised at how big it really is. The market opens into Grand Central Terminal and wraps around for several blocks to the east, past Lexington Avenue and over towards Third Avenue. The bakeries, delis, and cafes are mainly near the west entrance. The fruit and vegetable dealers are mostly concentrated on the other side, closer to the tunnels and docks for the barges that carry produce down the East River. You can find almost anything there. Ethnic food specialists are squeezed in among herbalists, soil mixers, insect farms, hydroponic growers, flower vendors, seed specialists, vitamin re-processors, manure blenders, and urban gardens. Dhanye and I have always loved wandering through the Market on weekends, poking through the food stalls. It's a place where you can see a lot of people.

Or, if you were a maniac, it's a place where you could kill a lot of them.

The thought of the carnage that a bomb could do in the food market gave me the shudders. This market is much larger than the earlier market that was closed down in the 2030s during the food shortages. When it reopened, it was named for Rebecca Meyer, a rabbi who had presided over a congregation in New York for several years. Meyer was the only New Yorker among the Thirteen. She was an inspirational leader of Women for Peace, and she worked constantly for the breakup of the Uniworld food cartel. Without her and the others, the market might never have reopened.

In the early 2060s, New Yorkers mulled over an appropriate memorial for the thirteen fallen leaders, finally deciding to put a major exhibit about Women for Peace in the terminal alongside the new market. The exhibit became an archive for many historical documents, but the centerpiece was a holo-rama production that covered the period 2032 to 2048 with the deceptively bland name: "Women for Peace: *The Early Years.*" It was an instant success, and it still draws large crowds.

The first part of the exhibit focuses on the secretive, criminal world of the Cartel, but then it quickly switches to the decade-long effort of the Women for Peace leaders to build a popular worldwide movement that could fight back against that organization. In the center of the exhibit visitors find themselves in a holo-rama that reenacts the climactic six-day confrontation in 2048. It's that struggle that's now known as the Week of the People. Demonstrations during that week were carried out simultaneously on five different continents, generating a huge amount of video coverage. But the exhibit retains a sense of immediacy—you can still feel the danger and excitement.

The goal of the protests of that historic week in 2048 was to force the parliaments of the four major power blocs to enact legislation that would break up the food monopoly. The way in which the Women for Peace organization accomplished this goal has become a case study in twenty-first-century confrontational democracy. They mobilized more than four million people to wrap themselves around the key parliamentary buildings in Washington, Beijing, Brussels, and New Delhi beginning on the same day.

The holo-rama gives viewers the impression that they are standing in the middle of the demonstrators, as they line up hundreds deep, keeping vigil for twenty-four hours a day and bringing in replacements as needed. At one point, visitors can feel themselves walking next to Bishop Maria Balewa, one of the more outspoken members of the Thirteen, as she marches around the Parliament building in New Delhi, confronting wavering parliamentarians and pushing them to make a commitment. While their allies inside kept the parliaments in continual session, protestors outside mounted a non-violent blockade challenging anyone who tried to enter or leave. Self-propelled video cameras followed Cartel agents everywhere. Electronic communications between the Cartel and its agents were disrupted by a barrage of messages that overwhelmed the system.

The battle was also fought in the streets, and there it got bloody. The images of those moments in the holo-rama are so real that they elicit screams from many of those walking through the exhibit. The *Patria* organization—a gang of neo-fascist thugs—surfaced for the first time during that struggle, injuring several of the Women for Peace leaders. Melinda O'Connor suffered a concussion when she was attacked in New Delhi by a group of *Patria* goons who were in the pay of the Cartel. Aayan Yusuf and Gabriella Rodriques were beaten in Rotterdam as they led a labor march. While these struggles were going on, labor unions, farmers' groups, students, and other WFP allies picketed Uniworld warehouses in every major city and battled with gangs wearing the *Patria* insignia.

But in the end the Women for Peace won. By the time the Week of the People demonstrations were over, the Uniworld Cartel's hold on the world's food system had been drastically weakened. The legislatures had enacted measures that not only broke up the monopoly but began the process of going after the shadow corporations that hid the criminal operators. A three-dimensional photo over the door of the holo-rama exhibit shows an iconic moment: Rebecca Meyer flanked on either side by Deva Chandri and Rasa Malik, as the three of them were being released from a federal jail in Washington. Over her head, Meyer is holding a copy of the bill that had just won Congressional approval. A triumphant smile spreads across her face.

I WAS EXPECTING another call from the NYPD updating the bomb scare, but instead the call I got was from Maya. That was a surprise. It wasn't yet daylight in California. Why was she up at that hour? Maya anticipated my question.

"My sleeping has been kind of crazy lately. I sometimes nod off in the afternoon and wake up in the middle of the night. Maybe it's my age . . . Anyway, I decided to call because I thought I might have worried you last night with all of my talk."

"I wasn't worried." I lied a little.

She knew I wasn't telling her the truth, but she dropped the issue. She said she'd called because she had found a photo of me at age thirteen, and she wanted me to have it. She didn't think I'd seen it in a while. I hadn't, but I remembered the day it was taken.

"I think your friend Chloe took the picture."

It was a photo of me standing in the prow of a ferry boat. We were heading into San Francisco for a big peace march.

"That was a difficult day," Maya said.

It was. There are times when I think I can still feel the bruises.

THE PICTURE WAS taken in 2055—seven years after the Week of the People demonstrations. There was another crisis brewing, and again it involved the Uniworld Cartel. Even though I was only thirteen, I had my own small role to play in this one. We didn't know it at the time, but it turned out to be the Cartel's last grasp for power.

Maya walked around the house nervously during those weeks. A campaign was building for war against the South Africa Federation, and she was on the brink of despair. Maya told me over and over about other war-propaganda campaigns that she'd seen in her lifetime. She said she knew where this one would lead. The media campaign was relentless. The leaders of the major powers kept making statements about the South African Federation's secret terrorist camps and about clandestine laboratories for weapons of mass destruction. There were news reports about oppressed groups inside South Africa that were being tortured by the government—complete with interviews of some of the supposed victims. There were stories each night about possible shipments of tainted food and about nuclear material that was unaccounted for. Story after story kept making the case for war. But Maya was adamant: none of that was true. She said the world powers were trying to lie their way into war.

And she was proven to be right. In a last-minute attempt to forestall the threatened invasion, Thabo Nyrere, President of the South Africa Federation, asked the Women for Peace leaders to join him in a press conference.

As the press conference started, Bishop Maria Balewa, dressed in her full regalia, bounded to the podium, where she was flanked by the other Women for Peace leaders. Her message was blunt: the Cartel had rigged the whole thing. Balewa called it "an audacious move by the same old criminal gang." It was Uniworld's attempt, she said, to rebuild the food monopoly that had slipped through its fingers in the last few years, and their campaign was based on a tissue of lies. Bishop Balewa went through the evidence that her colleagues had accumulated: planted news stories, manufactured documents, bribes of high-placed officials, and outright threats of violence. She named names, detailing the trail of money that led from Cartel agents to government officials. The evidence she presented was hard to refute. Most of it had been handed to the Women for Peace leadership by people in lower echelons of the Russian, Chinese, and American governments who were appalled at what their own countries were planning to do.

Buried in those documents and transcripts was something more: the reason behind the invasion. According to studies at that time, the world climate patterns were shifting once again, making South Africa one of the most attractive areas for agricultural development. The amount of money at stake was enormous. South Africa didn't want to do business with the Cartel, but the Cartel wasn't taking no for an answer.

Despite these revelations, the war-makers didn't back down. The momentum toward war seemed unstoppable. I didn't know it at the time, but Maya already knew what was coming next. It was something she'd dreaded from the beginning. She knew that the Women for Peace leaders would be putting their own lives on the line to prevent the war. She was appalled at the idea, but she didn't know how to stop it.

As FOR MY PART in all of this, the story really began with the ferry boat trip. A lot has happened since then, and it's hard to sort out my memories.

I was just thirteen at the time. As I looked at the photo now, I knew it was me in the picture,. But I hardly recognized the person I was back then.

2055

SAN FRANCISCO

JULIA STOOD in the prow, leaning out as far as she could, letting the wind run through her hair. The sea air filled her nostrils. The birds bobbing up and down in front of her seemed to be floating on the wind. She tried to follow their movements, thinking they might be secretly leading the boat across San Francisco Bay. But when you're standing here, she decided, you don't worry so much about other things. This was the place to be, out in front, heading into an adventure, with everyone following her.

But the lead spot was hers for only a few minutes. Her friend Chloe was pushing for her turn in front. Their other two friends, Annabel and Flora, were crowding in behind for their turns as well. Julia finally had to give up her perch and grab a seat.

They'd met the boat in Larkspur, where people from their co-housing community got on board together. The seniors took most of the benches on the forward deck. Maya sat with them, but Julia wasn't sure why. Maya was sixty-eight, but Julia was pretty sure she didn't see herself as a senior citizen. The idea of that made her laugh.

Maya was always running around doing something. For the last six months, she had been director of their entire co-housing community. Before that, she'd been running their community garden and organizing the retired people who ran the childcare program.

Carlos sat next to Maya with his arm draped lightly over her shoulder; he had a special way of doing that. Maya called him her boyfriend, but Julia thought that was a ridiculous term for a guy who was almost eighty. They'd been together since his wife had died about five years earlier. Julia didn't know how a relationship worked between people as old as they were, but they looked happy enough together. Plus Carlos had been good to her as she was growing up. She knew he wanted to move in with them, but Maya kept putting him off. It made Julia sad to think that Maya might be using her as an excuse.

Maya's son, Antonio, was sitting a few rows back, huddled with his wife, Li-Jin. He was pointing at the Golden Gate Bridge, telling Li-Jin something very serious about the breakwaters and the tidal generators under the towers. Are lawyers always like that? You've only been married for a few weeks, Julia thought. Can't you see Li-Jin just wants to cuddle? Antonio's sister, Lara, was a few seats away, and she didn't look happy at all. Julia felt sorry for her. Her brother's happy new relationship was probably making her even more miserable about her own situation with her partner, Rick—what a creep.

Rick wasn't there. Thank God for that. Julia wasn't even sure he and Lara were still together. She hadn't seen him around recently. Everyone had a story about him. Rick didn't have any kind of a job; he just sort of hung out during the day. There was something about his skin—it was kind of pasty and flaky—that she found disgusting. Chloe and Flora had both heard that he'd been beating Lara. Julia figured that was true, because she'd overheard Maya talking to Antonio about having Rick arrested. Maya got a terrible look on her face whenever anyone mentioned his name.

Julia had had her own run-in with him. The last time she'd visited her mother in the psychiatric wing of the hospital in San Rafael, she'd seen Rick about a block away in an alley outside some dirty-looking place. Someone said he spent a lot of time there. He was tinkering with a motorcycle, and there were some sleazy-looking guys with him. Rick saw her, and he started screaming and running at her. She panicked. Then he broke out laughing and yelled at her: "What's the matter, little girl, did I scare you?" Rick made her skin crawl.

THE BOAT WAS moving in closer to the Ferry Building, and Julia saw a huge crowd that had gathered along the waterfront, wrapping its way around the Farmer's Market. That seemed to be the signal for Eloni to pick up her clipboard and start giving directions.

"Do you girls know what we're doing today?"

Julia was amazed by Eloni Ubaka. She was close to forty, Julia figured, and she looked good—trim, with lots of muscles. She was Maya's friend from a job she had years ago, but Julia hadn't really paid attention to anything Maya said about her. She just knew that Eloni spoke with authority: when she talked, you listened.

It was Flora who jumped in with an answer to Eloni's question: "We're trying to stop a war."

Eloni smiled. "That's pretty close. We're trying to stop a war before it starts. All these people are gathering at the Ferry Building and then marching up Market Street. There'll probably be 200,000 in San Francisco alone. You've heard about Women for Peace, haven't you? They've organized big crowds like this in cities all over the world."

"I just hope this march works better than the last ones."

It was Harry who said this. He was sitting a couple of rows back with the group of seniors. As he started to talk, Julia glanced over at Carlos. She was pretty sure she knew what Carlos was thinking: Harry talks too much.

"When you're in your eighties," Harry continued, "you've seen a lot of this stuff. My mother marched down Market Street in 1969, pushing me in a stroller, to protest the Vietnam War. I walked in a big march on Market Street in 2003 to protest the Iraq War. And what did we accomplish with all that marching?" Harry didn't wait for an answer.

"Not a fuckin' thing—they just went out and fought anyway."

Flora and Annabel both looked startled.

"Oh, you girls don't mind an old guy like me saying things like that, do you?" He gave them a funny wink.

"This is going to be different, Harry." Eloni was fuming. "These women aren't just asking them to stop. They've got a plan to stop the war before it starts. If you don't mind my saying so, they're not just sitting around on their asses like some I know."

Harry's voice dropped to a contrite murmur. "I actually admire those women. I just hope they don't get themselves killed."

THE LONG ROBOTIC limbs on the dock reached out with a soft whir and grabbed the boat as it gently touched the pier. As they reached the gangplank, Julia and her friends were dancing in anticipation. They ran down and plunged into the crowd, getting caught up in an atmosphere that was almost festive. Julia had never seen so many people. Nearly everyone had placards. She and her friends held signs that said *Peace Now* on one side and *Women for Peace* on the other. Brian and Devon, Flora's two dads, unfurled a rainbow banner that said *War kills children and all of God's creatures.* Chloe's mom and Annabel's mom each carried signs that said *Marin Mothers for Peace.* Julia's mood plummeted for a moment when she saw that: why wasn't her own mother there? But she knew the answer. Her mother was in the hospital again for yet another psychiatric examination. Maya said she might be out in a week, but Julia had heard things like that before. She caught herself before her mood turned any darker.

The March was a huge wave moving down Market Street. Some people started singing, and the crowd joined in with them. A man shouted, *What do we want?* The people around him responded, *Peace! When do we want it? Now!*

Over the crowd noise, Julia heard Eloni yelling into her vid-phone. "I'm at Drumm Street, near the cable car turntable. The flash-screens ahead of us aren't working . . . Nope, they're still not on; try it again . . . Good, now you've got 'em going!"

As Eloni spoke, a translucent picture sprang to life about ten meters ahead, stretching from one side of Market Street to the other. It hovered over the crowd. Julia was surprised at how clear it was. But as she approached the screen, the images got wispier, disappearing entirely when they walked under it. But another screen—with the same picture—was ahead of them near Beale Street, and another beyond that. Flash-screens were stretched across Market Street at block-intervals as far as she could see.

The screens showed people in New York marching down Fifth Avenue. They must have seen the marchers in San Francisco at that moment, because they suddenly shouted, *Hello, San Francisco.* The marchers around Julia gave a huge roar in response. Nighttime marches in Paris and Istanbul then flickered into view, alternating on the screen with vigils in Shanghai, Mumbai, and a few places Julia had never heard of.

A FEW BLOCKS later the scenes got more ominous. There were no more pictures of happy, boisterous peace marchers on the flash-screens. New, darker images appeared, and the voices describing them were somber. Julia felt a sense of worry crawling up her spine. According to the streaming news ticker at the bottom of the screen, they were looking at a flotilla of small boats being battered by a fierce wind and choppy seas in the Atlantic Ocean off the coast of South Africa. The scene was getting darker. The words at the top of the screen identified some of the leaders of Women for Peace in the lead boats. Their voices were drowned out by the storm, but their words were scrolling across the bottom of the screen: *This war can only be stopped if the people of the world stand together and oppose it.*

They weren't alone out on the water. In the background behind their boats Julia saw several larger vessels. These were dark, hulking images that looked like warships. Their silhouettes looked even more frightening in the deepening twilight. Julia guessed what was going on, even before she read it on the screen: the women had placed their boats between a large war fleet and the coast of Africa. The scene screamed out danger.

The fog started to roll in. The street was no longer sunny; the mood no longer festive. The crowd was still chanting, but the words had an angrier, more desperate tone. The flash-screens were showing the events that had led up to this confrontation. Most of it was lost on her. Julia could only think about how small the women looked in those frail boats. She looked over at Maya, trying to get a sense of what was really going on.

AT THAT MOMENT, Maya was fighting to keep herself under control. She felt a deep sense of fear, but she was determined to keep going. The marchers were now chanting the old slogan, *The whole world is watching*. Maya sensed the people on the street had finally caught up with her mood. The world was watching, but would that be enough?

The sight of the women in their lonely patrol boats out on the Atlantic made her unbearably sad. She saw things others might have missed—Marta's eyes darting back and forth; the way Gabriella stood when she talked. She knew those looks: they were scared, all of them, but they were determined not to show it. This wasn't like any of their other protests. The stakes here—and the dangers—were even higher. These women weren't young anymore; all of them were in their late sixties and early seventies. They had families and friends who were worried about them. Rasa was still limping from a beating she'd received when a *Patria* gang had burst through a line of demonstrators last year and kicked her to the ground. Annette had survived two serious bouts with cancer; Magdalena had had a heart attack a year ago and had been advised to take it easy. All of them had something that should have given them pause. But the role they had taken upon themselves was to be brave and to bring out the bravery in others. Maya knew all of this, but she wasn't sure how long they could keep doing it.

In the middle of the night Maya needed the reassurance of Deva's touch. But she knew that wasn't possible She had to make do with just her voice and the image of her face, both of which she found halfway around the world. But after they'd spoken, she was more worried than ever.

Don't do it; it's too dangerous.

—They've left us no choice.

The world doesn't need martyrs. It needs you to be alive and strong.

—We have to follow through with what we've started.

Do you know that I love you?

—Yes, and that keeps me going.

To Maya, the news stories about the Women for Peace leaders were starting to sound like obituaries. Many in the media were hinting at the same thing, observing that the WFP leaders were taking even greater risks just as their level of personal danger was rising. The *Patria* attack on Rasa Malik that had occurred last year was just the latest warning. And that same neo-fascist gang had instigated a near riot three years earlier when they'd charged into a Parisian march trying to get at the WFP leaders. Then a *Patria* group had attacked a group of strikers in Sao Paolo, injuring hundreds. A week later a man and woman who'd been working with WFP were found murdered on a London street. Abraham, the shadowy leader of *Patria*, had issued a statement at the time, stating that the Women for Peace organization should be "eliminated."

Intelligence reports suggested that *Patria* was working closely with the Cartel, but Maya knew that *Patria* was fully capable of fomenting the recent attacks on its own. The group's propaganda was chilling. Abraham was a master at playing on men's fears, constantly exhorting them to roll back the social gains that women had made. Many fundamentalist religious leaders around the world played along with him, publicly deploring his acts of violence even as they secretly applauded his efforts. More recently, *Patria* had developed a new tactic. Women leaders in three separate countries had recently been kidnapped and raped by gangs that left *Patria* markings. Maya found herself looking down every intersection as they marched, fearful of a sudden attack.

Maya was roused from her thoughts by Deva's voice addressing the crowd on the vid-screen. *If negotiations are not successful, the killing may soon begin. We must act now to stop it. If we must risk our lives, let it be for peace and not for war.*

As Maya stood on that chilly street, surrounded by protesters rapt in their attention to Deva's message, she felt far away from everything, fighting a sense of helplessness.

JULIA WATCHED MAYA out of the corner of her eye, and she was troubled by what she saw. She'd lived with Maya long enough to know when something was wrong. As the marchers reached Taylor Street, she felt a slight vibration on her skin that quickly turned into a low, more definitive, roar. The noise was coming at them from the direction of Golden Gate Avenue. Then she heard the same noise pounding its way up Sixth Street. Suddenly, Market Street was full of men on motorcycles—large, noisy machines that gave off an awful smell. There were rods sticking out from the axles, flailing at the marchers as the two-wheeled vehicles ploughed through the crowd. The riders wore dark helmets and handkerchiefs that covered their noses and mouths; on their jackets was the circle-and-arrow insignia of *Patria*. Three women near Julia were quickly beaten to the ground. As she tried to get to the sidewalk, the motorcycles cut her off. The cyclists started circling around her and Maya, drawing their ring gradually tighter and tighter.

"What are you doing here, little girl?" one cyclist hissed. He leaned over as he went by, and Julia smelled his strong, sour breath. "Didn't this nice lady tell you that carrying signs like that could be dangerous?" They circled again. "Those peace ladies you saw on those screens can't help you. They can't even protect themselves. Don't you know they're all going to end up dead sooner or later?"

A rider grabbed the poster out of Julia's hand and cracked it across his knees, throwing the broken pieces at her. As Julia reached out to protect Maya, she caught the eyes of another rider. It was someone she recognized. Oh, my god, she thought; I can't believe what I'm seeing.

Julia heard police sirens, but then she felt a sharp pain in the back of her neck.

She didn't remember anything after that.

THURSDAY, APRIL 23, 2082

TARRYTOWN, NEW YORK

JULIA

THE MAGNO-TRAIN always seems like a long, tapered cocoon when it glides into the Tarrytown station. As I stood on the platform ready to board, the pressurized doors opened automatically, emitting a slight sound of escaping air. I stepped warily inside, and the door swooshed closed behind me. Anything that automatic always arouses my suspicions. Once inside, I noticed that the solar panels of the buildings on the other side of the Hudson River were in full glow from the morning sun. The train was fast and slick as it moved smoothly along the river down towards Manhattan—a little too smooth for my taste. After years in the U.S. Army rolling around on military transports, I preferred a few vibrations.

I was still getting updates from the NYPD. They were searching the entire Rebecca Meyer Food Market building, but they hadn't made a public announcement about it. Anyone going in and out of the building was being checked, and this was causing delays. My train was headed into Grand Central Terminal, and I'd probably be held up with all the others.

I had a walk-through scheduled that morning with two of the contractors working on the new United Nations headquarters: Irena Castillo, the general contractor, and Noah Fawkes, the electrical contractor. They planned to show me how the nano-circuits embedded in the construction blocks would signal an alert if anyone tried to penetrate the building. This definitely aroused my interest. But after that meeting, I had a potentially long-winded conference scheduled with Madeleine and all the contractors and suppliers about their lax record-keeping. I was prepared for a lot of grumbling.

I had the car to myself until the train made a brief stop at Yonkers. An older couple got on. The man was using a walker, and the woman slowly guided him to the nearest seat, taking pains to settle him in comfortably. A young man followed closely behind them, switching his backpack from one shoulder to the other as he waited a little impatiently for them to sit down and get out of the way. A young couple and two small children were the last to board. The little boy, who was probably about four, gave a delighted whoop as the doors whipped closed behind him.

The young family grabbed the seats across from me. The little girl, who was probably close to three, wiggled her way out of her mother's arms and came over to sit by me. She looked up, and her big brown eyes stared intently at me. She didn't know the words, but I knew what she wanted to say: "Can I sit here?" I got a little twinge as I looked at her. Would my own daughter or son be this endearing a few years from now?

Her mother reached across the aisle to get her, and she started to scream and resist. I told her mother it was okay: she could stay where she was. Her brother wasn't having the same success. He'd moved next to the young man in the row in front of him and was trying to poke his hand into the pockets of the backpack. The young man pushed his hand away and shoved his backpack to the other side of the seat. By then the little boy's father had moved up the aisle to get his son and bring him back to sit on his lap.

We were due to arrive at Grand Central in a couple of minutes. The overhead screens gave a polite ping and then lit up over everyone's seat. A message appeared: *Due to security concerns, passengers should anticipate some delay at Grand Central Terminal. We will try to make the procedure as brief as possible. We apologize for any inconvenience.*

"What do you think that means?" The man with the walker was talking a little too loudly, trying to make sure the woman with him could hear him over the hum of the car.

"I don't know," the woman said. "Maybe it's another one of those bomb things like they had in Union Square."

I checked my security network and found that the search was still going on. They were screening all arriving passengers, but the delay so far was only minimal. After we stopped, the passengers from our car and all the others getting off the train were met by a team of NYPD officers. They were checking everyone, using dogs to sniff at packages. They had a full-body scanner nearby that they could use at a moment's notice, but the courts had limited the use of that device to cases where a person had done something to arouse the cops' suspicions. Nobody in this group was doing anything out of the ordinary.

The man with the walker and his companion had several bags, and the security team hand-searched them all. The family of four got through a little faster. The two kids tried to dance their way through the line, thinking the whole thing was great fun. The dog growled at the little boy as he reached out to pet it, and the cop quickly pulled him back. When it was his turn, the young man just lifted his arms as the police patted him down.

I was the last one. An NYPD sergeant with the name "Herrera" on his badge was standing near the security monitor. I asked him if I could put in my biometric identification. He nodded, and I placed my palm against the screen. He gestured me forward.

"Come on through, Director Moro."

I pulled him aside so we could talk. "I've been getting regular security updates from your people. Is there anything new I should know about?"

"Not really. We haven't found anything. We're trying to finish up with the sweep of the market, and we should be through in just a couple of minutes."

I nodded. Whatever happened, I told him, I would like to have my team meet with him and the others later in the morning.

"Sure thing." He sounded grateful for any help he could get.

"The terminal and market are now clear," Sergeant Herrera announced to the crowd a couple of minutes later. "You can go through. Thanks for your patience."

The passengers all filed past the checkpoint. I moved along with the others, heading into the tunnel that led to the center of the terminal. My plan was to go over to the Vanderbilt Avenue exit and then catch a robo-cab on the Park Avenue grid.

The young man who had been on the train with me was walking about ten meters ahead. He had his hands tucked into the front of his sweatshirt, but he was glancing back every so often. As he saw me looking at him, he tried to speed up without calling any attention to it. That false move caught my eye.

Then it hit me: *his backpack was missing.*

I started running towards him, yelling at him to stop, but he was already too far ahead. And now I had another, more pressing worry. I stopped and grabbed my vid-phone, punching at the inter-agency security line. My identification was confirmed immediately. A crisp female voice on the other end said, "Director Moro, what can I do for you?"

"Send an emergency alert to the NYPD. They need to put a security team at each of the Grand Central Terminal exits. We have a possible bombing suspect."

I quickly gave her the information I had: brown jeans, green hooded sweatshirt, light skin, brown hair; probably about nineteen years old, eighty-five kilograms, and 1.8 meters in height. While I was shouting into the vid-phone, I had already turned around and was running back in the direction from which I had come.

"Contact Sergeant Herrera and the bomb team immediately." I was puffing out the words as I ran. "Tell him the kid was carrying a backpack on the train, but he didn't have it with him when he got off. He must have left it there when he realized the police were inspecting passengers. The bomb's probably still on the train."

I rounded the corner and saw Herrera. He'd gotten the message; he was running back in the direction of the tracks.

"It leaves in five minutes," he shouted. "We're pulling the passengers off."

We got within twenty meters, and I pointed to one of the cars. "That's the one."

As the passengers were moving out of the train, an older man tripped over the leg of a woman who was moving past him. As he fell to the ground, I rushed over and got him to his feet. I had him in front of me as we stumbled away from the train.

I felt the blast before I heard it. I found myself sprawled across a bench with a sharp pain spreading from my shoulder; seconds later it was pounding in my head. I must have blacked out for a few minutes.

"Here, take a glass of water." Herrera leaned down to get a better look at me. I pushed myself up a little straighter on the couch.

"Do you know where you are?"

"As near as I can tell, I'm in your office." My head felt groggy.

"Are you okay?"

"Yeah."

He was still checking me out. I'd been cleared by the paramedics, but Herrera may have thought I was bullshitting them.

I may have been bullshitting myself too. Something was brewing in the back of my head, pushing at me from the inside. *Let me out,* it was starting to scream. It had happened to me before when I'd been under stress. I'm sure it's related in some way to the hypno-scan I went through when I as a kid. Maya warned me at the time not to do it, but, being as pig-headed as I was, I did it anyway. Now, sometimes a harsh blow can trigger it. I've had a few of those over the years. I can still remember the hit I took as a kid that left me sprawling in the middle of Market Street.

But the headaches don't always get the best of me. It's like taming a beast: sometimes I can calm it down, tease it back into its cage. I tell myself each time that I can stay on top of it. If I didn't really believe that, I'd have to admit that I'm not in control of my own head. I'm not ready to go there. There are times when I probably take my stubbornness too far. I try not to be a burden, but I sometimes wonder if I'm making it worse for everyone. It's one thing to see that look in the eyes of a cop, but it's much worse when it's on the face of someone you love. Sometimes Dhanye's eyes just look right through me . . . *Julia, I'm worried about you.* Usually, it's a look of total exasperation . . . *your nightmares, your headaches, your traumas.* Behind those eyes I can see the fear . . . *why aren't you willing to let anyone help you?*

I will. I know I will, but not right now.

I wasn't about to go into any of that with Herrera. For his part, he seemed ready to drop his quizzing about my state of mind and move on.

"The train car was damaged badly, but thanks to you there were no major injuries from the bomb."

I took another sip of water and nodded.

"We got the kid. He ran down to the lower level and tried to board another train, but one of the railway cops grabbed him."

That news got me sitting up taller. "Has he said anything?"

Herrera shrugged. "Mostly, he's been feeding us a lot of crap."

"Do you want to take a look at him?" Herrera walked over to the vid-screen and found the setting he wanted. The picture on the wide-screen showed the cement-block detention area in the basement of the terminal. The kid from the train was sitting sullenly on a bench, picking at a couple of bandages.

"Just ignore the burn marks. That happened when he tried to bust out of the room without paying attention to the warnings about the electronic barrier."

I gave Herrera a quick glance. He shrugged. "Things like that happen."

The kid sat with a slouch. He had stringy brown hair, gray eyes that lounged behind sleepy lids, and a half-smile that did nothing but highlight a crooked tooth. He was as nondescript as I remembered him. The closest resemblance I could think of was to some old pictures I'd seen of the man who'd assassinated Martin Luther King, Jr. in 1968: James Earl Ray. He was so bland that he could blend into the walls. This kid looked pathetic as he moaned and poked at his wounds. I've learned one thing over the years about terrorists like him: they're fearsome in what they set out to do, but up close they look empty, dull, and weak.

"His name is Myron Lott, and he was arrested last year for threatening to burn down a women's reproductive clinic in Atlanta."

"Does he live there?"

"Apparently," Herrera said. "He and the other three boys who were arrested with him at the time were all members of the Faith of Our Fathers church."

Herrera saw the look on my face. "I thought you'd be interested in that."

The name definitely caught my attention, but it did nothing to help my headache. The Faith of Our Fathers congregation was run by Reverend Rufus Clay, a nasty, unctuous creature who worked the hate circuit. He was headquartered in Atlanta with supposed branches in twenty other cities, but nothing about his church was easy to verify: Faith of Our Fathers was a fringe operation that most religious organizations wanted nothing to do with. Clay was a peacock who loved the sound of his own voice. He was always popping up on vid-screen inserts everywhere. Lately, he had taken to denouncing the United Nations as *the Harlot on the Hudson* and *the love child of a group of debauched feminists.* Those were the kinds of phrases that were guaranteed to bring him to the attention of our security staff. The consensus was that Clay's religious fervor was just a smoke screen: he was under investigation in three states for dealing in illicit weapons and stealing money from his own church.

I took another look at Myron Lott, thinking about how the Reverend Clay must have drawn him into his orbit. Guys like Clay have been seducing guys like Lott since the beginning of time. They prey on the lost. There's nothing more attractive than some bombastic character with a book in his hand, promising to make you righteous and powerful. I tried to gauge the brain power behind Lott's eyes. There didn't seem to be much of it. The NYPD had been pressuring this guy hard, but I didn't think they'd get much. There'd be plenty of cut-outs between this kid and whoever was really behind the attack. Somebody had paid him, but they'd probably done it in some untraceable way, maybe even using an old-fashioned method like cash in an envelope. He would have been told only what he needed to know: here's the bomb; New York is in that direction.

"You probably haven't seen the latest from the dear Reverend Clay," Herrera said. "Today, he issued a statement praising the actions of *Patria* from a few decades ago. I'm not sure why he's bringing up that old stuff now, but here's the quote: 'If we had listened to what *Patria* was saying then, we wouldn't be getting ready now to idolize these godless women at the United Nations.' Here's another one: 'Abraham should be considered a modern-day saint.'"

"Is there a connection with this kid?"

"He was wearing a shirt under his sweatshirt with a picture of Abraham—not his real face, just the usual computer image of him that news sources had used years ago. As far as I know, there were never any real photos of Abraham from when he was alive."

"How do we know he's not still alive?"

Herrera looked surprised. "The news media always—"

"They don't always get it right."

"The last time anyone heard of him he was in Baluchistan twenty-five years ago, right?"

"As far as I know."

I REACHED MY office in time to find Avram, my Deputy Director, in full battle mode. He'd received the details of the bombing from Sergeant Herrera, and he was moving quickly to fit it into our threat assessment. The media had gotten hold of my role in the story. Avram said there were a dozen or so news-bots out in the press room, ready to record an interview with me. I told him to get rid of them. With my growing headache, the last thing I needed was a conversation with a bunch of robots.

Madeleine stuck her head in the door and wanted to know what the flurry of activity was all about. I didn't much feel like talking, but I couldn't keep her in the dark. She'd heard about the bomb on the train, but she didn't know I was involved. She didn't know anything about the bomber and his background either, until I told her. She scowled when she heard it; she could see the implications immediately. Our meeting with the contractors was in a few minutes, she reminded me. We'd talk more after that.

Rufus Clay and his church had moved to the top of Avram's list of threats. Given what had happened this morning, it deserved the number-one spot—for now. Avram had already ordered the security staff to go over the information we had about the Faith of Our Fathers church, looking for anything that might be a lead. But we both agreed that Clay and his bunch didn't seem strong enough or sophisticated enough to mount an attack against the U.N. by themselves. It was one thing to attack an unprotected market; it was something else entirely to assault the level of defenses that we had planned for the U.N. ceremony.

Avram started going through the other threats on our list. There were other firebrands like Clay in the U.S., in the Middle East, and elsewhere, but so far they had just been making loud noises without any action. There were the remnants of the old Uniworld Cartel, but they were mostly fighting each other these days. There was also a handful of small, renegade states that had been suspended from the U.N. because they were controlled by criminal elements. They had their grievances, but neither of us thought they would resort to violence over trade sanctions or a suspension of voting rights. There were elements in the U.S. Army and other military organizations that still needed to be watched. At my insistence, Avram was looking for any strange troop activity near Fort Knox, Kentucky—I'd had a run-in with a rogue military group a few years earlier, and that was something I wanted him to keep an eye on.

I'd been fighting a slight blurring sensation ever since I'd arrived at his office, and the pain had gotten worse behind my eyes. Avram sensed my discomfort, stopping for a second to see if I was okay. I wasn't, but I told him to continue. He asked me a question, but I couldn't respond.

And then it broke through.

A light pounding in my head, getting lighter and darker, as the colors were flashing and changing . . . Noise screeching and painful . . . Voices. 'You've been weak; you've been pussies' . . . Images piled upon images, moving and moving . . .

And then it was over.

I was sprawled on the couch. Avram hovered over me, eyeing me closely.

"Are you okay?"

"I'm fine now."

"I've alerted the medical team."

"Call them and cancel it. I'm all right." I was shaky, but I didn't want to admit it.

"What happened to you?"

"It's a long story." I hesitated, but I realized I had to tell him something. "Years ago, I went through something called a hypno-scan—a memory recall process to help the police in an investigation of the *Patria* organization. And now I occasionally get flashbacks. The bump that I got on the head today probably triggered it. It's not so bad."

"When did you go through that memory recall thing?"

"In 2055—I was just thirteen."

Avram's jaw dropped. "You and *Patria* crossed paths when you were just thirteen years old?"

2055

BALUCHISTAN

WHERE AM I?

Where do you think you are, little Jesse?

He lunged for the side of the bed, grabbing the edge of the mattress. His fingers scrambled around on the chipped concrete floor, making manic, spider-like circles until they found what they were looking for. The cold of the pistol bit into his hand.

They were there, over by the wall: faces—two, three, maybe more. They looked soft and soothing, but he saw the evil surging to the surface. His brain-on-fire took over: he fired once, twice, at the wall.

A pair of guards hurled themselves through the doorway, rifles at the ready, pivoting rapidly. Their eyes darted from corner to corner and up and down the walls, looking for the intruders. There was nothing there. They relaxed the grip on their rifles and stared into the darkened corner where the gunshots had come from.

"What are you looking at?" a voice barked. His brain-in-charge was ordering things now. "There's nothing to see. Get out of here."

The guards glanced at each other and then backed slowly out of the room.

HAD HE BEEN asleep? He'd been disoriented, trying to remember where he was—even *who* he was. A sick feeling had gnawed at him. For a while he was someone he wanted desperately not to be. *Are you always going to be a little pussy?* Something bad was going on. *Even little babies have balls.* In a dream—was it a dream?—he was locked in a closet, pounding on the door to get out.

IT WAS THE cry to prayer that woke him—the sing-song tones of the *muezzin* from Mardan, the town on the other side of the hill. He'd been there long enough to know the differing sounds of the five daily *Salah*. This one was *Dhuhar,* the midday prayer. What did the words of the chant mean? He didn't much care.

Islam didn't bother him any more than Christianity or Judaism. None of those religions meant anything at all. They just masked the truth. All you had to know is that darkness keeps drawing you in, promising you bliss if you yield to it. And it's all a trap: those soft, moist aromas only weaken you.

The ancient Hebrews knew that. Their stories about Eve's betrayal, Lot's faithless wife, Noah's timorous daughters were made up for a reason: mankind needed to be reminded, time and time again, to fight against the darkness. The Greeks had known it too. On wall after wall, vase after vase, you saw the same warning: Jason fleeing the harpies, Achilles battling the Amazon queen, Oedipus betrayed by his mother, Odysseus escaping the spells of Circe and the seductions of Calypso. And the greatest test of all: Zeus raging against Gaia, the supposed Earth Mother. Control was the only thing that mattered. If you wanted to worship something, you should worship that.

THE LEADERS OF the Cartel sent him a message in the middle of the night, demanding that he speak with them immediately. He made a special trip to the command room just to accommodate them. His brain-on-fire was seething, but he knew to be calm. He had the advantage. His sources told him the Cartel was in trouble. He'd seen the big peace marches earlier in the day just like everyone else. He'd watched those idiots out on their boats, and he knew that their protests were starting to have an impact. The Cartel's big war gamble over South Africa wasn't going well at all. The government ministers and other insiders they'd been paying off were getting cold feet. The peace protestors now had the upper hand, and this whiney bunch of Cartel leaders was worried. They were about to lose, and they were looking for a scapegoat. That made *them* weak.

They attacked him the minute he came on the screen. Where are you? *Who* are you? Is this Abraham thing just a mirage, or what? Why do you hide your face and keep scrambling your image? They wanted to know who ran his *Patria* network in different cities. All nine of them started throwing questions at him from different directions. He recognized the two major money men and the biggest of the drug lords. The men at the top of the food pyramid were there too, looking uneasy. The rest of them finally stopped talking and let Kolle, the fat one, do most of the questioning. He had the nerve to ask, "How do we know where our money is going?"

That infuriated him. Did these weaklings really think he would tell them anything? Did they think he was as stupid as they were? They'd grown soft. Without the muscle that *Patria* put out on the street for them, they would be too weak to do anything. He'd been nurturing his network for more than a decade, choosing which local leaders to pay, priming them with his messages, and scripting their actions. He'd slipped in and out of different cities, watching them perform, seeing if they could channel the anger of the men who were drawn to the *Patria* message. He had leaders in cities everywhere and thousands more who reported to them. There were millions more who hung on his every word. He had a network that was ready to do anything he wanted. All the questions and insinuations from these Cartel fools were an insult to him. They needed him more than he needed them.

HE'D SEEN THE real men who had started the Cartel thirty years ago. He began working with them—doing their enforcement work, the back-alley stuff no one else wanted to do—within a few years after they engineered the merger with Uniworld. Most of them were the fathers of this current group of degenerates. They knew what real power looked like. They would never have put up with the weakness of this crowd. If someone had exposed information about them—if a woman had humiliated them in public, like that so-called bishop did at a press conference a few weeks ago, she'd have been dead within hours. But this group of weaklings sat around wringing their hands. Those aggressive women are waiting in the wings, he wanted to yell at them. They're pushing and shoving with all their noise and publicity. They're itching to take over, and you idiots are going to let them do it.

This group had gotten sloppy and lazy, doing things their fathers never would have allowed. Their security was lax. They were careless about protecting their identities. They'd even squandered much of their financial power. Carnot, the glassy-eyed one, kept looking at him with an empty stare, clearly hooked on the same drugs that his syndicate was pushing. He was practically slobbering during their video transmission. The others snickered at Kolle, the fat one, behind his back, and made jokes about his child prostitution ring in Thailand. They knew what he liked. The only question was whether he preferred to do it with little girls or little boys.

These fools disgusted him. They'd had the Cartel handed to them on a silver platter; they never would have been smart enough to put it together on their own. Thirty years ago, Carnot's father had known which Bahamian and Caymanian officials to bribe to get key information about the black-money accounts in their banks. He could have stopped right there: that information alone would have made him one of the richest men in the world. All he would have had to do was team up with the crooked Chinese Party secretaries, hedge fund insiders, and other embezzlers, and they could have siphoned off a fortune.

But that original group had a bigger vision. They'd never hesitated.

Once they'd found all the hidden money around the globe, they knew they could link it into a powerful network. All the plutocrats around the world—the lazy sons of wealthy fathers—would either join them or get out of their way. The men behind the money didn't need to meet with each other or even like each other. They didn't even have to *know* each other. They only had to be linked together electronically and be disciplined enough to act in unison. That's how the original Cartel had put together the deal with Uniworld. None of them had ever met, and it was better that they didn't. Would the wealthy Arab who'd murdered his cousins to get the family petrol-dollar fortune have been able to stay in the same room with the Jewish financier who'd fleeced billions from his friends in New York? Would either one of them have been happy to break bread with the Camorra leader who had made a fortune using six-year-olds as slave labor?

The men in that original group were smart enough to stay away from each other. They didn't care how the others got their money. They focused instead on who needed to be bribed and who needed to be eliminated. They knew that if they used their power decisively, anyone outside the network would be forced to follow their lead. By the time they were ready to make their move, they had amassed enough wealth to buy anything—or anybody—and move every obstacle out of the way.

When the world food distribution system collapsed under the weight of the climate crisis, they grabbed their opportunity. They had a network of local-sounding enterprises and a well-scrubbed bunch of shell corporations ready to go. They had them dressed up with comforting resumes and impeccable balance sheets. And by the time anyone realized who was behind the whole thing, it was too late to stop them.

HE PUSHED HIMSELF down the hall, slamming doors as he did so. A couple of his lieutenants said they wanted to meet with him, but he wasn't going to do that now. *Should the local men be paid?* they wanted to know. *Pay them; don't bother me.* Didn't they carry the shipments from the drug fields down to the coast without any problem? *Pay them! The money should be there. Hamid will be coming around for his fat payoff, and he'll want another one for his brother, the Interior Minister. Pay them all.*

Over the past fifteen years he'd been watching the growing collection of pimps, cutthroats, and thieves that had found their way into the mountains to join up with his guards. There were enough of them now that they'd become something larger. But they were still the dregs of the world, and they swaggered around like they were something important —even calling themselves a militia. But he didn't trust them at all. He kept them, because he needed them—if not them, someone just like them. Someone had to guard his compound. And someone had to carry the drug shipments from the interior down to the coast. But he knew they had no loyalty to him or to anyone else. If he paid them well, they'd keep doing what he wanted. If he didn't, they'd probably slit his throat.

But those riflemen lounging outside his compound had no idea who he was—who he *really* was. There were rumors, but he wasn't going to do anything to confirm any of that. He paid them, and he expected them to do their jobs. If they thought about him at all, it was probably as someone they alternately feared and despised. He wanted them nowhere near the important things that he was doing.

His real followers were elsewhere. They were out there in the world in thousands of places. If his brain-in-charge and brain-on-fire agreed on anything it was that there was a world of men out there who were waiting for him to lead. They would rush to do what he said. They knew his name, and they would never forget it.

It was time to talk to them. He didn't want any interruptions. He checked the windows, making sure the locks and alarms were working. At the command room, he went through his security procedures again with the doors, closets, heating ducts, ventilation—everything. He settled into the feel of the room, sliding his fingers across the desk, fingering the equipment. He was just minutes away from convening his network—the one that circled the globe. He could feel the energy inside him struggling to get out. His brain-in-charge needed to be in control, but his brain-on-fire had its own explosive role to play. That fiery brain was tired of just pushing back against the voices. It was angry at being repressed. It was ready to expand and take over the room. At the crucial moment, that brain would mouth the words he needed and provide the power to slice through everything. His brain-on-fire was like a dog on a leash, straining to get loose.

He was ready to be Abraham.

HE DARKENED THE light and rotated the pictures on his vid-screen one by one. He was only a few minutes away from the gathering with his network. He had to find the right images. He angled the pictures, viewing them in different dimensions, searching for the characteristics he wanted. There, that's the one. He expanded the image and moved it closer. The young man in the picture had a head devoid of hair, except for dark eyebrows that wrapped around the sides of his eyes. They were penetrating eyes, angry eyes; there was no wasted emotion in that gaze. His neck was a pillar of strength that began at the base of the ears and angled out towards his shoulders. There were solid veins in that neck—strong, protruding channels that ran down either side. He activated the video and watched those veins as they pulsed and glowed. He wished he could reach out and touch them.

He found the other images that he needed—ten in all. He programmed their movements, putting in the right facial expressions, adding nuances of anger and power. He would be reaching out to the entire network in a few moments, and he needed strong faces behind him. He wanted everyone to see what he saw.

You're weak, and you won't be strong again until you act.
Your fathers and grandfathers—and generations of men before them—had power and respect. They had women who looked up to them.
What do you have?
He wanted to set a wave in motion that no one could stop.
They've taken your jobs, your status, and your role in the family.

They work without you; they earn money without you;
they live without you.
They sleep without you; they raise children without you.
They even conceive children without you.
They think they don't need you at all.
He wanted them to hear what they desperately needed to know.
They think you're nothing.
And you'll continue to be nothing, until you rise up and
take it all back.

2055

SAN RAFAEL, CALIFORNIA

JULIA'S MOTHER stood in the doorway. In the dark of the room, with the light shining from behind, she had a glow around her. She wore a dress that Julia remembered from years before, but she didn't know that her mother still had it. Her hair was gathered up the way Julia liked it, in swoops and strands with barrettes and pins holding it up.

Her memory of being hit on the street during the peace march was still hazy. She remembered the doctors examining her. And she knew that Maya and Carlos had hovered around her bed for a long time. By now, they'd probably gone home. But at the moment there was a new, wonderful feeling surging through her. Her mother was there.

"Hi, Mom. I haven't seen you in so long."

Her mother smiled. "I'm sorry I missed your birthday. I wanted to see you, but they wouldn't let me out. Are you okay?"

"I think so." Julia felt a twinge of pain, realizing that her left arm and shoulder were in a cast and sling. "I'm not sure what's going on."

Her mother was sitting now on the edge of the bed. Julia didn't remember her walking over towards her, but she was glad that she was sitting there.

"I missed you," her mother said.

Julia choked up for a second and found herself crying.

"Don't cry." Her mother reached forward, as if to brush back the tears. "I hate to see you that way."

Julia could the feel warmth of the gesture, even though her mother's hand didn't quite reach her face.

"Maybe we can read a story."

Julia hadn't seen a book in her mother's hand when she came in, but now there was one in her lap. She opened it for her. "It's one of your favorites from when you were a little girl. We used to turn the pages and watch the rabbit scamper up the hill and then down again. There was always another hill, each with its own color. The rabbit would go up the yellow hill, and then she'd go down; and we'd go up and down with her."

Her mother was turning the pages for her now, as Julia basked in her memories. Up and down, up and down. Julia watched the yellow line with its raggedy little spikes. It repeated the same pattern over and over again. The green pattern was different; its ups and downs were slower. There was a red one and a blue one and some other colors. They all had their own patterns: some were long and slow; others short and spiked.

All the lines seemed to be on the same page. Then Julia realized they weren't on a page at all. They were on the wall. She blinked a couple of times, trying to make sense of what she was seeing. The lines were part of some electronic pattern that was measuring something. She looked down at her chest and saw some things that looked like sensors. She touched one of them. One of the lines on the screen—the long, slow red one—started moving differently. The thing on the wall was measuring her.

It finally dawned on Julia that she was alone in the hospital room. Her mother wasn't there. Maybe she'd been there and left, or maybe she'd never been there at all. Julia was suddenly sad, and then she realized she was also angry. She tried twisting her head, getting dizzy from the effort. Then she saw a tube sticking out of her arm—the right arm, which was the one that wasn't in a sling. She traced it up to a plastic bag hanging on a pole. She tried to sit up so she could see the label. She felt herself getting woozy again, but she finally got close enough to read it. There was a series of drug names, but the only one she recognized was morphine. Whatever was in that bag, she decided, was making her stupid.

She tried to remember what had happened earlier, but she could only recall bits and pieces. There was the peace march, and then they'd been attacked. She was missing some important part; there was something she needed to remember, but she couldn't figure out what it was. The harder she tried, the less she was able to think straight.

She sat up on the side of the bed, trying to decide what to do. The clock over the doorway said 3:05 A.M. She looked down at the IV that was holding the tube in her arm and thought for a second. It didn't take long to decide. She pulled the tube out, yanking it with her teeth. She covered up the little cap to keep the blood from escaping.

She stood up and tried walking. After the first few steps, she felt steadier. The wall screen was still flashing the colored lines with the same peaks and valleys. Apparently, the wireless sensors on her chest sent the information to the screen whether she was lying down or walking around. She realized there was probably a screen out at one of the nurses' stations displaying the same information. She wondered how far away she could get from the bed before all the lines and squiggles disappeared.

She hated the hospital gown. She poked around in the cubby-hole across the room, trying to find her own clothes. Her underpants were at the bottom of the pile. She struggled to put on her pants, shoes, and socks with one hand, but she didn't even try to put on her bra. Her sweatshirt was baggy enough that she was finally able to get it over her head, managing to put her right arm through a sleeve. She searched around for her vid-phone, but it was missing. The nurses probably had it stashed away somewhere.

Now what? She walked over to the door and peeked out. There was nothing there except two huge screens, one at either end of the corridor, churning out news and other programs to an empty hallway. She took a few steps down the hall and started getting dizzy again; her shoulder was beginning to hurt. But she wasn't going back. She was on a mission. She realized how shaken she was from that earlier scene. She missed her mother. That hallucination, or whatever it was, had made everything worse. They'd been together, and then suddenly everything had disappeared. As she got closer to the elevator, she knew what she had to do. She remembered that her mother was in the psychiatric ward down on the second floor. She was going down to see her.

She leaned on the side of the elevator car to steady herself, happy that it had a railing she could grab. A news-screen was running in the elevator; she tried to ignore it until she saw scenes of yesterday's peace march. Was she anywhere in that picture? A news flash scrolled across the bottom. *After an all-night session, the U.S. Congress is voting on a bill to withdraw funding from the war.* The screen then shifted to scenes of Deva Chandri and Yoko Nakamura talking to the cameras. Julia knew this was important news, but she was too woozy to grasp what it meant.

She got off at the second floor, where she was met by a metal door that stretched across the hallway. A sign read: "Psychiatric Ward: Authorized Admission Only." She tugged at the door, but it was locked. She stood there, frustrated. She realized that she'd have to see her mother another time, wondering if that door might ever be open to her.

But she'd come this far, and she had no intention of going back to her room. She took the stairway down to the ground floor. It was empty except for a maintenance man at the far end. With no one to stop her, she walked past the darkened shops and the vacant admissions desk and continued straight out the front door.

MINUTES LATER, SHE was a block away from the hospital, sitting on a bench near the transit stop and trying to figure out what to do next. There were no trains at that hour. Her house in Larkspur was just over the hill but, given her condition, it was too far to walk. The thing with her mother had her completely disoriented. Why did everything she tried to do with her mother go wrong? She thought about going back and sneaking into her mother's room, but she knew it wouldn't work. They'd stop her and put her back in her own room. They'd attach her back to that bag, and she'd feel dumber than she felt right now.

She got up and started walking. Her shoulder was throbbing, but it felt better when she was moving. She didn't have a destination in mind, but after a few moments she found herself going in the same direction as the last time she'd visited her mother. Her feet must have gotten her brain working, because she felt a thought coming to her out of the haze—it was the thought that she hadn't been able to recall earlier. Suddenly, she remembered. It was the men in the handkerchiefs, the attackers on the motorcycles. She'd recognized one of them. He was Lara's ex-boyfriend, Rick.

She knew then where her feet were taking her—to that building; to the place around the corner where Rick had chased her last time. But this was dangerous. Her mind, even in its messed-up state, knew that. She told herself to stop, but she didn't. Her legs must have been listening to that other part of her brain that was angry: this man hurt me. She heard something inside her shouting, *who's going to do something about that?*

She reached the building and stopped. Is this the right one? In the dark, these old buildings looked alike. But she recognized the side door; it was just across from where the motorcycles had been parked. She could hear Maya's voice inside her telling her to stop. *Show the cops where it is, and they'll arrest Rick. Don't get any closer!* But Julia kept walking anyway. She didn't have her vid-phone, so she couldn't call anybody. And she seemed unable to just stop; her body was determined to keep going. She told herself that if she kept going maybe she'd find out what was inside.

She turned down the alley and started to walk past the side door. But as she looked more closely at the windows, she realized they were covered with some sort of blackout paper. Then she saw that there was a light moving behind them.

Oh shit, she thought, I have to get out of here.

She began heading north, up the alley, moving as fast as she could. But then she heard a roar ahead of her. It was the sound of a group of motorcycles. She saw the flash of their headlights and watched as they started to make the turn. They were coming down the alley towards her. She dove for the side of the alley and pressed herself against the wall, her heart beating rapidly. With her back against the wall, she tried side-stepping back the way she'd come, hoping they wouldn't see her. Then another sound sent her into a panic: more motorcycles. These were turning into the alley from the other end.

Both ways! In her mind, Julia was screaming her head off: They're coming both ways! She pressed tightly against the wall, reaching out instinctively with her free arm. As her hand touched the side door, it slid down to the handle. She gave it a twist; it opened. She hesitated for a second. I can't do this. But what else could she do?

She slipped through the door, quickly locking it behind her. Had any of the cyclists seen her? She didn't know. She probably wouldn't know until the minute they grabbed her and . . . she didn't want to think about it.

She was in a small hallway. The light she'd seen was from a room off to the left, but the hallway itself was dark. She had a chance. She turned right, moving away from the light. She needed a place—any place—to hide. She tried one door, and it was the bathroom. She couldn't hide there; those guys would probably go there the minute they walked in. There was another door just beyond that. She opened it and found a closet. She had no idea what was in it, but she couldn't take the time to find out: they were outside in the alley right now, parking their motor-cycles. She squeezed her way in and pulled the door closed behind her. There was barely enough room for her.

Julia heard a pair of loud thumps. Someone was pounding on the alleyway door.

"Hey, bro', open this fuckin' thing," a deep voice shouted. "'You ex-pect us to cool our asses out here all night?"

Julia heard footsteps coming down the hall and then a voice. "Okay, you assholes, quit making so much noise." It was Rick. "I thought I left it unlocked for you."

She heard a jiggling of the handle. "Does this sound unlocked to you?"

The door opened, and Julia heard the sound of heavy boots tromping through the hallway. Shouts flew back and forth. They all seemed to be standing just outside her door. Her shoulder was throbbing even more now, and her head was starting to hurt. She began giving silent instructions to the men in hallway: *Keep going . . . You've got to keep going . . . you don't need anything from the closet.*

"I have to take a piss, before I do anything else."

Everything was loud, even the splashes from the man with the high-pitched voice standing at the toilet.

"Hurry up," another one shouted. "I'm right behind you."

"Don't get too close with that damn thing," the first one said.

"Doesn't matter if he does or not," another one yelled from the hallway. "It's so small, you won't even notice it."

There was a roar of laughter and fists pounding against the walls. How much longer could she stand the noise, the heat, the pain, and the suffocation in the closet? Was there room enough on the floor if she just collapsed?

"I could use some blow," the deep-voiced one demanded. "If you've got crank, I'll take that instead. But I won't be able to listen to all this shit without a little something."

She heard Rick mumble a response. Some of the others took up the argument. "Why are we here so goddamned early?" one of them growled.

"You didn't complain when I was passing out all the money," Rick answered.

"But we had a nice little piece all juiced up, and she was ready to celebrate with us. She was just getting warm, man, and then we had to leave."

One of the others gave a long, guttural howl. "How about it, Rick? Are you stashing anybody around here to entertain us? Do you have anything in the closet?"

Julia held grimly to the wall with her good arm. She was afraid she might faint.

After a few minutes the sounds in the hallway died down. Julia pressed her ear against the door, trying to hear what they were doing. The sounds were coming from a room at the other end of the hall. Were they all in there talking? She couldn't be sure. Now there were more sounds and different voices. Were they looking at a vid-screen?

Sooner or later, she told herself, she would have to open the door and make a run for it. The alleyway door was between her and the men in the other room. Maybe now was a good time, while they were distracted. She opened the door a crack, trying not to make a sound. She saw lights at the end of the hall. She couldn't wait any longer.

She opened the door wider and slipped through.

She immediately wished she hadn't.

At the end of the hall was an eruption of angry men in throbbing electronic images, many of them hovering just above the surface of the walls and the ceiling, overwhelming everything else in the room. There seemed to be hundreds of men flashing in and out, getting larger and smaller. Some were shouting; others were just glaring. They were indoors and outdoors, in light and in shadow, in small groups and larger packs. Many of them were talking back and forth, with words flying from one vid-panel to another. Some images disappeared and then came back again. A man in one panel was suddenly gone, replaced by the image of an angry group of men shouting obscenities.

WHO ARE THEY, Julia screamed to herself? *Where* are they? Here? Next door? Somewhere else around the world? The men in the room—the ones she feared the most—were talking to the images of the men on the wall. The men on the wall acted like they could see them. Could they see her too? She had to get out, but she was glued to the spot. She tried easing herself down to the floor, hoping to make herself invisible.

"Hey, Rick, what's with the Bible?" one of them shouted. "Are we going to start saying prayers?"

"You ignorant prick," Rick sneered. "That's how we get our access code. He sends it to us in Bible verses."

Moments later, the room in front of her became quieter. The lack of noise was suddenly terrifying. The outside door was three steps away, but it might as well have been three blocks. She started to panic. She might be losing her chance to run for it.

The earlier images had disappeared from the end wall, and a new, larger one had emerged. The men—the ones in the room and the ones on the walls—had quieted down and were now looking at this new scene. None of them said a word. A line of ten young men appeared on that end wall. They were unsmiling men, each with a hard look in his eyes. There was a mist around them, like they were walking out of a fog. The music behind them had a heavy, pounding beat. They were wearing jackets, all with the same symbol that she'd seen yesterday on her attackers' jackets: the circle with the arrow running through it.

A murmur went through the men in the room, as another man, an even stranger looking man, appeared in front of the others. Julia had never seen anything like him. His face kept changing, altering itself in moods and colors. She realized she must be looking at a computerized simulation of a face.

He began to speak. Within seconds, Julia was cringing. Was that Abraham? She'd heard stories about him. Annabel and Flora had told her what they knew about him—how he hated women, especially the Women for Peace. But nothing had prepared her for this. These men were hanging on his every word. What he was saying made her nauseous.

This man hated women.

He hated girls.

He hated her.

Julia jumped out of her crouch and headed for the door. She reached for the handle and gave it a twist. The door opened, and she raced out into the street, moving as fast as she could while holding on to her throbbing shoulder. She could hear the men in the room shouting after her.

She reached the corner and saw a police car cruising through the next intersection. She headed for it as fast as she could. The car slowed down as soon as the driver saw her running. One of the policewomen got out and opened the back door. Julia dove into the backseat, trying not to land on her sore shoulder.

"Are you Julia Moro?" the officer asked.

"Yeah, how did you know?"

"The hospital's had us looking for you for the last hour."

MAYA GOT A call from the hospital at 4:15 A.M., telling her Julia was missing.

She fought a sense of panic. She started berating herself for not staying with Julia all night in the hospital room. Memories of another young girl—one who had disappeared in much the same way—came roaring back into her head. She was unable to move, not knowing whether to rush to the hospital or wait and hope that Julia might find her way home. She stayed that way, frozen in helplessness, until the hospital called to say they had found her. Julia was safe and back in her room. Maya let out a sigh.

"Where was she, somewhere else in the building?"

"No, the police found her a few blocks from here. She apparently wandered off."

"Wandered off?" Maya felt the tension rising again. "Where did she go?"

"The police need to talk to her some more to find out what happened. But she apparently had a run-in with a motorcycle gang."

Maya's emotions were ready to burst. *Don't do anything until I get there!* When the woman on the other end hesitated, she repeated it with more force.

"Do nothing! I want you to wait until I get there."

She slapped the vid-phone shut and grabbed a coat. The debilitating fear was gone. She was all action now, moving with a seething anger. Minutes later, she was at the hospital. A security guard eyed her as she walked through the front door, but she didn't bother to slow down. *Where were you earlier?* she wanted to yell at him. Her mind was racing as she waited for the elevator.

No—not again; it's not going to happen this time. She kept repeating that to herself, as if by force of will she could rewrite the history of the last few hours. The elevator stopped at the second floor, where a nurse stepped on. As the door closed, Maya stared down the hallway at the door to the psychiatric ward. She thought about Amy enclosed inside—Amy, who'd spent most of her life in and out of hospitals, fighting her demons. No—not again, she told herself. That wasn't going to happen to Amy's daughter—it wasn't going to happen to Julia.

Maya had an appointment with Amy's psychiatrists in a few days to find out what, if any, progress they'd made. She'd find out if they might release her. She'd learn if they'd found some miraculous way to restore her mental health. But she knew one thing for sure: the doctors could never undo the rape that she had endured at the hands of a group of misfits—a motorcycle gang that had tossed her around like a piece of meat.

No—not again. That couldn't happen to Julia.

Maya strode into Julia's room, hovering near her bed as a nurse checked Julia's IV tube. After a few moments her patience ran out.

"Is there any way you can do that later? I need to talk to Julia."

The nurse saw the look on her face. She said she'd be back in a while.

"Julia, are you okay?"

Julia looked scared, but she nodded yes.

"Tell me everything that happened."

Maya could see she was reluctant to talk. Her voice was softer than usual, and it drifted off. She stared at the sling around her left arm, picking at a couple of loose threads. Her descriptions got more and more vague. She was tired, she said. She wasn't sure she could remember everything. She looked everywhere but at Maya.

Maya had seen the passive resistance tricks of teenagers many times, and normally she'd just wait it out. But right now she had no patience. She wanted answers.

"Julia, you have to tell me exactly what happened."

Julia protested, but piece by piece Maya succeeded in getting the story out of her. She told Maya of the hallucination about her mother. Then she told her about Rick—that he had threatened her before, and that he'd been one of the attackers at the march. Rick and his friends were hooked into something that looked like the *Patria* network. And Julia had spent many harrowing minutes caught in a room with them.

"Did Rick touch you?"

"No."

"Did any of the others touch you?"

"No."

"Did any of them pull down your clothes or try to do anything to your body?"

"No! Why do you keep asking these questions?"

Maya stopped. She suddenly realized she might have gone too far. She saw tears in Julia's eyes. "I'm sorry," she said. "I didn't mean to get you upset."

She heard a noise and realized that Antonio was standing in the doorway.

"Mom? Are you okay?"

Behind him were a couple of uniformed officers, waiting to walk in with him. She'd awakened Antonio on the way into the hospital, asking him to get to the hospital as quickly as he could. Now he seemed hesitant to come into the room. Had he heard her from the hallway?

"These officers are here to talk to Julia."

Maya told them to come in. Suddenly, she just wanted to be out of the way.

"Maybe only one of us should stay while they do the questioning," Antonio said.

Maya knew what he meant: he was the lawyer, and he should stay. She should go.

MAYA FOUND A café across the street from the hospital and almost collapsed into a chair. She was exhausted. She knew she should call Lara and Carlos. They'd both be worried, but she needed time to think. She ordered a cup of tea and a scone, but the scone sat like a rock inside her. The tea wasn't any good either.

Her anger with Rick and his friends knew no bounds. He had ruined her daughter's life. Now he was starting in on Julia. What was he doing with the *Patria* gangs? As much as she hated Rick, Maya hadn't realized he'd sunk so low. She tried to come to grips with this new piece of information about him. He was probably holed up now in one of the gang camps near Santa Rosa, getting his fill of drugs and whores.

Maya got depressed when she thought about what had happened to Lara, an intelligent, lively woman who had somehow fallen for a complete loser. But why should she be so surprised? She'd done the same thing herself. She thought she could help her daughter avoid such a mistake, but the opposite had been true. Every time she suggested that Rick was abusing her, Lara got angry and said she was just projecting her own problems. Lara rushed to defend Rick. He was under a lot of pressure. He couldn't find a job, and he was upset by her two miscarriages. Lara had fallen for the whole line of rationalizations right up to the point when Rick had started hitting her. Now, she was terrified of him. She lived in fear that he would come back and attack her again.

The more Maya thought about it, the more she realized that Rick fit the *Patria* profile. He resented their co-housing community and everybody in it. He was scornful of the women, particularly the ones who were living alone or with other women. Men who were raising children on their own, like Flora's two fathers, made him seethe.

The Governor's Commission Report of 2054 had called men like him "rootless males"—underemployed, alienated from their families, and deeply resentful of a society they considered "feminized." When the Report had come out, Maya had organized a meeting to discuss it, sensing even then that she had a problem of her own with Rick.

The problem was partly economic, the Report said. In recent years women had adapted better than men to the available jobs. But it was more than just that. The Report noted that the status of men as "head of the family" had seriously eroded. The Report included one statistic—a hundred-year comparison—that stuck in Maya's mind. In 1954, a huge majority of children had grown up in families in which the parents were married and there was one male wage-earner. By 2054, however, fewer than ten percent of family units fell into that category. The Report cited all kinds of factors, including economics, reproductive technology, and changing women's attitudes. The nuclear family had declined as the national standard, while group arrangements, like co-housing, were on the rise. Most men had adjusted well to these changes, the Report said, but there were many on the fringes that either couldn't adapt or chose not to. They were usually men with low self-esteem and big hatreds. That seemed even clearer now. The Report was talking about men like Rick.

MAYA LEFT THE remains of her breakfast and headed outside for some air. She had to get her mind off Rick and all the rest of them. She found a park near the hospital and just started walking. She hoped she wouldn't run into anybody she knew. She'd left the house in such a hurry that she hadn't even combed her hair; she was wearing one of her rattiest coats. But she didn't want to talk to anybody anyway. She needed time to think.

Lurking behind all her anger at Rick and the rest of the world, she realized, was her anger at herself. She'd handled the thing with Julia all wrong. Her reaction had had less to do with what was actually going on with Julia and more to do with her fear that Julia would end up like her mother. It was an instinctive response that had just overwhelmed her. But the more she thought about it, the less sense it made. Amy was mentally ill—a victim of a childhood disease compounded by the neglect of someone who had left her to die. Julia was a bright, sensitive child. She was headstrong at times, but so what? She was never going down the same path as her mother.

Maya sat down on a bench and tried to make sense of what she was feeling. She was face-to-face with a thought that had probably been there all along: she was obsessed by her failure with Amy. It had been weighing on her for years, she realized, nagging her with a sense of guilt. During all those years, nothing seemed to work. She had learned all she could about Lynn-Taksin disease and how to treat it. She had consulted with all the doctors who specialized in it, but it hadn't done any good. She remembered the sleepless nights and the days of bitter disappointment, as she tried to reach out to a child who needed so much love. But the problems had been more than she could fix. There were times when Lara or Antonio had to take her aside and remind her to take care of herself. And then, one day, Amy's childhood was over, seemingly before it had begun. She plunged into an early and sad adulthood. There was no logical reason for Maya to feel guilty. She'd done what she could for a troubled child. But logic didn't matter. She'd taken responsibility for another person's life, and that life seemed to be drifting away piece by piece. She felt her failure on an emotional level that reason couldn't touch.

She saw now how those feelings had spilled over. They were starting to seep into her relations with others. Julia's hallucinations about her mother being in her hospital room shocked her. Maya realized she might have made a terrible mistake. She'd been trying to keep up the pretense that Amy and Julia might someday enjoy a normal mother-daughter relationship. She wanted Julia to feel good about her mother, but now she realized Julia may have become obsessed with her. What could she do now that wouldn't cause even more harm?

Maya wanted to sit in the park a little longer, but it was time to go back. When she reached the hospital, she saw that the main floor was now crowded with people coming and going, but the biggest group was gathered around the large vid-screen. Maya stopped to watch, her nervousness growing. There was breaking news. Maya held her breath. A news flash began scrolling at the bottom of the screen. *Congress has just voted to cut off all war funding. The President has ordered the invasion fleet to stand down.* The screen showed pictures of U.S. warships gleaming in the South Atlantic sunlight, as they turned and headed away from the South African coast. Those pictures gave way to scenes of Thabo Nyrere, who was laughing and talking to the press. He was flanked by a group of people, including a smiling Yoko Nakamura, Maria Balewa, and Deva Chandri.

Maya pushed her way past several people to find a chair. She needed to sit down. She suddenly realized how much of her life had been tied up in knots, hoping for the news she had just heard. Within minutes, she found herself starting to cry. People turned to look at her, but she didn't care. A huge weight had been lifted from her shoulders, and she let the tears flow without restraint.

THE TWO POLICE officers were anxious to tell Maya about what they had learned from talking to Julia. But her mood had gone from grim to exultant that morning, and she didn't want to be dragged back down. Yet she knew she had to listen.

From what Julia had been able to tell them, there were apparently several gangs and militia groups from around the world that had been linked to that meeting. The police had even been able to identify some of the leadership of urban terrorist groups in Brazil and Russia on the basis of her description. She'd seen some of the *Patria* groups in action. She was one of the few outsiders who had ever witnessed this.

"Our little Julia here is quite an observer," the older cop said. "We're just hoping she can tell us more."

Maya found his manner annoying. What was he talking about?

"Julia saw more things than she can remember right now," the older cop continued, as if in answer to her silent question. "If we can find out everything she saw, we could get even more detailed identifications."

If they had more complete information from her, they could probably triangulate the access point of some of the groups and find their location. Then they could work backward from there to unravel the network. He stopped there, apparently trying to let it all sink in.

"So, what do you want?" Maya asked.

The lead investigator glanced at his partner. "We'd like Julia to submit to a hypno-scan to find out everything she saw but can't remember."

Maya looked at Antonio. "Should she do that?"

Antonio shrugged. "I'm not sure."

"What do we know about this procedure?"

"The hypno-scan technique uses induced images to create a computerized reproduction of the subject's entire memory."

The other cop began an explanation of the procedure. He talked a little too quickly, as far as Maya was concerned. The hypno-scan had been in use for over three years, he said, and it was perfectly safe. It picked up images that had been seen, but later forgotten, as well as images that had been blocked out. It gathered everything that was still lodged in the person's memory. There was no danger to the subject.

"The images go directly from the brain to the computer. There are no ill effects. She won't remember the details of those memories any more than she does now."

"How do you know there are no ill effects?" Maya asked.

The cops looked surprised. "There are no reports of any," said the older cop.

"How about years down the line? You've only been doing this for three years. You don't know what kind of memory flashbacks someone could have in the long term."

"The scientists say nothing like that could happen."

Maya shook her head. The more they reassured her, the more skeptical she was. "We want to help you. We want to get Rick and all those other thugs as much as anyone, but I don't know. This seems like it could be risky."

"Maya."

She turned and saw a serious look in Julia's eyes.

"Maya, I want to do it."

THURSDAY, APRIL 23, 2082

TARRYTOWN, NEW YORK

JULIA

I WAS RUNNING late. Teki met me at the door of my office with a stack of documents in his outstretched arms, gripping them tightly between his finger joints. He appeared to have what I needed for the meeting.

"Did you check with Toki about this?"

Teki blinked yes.

"Did he tell you everything I wanted?"

There was another blink: yes.

As I took the documents, Teki was churning out a message. It was one he had given me before. He and Toki, the message said, were programmed to be gender-neutral, so my reference to him as a "he" was not technically correct.

Maybe, but I had to call them something. They just seemed like a pair of "he's" to me.

MADELEINE WAS ALREADY in the conference room when I arrived. She scowled as I walked in. She wanted to talk to me privately, that was pretty clear. But she wasn't going to get the chance until the meeting with the contractors was over.

Irena Castillo sat next to Madeleine. Technically she was running the meeting, but she'd probably turn it over to me once we started talking about security issues. Castillo ran the meetings with a light hand. She was a genial woman who was politically savvy enough to survive as the general contractor on the U.N. building project. Because of the balancing act that had gone into the selection of the subcontractors and suppliers, she had to be very diplomatic. These people were all politically connected.

Madeleine had briefed me about each of them months earlier. As I looked around the table now, I could hear her capsule summaries running through my head: Vassily Gregor (he's got the plumbing contract . . . he's in solid with the Conservative bloc of the Legislative Assembly . . . the only Eastern European on the project . . . can be suave but a little unctuous . . . watch your wallet). Gregor was now smiling at me with his ready-to-please look, probably sensing my upcoming complaints about his security procedures.

It was the same for the other problem cases: Nakia Coombs (specialty caterer . . . a close—very close—friend of the Secretary-General's brother-in-law . . . charming, but vicious); Waklin Ming (a good tile contractor, but a bad judge of character . . . be prepared for some unexpected gifts); Rogier Theroux (knows carpeting better than anyone . . . don't look too closely at his sources).

"These are all people we have to live with," Madeleine said. "Each one of them has an important relationship somewhere within the organization."

"So, what do you want me to do, just ignore them?"

Madeleine and I had gone around on this issue more than once. "We've found gaps in some of their procedures," I said. "Some have employees with no biographical records at all outside of the employer's database. A few even have employees who've tried to alter their basic body biometrics to create a new identity."

"Just try to go lightly," Madeleine said. "Remember there might be other issues than the ones you're concerned about."

"The electrical contractor, Noah Fawkes, is a good example of what I'm talking about," Madeleine continued. "It's easy just to dismiss him as an old bearded guy who can be gruff and rude at times, but his May 4th Foundation has provided the largest share of the funding for all of the commemoration ceremonies. Without him, we wouldn't have Laria Kwon's sculpture or the chandelier to illuminate it, or much else, for that matter."

By the time I sat down, Madeleine was already eyeing everyone around the table, trying to anticipate problems, worrying that I might tread a little too heavily. Fawkes and Gregor were already giving her sour looks. She wouldn't be happy about that.

Politicking. I was glad it was her job and not mine.

WHEN I GOT to the restaurant an hour and a half later, Madeleine was seated at her favorite table. The maitre d' always put her in the rear, where she could sit with her back to the wall and watch who was going in and out of the Madison Avenue entrance. The menus were already illuminated in the center of the table. She stopped reading when she saw me. She wanted me to sit down immediately so we could talk.

I jumped in first. "How do you think the meeting went?"

Madeleine gave a shrug and brushed off my question. "About how I expected."

"That's not what I want to talk about," she said quickly. "I want to hear about the bombing at Grand Central. But before that, I want to know what happened to you back in Avram's office. I heard you blacked out."

I was annoyed that the word had gotten around so quickly. "If you know something happened, then you must also know it was nothing."

"Listen," she said with an edge to her voice, "With something like that—"

She stopped quickly when she realized someone was standing next to her.

"Have you ladies had a chance to look over the menu?"

Madeleine looked up at the waiter hovering over her. She gave him a withering look, but he kept on smiling. He was tall, passably hand-some, and totally clueless.

"We have some specials; I'll let the chef tell you about them." He reached over to the menu screen and pressed a button. A man with a white jacket, chef's toque, and a heavy European accent appeared on the screen and began explaining his latest creations.

"Forget about that," Madeleine interrupted. "Just give me a Caesar salad."

"Good choice," the waiter purred. He reached towards the menu screen again. "I'll have our produce team explain the sourcing of the ingredients."

Madeleine grabbed his arm before he could push any more buttons. He looked surprised. "Just bring us two salads."

Madeleine glared at him as he walked away, then she turned back to me.

"Okay, what happened in Avram's office?"

"It was a memory flashback that gave me a headache. It went away on its own."

She didn't look convinced. "Avram said you were totally out for a minute or so. He said it was like a trance."

I found myself squirming. "I get headaches sometimes, okay? You know that. The last one was two years ago in Baluchistan. You certainly knew about that one."

"But I didn't know it was that bad."

"It wasn't," I admitted. "This one was worse. I don't know why."

Madeleine continued to stare at me.

"Look, I'm not sick. Can we talk about something else?"

Unrelenting, Madeleine asked what caused my flashbacks. I finally told her.

"So, you were thirteen when all this happened," she said, trying to process the information. "What did you remember after going through the hypno-scan?"

"Do you want to know what I remember or what the computer reproduction says I remembered? They're two different things. The computerized file of my memory has all sorts of details that I can't really recall: where the men were standing, what was in the background, the languages they spoke. I even had pictures in my mind of the clothes that Abraham and the others were wearing."

"Have you seen the whole thing?"

"No. I tried once, but I could feel the pain start to pound in my head. From the little bit I saw, however, I'd say it was like someone else's memory, someone who was not quite me. There's a copy of it in the U.N. Criminal Justice files, if you want to see it."

"Did any of this help their investigation back then?"

"Maybe. The police were already starting to crack down on *Patria* gangs in several countries. Their activity level went down further after that, so I guess the stuff they picked out of my memory helped. That's what they told me, anyway."

Madeleine fiddled with her fork, not saying anything. I couldn't stand the silence.

"Madeleine, you're acting like I'm damaged goods or something. I told you before you hired me that I had some issues to deal with. Don't you remember that conversation? We skipped the normal psychological screening because you were so anxious to have me come and work for you."

Madeleine nodded, trying to downplay her reaction. But I was still upset.

"Look, I can do this job fine, but I can't do it if you're worried that your entire security operation is being run by someone who is mentally unstable. I can handle the memory flashback thing."

Madeleine shook her head; I didn't need to go any further.

"I once told you that I'd trust you with my life," Madeleine said. "I still do."

I COULD HAVE told her about the good parts of my childhood, but she probably would have been bored. The year after my run-in with the *Patria* gang was one of the calmer periods—calm by the standards of my teenage years, anyway. Maya decided I should learn more about our co-housing community, so she took me on her daily walks.

She began those walks years earlier when she was chairing the co-housing council, but later she just kept doing them. Her walk took her through the vegetable gardens and over to the other side of Magnolia Avenue, around the back of the older hillside homes. Those houses had all been retrofitted with solar power and catch basins when their ground-ownership was transferred to the co-housing community years earlier. Now their role was vital. Without the water run-off they captured, we wouldn't have had a sustainable garden. For Maya, that would have been a tragedy.

It was around that time that we got some good news. Antonio told Maya that Li-Jin was pregnant. The prospect of another grandchild gave Maya a lot to think about on those afternoons while she sat on her favorite bench overlooking Corte Madera Creek. The other news we got was both good and bad: my mother was released from the hospital. She'd be living in a small apartment close to those who would be supervising her. That news should have made me happy, but instead it just highlighted how sad our relationship was. Because her problems were psychological, I couldn't really grasp what was wrong with her. In my own clumsy way I kept making things worse. Maya and the others debated whether I needed counseling in order to deal with her. Then I did something that forced their hand. I had been selected for the World Youth Holo-Conference that was sponsored by Women for Peace. It was an honor, but in the end it brought out the worst in me.

I got word that my essay had been selected and that I would be one of only ninety teenagers participating in the conference worldwide. I was feeling pretty good about myself, and I wanted to tell my mother first thing. But when I raced over to her apartment to see her, she wasn't there. I couldn't believe it. I just stood in front of her door with the excitement draining out of me. I was sure I'd told her I'd be coming by. I tried to tell myself not to be disappointed, but I sank down in the hallway anyway and tossed my books around in frustration. Just once, I kept thinking—couldn't it work out just once?

TWO WEEKS LATER I found myself sitting at a small table in an empty room, wondering if the conference was really going to happen or whether I would just be staring at a blank wall all morning. It was the first time I'd ever been part of anything like that, and I was pretty nervous. Finally, I got word from Eloni over my vid-phone that it was about to start. She was in the room behind me, monitoring the conference on a vid-screen and preparing to send me messages if I needed them. Maya was there, and at my insistence they'd arranged for my mother to be there with them too.

Suddenly I was in the middle of the conference . . . or was I? Seconds before, I'd been all alone. Then the lights went down and the holo-projectors went on, and the room became filled with people. If I stared hard enough, I could see the shimmering edges of the images. But my eyes were already starting to adjust. Eloni had said not to turn my head too sharply, so I tried looking out of the corners of my eyes. The other kids were looped around in an arc in both directions. Some were stealing looks at me; I must have seemed just as wide-eyed to them as they did to me. Across from us, there was another arc of chairs with the thirteen leaders of Women for Peace seated in them.

The vid-phone lit up with a message from Eloni. *I'm looking at the same screen that everyone around the world is watching. I can see you, and you look great.*

I've been in dozens of holo-conferences since then, but I still remember the excitement of those first few moments. Deva Chandri was there, right in front of me. She introduced the group, and then asked Rasa Malik to talk about why we were there. Rasa explained that their movement belonged to all the people around the world who want peace and justice. "It's especially important that we hear from young people."

The students were shy at first, asking only a few questions. *What was it like to protest against a war? Were they scared?* several wanted to know. Marta Kwon finally intervened and gently moved the conversation in another direction. "We want to know what problems are bothering you in your communities," she said. "We're here to learn." That opened the door to all kinds of questions. I remember one girl pleading passionately about the problem of child prostitution in Thailand and asking if they could do anything about it. But many of the comments were about problems of which I was only dimly aware.

My most vivid memory is of the women themselves. This was the first time I had ever seen them, and I was never to see them again. Deva Chandri sat in the center of the group, dressed in a sari with overlapping layers of soft peach and tan, her gray hair pulled up in a bun. Her eyes were even more penetrating than they appeared in her pictures. Those eyes served as a gentle beacon, directing the meeting, finding the right person to speak, seizing the right note to move the conversation elsewhere. Each of the women moved effortlessly to add her voice to the conversation. They seemed to weave in and out of the discussion without script or direction. The effect was mesmerizing. Each had her own distinctive personality, but as a group they had a charisma that reached another level.

A boy inadvertently underlined that point when he asked, "How come there aren't any men in your group?"

A couple of the women grinned, and that got all the students laughing. The boy sat there looking sheepish, until Ayaan Yusuf came to his rescue. "No, no. We shouldn't laugh. In my country of Somalia, I'm always asked that question."

"Let me say, we work very closely with many men. They've stood by us in the most dangerous things we've done. But the thirteen of us have been working together for years, and we know instinctively how the others think. In the work we do, we have to know immediately that we can speak with one voice."

I SAW A hand raised at the seat just to my left. I hadn't noticed it before, but in the years since, I have thought a lot about that moment.

Deva pointed in the direction of the raised hand. "Yes . . . Oh, good heavens, it's Dhanye! What a wonderful surprise! I had no idea that you were part of this group. Whose idea was this?" She looked down her row of colleagues.

Franca Peres answered her with a big grin. "We thought we should include one of your brilliant grandchildren, and then we decided to make it a surprise."

"That's wonderful." Deva clapped with glee. "Dhanye, where are you?"

"Mumbai."

"Mumbai! I can't believe it. I think my brain is too old to figure out how these holo-conferences work. It seems like you're right here."

Right here, only a meter or so away—almost close enough to touch. It was like seeing Deva Chandri's eyes in a younger, leaner face. At that moment, those eyes were wet with embarrassment over the fuss being made.

That brief encounter has become part of our personal history. Dhanye and I have talked about it many times since. Our eyes made contact in those few brief seconds, and we exchanged shy smiles. Something passed between us—we both knew it. But neither of us knew what it was at the time. What would have happened if we had gotten together then? Could we have built a relationship like we have now? Dhanye thinks so, but I know it wouldn't have worked. I was far too immature at age fourteen. I had many more anguishing moments to go through before I could jump into someone else's life. I'm convinced that my first meeting with Dhanye was just a note that my soul would be sending to me sometime in the future.

"What is your question, dear child?" Deva asked.

Dhanye glanced down at some notes before speaking. "Of all the many issues that Women for Peace is working on, which is the most important?"

Franca laughed. "See? I knew we'd get a question that would make us think. I would have to say the most important issue is the New Charter project for the United Nations. Do the rest of you agree? Maybe Yoko should explain it."

Before I heard Yoko Nakamura's explanation of the Charter Project that day, I had been only vaguely aware of its importance. But her passion for the project made it come alive. Looking back now, I realize the New Charter of the United Nations has defined the Women for Peace's place in history.

"The New Charter would allow the U.N. to act on behalf of all of the people of the world," she said. "It would have the power to prevent wars, control international cartels, regulate the environment, and protect human rights. These are things that we fight for every day, but right now we have to fight as outsiders. If the New Charter is adopted, we will have the institutions of government on our side."

I WAS ONE of the few students who hadn't spoken, and I was beginning to realize that I had to say something. Deva Chandri looked over at me expectantly and said, "Julia, did you have something you wanted to add?"

If I hadn't been so wrapped up in my own thoughts, I might have thought it odd that she knew who I was. I realize now that Maya had probably told her everything about me. But at that moment, I knew none of that.

I hesitated for a moment, and then I blurted out what had been bothering me. "I'm concerned about you and the other women."

I thought I heard the other students gasping, but in a room full of holograms I couldn't be sure of anything. However, my concern had changed the mood of the conference. I could feel it.

"Why is that?"

I took a breath and then plunged in. All of my anxieties came pouring out. I told them about the men screaming from the walls at the secret meeting, about the gangs that had attacked us on the march, and the lurid images from the hypno-scan. Before anyone could respond, I asked another question.

"How can you do all the good things you want to do when there are these people in the world who want to kill you?"

Well, I thought, it's out there now.

For a moment, no one said anything.

Deva Chandri looked at me intensely, and I got caught up in her gaze. It was as deep and sorrowful as anything I'd ever seen.

"Julia, I'm so sorry. It makes me sad that you had to go through that."

The seconds ticked by, and the moment seemed interminable. I could barely bring myself to look at the other students.

Finally, she spoke again. "Julia, I'm so glad you brought this up."

As she said it, I remember feeling a huge weight come off my shoulders.

Her tone was somber. "It appears that you have seen firsthand the work of the *Patria* organization. I'm sorry about that. *Patria* is a network of some very dangerous groups. We know we must be careful in dealing with them."

She turned slightly and directed her words to the others.

"But I urge all of you not to live your lives in fear. If we stop working for peace and justice because we are afraid of those who oppose us, we will lose even before we begin. Our opponents will win without lifting a finger."

She paused for a moment. "Please don't let that happen . . . you deserve better than that. One of the most rewarding things you can do in life is put yourself in the service of a good cause. Remember the words of Mohandas Gandhi, who once said 'Be the change you wish to see in the world.'"

"Julia, we can't thank you enough for your comments."

THE MEETING ENDED, and the room was suddenly just another room. The students on either side of me were gone; the panel of women in front of me had disappeared. The words and faces were replaced by ordinary white lights shining against an empty wall. I remember being startled by the sudden emptiness.

The Women for Peace were no longer sitting in front of me, but their words were echoing in my ears. "Be the change you wish to see in the world." The excitement was flowing through me. The question I had hesitated to ask had become an important moment in the conference. Deva Chandri herself had said so.

But I had no idea of the harm that my words would inadvertently cause. Nor did I have any idea what anguish my heady sense of achievement would cause moments later when it butted up against my neediness. I was about to find out.

ELONI CAME UP behind me and gave me a hug. "You were wonderful. I've been monitoring the audience comments and reactions. They've been great."

I glowed for a moment, as Maya added her own praise of my performance.

"We're all so proud of you."

Then I looked around the room. "What did my mother think . . . where is she?"

"She's not here." I could see Eloni and Maya were uneasy with the question.

"She left."

"Did she see anything at all?" I felt myself getting angry. It was a shameful emotion that, even then, I knew was wrong, but I couldn't control it.

"I don't know."

"Don't make excuses for her! She wasn't here at all, was she?"

"Julia, don't get yourself upset about this."

Maya was trying to calm me down, but I was in no mood for it. "Where is she?"

I raced out the door and headed down the block, cutting over towards the street where I knew my mother liked to go. I saw her from the back, sitting on some rocks. I began shouting at her as I got closer.

"You couldn't be there for me just this one time! I wanted you to be there, and you wouldn't do it. Don't I mean anything to you at all?"

I continued my outburst, unable to control the flow of my anger. I realize now that it had been building up for years, and I couldn't stop it. I heard someone coming up behind me, breathing heavily, and I realized it was Maya. She must have been trying to catch up with me.

"Please stop." Maya grabbed me by the arms and shook me. "Please. I know you're upset, and I know why. But there are things you don't know, things you probably need to know. Please."

Maya put her arms around me and eased me over towards my mother. She still had her back to us. She hadn't moved a muscle during my outburst. Now, I could see that she was crying heavily.

I don't ever remember feeling worse about myself than I did at that moment.

2056

SAN RAFAEL, CALIFORNIA

SO YOU'RE the daughter," Dr. Mortimer said, eyeing Julia up and down. "I probably have a couple of minutes I can spare to talk to you."

Maya insisted that Julia talk to a therapist who could help her deal with her mother. The first stop was Dr. Melissa Mortimer, her mother's psychiatrist. Julia disliked her from the first words she heard out of her mouth.

When Julia tried to say something, Dr. Mortimer pretty much ignored her. It didn't get any better as the minutes passed. She said she couldn't tell Julia anything directly, because that would breach doctor-patient confidentiality. But maybe they could share some information with her indirectly by providing her with her own therapist. That makes no sense, Julia thought: you're either going to tell me things or not. Why the roundabout stuff? The therapist they chose was Dr. Paola Bertani. Paola and her partner, Naomi, lived in the community, and Julia knew her. She had gone to school with their son, Josh. That arrangement was okay. She liked Dr. Bertani a lot more than she liked Dr. Mortimer.

"Your mother is mentally ill," Dr. Bertani explained in their first session, "And her interactions with others can make the illness worse. People around her can trigger a crisis without realizing it." She reminded Julia that her mother was very immature and, in a certain sense, hadn't grown up at all. She had her high moments, but things could change suddenly. She'd spend months at a time in hospitals until her doctors thought they could release her and control her behavior with medication. That would last until something triggered a relapse. Sometimes she'd refuse the medicine. During those periods she might wander off and suffer a blackout. Later she would just get deeply depressed. When things were at their worst, she would try to kill herself.

Julia was beginning to realize how much she might have contributed to her mother's pain without knowing it. She kept asking what she could do.

"You can't cure your mother all by yourself. If you're going to help her, you have to protect your own mental health," Dr. Bertani explained. "You've been living in a state of perpetual wariness, and that can take its toll."

Julia recognized the truth of that immediately. She'd known since she was a little girl that the rug could be yanked out from under her at any time.

Her mother's condition was hard to deal with, Dr. Bertani said, because it was caused by a combination of things. But the event that had triggered everything was a horrible incident of abuse early in life. The effects were both psychological and physical. She had been left alone for more than two days under circumstances that magnified her sense of abandonment. The physical effect was even worse. She'd gone without food and water, and when she was found she was partially unconscious and seriously dehydrated. Worse yet, she'd been deprived of the medication she desperately needed to combat a new and deadly virus, Lynn-Taksin disease. Her doctors were convinced that the lack of medication had left her mother with brain damage, from which she'd never totally recovered.

How could anyone do that to her mother? The thought of it left

Julia feeling sick. She pushed for more information. What had happened? she wanted to know. Who had done it to her? She wanted more
answers, but she didn't get them. Julia got the feeling that Paola Bertani
may have been told to hold back on certain things. Everything was
vague; it was like a big wall that Julia couldn't climb over.

A few weeks later, Dr. Mortimer showed up again at one of their
sessions. "Why are you here?" Julia asked. "I thought you weren't supposed to talk to me because of some sort of privilege?" Dr. Mortimer
gave her a thin smile and said they planned to talk about things they
had learned through independent investigation. Julia didn't think that
made any sense, but what choice did she have?

Dr. Mortimer wanted to talk about her mother's blackout
incidents. Julia felt a pang of misery as she listened to the details. But
after a while she realized they were tiptoeing around one particular
blackout period. "Why are you doing that?" Julia finally asked. Dr.
Bertani seemed uncomfortable with the question. Dr. Mortimer, however, jumped right in to answer her.

It was during that blackout period, Dr. Mortimer said, that her
mother had wandered off and gotten herself pregnant. She was only
fifteen. She later had no recollection of the father; her only memory
was of being surrounded by some men. She was as surprised as anyone
to find out she was having a baby. Her doctors and the police tried
to determine who might be the father, but they never came up with
an answer.

"Gotten herself pregnant"—the words were so remote that it took
Julia a second to realize they were talking about her. This wasn't just
another incident in the life of a mentally ill woman, this was her own
past. She blurted out the first thing that came into her head: "How
could she have a baby when she was only fifteen?" Then she realized
how stupid it sounded. With babies, you're not allowed or disallowed.
If you get knocked up, you have a kid. That's how it goes.

But Dr. Mortimer took her question literally.

"You should know that she was strongly advised to terminate the
pregnancy. Given her age, her immaturity, and the precarious state of

her health, we thought it unwise for her to carry a baby to full term. But she insisted on doing so."

Dr. Bertani was visibly angry with Dr. Mortimer's answer, but there was nothing she could do. The words were sitting out there, Julia thought, like a piece of rotten meat that no one wanted to touch. She knew what Dr. Mortimer meant: she, Julia, was there, but she really shouldn't be. She had been "strongly advised" to be nothing. And that was exactly how she was starting to feel.

"Where did they find her?

"It really doesn't make any difference."

"I want to know where they found her after she blacked out."

Dr. Mortimer squirmed a bit. "Julia, we don't know who the father was . . . or, I suppose, 'who the father is.' If you're referring to questions about your own—"

"I just want to know where she was."

The answer came grudgingly. "They found her up near Santa Rosa."

"Near where all those gangs have their camps?"

"Near there, yes."

She had visions of her mother walking around in a daze, being casually raped by every vicious man who saw her. The faces of the men on the motorcycles sprang into her head and clung to her like the acrid smell of their breath. The craziness of this was swirling out of control. A crazy woman gets raped and gets crazily pregnant and then makes the crazy decision to have the baby. Crazy plus crazy plus crazy equals what—her?

IT WAS ALL Julia could do to drag herself home after the therapy session. As she walked through the kitchen, she heard Maya on the vid-phone with Paola Bertani. Paola was trying to explain what went wrong during the session, and Maya looked furious. But Julia didn't really want to talk about it. She just snuck off to her room. Dr. Mortimer had pretty well crushed everything out of her.

Maya came into her room a few minutes later and sat on the edge of the bed. At first, she didn't say anything. The longer that went on, the more nervous Julia got. Maya seemed to be mulling something over in her mind, trying to decide how to phrase it.

"Dr. Mortimer shouldn't have handled it that way," she finally said, letting out a long sigh. "These sessions with the psychologists are over for now, okay?"

Julia nodded.

"Julia, you're never going to know who your father was. It's just best that you accept that and try to move on."

Maya nodded at her, trying to get a response. Julia nodded back, even though she wasn't so sure she agreed. What Maya said next came as a complete surprise.

"When I was growing up, I never knew who my father was either."

Her mother was in the country illegally, Maya said, and she was afraid of everything. She always feared retaliation from the man who had gotten her pregnant.

"I finally found out a few things about what happened, but I never really learned if she was raped, threatened, coerced, or . . . what was going through her mind at the time I was conceived." Maya's face turned sadder. The volume of her voice was down to a point where Julia had to strain to hear her. "I don't think it was love. She would have told me that."

Maya was too choked up to talk. She opened her arms and motioned to Julia to come over and sit next to her on the bed. She wrapped herself around her, and the two of them rocked back and forth for a few moments. Julia was soon caught up in Maya's tears.

"Sometimes when awful things happen, I think the world is going to fall apart." Maya whispered the words, just a hair's breadth from Julia's ear. "That's how I've felt with everything your mother's gone through." Her words were slowed a little by her sobs. "But no matter how bad things get, sometimes something good can come out of it—something you least expect." She gave Julia an extra squeeze, finding the thought she was groping for. "In this case, that something is you."

They held each other for several minutes, neither of them saying a word.

Maya offered to fix them a snack. Julia thought it was her signal that they needed to calm their emotions down a bit. They moved into the kitchen, where Julia grabbed some plates to put on the table. Maya took some bread and cheese and a little plate of olives out of the refrigerator. Julia realized she was starting to feel better. There was a message here. You just keep going.

SUNDAY, APRIL 26, 2082

TARRYTOWN, NEW YORK

JULIA

I AWOKE WITH competing memories that were circling around my head like a pair of cats, fighting to gain control of my mood. In my semi-awake state, I cheered hard for the brighter vision—the cherished memory of the first time Dhanye and I met. But I knew that the other, sadder memory was still there, winding itself slowly around the happy one, trying to drag me to a darker spot.

MY FIRST MEETING with Dhanye wasn't a romantic occasion—far from it. The death of Dhanye's brother was still fresh in both of our memories, and it drew us together like a common wound we both needed to heal. I wanted desperately to share my story of Raji. Sad as they were, our differing memories of him gave us a strange form of intimacy that continued into the next time we met. It was difficult for me to open up, but there was no time for awkwardness; our shared grief wouldn't allow it. We talked about our overlapping histories, and our reminiscences filled the room, until we were completing each other's thoughts.

Death seemed, in some strange way, to be a source of deep connection.

How did sorrow turn to passion? I'm still not sure.

That first evening we met at Dhanye's office at the History Department at NYU, and we wandered over to a French bistro on West 10th Street, where we talked for a long time over dinner. We had other meals after that, but most of our conversations were by vid-phone. Often, we were each just a figure on a screen in the darkness of the other's bedroom. It stayed like that for a few weeks until Dhanye invited me up to Tarrytown for dinner. While I was riding the train up the river, I sensed that that evening would be different. These were uncharted waters for both of us. My heart had never felt so open—or exposed.

"What would have happened if we'd actually met during the holo-conference?"

"I don't know."

"It felt very close."

"I know it did."

"What would have happened if I could have reached over and touched you?"

The question hovered over the table, somewhere between the dessert plates and the espresso cups. Seconds passed, and the thought took on a life of its own. Neither of us moved. Then, as if reading the other's thoughts, we each brought a hand to the table, one laid lightly over the other. The feeling that ran through my body was electric. We were looking at each other closely, our faces just a whisper apart. Dhanye's fingers stroked my cheek—downward with the tips and then slowly upward with the fingernails. Such beautiful eyes, I thought. I could live in those eyes.

The first touch of our mouths was just the hint of a kiss, the next a dance of the tongues that circled our lips. I felt a warm hand running through my hair, as the moisture built up inside me. I pulled back for a second. I wanted to look into those eyes again, to be sure of what I'd seen. It was still there, a promise that seemed to stretch to infinity.

I brought Dhanye's hand to my lips and then slowly guided it around my body, introducing it to all of my places. We were starting to move faster, and I told myself to slow down. There was a feeling in the air that we had all the time in the world. I found an ear nestled against my cheek, and I breathed into it, twirling the hair behind it with my finger. My hands and lips were moving now, blowing kisses through the light clothing, probing around the edges. I felt warm hands on my legs, my neck, and my breasts.

"Come with me—please."

The area downstairs was lit by soft, indirect lighting in the walls and shimmering lamps at the bottom of a pool. It felt like we were in some ancient, magical grotto. Without a word being said, I was invited to disrobe. I took off my clothes and left them in a pile. As I did so, I realized—for the moment, at least—I was leaving my fears and night-mares with them. I stepped over the edge.

I'd never seen anything as wonderful as the shy, backlit woman wading towards me. She had a beauty that was wholly unique—soft skin, graying black hair, eyes glistening in the subdued light, a mouth that seemed poised to say the most important words of our lives. I was certain that none of this had ever existed before. It seemed that love was being created at that very moment just for the two of us. I thanked God—really, the goddess of lovers—that we were both there to receive it.

The water lapped around our thighs, and we waded to the corner where a light waterfall settled over us. We held each other around the waist—legs to legs, belly to belly—while the water trickled through our hair. *Yes, my darling. Yes.* We gazed at each other again. *Give me your fingers . . . Yes.* I couldn't stop looking. *I love you.* Each time, I found something new that touched my soul. *I love you so much.*

BY MID-MORNING AN older, darker memory had caught up with me.

My last visit to see my mother in the hospital was as sad as all the others—in retrospect, even more so. She'd had another breakdown, and this one seemed more serious than the others. As the emergency medical team was taking her to the hospital, she kept repeating the phrase, "Please don't hurt her. Please don't hurt my mommy." They put her in the same psychiatric ward on the second floor where she'd been before. It was 2057, and I was fifteen.

As I got off the elevator, I found myself staring at the same forbidding door. The attendant peered at me through the paneled window and finally dragged himself away from the vid-screen he was watching to let me through. I was just a kid, and he was apparently not in a hurry to open any doors for me.

My conversation with my mother was short and painful.

"Hi, Mom. How are you feeling?"

"Oh, well, I'm . . . " She was struggling. She couldn't make the connection. I couldn't tell if it was the drugs or what it was.

"It's me, Julia."

"Oh, yes, Julia." Relief crossed her face, followed by a glimmer of doubt. "Do you know why I'm here?"

"It's for your own good, Mom. They can take care of you."

"Oh, yes." She was starting to drift off. "Then, I guess it's okay." She had a strand of her long brown hair wrapped around her finger, and she kept twirling it.

I found myself just sitting there helplessly. My instinct was to jump on the bed and hug her, but I knew the nurses would see that on the monitor and come running into the room. I talked instead about my friends and my classes, finally wandering off into trivia. Nothing seemed to register. I told her Chloe had a new boyfriend. She nodded like she might know what I was talking about. I said I had just seen Annabel and Flora at the café, and they wanted me to give her a hug. She smiled slightly. When I talked about my classes, about my track team, about the other people in the Community, I could see her mind drifting. There was no reaction even to the one bit of real news that I had: the police were searching for Rick, but he had fled the country and was apparently in Central Asia. I finally realized that my whole conversation with her had become a monologue. I was only talking to myself.

I wanted to do something, anything. I wished we could get out one of the old books and talk about the hungry caterpillar or look for the mouse hiding in the bunny's bedroom. But those days were gone, and part of me had disappeared with them. I wasn't a little kid anymore. And my mother? She was thirty, but she looked more like sixty.

"I love you, Mom. Do you know that?"

She smiled like it was a totally new idea.

I felt useless. The more I sat there, the more my mind began drifting to places where Paola, my therapist, and the others had warned me not to go. They said it could jeopardize my own mental health, but at the time that didn't stop me. An idea was growing inside me. I didn't have a name or a face or anything else to put with that idea. But I realize now that I was about to start down a path that would change my life. I was determined to find whoever had done this to my mother and make him pay.

PART FOUR

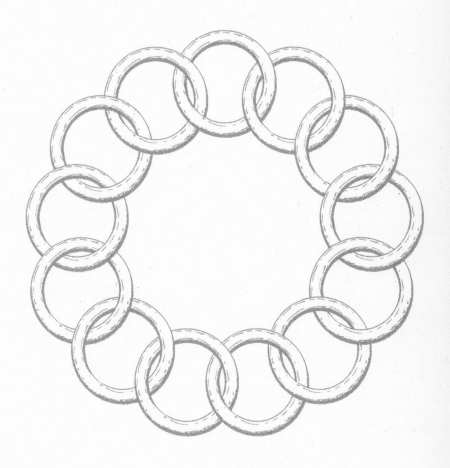

MONDAY, APRIL 27, 2082

NEW YORK CITY

JULIA

THE CHAIR OF the Council of Ministers stared at her personal vid-screen, brushing back a few strands of grayish-brown hair that kept getting in her eyes. She was reading everything carefully, moving slow-ly, living up to her reputation as someone who got her facts straight. If there was a hole in our security plan, I knew she'd be the one to find it. She looked up from her reading and put a question to the Secretary-General. He'd been fielding requests all morning from the Chair and the other Ministers, and by the look on his face he seemed eager to give them the answers they wanted to hear. They were down to the last item on the agenda. That was the one that made me squirm.

"Are you convinced that the security procedures for the dedication ceremony next week are as strong as possible? Perhaps you could sum-marize the plan for us."

The Secretary-General was a genial but cagey survivor of many years of political warfare, and he was smart enough not to stray too far from a few generalities. His answer was laced with phrases like "every precaution" and "complete cooperation" and "latest technology." He turned his eyes to the side of the room where Madeleine sat with a clipboard in her lap. She looked back at him impassively. If he was looking for her to jump in, she didn't oblige him. But after a few more verbal flourishes, he tossed the Chair's question to Madeleine anyway, hoping she'd give the Ministers the answers they wanted. I was expecting Madeleine to turn right around and toss it to me.

I wasn't sure how I would answer them. I might not be too reassuring. None of the anonymous warnings had been tracked down. In a couple of cases, our security team had found that the messages were coming from high-powered replicators that simply gathered trillions of bits of data from everywhere and pushed it in all directions. The police had yet to show a connection between any of the messages, let alone a real source. To me, none of that was good news. It probably meant that any potential plot was more deeply embedded than anything we'd probed.

The NYPD wasn't doing much better with the bombing incidents. They were working the leads, but the results were frustrating. The bomb seized from the NYU trash can was different from the bomb fragments found in Union Square or on the Magno-Train; and the chemical composition of those two sets of bomb fragments differed from each other as well. None of them were sophisticated devices, but that made the job of tracing them all the more difficult. Each of them used common synthetic chemicals that could be combined in almost any home food-processing equipment. The NYU bomb—the one they found intact—was probably the easiest to trace, but the police had only limited the possible sources to thousands of locations within a fifty-kilometer radius.

The cameras provided even less help. The Washington Square bombers had either found a flaw in the coverage plan for the park cameras, or they'd simply gotten lucky. The only photos showed the backs of two hooded men running from Washington Square at about the time the police believed the bomb had been left there. The Union Square pictures were even more maddening. The area was blanketed with security cameras, but no one had checked recently to see if they were working. The one at the bomb site had been inoperative for seventy-one hours prior to the blast. That meant the police had to sort through about 20,000 random pictures of people who'd wandered through that general area during the three-day period in question. They were still going through the images without much success.

That left Myron Lott, the train bomber. Our whole staff was working along with the NYPD, trying to nail down the link with the Faith of Our Fathers church. The U.S. Attorney in Atlanta had a whole team working on it. But a search warrant only showed that he had once been a member of the congregation. Lott himself was still sitting in his cell, staring at the wall and saying nothing.

I was trying to figure out how to put a happy face on all this for the Council, but Madeleine surprised me by answering the Chair's question herself. She laid out our building security plan in depth. I was impressed at how thoroughly she had mastered the details. She spoke with such a sense of assurance that she got hardly any questions. She even managed to throw a few accolades in my direction, telling them that their security was in good hands. It reminded me again why I loved her.

As the meeting broke up, I thanked her for what she'd said about me.

She nodded, giving me something that was not quite a smile. "Don't make a liar out of me."

BY THE TIME I got back to my office, Avram, my deputy, and Omar Khaled, our Director of Electronic Intelligence, were waiting excitedly to show me the new version of the Mother Grid, the device that controlled surveillance in the building and for a wide radius around it. They had one of the Grid's self-propelled cameras in full operation, swooping around the outside of the building and checking the air-pocket insulation in the four-layered exterior walls. They pitched it upwards and then angled it down, zooming in on some of the 20,000 square meters of plants and photo-voltaic cells on the roof.

Avram and Omar swore they weren't just having fun, but they seemed to take great delight in sending the camera out several kilometers over Central Park and doing quiet, electronic frisks of passersby. I finally saw enough to be confident that the new Mother Grid was working properly. I didn't feel like playing with it anymore.

SOMETHING ELSE WAS nagging at me. We'd been assessing every threat; we'd rehearsed every contingency. What if we were missing something totally different from what we'd anticipated? Were we planning for the wrong thing? Wasn't that what had happened twenty-five years earlier in 2057—when no one expected the events that led to the death of the Thirteen?

At the time, law enforcement agencies had done what they thought was a thorough analysis of the threat from *Patria*. They knew that its main strength was in the larger cities and that it drew its recruits from urban gangs, paramilitary groups, and the mass of chronically unemployed men. *Patria* had taken the grudges of an urban underclass and honed them into an instrument of terror. It had some powerful corporate paymasters, and enough of that money filtered down to the men who did the dirty work to keep them happy. But for the thugs out on the street, the attraction was more than just money. The constant propagandizing about *Patria*'s muscle gave them a swagger. City residents never knew when *Patria* toughs might appear on their block and launch an attack on a group they didn't like—or maybe even kill someone. Law enforcement units were geared up for that kind of urban warfare.

But what actually happened had caught them totally by surprise.

2057

BALUCHISTAN

JESSE, YOU *can't hide. They're going to find you.*

Hamid was in his outer offices, and Jesse knew something was wrong. Hamid should have been held at the door. Had there been another security breach? A few days earlier he had had to get rid of all the old guards and replace them with new recruits: some biker toughs from California and mob thugs out of the Ukraine. Could Hamid have bought them off that quickly and put them on his own payroll? He knew Hamid wanted a bigger cut of the drug money, but could he have found out about the *Patria* network as well? Had he suddenly realized who was in his midst?

Jesse's brain-on-fire was already starting to curl his fingers, surveying Hamid's throat for the right spot. But his brain-in-charge said no. He's the Interior Minister's brother, and, for now, you have to keep dealing with him.

As always, Hamid had the same maddening smile.

"I've brought you a present."

His unease was growing. He hated presents.

"It's from the Communal Council at Mardan," Hamid said. "The elders are appreciative of the help you've given them in putting down that so-called women's revolt. The trouble those women stirred up was very unfortunate."

"Are you telling me it's over?"

"Well, we'll see." Hamid smiled with a repulsive display of teeth. "I think the Council has the situation in hand."

The conversation was headed somewhere, but he didn't know where. "What's this present you're talking about?"

"It's really more of an honor."

Hamid nodded towards the darkened doorway, where a young girl was crouched behind the door. Her head was covered in a scarf that had been partially torn. From the look of her clothes, she'd been dragged through the dust.

"What's she doing here?"

"She's your present from the Council."

"I don't want her. Take her back."

Hamid smiled without moving his eyes. "You can't do that. The tribal leaders would be insulted."

"Who is she?"

"She's the sister of one of the ringleaders of the group. Because of her age, they're being more lenient with her. The others will be put to death—after their trial, of course. But she'll be banished from the community and forced to live on her own."

"Meaning—"

"Meaning, she'll have to live the only life left open to her."

"Prostitution?"

"That would be her decision."

"How old is she?"

"I don't know. The important thing is that you have the honor of being the first."

So that's how it's going to be, he thought as he watched Hamid leave. He was left with the girl whether he liked it or not. But he wasn't fooled. This was part of Hamid's plan to move in on him, maybe carve out a bigger piece for himself. Jesse knew the rumors. They were setting him up; he was sure of it. If this girl just walked out without anything happening to her, word would get out. Have you heard? That fresh, young, beautiful flower was there for the plucking, and he refused it. What kind of a man is that?

He moved closer to get a better look. He grabbed her chin and forced her to look up at him. Nothing. This was disgusting; there was nothing there he wanted. He felt his legs growing weak, a sudden shakiness, as he tried to figure out what his choices were.

Then she did him a favor. She looked him in the eye and spat.

He slapped her hard, and she shrank back to the corner. His brain-on-fire screeched in anger. He reached over and dragged her from the room, forcing her along the hallway and into his bedroom, shoving her until she hit the table. She fell down screaming to the floor. She sat there, massaging her arm, looking up at him defiantly.

The stupid bitch, if she had any brains, she would be soft and sweet and seductive. Then she'd be so repellent that he'd probably leave her alone. But she wasn't smart enough for that. She'd keep fighting him and resisting him. He forced her to stand up, as he ripped off her clothes. Good god, she had no pubic hair! Her breasts were no bigger than a boy's. How old was she? Maybe eleven? If he didn't hurry up and get this over, he wouldn't be able to do anything. He threw her on the bed, mounting her as he did. He fumbled with a half-hearted erection, trying to force it somewhere it didn't want to go.

Out of the corner of his eye he saw a flash. A knife! She must have pulled it from her shoe while he was wrestling with her. He grabbed her hand as she was ready to plunge it in, twisting her arm until the knife finally fell to the side of the bed. But with her free hand she suddenly reached at the medal around his neck, breaking the chain that was holding it and sending it flying across the room and under the furniture. He let out a roar that brought the guards into the room.

"Find that," he pointed to the broken chain, "and then get out of here."

He saw the fire go out of her eyes. When she realized that the guards weren't going to help her, she started to weaken, her body tensing up rather than fighting back. He couldn't wait to get rid of her. He reached down between her legs, probing for the spot, and then gave a sharp pull. Now there'd be something to show to anyone who cared to look. She screamed with pain, but he ignored her.

SOMETHING HAD CHANGED.

When Hamid walked into the compound later in the day, he made no complaint when the security team stopped him. He had no reaction at all to the sight of the girl lying in the corner whimpering. He just muttered something about taking her when he left. What was different? Hamid didn't strut around the room in his usual manner, marking off his claims to that territory. He was quieter, but his smugness had an added twist.

"What's going on?"

Hamid gave a slight grunt. "With all your sophisticated equipment, I thought you'd already know." He walked over to a vid-screen. "If you'll permit me, I'll show you." Without waiting for an answer, Hamid turned on the screen.

"It's a press conference. Can you see where it is? Do you recognize the place? They're in Gwadar in a building right on the coast. I've been in that room they're using, it's a nasty little place, but I guess that's all they could find on short notice."

Hamid eyed him coldly, apparently trying to draw a response.

"They're less than a kilometer from the port where your men drop their shipments. You didn't know that?"

The same sneer. This time the teeth were back.

"Do you see who's running the press conference? Take a look."

He could see. The images were already exploding in his brain.

"That's Deva Chandri speaking right now. She's been talking to those reporters and news-bots for the last twenty minutes or so. Do you hear what she's saying? She's telling them that her so-called Women for Peace group is planning a protest right here. They're coming right *here*—to this town. They're supposedly going to tell the world how the local women are being mistreated."

Hamid kept pointing the women's provocations out one by one. When he didn't get a reaction, he turned more insistent. His tone got almost gleeful, as he goaded his host. "What are you going to do about it?"

Jesse, where are you?
They're looking for you.
They're going to keep on looking and looking until they find you.
You can come out now, Jesse, you're safe with us.
No. They're not coming *towards* me, they're coming *at* me.

HE OPENED HIS eyes and blinked. His knees were shaking. He sat down for a second to steady himself, as he crawled back from wherever the voices had taken him. Where had he been in the minutes since Hamid had left? He didn't know.

His brain-in-charge was trying to get things under control, struggling to come to grips with what had fallen into his lap. This wasn't part of his plan, so it must be part of someone else's plan. It was part of *their* plan. But what was it? He replayed the interview scenes over and over, trying to understand what these women were really doing:

FIRST REPORTER: *Can you tell us what you're planning to do?*
DEVA CHANDRI: *We're leading a small caravan of vehicles out of Gwadar up into the interior. Our destination is the town of Mardan.*
SECOND REPORTER: *Why are you going there?*
DEVA CHANDRI: *We've had an urgent plea from the women in that town. They've been subjected to terrible treatment, Now, they are being threatened with execution. We're hoping our presence will spark an interest in their plight and convince the local government to release them.*
NEWS-BOT: *What exactly do you women think you can do?*
GABRIELLA RODRIQUES: *We want to put a stop to the brutal practice of 'honor killings.' That's what's behind all this. Women*

who have been raped are now being put to death, because some-
one claims they have dishonored their family. There is nothing
'honorable' about any of this. It's just plain killing.

What are they *really* doing?

It can't be just that, his brain-in-charge said. They can't just be
walking up to his doorstep and lying down. It has to be a trap. It was a
surprise, and he hated surprises.

REPORTER: *That's pretty rough country. It's the same country*
that Al Qaeda and the Taliban operated in forty years ago. We've
heard rumors that Patria may have forces in the region. Have
you thought about the danger?
MARTA KWON: *We plan to be cautious. We've been in contact*
with the Interior Minister of the government of Baluchistan, and
he's assured us that there are no guerilla forces in that area. He's
offered us safe conduct.
NEWS-BOT: *The Baluchi government has a reputation of being a*
narco-state. Do you really trust them?
MARTA KWON: *It's the government in power, and we have to deal*
with it. We don't carry weapons, and we're hoping no one will see
us as a threat.
NEWS-BOT: *What about your campaign against child prostitu-*
tion? Won't you have to revise your plans for the big demon-
strations you've planned in Bangkok next month because of this?
Won't this change your timing?"
MARIA BALEWA: *No. The Bangkok demonstrations are going on*
as scheduled. Why should we pull back on anything we're do-
ing? Today we're battling against the killing of women. Tomorrow
we're fighting child prostitution. Those are just two sides of the
same issue.

His brain-in-charge was churning, trying to sort things out. They
were coming here; they were going to be right in his backyard. Any-

thing he did now would be visible to everyone. How would this affect his Network? What would happen to his funding? He needed time to think. He had to be cautious.

But his brain-on-fire had no such restraints. It shouted at its timid brain-mate, mocking it for being so weak. *This is it,* his brain-on-fire screamed. *This has to be it! This is what you've been waiting for.* His heart was beating fast and listening to this insistent brain. *These women are the worst of the worst, they're everything you hate. They're the most arrogant bitches of them all, and they're coming right towards you. What more do you need? They're walking into your arms!*

The battle went back and forth in his head. It was more intense than it had ever been. He worried that he might slip back into the darkness where he'd been moments earlier. *Stop and plan,* one brain said; *no, act now,* replied the other. His heart was racing; his sweating was worse. *Take time to find out what they're up to.* He had to decide. *No, kill them while you have the chance!*

He went back to his vid-screen and fiddled nervously with the pictures, looking for the right one. He found what he wanted: an image of the thirteen women standing behind a table looking at a questioner. He enhanced the picture. Then he rotated it and projected it to the center of the room. He walked around it slowly, staring at it from all sides.

He reached over to the controls and began to slowly manipulate them. That's it, he realized. This was what he needed to do. He wasn't nervous now—no, not at all. Now, he was becoming excited. He focused on the women as they talked earnestly to the audience in front of them, unaware of the dark patches of color that were closing in around them. He held the controller tightly. He stroked it; he loved the feel of it in his hand. He teased the patches of color, watching them grow darker and wider. He breathed along with them, as the splotches pulsed and grew. He moaned, as the giant waves overwhelmed the women, finally covering everything in sight.

The debate in his brain was over. The decision had been made somewhere deeper.

SIX DAYS LATER

THE PLANE GREW larger on his vid-screen. His brain-in-charge was running things now, as he made contact with the plane's cabin by audio/video imagery to verify that the passenger was who he claimed to be. He'd given them permission to land, and he'd sent a team of men to bring the passenger to him immediately.

But now the leaders of that team were standing in the shadows of his outer office, seemingly afraid to say anything. One of them—the pasty-looking gang member from California—seemed to have his words caught in his throat. "What is it?" he demanded. They finally blurted it out: Hamid's men had moved into the landing area first.

"How could you let them do that?" he screamed.

He pushed the two of them aside and rushed out to the landing space just as the aircraft retracted its fixed wings and unfurled the rotary blades. It hovered for a second and then slowly settled down into the space surrounded by Hamid's troops. His own troops were standing in a ring beyond them, looking on helplessly. As the door of the plane opened, Hamid raced up the retractable stairway and stepped inside the plane. The seconds ticked by. Jesse's fingers were twitching. *Kill them*, his brain-on-fire was screaming. It was getting harder and harder to argue with that thought.

The door of the plane finally opened. A happy-looking Hamid emerged, followed by an overweight man in a white suit. Hamid brushed past the guards, dragging his uncomfortable-looking guest with him. He was all smiles as he reached the edge of the landing pad.

"Ah, here you are. I wanted to be sure our distinguished guest received a proper welcome to Baluchistan." He turned to leave. "Now, I'll let you discuss your business."

With Hamid gone, the other man looked around nervously. The

gusts from the rotating blades had mangled his hairdo. He was breathing heavily—probably as much from being overweight as the altitude. His suit was in a style favored by gangland pimps in Bangkok, and sweat stains were forming under his armpits. Jesse knew what he looked like from their video meetings, but in person Kolle was even more odious.

"At last we meet," Kolle grabbed him in an awkward embrace. "Talking by video all those times was less than satisfactory, wouldn't you agree? The others—those would-be colleagues of mine in our little cartel—sometimes showed no sense."

"May I call you by what I believe is your real name?" Kolle asked. He waited for an answer until he realized he wasn't going to get one. "Well, perhaps, that's not such a good idea. . . .What is this place? Was it not once part of Afghanistan?"

"It's still disputed. The Baluchistan government controls it at the moment."

"My staff tells me there's an important dam nearby."

"The Kajaki Dam. It's near here." He gestured to his right.

"And your guests are there?" He gestured in the same direction.

"My guests, as you call them, are in the canyon a few kilometers from here."

"And they are in that particular canyon because—"

"—Because that's the easiest place to hold them. My men have cut off the exits from the canyon, so they aren't going anywhere."

"I see, I see." Kolle nodded his head and puckered his lips. It was a gesture, one of many, that Jesse found disgusting.

"That's very inconvenient for them. They probably didn't think they would end up there when they set out on their little caravan earlier in the week."

This small talk was getting on his nerves. "What are you after?"

"Maybe there is someplace we can go that will put us in the shade. Can we sit down and get something to drink? Is such a thing allowed in this country?"

The nearest place was just a lean-to, but once they arrived there, Kolle seemed content to squirm his way into a rickety metal chair. He took a sip of beer, wrinkled his nose, and then took another. "Thank you for adjusting to the ways of someone a little more urban in his habits."

His associate, who had been tagging along behind him, brought him a case with a control panel and a portable screen. Kolle flicked a couple of buttons and turned the screen towards his host.

"Just a little relaxation before we get down to business," he said. "Here are photos of some of our newest offerings. If you see one you like, we can arrange for her to be with you whenever you come to Bangkok."

The bile rose in Jesse's throat, but he said nothing.

"I can see these are not to your liking." Kolle turned the screen back towards himself and deleted the images. "We have them a little younger. Or maybe you prefer, how should I put it . . . a different body type altogether."

Kolle reached again for the control panel but found a hand gripping his arm.

"Forget all that. Tell me why you're here."

Kolle looked up from his screen and gave a small shrug.

"Well, as you know, we are very much interested in your guests. I'm surprised you didn't contact us to see if there was something we could work out. You know how we feel about them and their plans for Bangkok in the upcoming months. This would seem to be a good time to take care of all that."

"Are you sure you want to pay me? I heard that you were ready to pay them."

Kolle stared at him, toying with his beer glass. "Well, it appears that we must have some sort of leak in our organization."

He scratched at his nose for a second. "I suppose there's no reason to deny that. Yes, we offered the Women for Peace organization a substantial amount of money if they would stay away from Bangkok and not interfere with our business."

He ran his finger over his upper lip, moistening it slightly. "We're businessmen, as I'm sure you realize, and we have to do the most cost-effective thing. Paying them would be the smart thing to do. After listening to their press conference, we thought we could ease them out of some of their other commitments. So we offered them ten million dollars to call off their Southeast Asia campaign."

"I heard it was fifty million."

"Was it?" Kolle said. "Well, maybe your information is better than mine."

"Did they take it?" His disgust with this weasel was growing by the minute.

"No, I'm afraid they didn't," Kolle said. "They were actually quite rude about it. One of their spokespeople, I believe it was Maria Balewa, told us to 'shove it.' I thought that was a pretty shocking response, coming from a bishop."

"Now what do you want?"

"Well, it's a shame that they didn't take the money and leave us alone, because that would have made it easier for everyone. But if I understand what's going on here, we can accomplish the same thing in a different manner. The fifty million dollars are available to you, if you can make this problem go away for us."

"It will cost two-hundred million."

"You drive a hard bargain, my friend." Kolle grunted and fingered his vid-screen. "I'll have to confer with my associates." He typed something and waited for a response.

"Okay," he said after a couple of minutes, "you will have your money. Your account number is the same, I presume?"

He nodded okay.

"Check your account," Kolle told him a few moments later.

He typed in his code and opened the screen. The money was blinking back at him. Now, he wanted Kolle out of there.

"Well, I guess that's it. I should be going, but let me tell you one more thing."

He wanted him to go immediately. He didn't want to listen to 'one more thing.'

"I realize you don't like me. That's okay; I don't take it personally.

But just remember something: we want results, but we don't want a lot of attention focused on those results. This has to be done in a way that will blow over quickly."

"I expect to turn on a vid-screen in a few days and hear about a tragic, unexplained accident that took the lives of some beloved women. We'll all weep for them, but we'll get over it in a few days. I'm sure your friend Hamid feels the same. His government doesn't want the wrath of the world at its doorstep any more than we do."

"So, do we have an understanding?"

Kolle waited for his answer, his agitation growing as the seconds ticked by.

MONDAY, APRIL 27, 2082

NEW YORK CITY

JULIA

WHY DID THEY do it? Why had the Thirteen walked into the arms of Abraham and almost certain death?

As the twenty-fifth anniversary of their deaths drew closer, their story was everywhere. I walked into two successive stores on Lexington Avenue and then walked right out again. I was in no mood to see a documentary on the events of May 4, 2057, but those scenes were filling the wrap-around screens in both places. And in each case the same question came up: Why? The story was even dominating the flash-screens outside the buildings, as pedestrians on 86th Street kept adding insets from their own vid-phones with their remembrances and speculations. I had to walk two blocks before I could get away from everyone else's thoughts and concentrate on my own.

Eloni had a theory of why they had done what they did. She had told me once over dinner, and we'd agreed it was probably closer to the truth than any other theory either of us had heard. At the time the events in Baluchistan had occurred, Eloni had been a regional director for Women for Peace. When she and the other regional directors had found out what their leaders were planning, they'd tried desperately to talk them out of it. They couldn't believe they were planning to make the trip alone. Everyone was concerned for their safety. "It's too dangerous," the regional directors had argued. "They should at least put together a bigger group or arrange for some security." Several of them had offered to drop what they were doing and go to Baluchistan with them.

But the Thirteen wouldn't be deterred. They said there wasn't enough time to do it any other way. If they waited for others to join them, it would jeopardize the women they were trying to help. They thanked all the people on the conference call for their concern, and they promised to be careful. But they were going to do it alone.

"You saw how they were," Eloni said. "They never asked anyone to do anything that they weren't willing to do themselves. But in this case, it was something more: they knew the risks they were running, and they didn't want anyone else running those risks with them. They wanted to protect us from ourselves. It was their last gift to the organization they'd founded. They wanted to make sure that the others would be there to keep up the struggle, even if they were gone."

That answered part of the question but not all of it.

There was one question at their last press conference that had stuck in my mind. I had seen the video of that conference several times over the years, and each time I could sense the dread hanging over the room. What I always remembered most was a question near the end. A reporter had asked them why they had made the choice that they had.

"There are lots of terrible problems in the world that need your attention. So why are you focusing on this one? Why here? Particularly, since this place looks so risky?"

Deva Chandri looked back and forth at the women at the table, finally deciding to answer it herself. "The reason is simple," she said quietly. "They asked for our help."

Was that it? The first time I'd heard it, I couldn't make sense of that answer. Would they go rushing off to save just any group of women who asked for their help?

"But it's really more than that, isn't it?" the reporter continued.

There was a sudden chill in the room—it was the tone of the question.

"Don't you feel you're somehow forced to do this? Let me read from the communiqué they sent to you."

We saw your Youth Holo-Conference last year on the vid-screens here in our village, even though the Council tried to stop us from watching. We heard your words encouraging people to stand up for our rights. We heard you recite the words of the great Mohandas Gandhi, saying 'Be the change you wish to see in the world.' We listened, and we decided to assert our rights. Now there are several of us who are under a death sentence, and we beseech you to help us.

"Isn't that what's going on?" the reporter asked. "Don't you really feel you got these women into this danger and now you have to get them out?"

MY RECOLLECTION OF those events in 2057 isn't pretty. Although it happened twenty years earlier and I was a teenager at the time, the memories are still too fresh and brittle. When I walked into our community room at the co-housing complex on May 4th, the room was filled with people sitting on the floor and children sprawled everywhere. It didn't take long for me to realize that something terrible was going on. I knew most of the people in the room—Carlos, Naomi, Paola, Harry, Lara, Li-Jin, Antonio. We'd shared meals in that same room; many of these people had taken care of me as a child. Whether I realized it or not at the time, they were my family. And right now they all looked stunned. Maya looked the worst of all. I didn't know what was going through her mind at that moment, but I could see that it was something terrible. I'd never seen her like that—not before, not since.

Local news from Baluchistan was slow in coming in. The news teams following the Women for Peace caravan had been forced to leave after the women were captured. News-bots trailing the story had been destroyed or dismantled. A European Union reconnaissance drone finally began providing video coverage, and the people in the room gasped when they saw the pictures. The drone zeroed in to a level of about thirty meters. The picture showed what looked like the Women for Peace leaders sitting on some rocks in a circle, looking frail and pitiful in the harsh environment. The drone confirmed what the earlier reports had said: they were trapped near the base of the Kajakai Dam.

Information about the area soon came pouring in. The news feed along the bottom said that the area near the Kajakai Dam had been attacked by U.S. bombers in 2001 and had been the scene of fighting in 2007 between NATO and Taliban forces. On both occasions there were fears that the dam might be breached and the area flooded.

The E.U. drone scanned up the side of the dam, reporting back a steady feed of information. The video stream showed what appeared to be explosives, which had been placed at vulnerable points along the structure. Militia troops were stationed at several locations around the dam. The drone was following those troops as well as the government troops that were shadowing them. From all of that coverage, one fact stuck in my mind: the dam had a storage capacity of over a billion cubic meters of water.

A bulletin flashed on the screen, saying that the U.N. Security Council would be meeting the next day in emergency session. But that announcement was met by groans around our community room. *That will be too late. Why are they waiting?* Everyone in the room sensed that the response of the world's governments was far too weak.

COULD ANYTHING HAVE been done to prevent the disaster that occurred? We studied those events for almost a week during my second year at the U.N. Academy. There were no definitive answers. One of the major powers might have tried to send in a military team to rescue the women—maybe the U.S. or China, possibly even India or Russia. But it probably wouldn't have worked. There were people in all of the major governments who admired and respected the work of Women for Peace. But there were just as many high-placed officials who considered them a nuisance. Although nobody wanted to see them harmed, there seemed to be a fatal hesitancy in each of the world's capitals when it came to acting on their behalf—an inability to do anything until it was too late. Events had simply outrun the ability of the governments to respond.

And what exactly were those events? Among historians, there was little doubt that it was Abraham in charge of that militia and that he was the one who'd ordered the explosives placed on the dam. But why? Abraham disappeared afterwards, and the Baluchistan government wouldn't let investigators in for any kind of forensic examination. So the record of why things had happened wasn't clear. Most historians thought that the actual ignition of the explosives had been a miscalculation or an accident—maybe caused by a stray round from one of the government planes. But they were guessing. The reason most people thought that, I was convinced, was because blowing up the dam was an irrational act that was far out of proportion to anything that someone might have hoped to gain from it. You had to imagine a mind so warped that some fiery, irrational demon could rise up from the depths and seize control of it. That was a level of madness most people didn't want to think about.

THE RUNNING COMMENTARY at the bottom of the picture on that fateful morning announced that the drama of the women's captivity was being watched on an estimated ninety-one percent of all of the world's vid-screens. The news media showed candlelight vigils in Paris, London, Istanbul, Tel Aviv, Cairo, and Johannesburg. There were large crowds in Beijing, New Delhi, Mumbai, and Tokyo, even though it was almost morning in those parts of Asia. An estimated 300,000 demonstrators had blocked the area near Times Square in New York. In San Francisco, a huge crowd had gathered on Market Street.

Baluchistan had seemed to be feeling the pressure: it announced that it had persuaded the town council to commute the death sentences of the women whose fate had sparked the Women for Peace intervention in the first place. But that was the only good news. Networks reported apparent gunfire between the Baluchistan army and the guerrilla troops. They also began to report that the troops were apparently part of *Patria*.

A news bulletin a few minutes later from India Air Control sparked another wave of anger. It reported that a hover jet had been tracked a day earlier flying from Bangkok to the area near the dam. That event had occurred just a few hours after the women had been seized. Several networks began speculating that criminal elements behind the prostitution rings in Thailand had something to do with the capture of the women.

Moments later, Eloni sent word from her office that an electronic petition with almost a billion signatures had been delivered to U.N. headquarters, demanding action. At the same time the Episcopal Bishop of Washington, D.C., announced that she and a group of her fellow bishops were heading to Central Asia as a show of support for Bishop Balewa and the others. Another report said that rabbis and other colleagues of Rebecca Meyer in New York were expected to have a similar announcement within the hour. News cameras showed the Dominican Sisters, Magdalena Garcia's order, holding a huge vigil at that moment in Rome. Their statement said this was a moment of solemnity for the women of the world.

Then the networks cut in with a news flash, reporting that the captors had apparently freed all of the drivers and support staff that had accompanied the Women for Peace caravan. This was confirmed by aerial surveillance. Pictures flashed on the screen, showing happy Baluchi truck drivers and porters, smiling and cheering as they were being reunited with their wives and families.

A cry of joy went up around the room. But that was soon followed by a howl, as Maya started to sob uncontrollably. It took the rest of us a few seconds to realize what Maya had sensed immediately: the captors were just clearing the decks. What they had in mind only involved the thirteen women.

I remember Carlos trying to comfort Maya, asking her if there was anything he could do. She stared at him blankly. He repeated the question, and she slowly nodded her head no. Her blank expression at that moment seemed worse than any horror I could imagine. I didn't know at the time how close she was to the events unfolding in front of us. How could I? It wasn't until years later that I would learn the full agony of what she was going through.

Maya had been reliving the memory of when they had all met—a memory that had just turned to despair in front of her eyes.

2032

SAN FRANCISCO

DEVA SLID back the security bolt, loosening the other latches with her free hand. She threw open the door, wrapped her arms around Maya, and held her there for a few seconds. Maya's arms were loaded with bags of food, so she couldn't do much more than accept the warm embrace.

"What do you have there?" Deva grabbed one of the bags, poking her hand into it. "Maya, this is beautiful!" She pulled out two large heads of butter lettuce and admired them. "I haven't seen anything this good in months."

"There was a produce truck from a little farm in Portola Valley that parked on our street this morning. By the time the guy got the cartons out of the bed of the truck, I thought he was going to be mobbed by my neighbors."

Deva grabbed Maya's hand, giving it a squeeze. "Let's get this all into the kitchen. It seems like ages since I've seen you."

Maya laughed. "It can't be that long. I only met you two weeks ago."

"Oh, I know," Deva smiled, "and I know you were just here the day before yesterday. But it always seems like we have so much to talk about."

Maya helped Deva unload the bags on the small kitchen sink, holding up one small sack like a trophy. "I almost got into a bidding war over these tomatoes."

"Does Verafoods know about this guy's business?"

"I hope not," Maya laughed. "They'd try to shut him down for sure."

"I didn't know what you had planned," Maya said. "But you're such a good cook that I figured you could make something out of anything I grabbed. Did I get enough?"

"More than enough," Deva said. "We'll have food for days. There are only six of us here tonight for the meeting. The other eight will be on video hookups."

Maya put most of the food in the refrigerator, shoving aside the leftovers of a meal they'd had two days earlier. On the counter, she found some loaves of bread that Deva had baked. Maya took a deep whiff as the aroma tickled its way through her body.

"When Amy found out where I was going, she wanted to come with me."

"You should have brought her!"

"No, you needed a break for a few days," Maya said. "Besides, Lara loves having her there. Antonio is too old to boss around anymore, but Amy's just the right age."

Maya savored a thought for the moment, trying to articulate something she had been feeling ever since the two of them had found Amy. "You know, watching you go out of your way to give so much kindness to that little girl really touched my heart."

"Thank you," Deva said. She gave a little laugh. "I'm smiling, because I was just thinking the same thing about you."

"Let's go into the living room for a few minutes. Do you want some tea? Or I have wine, if you'd like."

"I don't know," Maya said, "a glass of wine at this time in the afternoon, and I might be ready to take a nap."

"You can do that too, if you want. We have lots of time before the others get here."

"What are you having?"

"I think wine sounds good," Deva said.

While Deva searched for the bottle and glasses, Maya glanced at a couple of manuscripts on Deva's desk that she was editing. Next to them were some pictures. "I haven't seen these pictures of your family. This one must be your husband and daughter."

Deva took the picture Maya was holding, brushing some nonexistent dust from the surface. It showed an older-looking man and a girl who appeared to be in her teens.

"Yes, this is Dhriti; she's so wonderful. This picture was taken right before she left for college." Deva paused a second. "And this dear man is Madhu. It was just two years ago that he died."

Maya offered her condolences. Deva accepted them with slightly moistened eyes.

"As you can see, he was a good deal older than me—seventeen years, to be exact. Still, we were very close."

"You're very lucky."

Maya realized immediately she might have said something insensitive. "I don't mean that the way it sounded. I just mean you're fortunate to have a loving memory that still lives on in you. Sometimes, I'm a little clumsy about saying what I really mean."

Deva smiled. "I knew what you meant."

Deva added a splash of wine to Maya's glass and poured some more for herself. She adjusted the sound system, and soft music began flowing into the room. Maya thought it was a Handel sonata, but she couldn't be sure. Her mind was on something else. Deva moved her chair in a little closer.

"Maya, I know how difficult it was for you to sit here the other night and tell me about your childhood and all the things you went through. It must have been terrible having to hide all the time because your mother was an undocumented immigrant."

"Have I been that awful to listen to?"

"Of course not," Deva said. "We've had some wonderful moments together."

"We've laughed a lot more than we've cried." She teased a smile out of her. "But I don't think you realize what a wonderful gift you've given me."

"I didn't give you anything," Maya said. "Most of the time I felt like a fool."

"No, you're wrong. You gave me your trust. It was something very intimate."

Maya looked up. Deva's eyes were pouring through her.

"Each secret you shared with me—no matter how painful it was at the time—helped build something between us. It was another piece of you."

Maya was almost afraid to look at her.

"Maya, that's the way love is built, one piece at a time."

"IF YOU WANT to put together a movement, I'll tell you were to begin." Maya listened eagerly along with the others as Annette Dubois smiled at them from the vid-screen; her face was highlighted by her spiked, blonde-gray hair. "From my window, I see about five thousand people camped out on Figueroa Street. They've taken over every vacant lot and alley. There are enough homeless people in the Los Angeles area to create a people's army. That's probably true in most major cities."

Franca Peres sat on the edge of her chair, nodding as Annette spoke. She'd started writing down everyone's ideas. Annette's description matched what the others had been saying. Wang-Li Minh, on the vid-screen from Hanoi, said a lot of the homeless people in her area were living on rickety boats because the rising waters had overrun their homes. Melinda O'Connor, speaking from her office in Melbourne, said Australia was facing both a food shortage and a water shortage. That brought a laugh from Rebecca Meyer, who said New Yorkers would be happy to share some water with Australia.

"We've had five hurricanes in the last two years. The experts say it'll be at least eight years before the new techniques of bio-seeding clouds can reverse the pattern."

Aayan Yusuf, speaking from her tiny kitchen in Paris, seemed to sum it up: "We either have to turn things around, or whatever's left will collapse."

Yoko Nakamura, speaking from Geneva at the International Labor Organization, had her own thoughts. She'd been following popular movements for the last couple of months, and she'd seen signs of change. There'd been dozens of demonstrations against Verafoods and Uniworld in places you would least expect, she said. Some of them were still going on. "This gives me hope. With the right leadership, we could move forward," she enthused.

"Are you saying we should turn our whole focus to this Verafoods/Uniworld outfit?" Franca sat up straighter on her chair so the camera could see her asking the question.

"Something like that," Yoko said. "At least at first."

Franca shook her head. "That's quite a challenge."

"It may be an impossible challenge, for all I know." Gabriella Rodriques was on the vid-screen, speaking from her living room in Sao Paolo. "But I was there in San Francisco a few weeks ago when we marched against Verafoods. I could feel the passion in people. I hadn't seen anything like that in a while. I think Yoko's got the right idea."

The thought went around the room, as each of them added to it.

"I agree," Rasa said. "Fighting the Verafoods food monopoly would be more than just a symbolic gesture. It would go right to the heart of what's wrong. Someone has to break the power of the Cartel before any real progress can be made. Fortunately, Uniworld is so hated around the world, it could give us a powerful organizing tool."

"Ah, yes, organizing." Maria stood as she spoke, extending herself to what the others lovingly called her "full Bishop Balewa presence."

"Most of us have worked together in one way or another for years. We know each other; we trust each other. We know how each of us thinks. But now we're talking about something much bigger. Do we really know how much bigger? By my count, there are just fourteen of us. We'd have to pool all our resources. And we'd have to call on everyone we know in all the groups we've ever been involved in, and even that wouldn't be enough. We'd need to build much larger networks on top of that. And we'd have to commit ourselves to providing a dedicated, long-term leadership at the top. We'd probably spend so much time together that we'd get sick of looking at each other."

"Are we ready to do that?" She looked at each of the women in the room, continuing her long, slow stare at the others on the vid-screen. "Are we?"

The seconds ticked by.

It was Maria's own face that was the first to break into a big smile. "Well, I am. Let's get started."

DURING A BREAK, someone opened a window to get some air. Maya felt chilly, and she went looking for her wrap to put around her shoulders. She found it behind a cushion in Deva's bedroom.

As she turned to go back, she saw Marta Kwon looking at her though the doorway. Maya felt immediately embarrassed.

"I'm so glad you've become part of this group."

"I'm just happy to be here," Maya stammered. "I hope I can contribute. I've never seen women with so much energy and so much affection for each other."

"Most of us have worked together for a long time, so we're pretty close." Marta said. "I'm sure you know Deva's very fond of you."

Maya found herself blushing.

DEVA WENT AROUND the room thanking them for being there, repeating it for each of the women on the vid-screen.

"This has been an inspiring meeting. I'm always deeply moved when I'm with this group. I think we've accomplished a lot."

During the break, they'd checked their calendars and found a date when they could meet in San Francisco. "That meeting will be very important," Rasa said, "but we have an enormous amount of work to do first." She'd put together a quick list of some of their contacts: Marta's labor organization in Korea with its local organizers all over East Asia; Gabriella's Peace Institute with its branches in world capitals; Rebecca,

Aayan, Maria, and Mag with their contacts in religious organizations around the world.

"There are lots of resources—even financial resources," Rasa said. "The question will be whether we can pull them all together."

"Can I say something?" Magdalena Garcia asked. She was seated behind her desk at her office in Rome.

"Of course," Deva said. "Mag, you've been awfully quiet during the meeting."

"Well, it's because I agree with most of what's been said. But I just want to add something. Let's make sure that in all of our organizing we don't forget the most important thing: our moral commitment. That's the key to what we're doing."

She lowered her voice slightly to make her point. "We're just a small group of women. The only chance we have to make a difference is to appeal to everyone's better nature. That's an enormous challenge, but we can do it if we remember that a moral commitment is the key to any social change. We have only to look at Mohandas Gandhi or Martin Luther King."

Maria Balewa had her hands over her eyes, slowly shaking her head. "We better not look too hard. They both got assassinated for their efforts."

The room was quiet. Maya felt a chill go through her.

Finally, Rasa said, "Let's try to skip that part."

FOUR MONTHS LATER

MAYA UNPACKED THE carton of notepads and other supplies for the meeting, while Deva brought the food into the kitchen. Both were in a state of disbelief.

"Maria, this house is incredible," Deva said. "When you said we could have our next meeting here, I never realized it would be so luxurious."

Maya and Deva poked their heads into the various parlors and libraries. There were valuable paintings on every wall and spectacular views from most of the windows. A pool and atrium ran along almost the entire ground floor.

Maria offered one of her big happy grins. "When you live on these four blocks in Pacific Heights you don't let a little thing like an economic collapse stand between you and the benefits of real money."

"What are you doing here?"

"You mean I don't look like I'm part of the economic elite?" Maria feigned indignation. "Well, it so happens that the people who own this mansion are members of Grace Cathedral, and they have graciously allowed their visiting Bishop—that's me—to live here while they are out of the country."

"Thanks for letting us meet here," Deva said.

"No problem. This place is so big that it sometimes gets spooky being here alone."

"Madame Chairwoman," Melinda said, "I have a motion."

"A motion? Why?" Rebecca stared down at Melinda from the other end of the long table where they had been meeting. "We've gone all day long without using parliamentary procedure. Why start now?"

"But you haven't heard my motion," Melinda said. "I want us to get our bodies in motion out of these chairs and get into that beautiful pool we've been gazing at all day."

"On a hot night like this, you'll get a lot of seconds on that!" Gabriella laughed.

"What does everyone think?" Deva asked. "We're pretty much through with our business." But by that point she was already just talking to half-empty chairs.

"Shall we just strip down and go in? That's how we'd do it in Australia." Melinda started undressing, and then looked around. "Unless you want to stand on formality—"

"—No!"

As the others slipped out of their clothes and into the pool, Maria fiddled with a panel of buttons behind one of the columns. "Wait until you see this."

The lights lowered until they had reached a soft glow. Then the ceiling began sliding to either side, revealing a clear night sky with the moon peeking over the wall. Maria announced that the pool was filled with recycled water and heated through solar panels. "So, no one should feel guilty. As far as I know, you can work to save the world and still be a bit of a hedonist."

"This feels wonderful," Wang-Li said. "Why did we sit around that table all day?"

Maya took off her clothes and left them in a pile on her chair. She felt a little shy about the whole idea. She and Magdalena were the last two into the pool.

"You look like you've never seen a naked nun before?" Mag dead-panned.

"Actually, I haven't."

Mag stared down at herself. "I think I look like everyone else."

"You do," Maya replied, laughing. "Maybe even a little bit better."

Most of the women lay with their backs against the tile walls, kicking their feet lightly out into the water, delighting in the sensation. A few tried to swim laps, but they soon settled back with the others. They were close enough to lean against each other, as they shared their new-found buoyancy. By now, the moon had risen high enough in the sky that the light began to glisten off their bodies.

They were soon grouped in clusters, chatting aimlessly. No one wanted to talk business. This was a side of these women that Maya had never seen before. In the past few months she'd gotten used to watching them in motion, like coiled springs, jumping into action. Now, she was seeing them relaxed.

Franca tried to say something, but she began to laugh as she found her wet hair dripping in her face; Gabriella floated over behind her and helped gather it out of her eyes, pulling it back, strand by strand, slowly weaving it into a ponytail. Annette lay against the side of the pool, listening to the Vivaldi concerto that was flowing through the atrium. She invited Melinda to lean back against her, so she could massage her neck and shoulders. Melinda's sighs were so audible that some of the others laughed; they wanted their turn to be next. Maya found herself sitting next to Deva, leaning on her shoulder, hoping she would never have to move. She couldn't ever remember feeling so contented. She reached her hand through the water and gave Deva's hand a squeeze.

Maria activated a projector, and a smiling pair of dolphins appeared, glimmering on the wall at the end of the pool. "They may not compare with the Renoirs and Matisses in the other rooms, but these two always make me happy when I'm in here swimming."

"They're beautiful, Maria." Yoko said. "They're frescoes at the palace at Knossos, aren't they?"

"You know Minoan art," Maria said. "Here's my favorite."

"Oh, I love that one," Yoko said, "the Woman of Thera. She's gorgeous. I love the way she stands there, with her boobs sticking out, picking flowers. She looks like she's on top of the world. I'd love to have lived then; it was a very egalitarian culture."

"Who knows?" Aayan said. "Maybe we'll see that again." Aayan had a philosopher's instinct, always nudging the others to take the next intellectual step. "I think we might be at the end of a thirty-five-hundred-year cycle. It could be that we just have to give it one more push."

"Do you really think that?" Marta asked.

Aayan had her head resting against the side of the pool. Her legs were beating a long kick that added a rhythmic intensity to her words.

"For years I've had the theory that equality for women is the key to everything else. I'm talking about true equality across the board—not just equality for western women; that's too tenuous. But if you can achieve the kind of equality I'm talking about, then all of the other problems of the world become easier to solve. If you don't, then society just keeps repeating the same mistakes."

"Maybe it's just a dream," she said, "but we could be at a point where that kind of change could happen."

"You really *are* an optimist," Rasa said.

The thought worked its way around the pool. How optimistic, really, were any of them, Maya wondered? Could they accomplish even half of the things they wanted to do? It was the work that was important to them. None of them acted like the changes they wanted would all occur in their lifetimes—Deva least of all. Maya realized that Deva was always focused on some moment that lay just beyond everything else.

"I don't want to spoil a wonderful evening," Rebecca said, "but I'm a little more of a worrier. We can talk about peace and justice and equality for everyone, but there are a lot of pathologically insecure men out there who will look at us and see only one thing: a bunch of women who are trying to change *their* world. They'll be deeply threatened."

"That's a sad thought," Aayan said. "If you're right, what can we do about it?"

MAYA ALMOST MISSED the signal. She crawled out of the pool and found her vid-phone on a chair buried under her clothes. The call was from Lara. Maya could tell she was panic-stricken. She listened and then dressed quickly. She hurried back over to the pool and knelt down next to Deva.

"What is it?" Deva asked. "I saw the look on your face. Here, let me help you."

"I've got to go," Maya said. "It's Antonio. There's an ambulance at the house right now taking him to the hospital."

MONDAY, APRIL 27, 2082

NEW YORK CITY

JULIA

I KNEW NONE of that at the time.

As I sat there in our stifling community room on May 4, 2057, watching the noose tighten slowly around the Thirteen, I knew nothing about Maya's earlier involvement with them. I didn't even know that she knew Deva or any of the others. But I was soon to find out that very day—and in a way that would shock me.

But it wasn't until many years later that Maya would tell me the full story of her relationship with Deva. By then, it was 2067, and I was twenty-five years old. I had just graduated from law school at UC Berkeley, and I was getting ready to enter the new Military-Legal Academy of the United Nations. Maya was celebrating her eightieth birthday.

Maya wanted a simple birthday celebration that day, so her friends were cooking a special dinner for her in the community kitchen. While that was going on, she and I walked down to her favorite bench by Corte Madera Creek. She said she wanted to talk to me about some things she hadn't discussed with anyone in years.

She wanted to tell me about Deva.

MAYA DESCRIBED THE five or so months that she spent with Deva the way an artist might paint a garden—a memory here, some laughter there, a touch of sadness around the edges. Everything had been a revelation for her during that brief period in 2032. She said she saw things that she had never seen before, and it all seemed to gleam in her mind in bright colors. Working with the other thirteen women had given her a new sense of purpose. Even the joint task that she and Deva had undertaken—the one of caring for my very troubled mother, Amy—seemed somehow lighter when the two of them were together. At the time Maya was sitting there telling me all this—a moment when her friends were preparing for her eightieth birthday—the days she had spent with Deva were already thirty-five years into the past. But in her telling, it all sounded like it had happened just yesterday.

Things had begun to change, however, that night during the meeting when Antonio was rushed to the hospital. Maya said she remembered the next few days as a living nightmare. Once they allowed her into the quarantine perimeter around Antonio's room, they wouldn't let her out until the doctors were sure what kind of a disease they were dealing with. He was running a high fever with convulsions. "I moved a chair close to his bed, and just sat there, living on instinct, trying not to let my imagination run wild." After forty-two hours, the doctors thought they had it under control. They said it was okay for her to leave for a while.

"As soon as I stepped out into the corridor," Maya said, "I saw Deva standing there. She was as close to the room as the medical staff would allow her to go. She'd been there for hours, keeping a vigil—almost from the time I'd rushed into the hospital. She'd taken a break to go to my apartment to see if everything was okay with Lara and Amy, but then she'd picked up a change of clothes for me and had come right back."

"When I saw her, all I could do was grab her and hold on. I don't know how long we stayed that way. I just held her and kept crying and crying. All of my emotions of those last few days came pouring out. People must have thought we were crazy, but neither of us cared."

Maya stared out over the water as she talked to me. "I hadn't realized until then just how much I loved her." She bowed her head for a second without saying a word.

"What was wrong with Antonio?" I asked. I had to say something to bring her back from where her thoughts had wandered.

"We never did find out exactly," Maya said. "It was probably some allergen from a contaminated food shipment. Thank God, there were no long-term problems."

She hesitated, seemingly trying to decide how to describe what came next.

"Despite the love I was feeling just then, I remember the moments that followed as being very painful."

It wasn't the wrenching agony that she had just gone through, Maya said. It was an emotion that seemed almost self-indulgent after she had been worrying about the life or death of her child. It was a more wistful sadness, like the loss of one's dreams. As quickly as she had found someone she loved, she realized she was about to lose her.

Maya remembered the conversation as if it had only been a few days earlier.

"Deva, I can't do it."

"I know what you're going to tell me."

"I can't go on with you and the others and be part of what we're planning. I can't leave. I don't know why I ever thought I could do it. It makes me sick to say it, because I feel alive when I'm around you—when I'm around *all* of you. But I just can't do it."

"I know that," Deva said. "I know what kind of a person you are."

As she said those words, Maya remembered Deva taking her hands, coaxing her to lift her head until they were eye to eye. "Listen to me. I want to say this before you have me crying too. I love you. Nothing's going to change that. But I know you can't be with me."

Maya found it hard to listen. Every word was true; every word was painful.

"You have responsibilities you can't put aside," Deva said. "You can't just leave your children. My daughter is grown and in college; the same is true with the others. We can do what we're planning to do without hurting our loved ones."

"You can't do that. There are those who are counting on you right now. Women can't change the world by leaving emotional disasters in their wake."

"That doesn't make it any easier."

"Maya, if you were the kind of person who could pick up and leave the people who need you, I wouldn't love you the way I do."

"I'm going to miss you so much."

Maya remembered resting her head on Deva's shoulder, running her fingers through her hair, absorbing the richness of it. She felt the moisture on Deva's cheeks, and she knew Deva's tears were beginning to flow and mingle with her own. At that moment—maybe, it would be only for that moment—she and Deva were together as one.

"You are deep in my heart," Deva murmured. "I'm eternally grateful for that."

She lifted Maya's face between her two hands. Then she quietly closed the gap between them and kissed her. It was a kiss that would have to last awhile.

MAYA STOPPED TALKING for a second. I offered her a tissue to wipe her eyes. She thanked me, and then she continued with her story. She was determined to tell me all of it.

The thirteen women all left San Francisco a couple of days later, Maya said. Deva went to London and spent the next six weeks in Europe, meeting with sympathetic groups. The others split up temporarily, traveling to other cities to enlist supporters. Maya was getting reports that their movement was starting to build.

"Neither Deva nor I wanted to shut the door completely on our future. Things could change, we said. And when they did, we would still be there for each other."

Things did change, Maya said. The opportunity arose for her to move to a new type of co-housing community—"this place, right here." Her first house was just on the other side of Magnolia Avenue. Compared to their cramped apartment in San Francisco, it was huge.

"Your mother came with us too. Deva thought at the time she should help take care of Amy, but I insisted she stay with me. She was already part of our family."

"Deva and I kept up the hope that we would get together again," Maya said. "Then, three years later in 2035 the National Co-Housing Organization announced that Deva would be a guest speaker at our national convention in Washington, D.C. I was already planning to attend as a delegate, and we realized we would be seeing each other."

For weeks leading up to the meeting, Maya said, they chatted on the vid-phone every day, talking about what they would do with the little time they had.

"I was on a panel about integrating child-care and housing for retired people into co-housing communities. You know how strongly I feel about that. But as I was speaking, Deva walked into the room. I got so excited I forgot what I was saying."

When Deva spoke to the convention later in the day, Maya said she got a rousing ovation. She outlined the plans for what was then being called Women for Peace. "The funny thing is, I was the one who thought of that name at one of our meetings."

Later that night, Maya said, the two of them had dinner together and spent the late hours walking around the city, talking endlessly. "We were both nearing fifty, but we were giggling like a couple of schoolgirls." They finally reached Deva's room, where they crawled into bed together.

"We lay there, cherishing what was left of the night, wishing the dawn would never peek through the curtains."

Maya squirmed a little on the bench. All of a sudden she was having trouble getting comfortable. "I've gone this far, I suppose I should tell you what happened next."

I waited.

"Well, nothing, really. I went home, and Deva went on to New York, where she had a meeting." She paused for a second, looking for the right words. "We decided—or maybe, I decided—that our relationship couldn't continue like that. We were still very fond of each other, but we shouldn't complicate things by trying to meet that way. We talked all the time. We were each other's best friends, but we left it at that."

Maya said they talked every day, usually late at night when neither of them could sleep. In the middle of the night they be could be as intimate as they wanted without anyone overhearing them.

"We talked when you were asleep," Maya said.

"When I was growing up, I didn't even know you knew her."

"I know. I tried to keep it that way."

Before I could ask why, she shifted to something else, something that was bothering her. "It was different with your mother. I think she knew what was going on."

I waited. There was something painful in this.

"I guess I never realized until too late how attached Amy had become to Deva. They only really saw each other for those first few months, but maybe that was enough. Your mother may have needed her, and she might have thought I was keeping them apart. Maybe things wouldn't have happened the way—"

"Maya, please. Don't do that to yourself." I couldn't let that go on any longer. "You did everything you possibly could for my mother, just like you've done everything for me. Nobody could have asked for anything more."

"I suppose." She was crying. I moved closer and put my arm around her.

THERE WAS SOMETHING else she wanted to tell me, but she was waiting for me to ask. "Was there more to your feelings about Deva than you've told me?"

"Yes," she said quietly. "I wanted desperately to be by her side and to have her with me, but I knew it wasn't going to happen that way."

"Why? Didn't she want that?"

"No, just the opposite. She would have dropped everything and come with me, if I'd asked her. But I couldn't do it. I saw what she was doing, and I knew how important it was. I would never have forgiven myself if I'd taken her away from her work."

Maya stared out over the water. "Deva belonged to the world."

She sat for a second. I could see she was trying to find the right words.

"A few days after that night we spent together, I told her that I thought we just weren't right for each other in that way. But I had to turn away from the vid-screen as I said it. I couldn't bring myself to look at her."

"What did she say?"

"She pretended to agree with me, but I know she saw right through what I was doing. But it doesn't make any difference now. We never talked about it again."

But it still hurt. I could see it all over her face.

"There are times—even now—when I think I can still feel her near me, whispering softly in my ear."

WOULD I HAVE acted any differently if I'd known all of this on that dismal afternoon in 2057 as I watched the women being held captive? Maybe, if I had just turned and gone the other way . . . But, no—I can't do that. I was emphatic in telling Maya not to blame herself for what happened to my mother. Why can't I follow my own advice?

THE NEWS ABOUT the women's captivity kept getting worse. The room became oppressive. My confusion was unbearable.

I remember thinking I had to get out of there. I stepped over a couple of our neighbors and pushed my way through the door. Outside, I took a deep breath, trying to exhale what I'd seen. I started running, hitting full stride when I got to the street. I thought about turning north and heading to Marin Hospital, but at that moment I couldn't handle another one-way conversation with my mother.

I turned south down Magnolia Avenue. I was trying to get as far from the scenes on those vid-screens as I could, but I was still carrying them around in my head. Activity on the street had almost stopped. People were crowded into the café, staring at a wide screen behind the counter. The whole town, maybe the whole world, was caught up in the same awful news about the Women for Peace. I ran past everything, using my long strides to get through the middle of town, away from anyone I didn't want to see.

I turned right on Madrone Avenue, racing past a grove of redwood trees, toward the direction of Mt. Tamalpais. After a couple of kilometers, the street dead-ended against the foot of Mt. Tam, and I veered to my left, breaking stride for a second as I hit the dirt trail. After another kilometer of hard running, I reached the Southern Marin Line Road and turned left. The trail got more difficult. By the time I reached Old Railroad Grade and turned west up the mountain, my pace had slowed. I dodged branches and rocks and leaped over small rivulets from a recent rainfall. I didn't mind any of that. At that moment I felt I could deal with almost anything but people.

After about thirty minutes of hard running, I reached my favorite spot. It was a small clearing with a couple of large logs. When I hoisted myself to the top, I could see the whole expanse of San Francisco Bay. I liked Mt. Tam because of its odd shape and the story behind it—the "sleeping maiden" of Miwok tradition. I remember thinking that maybe that was me. I'd been sleeping too long, and it was time to wake up.

As irrational as it sounds, at the time I was blaming myself for the whole thing. I was the one who'd asked the question at the holo-conference that had seemed to encourage the women in Baluchistan to stand up for their rights. Maybe, I had inadvertently set the whole sequence of events in motion. The idea that I might be responsible for all of this was eating me up. But an hour alone up on the mountain cured me of that thought. I started to realize that what was going on at that moment went far beyond what any one kid might or might not have done somewhere in the world.

By the time I headed back, clouds were creeping down the canyons of Mt. Tam. There was a flash of lightning, followed by a peal of thunder. I was running with less fury than before. My desire to get back was a lot weaker than my earlier need had been to get away.

I slowed to a trot when I reached the street, easing up as I passed the café where I'd spent so many hours talking with my friends. Through the window, I saw Chloe seated at a window table. When she saw me, she motioned furiously for me to come in. Annabel and Flora were with her. Their normal chatter was missing. Flora had her head down on the table, cradled in her arms; Annabel looked like she'd been crying. I remember glancing around the room and seeing that everyone, even the staff behind the bar, was glued to the vid-screen.

"What's going on?" I found myself whispering without knowing why.

"It's them," Chloe blurted out, pointing up at the screen.

It took me a few minutes to realize what I was seeing. The live, multi-dimensional scenes of Mt. Tamalpais that normally flowed across the screen were gone. In their place was a flat montage of images, all of them as dark as the gathering clouds outside. The side screens were carrying some of the same aerial surveillance pictures that I'd seen earlier, but the mystery was contained in the large, central screen. The pictures were so dim that it was hard to see them. It wasn't until a figure emerged from the shadows and walked towards the camera that I knew what I was looking at. It was Deva Chandri.

"The pictures of them started coming in about an hour ago," Chloe whispered, choking back her tears. "There was no warning, really. The women just showed up on the screen. Since then, they've been taking turns talking, giving messages to their families, trying to sound all positive and everything."

She stopped, as her crying got the best of her. "It's awful, Julia! They're probably going to be killed. They must know that, but they're so upbeat. I can't take much more of this, but I can't stop watching."

Neither could anyone else. The side screens showed pictures of large crowds in New York, Chicago, and San Francisco. The camera panned over thousands of faces, all of them quietly looking at giant vid-screens, seeing the same images that we were seeing. The emotions were all the same—sadness, anger, and a look of utter helplessness.

Deva Chandri stepped closer to the camera and began to talk. Her eyes were as I remembered them, alive and flashing. If she'd been crying or distressed, it didn't show.

I feel so much love at this moment for all of the millions of people who have been watching, waiting, and praying for us. As my sisters have said before me, no matter what happens to us, we have all been extraordinarily blessed.

I gripped the edge of the table, determined to keep my composure while I listened. The room was deathly silent.

We know about the efforts being made to rescue us, and we know how difficult that would be. Now that we have this vid-phone working, we've been able to see the same pictures that many of you are watching. We know that we are at the foot of a dam that could explode at any time. If anything goes wrong, we will be covered with water in minutes. If we were all forty years younger, we might be able to crawl up the walls of this steep bunker in which we find ourselves and find a way to escape. But I'm afraid that isn't an option.

We know there's been a huge outpouring of support around the world, and we are forever grateful to those who have lent their voices in our behalf. Many wonderful people are working hard to bring this to a happy ending. We hope they are successful, not just for ourselves but for the many thousands of people who depend upon this dam for their lives and livelihood. But we're realistic enough to know that may not happen. So, all we can do is wait. I want to say, however, that we are gratified to hear that

the village women who sought our help are likely to be released.
It makes us happy to know that this mission—which may be our
last—was, in that sense, a successful one.

She began giving personal messages to her family and friends. She
wasn't saying goodbye, but everyone knew that was what she meant. It
was hard to listen, but it was impossible to move away.

Flora leaned over towards me. "The others all gave the same kind
of messages before you got here. It's so awful."

I gave her hand a squeeze; I couldn't think of anything to say that
would make the moment easier. Then I heard a message that I probably should have anticipated.

. . . and to my dear grandchildren, Dhanye, Indira, and Rajiv—

My heart dropped. "Dhanye!" That beautiful face that I had seen
next to me at the holo-conference was suddenly a portrait of agony. I
tried to imagine her pain, but it was beyond anything I could understand at that moment.

While Deva spoke, the vid-screens next to the main screen were
showing pictures of battles raging near the dam. It was an eerie scene.
The drones hovering above the armies captured only the pictures
without the sounds. But those same sounds of battle formed the background noise for the small, almost pitifully fragile, vid-phone that was
linking the women to the outside world. Explosions could be heard
after almost every word Deva uttered.

Deva had reached the end of her personal messages. But there was
one more—one I could never have expected.

To my wonderful soulmate, Maya Flores. You have been so close
to me over all these many years. There are worlds that might
have been, and I truly believe they will always be there for us.
You are in my heart forever.

DEVA CHANDRI HAD more to say on that last day, but I didn't hear it.

I was so stunned by what she had said about Maya that nothing more could penetrate my brain. Deva's message to Maya came as a total surprise, and it left me disoriented, almost gasping for breath.

But the remainder of her words weren't entirely lost. Like most people, I've heard them later on—many times. The last words of Deva Chandri and the rest of the Thirteen were destined to be played and analyzed and discussed, over and over again, for years to come, as people tried to come to grips with what had happened and what it all meant.

In the last few hours, my sisters and I have been hugging and kissing and telling each other stories. We've looked into each other's eyes, and we've shared our dreams and hopes. We are so lucky to be with people that we love at a time like this. We've been listening to beautiful music, and the words of one old song have lifted our spirits: "Don't lose heart," the lyrics say, "it's the beginning not the end." We truly believe that. We want to share that message with the world.

We've seen a love in each other's eyes that will never die. We feel a joy and a power that can never be crushed. We feel a wonderful sense of eternity. We've seen the face of God, and she is beautiful.

THE END CAME suddenly.

The screen showing the top of the dam was suddenly ablaze from the light of an explosion—a terrible, soundless light show. It was followed by more blasts, as the surging water lifted itself majestically into the night air in search of its natural level. A sound began in the café. It was an instinctive, animal howl that went around the room, as people reached out in every direction for someone to hold, someone who might protect them. That sound was matched by moans coming from the crowds on the vid-screens. Heartrending noises were sweeping through the streets of New York, Chicago, Paris, Rome, London, and all the other places where people were watching.

The most chilling sound of all came from the center screen, where the noise of the exploding dam could be heard at that moment in the background—an ominous, offscreen presence that would soon come crashing into the picture. But for that brief moment the center stage belonged to the women, still clad in their thin dresses, standing in a circle and hugging each other tightly. It was that moment—only seconds in length, but eons in its agony—that became seared into the minds of millions as the Circle of Thirteen. It was the picture of thirteen women, holding each other closely, waiting to meet their fate. They were frail, human, but somehow undefeated.

WITHIN MOMENTS IT was over. The center screen suddenly went blank.

It stayed that way for several minutes, a formless, screeching picture of static. It was as if the news producers didn't have the heart to remove it from the screen and, with it, the last remnant of hope.

I found myself hugging Flora, feeling her quiet sobs on my shoulder. Annabel and Chloe were holding each other, both at a loss for words. Without thinking about it, the four of us ended up huddled together, squeezing each other tightly, allowing ourselves to cry without restraint, vowing between sobs that we would always be as strong and as faithful to each other as the women we had just seen.

New pictures began appearing on the screens. Drones were tracking the progress of the raging water through the river valley, watching it wreak havoc on everything in its path. The emotional impact on the audiences watching the news was palpable. News channels began switching to commentators, newscasters, and anyone else who could talk about what had just happened and try to make sense of it. The commentators were having a hard time saying anything coherent. Some tried historical analogies, comparing the emotional impact of that moment to the Zapruder film of the murder of JFK or the pictures of people leaping off the burning towers in Manhattan. Others speculated about the long-term political effect of the tragedy. Still others talked about psychological damage to children and the mentally unstable, warning against everything from irrational attacks to attempts at suicide.

We couldn't watch any more of it; we were simply numb. My friends and I finally got up and left, walking without ever deciding where we were heading. We had nowhere else to go, but anywhere seemed no better or worse than where we were at the moment.

By 10:00 P.M., my friends had all gone home. We were all exhausted. I went by the community center on the way back to our apartment. Almost everyone was gone and the lights were off, but I saw two people in the corner of the room: Carlos and Maya. As I walked in, Carlos brought his finger to his lips, gesturing that I should be quiet. I tiptoed over to him. Maya was lying next to him asleep.

"How is she?" I whispered.

"She finally cried herself asleep about a half-hour ago," Carlos said quietly. "Did you hear—"

"Yes," I interrupted. At the moment, I couldn't bear hearing about it again. Carlos nodded. He laid his hand lightly on Maya's sleeping shoulder.

"It was rough on her, but I think something changed when she heard Deva mention her name. After that, I guess she was finally able to let go."

"I think she's going to be okay." He rubbed his hand gently across her shoulders. "She didn't think I knew, but I did."

THAT NIGHT I hit bottom.

The storms had returned, bringing with them thunder and flashes of lightning that hammered at my fragile sleep. The killing of the thirteen women played itself out in my head all night long, with walls of water breaking through everywhere and battering against helpless, screaming people. I was alone in the apartment. Carlos must have been with Maya somewhere, probably at his place, trying to comfort her. The foreboding I'd felt all day long was still with me.

I've gone over and over my memories from that night, and I still can't distinguish between sleeping and waking. How much of what happened was a troubled dream, and how much was a waking nightmare? The dark, ominous empty spot that I sometimes see in my dreams began that night. I've berated myself about it for years afterwards. Should I have realized? Should I have been more awake? Should I have gone north when I reached the street instead of heading south? What should I have done? What *could* I have done?

I finally woke up for good with my heart beating rapidly. The last dream was the most harrowing; it jolted me upright. I couldn't recall what it was about, but I knew it was desperately important that I try to remember. I looked at the clock: it was 4:05 A.M. I flicked on the light and started to get out of bed.

Then I looked down and saw a pool of water in the middle of the room. There was water on my bed as well. I looked up to see if there was a leak, but the ceiling was dry. Then I saw more water leading towards the door, and a horrible thought began to creep in. When I reached the door, I realized that it had been left open. Then the dream came rushing back to me.

I raced to the vid-phone and punched in the numbers furiously.

"Is Amy Moro in her room?" I blurted the words out to the nurse in the psychiatric ward.

"It's 4:00 in the morning," she responded, "and our patients aren't allowed to take calls."

"I don't want to talk to her. I just want to know if she's there."

"Our patients are not allowed to go anywhere at this time—"

"Look," I said quickly, "this is her daughter calling, and I want to make sure that she hasn't left the hospital. I'm worried that she might have gotten out."

"I'm sorry, but we can't—"

"—Of course you can," I screamed. "Just look above your desk at the video monitor. Do you see her in her room?"

"Well," she answered, "I don't know if I see her or not."

"Please, please go look."

"Okay, hold on."

The dream was clear to me now. My mother had her arms around me. She was dripping wet from the rains, whispering something in my ear. A feeling of guilt began building up inside me. If only I had woken up, if, if, if—

The nurse came back to the phone. "I'm afraid she's not there. I've alerted security."

"Were the vid-screens working on your floor last evening?"

"I don't see why—"

"Just tell me. The news-screens at the end of the hall—were any of the patients watching what was going on?"

"Well, yes. Everyone here was glued to the screen. It was so awful."

It hadn't been a dream. My mother had come to my room to tell me goodbye.

I WAS STILL staring at the window at 5:30 A.M., trying to blank everything out of my mind, when I heard Antonio at the door. I'd called him earlier. I didn't know where else to turn in the middle of the night.

"Julia, I have bad news."

I knew what he was going to say before he said it.

"I don't know how to make this any easier."

"Tonio, please. Just say it."

He exhaled slowly, nodding his head.

"The Coast Guard says that a woman jumped off the Golden Gate Bridge at about 4:55 this morning. They've now recovered the body. It was your mother."

MONDAY, APRIL 27, 2082

NEW YORK CITY

JULIA

I WAS LATE getting downstairs. It was a meeting that had been arranged weeks ago. Madeleine was already there with the others, and she gave me a disapproving look as I walked in. It's a look I've come to recognize: *Where have you been?*

I ignored her. She'd want to know what I'd been doing for the last few hours, but there was no way I could tell her. What could I say— that I was lost in my memories? That I'd been caught in the grip of the past? That I couldn't break loose?

Madeleine and her group were taking a tour of the Hall of the Charters on the second floor of the new headquarters, giving it a thorough walk-through before it officially opened. The Secretary-General and a few of his aides were there, along with several other dignitaries. Noah Fawkes, looking rather bored with the whole thing, had been invited as well. Madeleine thought inviting him was the right thing to do, since his foundation had provided most of the money for the exhibit. That was just the latest of the many funding coups that she'd been able to pull off.

The Hall contained the original 1945 Charter as well as the New Charter adopted in 2058. The display took up a lot of space. Both of the Charters were written in five official languages, and there were ratification documents from each of the national parliaments. The collection of historical documents was impressive. There were some original papers on loan from the FDR Library in Hyde Park that talked about the founding of the U.N. in 1945. The curator had also found an early draft of the New Charter with Yoko Nakamura's margin notes from a 2053 meeting in London.

The Secretary-General and the others were giving the documents a thorough look, focusing on the layout and the flow of the exhibit. While they were doing that, I decided it was time to put my mind back to work. I checked around and confirmed that there were no isolated corners or hidden angles where anyone could hide. The floor and the walls were solid enough. The skylights were made of the strongest glass we could find, and they seemed to be securely bolted. The nano-circuits built into the glass would activate the alarm on the Mother Grid if there was any attempt at penetration. By my standards, the exhibit appeared to be a success.

The Secretary-General seemed intent on examining each of the ratification documents from the national parliaments, shaking his head slightly as he did so.

"I'm still astonished. Even twenty-four years later, it's hard to believe how quickly the major countries acted to ratify the New Charter."

He paused, savoring the recollection, trying to answer his own question. "There was so much public outrage in those first few months after the death of the Women for Peace leaders, I think everyone was just looking for a way to make things better. Don't you agree?"

He turned to Fawkes for confirmation of that thought. He got a slight nod.

Then the Secretary-General looked at me. "Do you remember those days?"

I told him I did.

I LIED.

That was my lost year. I don't remember much of anything.

Of all my teenage years, that one—the year after my mother's death
—is the most difficult to bring into focus. I was fifteen. As the months
went by, I grew more and more withdrawn, more distrustful, less and
less sure of anything. Maya told me later that she'd worried that I was
digging myself into such a deep emotional hole that I'd never get out.

Poor Maya. As I think about it, she had less than eight hours that
night for her own grieving. Carlos said she awoke several times shiver-
ing and screaming. He tried to calm her down, but there wasn't much
he could do. She said later that they came to her in her dreams—all
thirteen of them, talking to her one by one. Their words were strangely
intimate and calm, their voices echoing from someplace far away.
Then, she would wake up with a jolt. Within seconds the serenity of
those dream-words would come crashing up against the reality of
her pain.

But her grieving was cut short. She had to take care of me.

Antonio reached her around 5:45 A.M. to tell her about Amy's
death, and Maya was forced to drag herself out of her misery. She knew
I couldn't handle it alone. Years later, she told me she wasn't sure if she
could do it. But she swore she heard Deva's voice whispering in her ear:
"Go to her; she needs you."

MAYA WAS DETERMINED that we would all have a new beginning.
There would be no more nights at home alone, no more feelings of
guilt. She asked Carlos to come live with us, and he moved in within a
couple of days. I was glad he did. There were times when it took both
of them to handle my moods.

Maya soon had something to be happy about: her new grand-
daughter. She broke into tears when she heard the little girl's name:
Deva. Antonio swore they didn't give her that name just for Maya's
sake. He pointed out that thousands of babies had been named Deva
since the death of the Thirteen, many of them little boys. But Maya

knew what he and Li-Jin were doing, and she was grateful to them. Little Deva's presence in the house, her uninhibited squeals of joy, renewed Maya's faith in the future.

IT WAS A pivotal year for the world, but my memory about what happened that year is the last thing anyone should trust. Maya and Carlos would sit there for hours, watching the unfolding drama on the vidscreen, but I couldn't bring myself to do it. I saw a few brief scenes, but that was only when I was passing through the room on my way from one ugly thought to another.

Years later, I realized I still didn't know many of the details of what happened that year. I started reading anything I could get my hands on. Last year I even snuck into a course on Contemporary History that Dhanye taught at NYU, listening to her two-day lecture about the events of 2057–58. The public reaction, I learned, had been overwhelming. People seemed determined that something like that should never be allowed to happen again. Tens of thousands of volunteers flocked to Women for Peace offices around the world, offering to help. "If those who engineered the death of the Thirteen hoped to kill off the ideas of social justice that they embodied," Dhanye told the class, "they made a major mistake. The push for those ideas just became stronger."

The regional directors of Women for Peace met shortly after the death of their founders, vowing to carry on their work. Within days they launched a worldwide campaign to create a permanent memorial to them. They had only one goal in mind: the immediate ratification of the New Charter for the United Nations. The thirteen leaders had put their hearts and souls into the effort to adopt that charter. This would be a living memorial—something that would make a difference for generations to come.

The campaign succeeded. Ratification had been languishing for months, but the new Women for Peace leaders took it upon themselves to try to break the logjam. The struggle produced some dramatic media coverage. The WFP was shown lobbying parliaments in the larger countries, echoing the huge, mass campaigns that the Thirteen themselves had organized in 2048 and 2055. Electronic petitions with over a billion signatures poured into capitols around the world. Candlelight vigils were organized to coincide with key parliamentary votes. One video showed the new Women for Peace leaders, with Eloni in the front rank, leading a march of more than 250,000 people around the parliamentary buildings in New Delhi, waiting as the Indian Parliament went through the slow process of voting. Once the larger countries gave their approval, the others followed quickly. By February 2058, they had the majority they needed.

The success of the campaign came as a surprise even to Eloni. Years later, at one of our dinners, she admitted that at that time they were riding an enormous wave of goodwill beyond anything they expected. But sometimes history works that way.

"Maybe," she said, "we just got lucky."

MAY 4, 2058—one year after the death of the Thirteen—the New Charter was formally signed in San Francisco. With that gesture, the memorial for the Women for Peace was forever linked with their most cherished project.

But that day my mind was elsewhere. It was also the one-year anniversary of something else.

MAY 4, 2058

SAN FRANCISCO

SAN FRANCISCO was gleaming for the occasion, basking in its one-day role as the center of the world. Flags were flying on poles everywhere in the City, whipping around in the warm spring breeze. The area around the Opera House was full of people, crowding all of the side streets. Marching bands, choral groups, and dance troupes from hundreds of countries were breaking out in music everywhere around the city. It was a lively, colorful display that Maya found a bit overwhelming.

She walked up the carpeted steps from Van Ness Avenue, feeling slightly out of place. Videographers filled all the empty spaces along the sidewalk, taking pictures of everyone who approached the building, asking questions, looking for comments, trying to identify the guests. "Who are you, anyway?" one of them asked her. Maya didn't know how to answer. She felt suddenly old, a bit of a historical relic. She held on tightly to Eloni's arm as the two of them entered into the marble foyer of the Opera House.

Once the date had been set for signing the New Charter, there was no arguing with the choice of location. It was San Francisco where the Women for Peace organization had gotten its start, and it was San Francisco—the Opera House, in fact—where the original United Nations Charter had been signed in 1945. One hundred and thirteen years later, the dream of the U.N. founders would be given a new lease on life in the place where it had been born.

Eloni arranged for Maya to sit in her box at the ceremony. After winning a special election in California's 6th Congressional district earlier that year, Eloni had secured a place on the official U.S. delegation to the signing ceremony. She could have arranged a seat for Carlos, if he'd wanted one. But he had said no, this was Maya's day. He hated crowds. He was planning a quiet dinner for Maya and Julia later that evening.

The ceremony itself was both simple and moving. It began with a tribute to the Thirteen from Thabo Nyrere, telling in moving terms how they had saved his country from a threatened invasion. That was followed by holographic vignettes of them in happier days. Some of the scenes were so poignant, Maya had to grip the edge of her chair to keep from breaking down. But she was determined to get through the day without crying. As pictures of the thirteen women went by, she found herself whispering a silent prayer to each of them.

Following the tribute, there was the signing of the New Charter. The organizers had located the original round table that had been used at the United Nations founding in 1945, and they used archival photos to place it in the same spot on the stage. They surrounded it again with a semi-circle of national flags, most of them new additions since the original ceremony. As the orchestra played Beethoven's 9TH symphony, the representatives of the countries walked across the stage to sign the document. When the last signature was added, the new United Nations was officially born.

As she sat there, Maya was transported. She found herself wrapped in the warm memory of her friends who had now become a part of history. A few steps outside, and she was brought back to earth. There was a message from Carlos on her vid-phone.

"Julia is in jail."

A FEW HOURS EARLIER

"DID YOU ORDER me a coffee?" Flora asked, slightly out of breath.

"I got it for you," Annabel said. "What kept you?" She moved her chair a bit, so Flora could squeeze in between them. Julia moved in the other direction to make room.

"Kevin was down the street with some of his friends, so I went around the block to avoid him." She pulled her chair in even closer.

"You mean Kevin the Creep?" Chloe asked. "I thought you told him to get lost."

"I did, but he keeps bothering me."

"He's such a toad," Annabel said. "The guys he hangs out with are real throwbacks."

"Haven't you told him you want nothing to do with him?" Chloe said.

"Yes!"

"And he still keeps coming on to you?" Annabel said. "What a jerk."

"What am I going to do? He keeps sneaking up behind me, putting his hands on me, telling me I should go out with him." She leaned out over the table and looked down the street warily. "If you see him coming, let me know, okay?"

Flora finally calmed down and started sipping at her coffee. She glanced over at Julia and raised her eyebrows, as if to ask, "Are you okay?" Julia gave her a quick nod.

"I'm just glad we're all here today," Annabel said.

"Do you mean because of the big memorial?" Flora asked.

"Not just that," said Chloe. "We all need to be together—particularly today."

Chloe looked at Julia and grabbed her hand, giving it a squeeze.

Annabel and Flora picked up on the gesture, adding their hands on top of the others. They stayed that way for a few seconds.

"There's someone else we should be thinking about too," Chloe said.

For a moment, no one said anything. Julia stared at the table.

"DON'T LOOK NOW," Annabel said, "but I see Kevin walking this way."

A tall, thin boy strode into view, trying to act like he was alone. But he wasn't cool enough to pull it off. A surreptitious glance over his shoulder at his friends gave the game away. As he approached the table, Julia saw him look beyond their group and then off to the side, focusing on them only at the last moment. His slow, studied gait was just short of a swagger. He leaned back against a small railing, sliding his legs forward until they were close to the table. His arms were crossed in front of his body.

"You looked like you were avoiding me back there."

"I didn't feel like talking to you," Flora said, "if that's what you mean."

"I don't know why not," Kevin said. "I told you there's a cool party tonight, and you know you want to go with me."

"What gave you that idea?"

"Because I know what you want." He leaned over and started rubbing Flora's arm. Flora flinched and moved away.

"What's the matter?" he said. "Afraid to show a little affection in front of these friends of yours?"

"She doesn't want to talk to you," Chloe interjected. "Why don't you just leave?"

"Who the hell's asking you?" He gave Chloe a nasty look, followed by a quick glance back in the direction of his friends. Julia watched, as they moved closer.

"Look," Annabel said, "the four of us are just sitting here, enjoying the holiday, and we'd rather be alone."

"'Enjoying the holiday'—are you sure you're not just sitting there mooning over those women that got themselves killed last year?" He looked at Julia first and then glared back and forth from one girl to another, trying to get a reaction. "As far as I can see, they had no business being there in the first place."

"Please leave," Flora pleaded. "Can't you see that my friends don't want you—"

"—And do you take orders from them? Are you going to just sit here like them and wring your hands over some dead women?"

"You asshole," Julia muttered under her breath.

In an instant, she was out of her chair and had Kevin around the neck. Her forward thrust carried the two of them over the railing and across the sidewalk to a planted area along the curb. As they landed, she kept her hands around his neck and was pounding his head into the dirt.

Julia heard her friends yelling at her to let go. A couple of passersby had their hands on her arms trying to pull her loose. From down the street, she could hear the sounds of Kevin's friends running towards them, hurling curses at her.

She knew she would have to let go any second. But, for the moment, it felt good.

A WEEK LATER

"COME IN, JULIA. Please take a seat anywhere."

Julia eyed the table warily. Paola Bertani was sitting in a chair behind the others; it was pretty clear that she wouldn't be in charge of this show. Someone named Dr. Fong was at the table; she'd never seen him before. As usual, Dr. Mortimer was doing the talking, wearing her same snotty smile. Julia figured she'd be running things.

'Taking a seat' was probably the first test: she was sure there was a 'right' chair and a 'wrong' chair. Dr. Mortimer would probably have a comment about it no matter what she did. She took the seat closest to the door.

"Julia, we're worried about you."

She knew that was coming. She was worried about herself.

She also knew this wasn't going to do any good. The only reason she was there at all was because she'd promised Maya she would do it. After Maya and Carlos had gotten her out of jail a week earlier, Julia was in no position to object.

"I don't think there's anything to worry about," Julia said.

"We disagree," Dr. Mortimer said. "We've looked at your school records for the last year. We've seen your evaluations, grades, therapy sessions, interactions with others—the whole thing. We think you have a problem."

"It sounds like I have no privacy at all. Who gave you the right to do all that?"

"You've become withdrawn and antisocial. Even the little things point to that. You came in here today and took the seat closest to the door, which is a subconscious way of saying you want to get out of here as quickly as possible."

"I guess you have it all figured out."

"No we don't, but we are trying to help you piece it together," Dr. Mortimer grabbed a pen and started to point with it. "Now, about that instance when you attacked that boy the other day—"

"That's over with."

"But it's symptomatic," Dr. Mortimer said. "Look, we all know that was a difficult day for everyone. It was the commemoration of the death of the Thirteen—"

"—Fourteen."

"Excuse me?"

"I said 'fourteen.'"

"What are you—"

Julia moved to the edge of her chair and glared at her. "There were fourteen women who died that day. Did you lose track of my mother again?"

Dr. Mortimer threw down her pen in exasperation and turned to Dr. Fong. The two began an animated whisper.

"Julia, can we talk a second?" Paola came around the table and pulled up a chair next to her. She grabbed her hand; Julia avoided her gaze. "Please?"

"Dr. Bertani," Dr. Mortimer said, "We would think—"

"—Please let me handle this," she insisted.

"We know you've been trying hard to put your mother's death behind you. It breaks our hearts—all of us, Dr. Fong, Dr. Mortimer, and myself—to see what you've been going through. You've been brave, and you've been tough. We're all proud of you."

Julia forced herself to look up at Paola. She deserved that much.

"But we just don't think that you're coping with it very well. We're worried."

Julia broke away from her gaze and looked around the room in frustration. "Well, what am I supposed to do? All you've done is make me feel worse."

"I know," Paola said. "That's why we're thinking of trying something different."

That caught Julia's attention.

"It's risky. We've been debating it for the last few weeks. You might react to it badly, and it might set your recovery back even further."

"What are you talking about?"

"We have something to show you that might explain why your mother was so mentally disturbed." Paola waited to see her reaction. Julia hung on her words.

"Your mother was deeply affected by an event early in her life that left her traumatized. In the end, we couldn't do anything to cure it. There was a period of time when she was neglected and left without food or water. There was medicine she was supposed to take, but she didn't—"

"—You told me all this before," Julia interrupted. She was getting wary about where this was going.

"But this is different," Paola said. "We have a video recording of it."

Julia was dumbfounded. "Why haven't you shown it to me?"

Dr. Mortimer jumped in. "We couldn't say anything while your mother was alive. There were problems of doctor-patient privilege and regulations about the use of—"

Julia had her mouth open to shout at her, when Paola put her hand up to stop her.

"Please," she said. "Let's not get into that. The question is whether we should show it to you now. Will it help with your recovery, or will it set you back?"

"I want to see it," Julia said without hesitation.

"Are you sure?" Paola asked. "It's very disturbing."

"Let me see it."

"WHAT YOU ARE about to look at," Dr. Fong explained, "is a three-dimensional enhancement of a two-dimensional video recording, because that was the type of camera that was used. It's only visual. No sound recording was made."

Julia tapped her feet nervously, wanting him to get on with it.

"There was a wide-angle camera embedded in the wall over your mother's crib. However, the quality of the images fade from time to time, probably because it was operating on an alternate generator. The country was experiencing enormous power shortages and weather-related problems in those years."

Please, she thought. Just start playing it.

The room darkened, and the image of another room came into view, filling the space at the far end of the therapy room. It was a shabby apartment complete with the image of a storm blowing outside the window. The image was frozen for the moment, but the figures looked poised for movement. Julia choked a bit as she thought about who they might be. Dr. Fong gave the command that started them in motion.

"The woman walking around the apartment is Cheryl Madsen," Dr. Fong continued. "We know that she is—or, should say 'was'—your grandmother."

Julia stared at the image. The woman was wearing jeans and a sweatshirt; she was young, pretty, seemingly lively—and a complete stranger. Her mother had never said anything about her; she'd never even mentioned her name.

"The little girl in the crib is your mother."

Julia had resisted crying, but now her eyes began to water up. That little girl was the mother she'd never really known. She was so beautiful, so lovable, and so lost.

"The unpleasant part is about to begin in a few moments. It will look like a happy occasion, but it gets bad very quickly."

"Julia," Paola interjected, "if you want us to stop this at any point, just say so."

She told them to keep going.

"The doorbell likely rings at this point. You can see Cheryl looking through the peephole. She's obviously very excited to see who's outside the door. Now she's opening the door. There. You can see how she jumps on him and kisses him."

"Who is it?"

"We believe he's your grandfather."

Julia looked at the forbidding man in the hooded parka, trying to get a good look.

"Does he ever show his face?"

"Not really. He's good at keeping it away from the camera."

"What's his name?"

"We're not sure. Your grandmother keeps calling him 'Jesse.' The New York City police had lip-reading experts look at this several times, and they're sure that's what she's saying. But there's a problem: at one point he denies that's his name. She keeps calling him Amy's father, but we don't know that for sure."

Julia watched as Cheryl and Jesse walked around the apartment, Jesse poking at things and Cheryl tagging along behind him, seemingly asking questions. At one point she dragged him over to Amy's crib, pointing at the child. He didn't show any interest.

"What's that?"

"That's a box of things that she had apparently been keeping for him," Dr. Fong said. "At least that's what we can get from the snippets of lip-readings we could pick up."

"What was in it?"

"That's what the police wanted to know. They went over this video several times. They zoomed in to see if they could read the words on the documents, but the resolution wasn't clear enough. They determined that there were some passports in the box and maybe identification cards. They also saw things that looked like military medals, but they couldn't figure out how they fit into the pattern."

"What pattern?"

"The police concluded that Jesse was involved in some sort of criminal enterprise and that he just came to the apartment to get that box. He was apparently so intent on getting into your grandmother's apartment that he killed someone to do it. When the National Guard finally broke down the door to the apartment days later, they were investigating the death of one of their guardswomen. She'd been strangled near the apartment. The police decided the two crimes were committed the same way."

"I guess I'm getting ahead of myself by talking about two crimes," Dr. Fong said.

He acted like he regretted what he had said, but Julia said nothing. She'd already guessed that something awful was coming.

"This is where it gets bad."

Julia watched as the man called Jesse turned and slapped Cheryl's face hard. A moment later they were struggling, but she was no match for him. Suddenly, he picked her up and heaved her against the wall. Julia tried to keep from screaming out, as she watched her grandmother's broken body crumple to the ground. Within seconds he was on top of her, his hands pushing down on her face and neck.

Julia's heart was pounding. She watched him pick himself up from her grandmother's motionless body and start walking towards the crib. He was heading towards her mother. He stared at the baby, avoiding a direct look into the lens. Then he reached up towards the camera, apparently trying to disable it. After a few seconds, he gave up and left.

"Could you run that part again?" Julia said.

Julia eased forward out of her chair to get as close as she could without distorting the image. It was only a top-down angle, so she couldn't see much. She wanted desperately to get a better look.

"We should stop here," Paola said. "You'll need time to think about all this."

"No," Julia said. "I want to go on."

"There's nothing to see," Dr. Fong said. "He doesn't come back. Nothing happens for the next fifty-five hours or so until the National Guard forces its way into the apartment."

"No. My grandmother's still there. My mother's still crying in her crib."

"It goes on for another two days," Dr. Fong protested. "You can't just stay here."

"I'm staying," Julia said, refusing to look up.

MAYA EXPECTED A call from Paola after Julia's therapy session, but not the one she got. Julia was still watching the video, Paola said; she wasn't planning to leave. They both agreed after the incident at the café that it might be a good idea to show the video to Julia. They knew they couldn't be sure of her reaction, but they hadn't counted on this.

By the time Maya got down to the office, Julia was still sitting there without moving, staring at the drama being played out on the wall. She seemingly had no intention of going anywhere. It was after closing time, and Paola had just gotten though quieting down the other two doctors and ushering them out the door. But she didn't know what to do now.

As Paola and Maya talked, Julia continued watching the video, ignoring them both. They agreed she was going through a kind of catharsis, but neither was sure how it was going to end. Maya told Paola to go home, saying she would take it from there.

Maya brought over some cushions and propped them up behind Julia, trying to make her more comfortable. Julia looked up for a second, giving her a nod of thanks, and then went back to the scene in front of her. Maya stood next to her, thinking she should do something more. Finally, she went back and got a chair for herself, placing it far enough behind Julia so that she could watch her without disturbing her.

She could only see the back of Julia's head, but she knew she was in quiet misery. The videotape was agonizing. Although it had no sound, it was impossible not to hear in your mind the loud, plaintive crying of the child. The words "Mama, Mama," couldn't have been any clearer if they had been written on the wall. She was reaching through the side of the crib, trying to rouse the lifeless body of her mother on the other side of the room. She continued like that for an hour or more until she finally sank to the bottom. Her face said everything. She was hungry and thirsty, her diapers were overflowing, and she was desperately lonely. She couldn't comprehend that her mother would never be able to pick herself up from the floor and give her the love she needed. Finally, she fell over and seemed to sleep, only to awaken and repeat the whole, heartbreaking ritual.

Around 9:00 P.M., Carlos came by with some sandwiches and a few more pillows and blankets. He offered to stay, but Maya sent him home. "There's no sense both of us being miserable," she whispered.

Maya tiptoed up to Julia and offered her one of the sandwiches. Julia nodded her head in thanks; she took it and ate it. A few minutes later she took a bathroom break, but she came right back to the same spot. Maya suggested that they could stop the video at that point and start it up again the next morning. It would be Saturday, she said; they could have the office to themselves. Maybe she should go home now and get some rest.

Julia shook her head no.

By 11:00 P.M., Maya knew they were there for the night. She propped up the pillows on the chairs and tried to get comfortable, but there was no good way to sit. She suddenly wished Deva was there with her. She needed her advice and the touch of her hands. She needed to hear her whispering in her ear.

THE SCENE IN front of them had changed only slightly over the last several hours. The apartment had gone from light to dark and then to light again as a new day dawned all those years ago. The baby was moving more slowly now. The bouts of crying were shorter and shorter.

She was getting weaker, and that weakness was beginning to show in longer stretches of helpless sleep.

Julia kept watching the screen without moving a muscle. Maya knew she was determined to see it through to the bitter end. By her calculation, it would be around forty hours before the National Guard would come bursting through the door on that distant morning to rescue baby Amy. She hoped she could last that long.

But until then, the child in that scene would continue to cry out to her dead mother.

And the child watching the scene would cry out to hers.

PART FIVE

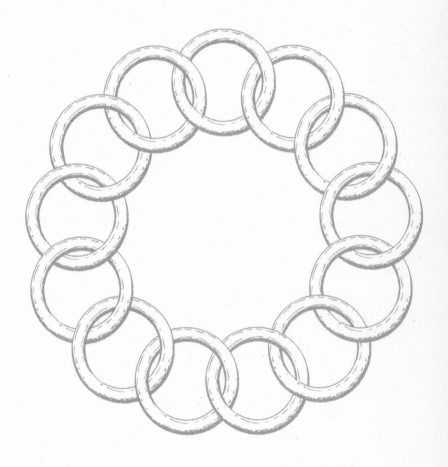

TUESDAY, APRIL 28, 2082

NEW YORK CITY

JULIA

THERE WERE RINGS under Madeleine's eyes. She probably didn't get much sleep. I knew the feeling.

We were getting ready to leave the building the night before, when the NYPD had flashed an urgent bulletin on the vid-screen. They patched us in to the video of an investigation in progress. Madeleine was in my office when the news came in, and it had caught both of us by surprise.

The crime scene was in Morningside Park just off of 113th Street. The police had set up temporary lights that gave off an eerie glow, but the scene would have been grim under even the best of lighting. A young woman was lying on the ground being tended to by an emergency team. The police sergeant talking on the investigation video said the young woman had apparently been raped. The police's preliminary assessment was that there might have been several attackers. A medi-cam was in place, and the EMTs were moving as quickly as they could to follow the doctor's videoed instructions. The girl was in bad shape.

Her clothes were torn, and there were patches of blood on her legs and abdomen; she appeared to be unconscious. The rest of the police team was moving carefully through the surrounding grass, combing the area for clues.

Two of the clues were in plain sight: on a wall next to the young woman, someone had drawn a *Patria* symbol, and under it they had scrawled a misspelled version of Abraham's name. And as if that weren't clear enough, they had also used the girl's own blood to write the number "13" on her forehead. Madeleine and I just sat and watched. We were both too shocked to move.

As the night wore on, more information trickled in. At 10:45 the police investigator put through a message, saying they had a lead on a possible suspect. About an hour later, we got some good news: the woman had regained consciousness and had confirmed the earlier description of one of the suspects. The police flashed a picture of a man matching the description from their video files: he was young, maybe seventeen, with olive skin and several small, vertical scars on his forehead. Neither Madeleine nor I recognized his face, but we knew the scars—they were gang markings. The slashes were the insignia of a band of punks who did the dirty work of a small-time criminal syndicate operating out of Bergen County across the river in New Jersey. At 1:28 A.M. the police contacted us again to say that they had captured someone who fit the description and had him at the station for questioning. They were squeezing him hard, trying to find out what he knew.

Between messages from the police department, our moods shifted back and forth. We were getting on each other's nerves. I was so tired I found myself arguing a point that I had just criticized Madeleine for bringing up moments earlier. The only thing we could really agree on was that someone was sending us some sort of sick message.

THE NEXT MORNING, Madeleine wanted to know if I was okay. I said I was fine, but the truth was I'd been awake a good part of the night thinking about what had happened.

"Madeleine, we need to talk this through. I think we have to assume that someone's getting ready to attack us."

Madeleine looked at me without showing much emotion. I knew she had the same worry. But she wasn't going to let it gain a foothold—not even in her facial expression.

"If you're right, how do you think they're going to do it?"

"I don't know how, but we have to assume they'll try to do it during the dedication ceremonies."

Madeleine gave a small grunt and stared at the window for a second.

"Who do you think is going to do it? Are those small-time crooks in Bergen County going to round up another band of cowards, like they did last night, and try to bust into the U.N. headquarters? Or is Rufus Clay going to stir up his parishioners in Georgia and march them up here to storm the ramparts?"

She was trying to convince herself, as much as me, that the idea was ridiculous.

"These are small-time people," she continued. "They're corrupt from top to bottom. If you pay them enough, they'll stir up all kinds of trouble, maybe even plant bombs or rape somebody. But they don't have the ability to mount an attack on us."

I nodded in agreement. "And that's what has me worried."

She was waiting to hear what I meant.

"I think we need to approach this from another direction. The link with these groups has to be money," I said. "Nothing else makes sense."

"Rufus Clay wouldn't send a kid up to New York to bomb a building without someone paying him to do it. You know how he operates. He's always working for the highest bidder. The same goes for the guy they picked up last night and all the other kids who've been doing the vandalism and graffiti. They all seem to have gang ties. None of them really cares one way or another about the United Nations, certainly not enough to attack it without being paid to do it. If we look hard, we'll find money changing hands. Someone is paying these people to create panic. Whoever's behind it is just trying to soften the target for whatever else he has in mind—like maybe attacking us."

Madeleine scratched at her chin, shaking her head slightly. "I'm not sure I buy your theory, but let's say you're right. How do you find out who it is?"

"That's the problem." She'd hit on the part that had really kept me awake.

"If we had enough time, we'd subpoena everyone's bank records and get search warrants to look for the money. Then we could try to trace it back to its source."

She finished the thought for me. "But you don't think there's enough time. The dedication ceremony is in six days."

"I've told Avram to have his team go all-out to find what they can about the money links. But no, you're right; I can't argue with you. It will probably take more time than we have." My mind had gone flat. "I guess I've failed you."

"Oh stop feeling sorry for yourself," Madeleine snapped. "What happened to the woman I worked with a few years ago? *That* woman thought she could handle anything."

"*That* woman was Colonel Julia Moro of the U.S. Army. She resigned her commission, in case you've forgotten." I could be as testy as she was.

Madeleine just looked at me, shaking her head. Neither of us said a word. The dead air between us threatened to grow more foul. Her remarks bothered me. Had I lost my edge? Would the woman I used to be have had a better handle on this? That woman was pre-Dhanye and pre-everything I now believed in. She had kept her feelings under such a thick layer of bravado that they never saw the light of day.

THE COLONEL JULIA Moro that Madeleine thought she knew so well was in some ways just a stand-in for the real me. I did my day job, and I was pretty good at it. I had worked my way up the ranks of the U.S. Army and spent my professional days officially working to preserve world peace. But my personal life was a mess. I spent my nights chasing the coldest of cold cases. Ever since that miserable day—almost three days, really—when I'd watched the video of my grandmother's murder and the beginnings of my mother's madness, I'd been determined to find the man who'd done it. It was my own private vendetta. I had spent more than twenty years chasing Jesse, and I'd come up empty-handed.

My life, in many ways, revolved around that search. I'd gone through high school intent on finding a college program in criminology. My step-by-step accumulation of skills had led from college to law school, and after that I was appointed to the first class at the newly-created U.N. Military-Legal Academy. That involved a simultaneous commission through the U.S. Army Officer Candidate School. Following that, I was given an assignment that was something totally new for the U.S. Army—a special unit to carry out military actions that were ordered by the United Nations. Whenever an Enforcement Order was issued by the U.N. Council of Ministers, I had to be ready to go. When that happened, I'd usually end up on the enforcement team reporting directly to Madeleine and her colleagues at the U.N. We'd gotten to know each other pretty well.

Throughout all this, I'd had a sponsor, someone who made sure I took the right career path. That was Eloni Ubaka. She'd been reelected to Congress several times and kept moving up in the leadership ranks. By 2076 Eloni had been appointed U.S. Secretary of Defense. During all that time, she insisted, she was "keeping an eye" on me. I don't know whether she thought I had a great potential or just a great potential to misbehave. I'm still not sure how much she had to do with my advancement. I never asked her for any favors, but I also knew I didn't have to.

WHILE MY CAREER trajectory in law enforcement proceeded on a grand, even international, scale, my own personal priority was a case that was about four decades old. The search had become part of my daily ritual, like eating or running. Most of the time I got nothing, but I kept looking. It took me months to get the video and the police report. Paola had agreed to it, but Dr. Mortimer and the others were just as pigheaded as ever. I'd finally made so much noise that they produced a copy, but the backup documents were still deep in the New York City police archives. No one would get them. Finally, when I was still in law school in California, I went to New York myself and pushed the NYPD until they found them in a warehouse.

Once I had all the pieces, I went through the video again, this time with the full report and the lip-reader's transcript at hand. I found myself yelling at it. Look, look there! He has his glove off; he just touched something. There might be a fingerprint, some DNA—anything! How about that thing around his neck? It looks like a ribbon of some sort. But there was no follow-up on that or anything else. Jesse was still a mystery.

It had stayed like that until I was commissioned into the Army. At that point, I gained access to the database of military records. I programmed the date of the murder into the system and found the name of the national guardswoman who had been murdered that day in New York City. After a little digging, I found the file. During the struggle, the woman had scratched Jesse's face and gotten some of his skin under her fingernails. The DNA test matched it to a pair of murders in Tennessee: a kid had killed his mother and another woman. I was shocked, but I wasn't completely surprised that Jesse had something like that in his past.

I cut corners to trace the records. As a military-legal officer, I had access to federal databases and to the criminal database of the U.N. Military-Legal Command. But there were rules against unauthorized searches. The files were there only for official investigations. My search for Jesse was anything but official. I was careful about it, but if anyone looked hard at what I was doing, I would probably have been court-martialed.

If I was going to find him, I had to get lucky. I checked every source I had, including research and profiling programs. I checked my biological grandmother, Cheryl's, background records, trying to find friends or family that might know something about her. I made a daily check of the databases to see if Jesse's fingerprints or DNA would show up somewhere in a criminal investigation. That was all I had to go on. More sophisticated methods, like iris or brain scans, wouldn't work, because there was nothing in his juvenile record to compare it to. Even age-enhanced photos would deviate more and more from his actual appearance as time went on. It was a process I repeated every night, and it had gotten me nowhere.

MY EMOTIONAL LANDSCAPE had very few landmarks during those years. The days around my thirty-fifth birthday were a little more vivid than most. I remember returning from a run around the base at Fort Monmouth, and I couldn't wait to rip off my sweaty running clothes. I told myself I'd shower and put on street clothes later. At that moment I just wanted to grab a beer out of the fridge and slap something between two pieces of bread. There was nobody around to watch, so I could just sit there in my underwear and eat it.

I noticed a vid-phone message. It was Chloe's face. She had her usual enigmatic smile—the one she wore when she'd caught me at something.

"The girls and I want to know how you're spending your big birthday. We're all certain you're doing something wildly romantic."

I knew that voice. She was certain that I was not doing anything romantic or even interesting. These were the years before I met Dhanye, and my love life—which Chloe described as "pathetic"—was a source of mirth for her and my other old friends, Flora and Annabel. But it was a mirth that bordered on concern. And it was starting to bother me as well. Chloe's message got me thinking for the first time that something was seriously wrong with my life. As I sat there dripping sweat in my underwear, I remember thinking I had no one to get dressed for. Worse yet, I had no one to get undressed for.

When was the last time anyone had touched me with affection? When was the last time I'd looked at another human being with anything resembling desire? I couldn't answer either question. My body seemed to have entered a sex-free zone. It had gotten to the point where I didn't even want to get intimate with myself. Potential partners were available; that wasn't the problem. After all, I was in the military. In an age when fewer and fewer people were getting formally married, the military was a staunch holdout for matrimony, family values, and righteousness—which made it a hotbed of married men who were constantly horny. I'd been involved with a few of them, trying, on principle, to stick to the ones who at least said they were between marriages.

At the time, those affairs had a certain appeal—probably because they were brief. Things went up, they stayed there awhile, and then they came crashing down. Each night was like a microcosm of the whole relationship. After a while, I always drifted away. Eventually I'd gotten to the point where I didn't know what the attraction was. Maybe I was doing it just to prove I could. I wondered if I was falling into the pattern that Chloe had warned me about years ago: I didn't really want to be with anyone who wanted to be with me.

But it was my relationships with women that puzzled me at the time. Twice I'd found myself involved with another woman, but I wasn't sure either time how I'd gotten there. In neither case did we start out with anything resembling a date, but instead the romantic feelings just seemed to have slipped in through the back door. Both times the relationship started out on some other level—it was an academic colleague in one case; a civilian contractor in the other. But in each case it changed into something else after we'd already become friends. The leaps to sexual intimacy astonished me. It was like alchemy; first it was one thing, and then it became something else. I liked the feeling. It was soft, gentle, and almost endless.

But—if I'm being honest with myself—that was what scared me off. None of my self-defense mechanisms worked. I'd never learned how to lie to women, or how to flatter them, or even how to take them for granted. Sincerity seemed to be my only option. I either had to make a real commitment, or I had no business being there.

In both cases, I did what my instincts had told me to do. I ran.

IF CHLOE KNEW what I really had planned for my birthday, she wouldn't have been happy. She thought I was spending far too much time on my obsession about Jesse. Part of me knew she was right. Nevertheless, I had arranged to spend that weekend visiting the town where his murdering spree had begun. The local sheriff's department had been cooperative, but the file didn't tell me much. One name, however, kept popping up: the officer who had followed Jesse all the way through the system. A supervising clerk gave me an address where he thought she might be living.

Jewel Murphy was in a retirement home in a town outside of Dallas. It was the kind of place that would make Maya furious: she hated age-segregated communities. But Murphy seemed happy enough. When I told her why I was there, she swung around in her wheelchair and suggested that we go over to a corner where we could have more privacy. Her eyes seemed to light up at the prospect of talking about it.

"My god, that case happened ages ago!"

"Ms. Murphy—"

"Please, it's been 'Jewel' all these years, so let's keep it that way."

I smiled. "Jewel, I know it's difficult to remember something that far back."

"Oh, it's not that hard. You don't forget cases like that."

"What do you remember about it?"

She jumped at the question. "You mean, aside from the fact that he killed two women and didn't show any remorse? Jesse was a manipulative little bastard. His father was another real son of a bitch, but my guess is that Jesse turned out worse."

"It sounds like you hated him."

"The thing of it is, I felt sorry for him at first. He was just a little kid when it happened. The night of the murder, he was too traumatized to talk. I figured the shock of it made him numb. But after a while, I realized he was a little schizo. You never knew what you were going to get. Sometimes he'd be spouting pure evil, and then out of nowhere his scared-little-boy persona would take over. I followed him through the whole juvenile detention process—more than ten years of it."

Jewel paused for a moment, and then admitted, "Yeah, I did come to hate him. I think I hated him most for what we—the system—let him get away with. He had a real thing about women. One time the guards had to pull him off a girl in the hall. He even attacked one of the women on the staff. But nobody did anything about it. They put him in one of the Bible study classes, and the teacher used to swear up and down at the hearings that he was a changed young man. I said he was bullshitting them, but they didn't believe me. He was smart. He knew what they wanted to hear, and he gave it to them."

I asked if there was anything that could identify him.

Jewel thought for a few moments. "Well, he had a scar right here." She drew a line down her right cheek. "That's one of the things that was so maddening. We knew damn well from our investigation that his father had beaten him and caused the scar, yet everything was so warped in his mind that he blamed his mother for it happening. He blamed her for killing his father and for just about everything else in the world."

"There's one other thing: he had a medal that his father had given him. It was an army medal from the Iraq War. He always used to wear it, but why anyone would want to be reminded of that damn war is beyond me.

"That's about all. And, oh yeah, he used to love to tinker with wires and set fires. He would have blown up the whole detention center, if he had the chance."

"So, what happened to him?"

Jewel told me what she remembered, which wasn't much.

"Once he became an adult, we had to release him."

I'd hoped for a fresh trail, but I was starting to see how difficult it would be.

"So, tell me, what's he done? I was in the sheriff's office for thirty-five years. I can smell an investigation from across the room."

I liked this woman. I decided to share everything I had.

"Oh, my god," Jewel said. "Here I'm on a rant about this guy, and it turns out that he might be your grandfather. I'm really sorry."

"Don't be. I already knew what he was like."

Jewel nodded. "Maybe there is some justice. He's responsible for bringing a smart young woman like you into the world, and you may be the one to take him down."

THAT WAS FOUR years ago. I loved talking to Jewel Murphy, but nothing I learned from her brought me any closer to Jesse. Her department had some early addresses, but they were way out of date. Jesse had no family. The only pictures of him were about forty years old.

Since no one else seemed to be looking for him, anything that might show up about him would only be by accident while some other crime was being investigated. I had to hope that a new set of fingerprints or DNA would wander into the system serendipitously. The results were tantalizing, but they didn't lead anywhere. The last time one of his fingerprints appeared in the system had been a few years ago, when the London police were searching for fingerprints in the men's room at Victoria Station after a shoot-out with a drug gang. His thumbprint, which was one of over eight hundred sets of prints found in the room, was above one of the urinals. That print only proved that he had been in that men's room at some point in his lifetime. But when? It could have been almost anytime.

I had the same problem with a tiny piece of skin found wedged between the elevator button and the control panel during a robbery investigation at a Washington, D.C., hotel. The building had been built in 2070, so that little piece of Jesse couldn't have gotten there any earlier than that. All I knew was that Jesse, along with thousands of others, had once been in that elevator and left a trace of his DNA.

I needed more information. I kept telling myself that somewhere, right at that moment, Jesse was touching something, leaving a trace of himself behind. I even found myself wishing—a little perversely—that he was committing some random crime just at that moment. I hoped that the police were being called to a scene where Jesse had put his hand just minutes earlier.

My search for Jesse was at a dead end, but I was unwilling to admit it. If I did, I would have to admit that my life was at a dead end as well.

THURSDAY, APRIL 30, 2082

NEW YORK CITY

JULIA

WHEN WE'D PLANNED it a month earlier, our scheduled walk-through of the U.N. building had sounded routine. It didn't seem that way now. I could feel our security plan staring me in the face, daring me to find the weak link.

The Secretary-General and Madeleine were both there. A small liaison team from the New York City Police had come along for the tour, together with a pair of security experts from the FBI. The general contractor, Irene Castillo, tagged along with us to answer any questions. The plan called for five members of our security team to be posted at each entrance and emergency exit, along with double that number from the NYPD. In addition, the security services from each of the national governments would be allowed to have their own people at each entrance. The NYPD would also have patrols throughout the park and covering a two-block radius around the building. There would be a thirty-person security team on the roof using the best surveillance equipment available.

The contractors had been directed to expand their normal safety procedures, checking to make sure that everything was working and that all nonessential personnel were out of the building well in advance of the event. Everyone would have to leave five hours beforehand, and the building would be scanned both electronically and with bomb-sniffing dogs before anyone would be let back in. We'd be sticking strictly to the invited guest list, and everyone in the building would be wearing an electronic name tag.

A couple of questions came up as we walked around the building. The NYPD representatives grumbled that they weren't getting the agreed-upon daily intelligence feed from the FBI. I intervened and said we would provide it to them. The FBI had its own complaint: they hadn't received a copy of either the plumbing grid or the backup electrical power system that they'd requested. Castillo said she would get the plumbing contractor, Vassily Gregor, on the problem immediately. Madeleine was seeing Noah Fawkes shortly after the meeting on another subject to discuss his foundation's donation, and she said she'd pass on their request.

There were several questions directed at me. My well-rehearsed answers seemed to keep everyone happy. External security? All fly-overs within fifty kilometers would be banned during the celebration. U.N. hover cameras would be kept aloft scanning the area, and they would be looking for any suspicious activities. Emergency services? The NYFD, NYPD, and other New York emergency services would be on alert starting at midnight. On top of everything else, the building would be wrapped in an electronic curtain to detect any suspicious movements. The Mother Grid would be keeping watch.

A SMALL GROUP of very serious-looking people were already waiting in Madeleine's conference room by the time we got back. They had the smug look of people who had given a lot of money to a project. One of them, a woman from a Beijing foundation, gave me a nasty stare, apparently assuming I might be the reason Madeleine was late. A man from the Carnegie Endowment, who was in town for the ceremony and the social events, was a little more polite, but he didn't do much to lighten the tension. Fawkes was there on behalf of the May 4th Foundation. I just hoped Madeleine wasn't counting on him to smooth things over with the others. I didn't find him very diplomatic.

MADELEINE HAD STEPPED into her inner office for a second before joining the group. And now she motioned to me to come in as well. She closed the door behind me.

"Have you seen this?" She drew me over behind her desk. A report from Omar Kahled, our Director of Electronic Intelligence, was visible on her vid-screen.

"That's the issue I asked Omar to look into," I said. "I'm supposed to meet with him right after this to go over it, but I haven't seen the actual report yet."

We both knew what Omar had been assigned to investigate. Madeleine and I had talked about it at length and had decided that if anyone were planning an attack, there would probably be an unusual pattern of electronic messages in and around the New York area. Maybe it would involve Rufus Clay's church in Atlanta or, perhaps, the front-businesses that were run by the Bergen County mob. If we were lucky, maybe there would be some electronic funds that we could trace. We were grasping at straws, and we both knew it.

But Madeleine had seen something on the screen. I looked where she was pointing and saw what had gotten her attention. There was a pattern of messages going back and forth from New York to Atlanta, Bergen County, and several other locations. One of them was Fort Knox, Kentucky.

We exchanged quick glances. We both knew what this might mean.

"I have to go deal with this group of donors," Madeleine said. "Let me know what you've learned after you talk to Omar and Avram."

OMAR WAS BEING Omar, talking in techno-speak. He sat across from my desk trying to explain what he had found. He wandered around a bit with his explanation, but I knew he'd get to the point eventually. Finally, I had to give him a nudge.

"So, let me see if I understand what you're saying. You've found a pattern of someone using Biblical passages as a coding device for messages?"

"Right," Omar said. "They're assigning the numerical values of each consecutive word as an entry device. The algorithm they're using has four variations—"

"—Omar," I interjected, "what's the Biblical passage they're using?"

"I have it here." He looked at his notes. "It's from Revelation 18:21: *Thus with violence shall that great city Babylon be thrown down, and shall be found no more.*"

I was excited: the choice of phrase was an important clue. The lunatic fringe had been calling the United Nations the "Whore of Babylon" for as long as I could remember.

"A lot of the messages using this coding have gone back and forth within the New York area, but several of them have also gone here and here." He pointed to the Atlanta area and to Fort Knox on the large electronic map.

"Was any money transferred?"

"Maybe," Omar said. "We saw the type of coding that usually signals an electronic funds transfer, but we can't be sure."

"What was in the messages?" I asked. "What where the points of origin?" Omar shook his head. His team hadn't yet figured that out. They just had patterns gleaned from a huge amount of electronic data from multiple sources. Pinpointing the source and the contents would take a lot more work. It might take several days. We didn't have several days.

OMAR'S NEWS REOPENED a wound that had begun in Fort Monmouth and ended at Fort Knox—at least, I thought it had ended there. I'd had Avram keeping an eye on activity in that part of Kentucky in case my lingering worries might somehow be justified. But this was the first inkling that something might really be happening.

The problem had begun three years earlier with Major General

Curtis Redmon, an old-school general who had been in the military for many years. His career may even have predated the adoption of the new U.N. Charter. In fairness to Redmon—not something that's easy for me to do—he was used to what he thought of as the good old days. He liked operating in an era when the U.S. military could do just about anything it wanted.

Redmon was the base commander at Fort Monmouth, and he was my commanding officer. Unfortunately, that wasn't all of it. He was also my stalker. His favorite place for targeting me was at the officers' club. He cornered me there often enough that I soon realized he had someone keeping an eye out for me. I figured out that his spotter was Brigadier General David Earl. Earl was Redmon's Chief of Staff—and he was also his chief lackey. Redmon's favorite trick was to come up behind me and place his hand on my rear end. The more he'd had to drink, the harder he would squeeze. I'd slap his hand away, but he would pretend that the incident had never happened, only to come right back and do it again a few moments later. If he was talking to other people in my presence, he couldn't resist putting his fingers on the small of my back and moving them around in circles. The message he was sending was that I was in his command—in more ways than one.

Redmon finally went too far, but it wasn't his harassment of women that ultimately caught up with him. This time he'd flirted with insubordination. One of the junior women officers on the base—one who had a name that was easily confused with that of a man—got a disturbing memo from an anonymous source. I did a little checking and found several male officers who had received the same thing. The memo was a rant about how assignment of U.S. Armed Forces to the United Nations command was a breach of our sovereignty and a victory for the "effeminate leadership" and "foreign influences" of the United Nations. The memo urged U.S. officers to resist foreign control by questioning their orders at every level. By doing that, they could show that these types of international peace-keeping forces are not workable. The rhetoric was pure Redmon. I'd heard him spouting these same ideas several times after a few drinks.

I had a back channel, and I used it. When I reached Eloni, she was seated behind her desk in her paneled office at the Defense Department. After reading over the memo, she seemed to ponder it for a few moments.

"Eloni, these kinds of things can cost lives. There were some unexplained slowdowns in the last operation we did under the command of the U.N., like delays in communication and equipment that didn't arrive. If you don't believe me, call Madeleine. She noticed it as well."

Eloni nodded. "We've noticed it here too. I've had investigators looking into it."

"It's nothing personal about Redmon, but I just don't trust him."

She smiled. I had talked to her earlier about Redmon's harassment, so she knew what I had been going through.

"Does Redmon know you came to me with this?"

"No, and neither does General Earl."

That's what I thought at the time. I realized later that I'd probably underestimated Earl's surveillance network.

I HAD SOME poignant memories mixed up in all this. A week or so after my call to Eloni, I was warming up before going for a run, when I saw a young man a few meters away, going through his own warm-ups. He was in his mid-twenties, with dark hair and flashing eyes. I nodded to him. He nodded back, showing a smile. A nice smile, I thought.

When I started running, I realized he was only a few steps behind me. "Would you like someone to run with?" I asked.

"That would be nice." He flashed the smile again.

"I'm Julia Moro." I offered him my hand without breaking stride.

"Yes, I recognized you, Colonel Moro. I'm Lieutenant Rajiv Rameau."

"Please. If we're going to run around here together and get all sweaty, we don't need to use titles. Out here, just call me Julia."

That drew another smile. "Then, please, it's Raji. My friends call me that."

We settled into an even pace. He was a little unsteady, but he kept up.

He said that he'd just reported to the military-legal command at Fort Monmouth as part of the Officer-Exchange Program. He didn't know which unit he'd be in. I knew, because the latest group of exchange officers, including him, had been assigned to me.

As I think back now, I probably should have realized who he was. But it was the last name that threw me off.

"I hope it's not rude to ask, but you have an unusual combination of names. It sounds like Indian and French."

"It is. I grew up in India, but my father was French. My parents were diplomats who died in a plane crash while brokering a peace agreement. One of my sisters lives in Mumbai; the other is in New York. Rameau was my father's family name. I know it's more common these days to use your mother's last name—that's what my sisters do—but I decided to honor my father by using his name."

We talked about a few things as we jogged. I found him more interesting than most of the people I'd met around the post. He told me he played the piano.

"There's a piano at the officers' club. You should play it some time. Right now, it's only used when some senior officer gets drunk and thinks he's God's gift to music."

Raji smiled. "Maybe, but I should be a little careful. Not everyone seems happy to have me and the others in the Officer-Exchange Program here on the base."

I came to a quick halt. A thought flashed into my head: Redmon—that shithead!

Raji stopped a few paces later, looking back at me.

"Listen to me. You and the other exchange officers are a crucial part of what we do around here. When an Enforcement Order comes down from U.N. headquarters, we're all in it together. Having you and people from other countries involved helps things run more smoothly. I should know; I'm the one who will be doing most of your training. If you ever encounter an instance of hostility, I want to hear about it, okay? I don't care if it's from a general or anyone else."

Raji seemed surprised at my vehemence. He nodded his head, saying he would.

"Good. Now let's get back to some serious running."

He told me he'd lived in Paris for a few years. That gave him a chance to get to know his cousins on his father's side. As I listened, I added it up, concluding that he'd lived in six countries and spoke five languages.

"Do you see your sisters very much?" I found myself making small talk, not something I've ever enjoyed doing.

"I don't see my sister in India very often. She has three small children and doesn't travel much. But I'm close to my older sister, who teaches in New York. It's odd, maybe, that we would be so close, because there's a big age difference. I'm only twenty-five, and she's thirty-seven."

Watch it, soldier, I wanted to say. You're in a minefield. That's my age.

There was a faint ring, and Raji answered his vid-phone. I found myself unaccountably wishing I could peek around and see who was on the screen. He spoke a couple of quick phrases and then hung up.

"It was my sister."

"The one in New York?"

"Yes. I told her I'd call her back in a while. She's just been through a separation from the man she was living with for the last four years, so we've been talking a lot."

"It's a good thing you're there for her."

"Yes, but the separation was probably for the best. There wasn't much keeping them together. She tried to have a baby, but she couldn't. Then they just drifted apart."

"That must have been rough on her emotionally."

"True, but I told her a few weeks ago that I thought she would be happier if she had a relationship with a woman."

I couldn't help but laugh. "Isn't that something she should decide for herself?"

"That's what she said," Raji grinned. "She also said that I was being a pushy little brother."

"How do you plead to that charge, soldier?"

"Guilty, I guess."

When we were back near the base, I pointed to a café I liked. "Can I buy you coffee? Maybe it will make up for the crappy reception you got when you arrived."

A WEEK OR so later, Sergeant Rutledge, who ran my office staff, flashed me a message saying that there was an officer who wanted to see me. Raji walked in and saluted. He stood there a little awkwardly until I told him to sit down.

"What can I do for you, Lieutenant?"

Raji hesitated for a moment and then produced a small electronic disk from his pocket. "You told me that if I found anything strange happening, I should let you know. This is something that I found in the back of a dresser drawer in my new quarters. I took a look at it, but I'm not sure it was something I was supposed to see."

I took it from him and then activated it on to the vid-screen in my office. After looking at it for a few minutes, I asked Raji to leave. He looked concerned, but I assured him, "No. No. You did the right thing, but I have to handle this myself."

What Raji had found was pretty shocking. It was a list of military officers in what Redmon was calling his "RWB" network, which stood for "Red, White & Blue." These were the ones who were being fed a daily dose of propaganda and scenarios about the military's response in case of a "collapse of the current international structure."

I contacted Eloni's office. Her mood settled into a silent stare after she saw the video herself. "We'll take care of it," she said quietly. Within a few days Eloni's response had become clear to everyone on the base. By order of the Secretary of Defense, General Redmon, General Earl, and several other high-ranking officers were being reassigned to the Army Records Center in Fort Knox, Kentucky. The rumor was that this was the first step in getting them out of the military entirely.

But that wasn't quite the end of it. Three days later I was in my office getting ready to shut things down for the day.

"Sergeant, is there anything else I need to sign before you leave?"

Sergeant Rutledge reached through a pile of documents. "Headquarters needs your real signature on this one, not an electronic one."

"Okay." I scratched my name on the form.

"I'm about done here," he said. "I'll be gone until 0800 tomorrow."

I headed back to my office. A large stack of folders was cluttering up my desk to the point of distraction. I had nothing planned for the evening, so I decided it was a good time to get them filed. I scooped them up in two hands, but they were so unwieldy I had to prop one knee against the file cabinet to keep them from falling.

A door opened behind me.

"Are you still here, Sergeant?" I asked.

The door closed. When he didn't answer, I realized it wasn't him.

Within seconds, there was another body—a man's body—up against mine, pinning me against the file cabinet. I forced my head around enough to see that it was Redmon. He had all his weight against me. His head was hovering over my shoulder, and I could hear him panting. The flag-and-cross tattoo on his neck was quivering, and he was bathed in a sweat that started at his scalp and was dripping down his face. I could feel the anger in his pores and the liquor on his breath.

"General, what are you doing?"

"What are *you* doing?" he hissed. "You've been trying to undermine me ever since you've been here."

He was muttering obscenities in my ear, grabbing at me with his hands. I pushed myself back against him, trying to give myself room to turn, but the folders in my arms went flying across the floor. I tried sliding out from under him, but my footing slipped on the loose papers. He grabbed both of my arms and pulled me back against the file cabinet. We were face to face, and the look in his eyes was poisonous.

"Don't think I don't know what you and that bitch in Washington are up to."

"General, stop now. If you don't, you're going to regret it."

"Am I?" He pushed even harder.

My options went racing through my mind. Shouting? No one would hear me. There were at least four vacant offices and a parade ground between me and the sentries. Alarm button? There was one at my desk, but he knew about that too; he'd never let me get near it. Fight him off? He had about twenty kilograms on me, and he was in good shape. The knee? That was probably my best choice, but he'd be expecting it. I'd have to wait until he was distracted. Submission? Not a chance.

"I've been watching you." He breathed into my ear. "You know you want it, and I'm going to give it to you."

"You're badly mistaken."

"I know a sex-starved bitch when I see one."

He leaned into me with his shoulder and freed up a hand to fumble with his buckle. He got it loose and began to rip at his zipper. He grabbed my skirt, pushing it up, and forced his fingers under the elastic of my underpants. As he slid roughly through my pubic hair, he made a grunting noise. I could feel him getting hard.

"Colonel Moro? Are you in there?"

Redmon heard the voice in the doorway at the same time I did. He hesitated for a second to listen. *Now,* I thought! I brought my knee up as forcefully as I could. Redmon's grip on me eased, as he howled in pain. He fell back against the wall, fumbling with his pants and belt. I pushed down my skirt and moved away.

"Colonel, are you okay?" It was Raji's voice. He poked his head through the doorway. "Oh, I'm sorry. I didn't realize there was someone in here with you."

"Lieutenant—" Redmon started to bellow at him, but then winced in pain. He tried again in a lower voice. "Lieutenant, don't you know to request permission before you enter the office of a senior officer?"

"Yes, sir," Raji said brightly. He snapped a salute. Redmon tried to return the salute, but he could only give a casual flip of the hand as he bent down again in pain.

"Excuse me, sir. I had no idea you and Colonel Moro were in a meeting. I only came by because we had arranged to run together when we both got off duty."

Redmon mumbled something as he made his way over to the door. He slammed it behind him, and I could hear his footsteps fading as he walked through the outer offices. I moved, a bit tentatively at first, over to my desk and sat down. I stayed there with my head in my hands for a few seconds before looking up.

"Are you okay?" Raji asked.

"We had 'arranged to run together'? Where the hell did that come from?"

Raji smiled. "I had to say something. I couldn't say 'General, I came in because I heard you trying to rape the Colonel.'"

I shrugged, giving him a half-smile. "What were you doing in my outer office?"

"I really came by to ask you to go for a run. The offer's still open."

I stood up, testing my legs for a second. I grabbed my jacket and looked over towards him. "Not tonight, I need a drink. Are you coming along?"

RAJI SAT AT the piano in the half-empty bar replaying the same song. Each improvisation seemed more soulful than the one before it. I had every reason to be in a bad mood, but I thought he seemed as depressed as I was.

"That's kind of mournful, but it's beautiful."

"Thanks." Raji picked up his glass of mineral water and headed back to the table. He'd ordered wine when we came in, but since then he'd switched to water. After a couple of Manhattans, I decided I better slow down.

"George Gershwin wrote it in 1937. It was the last piece he wrote before he died."

"I've heard it, but I can't think of the name."

"It's called 'Our Love Is Here to Stay.'"

It was like a little warning bell, the way he said it.

"He was pretty young when he died," Raji said. "I seem to be drawn to composers who died young—Gershwin, Purcell, Mozart."

"Why?"

"Maybe . . . " He shrugged. "Who knows? Maybe I'll die young myself."

"What a terrible thought!"

"I suppose. But it's hard to see myself at an age other than what I am right now."

"I've got to get some food in you, before you get too melancholy."

We ordered a couple of items off the menu and then ate quietly. I was hungrier than I thought. After a few bites, I sensed that Raji's mood had picked up.

"What are you going to do about what happened?" he asked.

I thought for a second. "I'm not sure. Do you know that Redmon and his clique are being transferred to Kentucky? They're going to Fort Knox."

Raji nodded. The word had already gotten around.

"So, I could just drop it and let the Defense Department defuse this guy in its own way. But if I were to play it by the book, I'd report him immediately and go all-out to prosecute him. If he's not stopped, some other woman will probably be attacked."

I gave Raji's arm a little squeeze. "She may not be as lucky as I was to have you walk in at the right time."

Raji responded with a shy smile. That smile is one of the things I still remember about him.

"Don't you think you could have fended him off anyway? You seem pretty resourceful to me."

"Maybe, but I'm glad I didn't have to try."

The food and wine had made me a little too reflective. That's actually a polite term for it—I was probably pretty drunk. But I kept on talking anyway.

"I really don't get it. I hate the violence that I saw in Redmon, but at least I could understand it. He wanted to humiliate me, and that was a good way to do it. It's the sexual arousal part I don't get."

People at other tables were listening. I tried to lower my voice to a whisper.

"The son of a bitch had an erection the entire time; he was getting off on the whole thing. I know, I know, I've studied rape cases. But I still don't understand how anyone can get sexual pleasure out of an act of violence."

Whispering or not, I was getting so shrill that I knew I should stop. "You're a man, can you explain it?"

Raji looked at me quietly. "We're not all like that."

Oh, my god, I thought, this is all wrong. I pushed my chair back and told him we had to leave right away. I was embarrassed at the time, and I'm still embarrassed when I think about it.

"I don't know what I was thinking. I shouldn't be sitting here talking like this. You're a junior officer in my command, and I'm way out of line."

Raji said he didn't mind.

"No, forget I asked you any of this. I mean, even apart from the rank thing, you're a sweet guy. You're not like Redmon. It's insulting, really."

Raji pushed back his plate. He hadn't eaten much.

"I hope you don't mind me saying so," I told him, "but you're looking a little peaked. I think it's time for both of us to get home."

He made no move to get out his chair. "I need to tell you something." He hesitated, and then he continued. "I've been diagnosed with Lynn-Taksin disease."

I sank back into my chair. The air had suddenly been drained out of me.

"When did this happen?" I struggled to keep calm during his explanation.

"I found out about four months ago, just before I was assigned here. It's in Stage Two. I could have had it in a latent form for years. Do you know the disease?"

I found myself choking up. What could I say?

"My mother had it as a child. It was one of the earlier mutations."

"What happened?" Raji asked. There was a slight tremor in his voice.

I hesitated. I couldn't bring myself to talk about it just then. "It's complicated," I said. "I'll tell you about it sometime, when I'm not so tired."

"The doctors say the survival rate these days is pretty good."

I told him I knew that. I forced the biggest smile I could manage. "Does the Indian military know about it?"

"No, I got diagnosed on my own. They might force me out, if they knew."

"Maybe that wouldn't be such a bad thing."

"There's no reason why I should leave. I'm not contagious; I can do my job."

"Who else knows about this?"

"Just my sisters and you—I've only told people I care about."

I felt my stomach rise up in my throat. I was wishing he hadn't said it that way. When I looked up, Raji was still looking at me.

"We better get out of here," I said.

FRIDAY, MAY 1, 2082

NEW YORK CITY

JULIA

WHAT DID WE have to lose?

Omar and his team hadn't come up with anything else since we'd met the day before. We knew only that there was an unusual pattern of messages coming out of New York and that some of them probably involved electronic funds. We knew that some of the recipients were in the Fort Knox area, and that the access code was in the form of Bible verses. That wasn't enough—not nearly enough. But it was either now or never.

I told everyone to be quiet and move out of sight, while I put through a connection on the vid-phone. A face appeared that I hadn't seen in two years. At that time, he had been trailing a grim-faced General Redmon around Fort Monmouth. Now he was sitting in his office at Fort Knox.

"General Earl, I see that you're still serving as General Redmon's Chief of Staff. It's good to see you."

He didn't look particularly pleased to see me. But his nervousness told me that I might be on to something. He asked me, rather tentatively, what I wanted. I eased into it slightly, and then I decided to go right at it.

"We know all about the money and the coded messages going back and forth, you know, the ones about the Harlot on the Hudson? The Whore of Babylon? Revelation 18:21? We're getting ready to blow the whistle on the conspirators, and I wanted to make sure you and General Redmon aren't involved. It would be embarrassing to everyone, if your names were dragged into it."

The reaction on his face said everything. I heard slight murmurs from the others in the room with me. They saw what I saw.

Earl hesitated. "Let me call you back on another line. Give me five minutes."

"That's fine," I said. "I can probably wait that long."

As soon as the call disconnected, my office came alive. I quieted everyone down and started assigning tasks. I told Avram to put in an immediate alert to Eloni at the Defense Department. Whether or not we got anything more out of Earl, she'd want to keep a close watch on Redmon and his friends.

When General Earl called back, he used a special encryption icon. To connect, I had to input the scrambling code that the message demanded, meaning I wouldn't be able to trace it or copy it. It would disappear within seconds after I closed the transmission. At this point, I needed to talk to Earl. I decided it would have to be on his terms.

"What do you have to tell me, General?"

"None of this is my idea, I want you to know."

He spoke hurriedly, dancing around things. The call might have been encrypted and self-destructing, but he still wasn't saying anything we could use against him.

"Redmon has been getting anonymous messages. Like everything else, they go across my desk as Chief of Staff. They're coded in biblical phrases. We received instructions on how to read them." He hesitated, probably looking for a phrase that would give him deniability. "One of them said there might be a crisis at some point soon and that the military should be ready . . . but only if necessary."

"Any dates, any times, any places?"

"No, no, nothing like that. It was just 'be ready for a crisis.'"

"A crisis? Was that the exact wording?"

"I'm not sure of the exact phrase."

He probably knew more, but he wasn't about to admit it to me.

Everything about it seemed authentic, he said. The message sender knew how to find Redmon, and he knew his sympathies. "Redmon's very excited about all this. He's waiting to see what happens next."

The more he talked, the more I realized there were more messages than we were currently aware of. Worse yet, they'd apparently been resent by Redmon to his friends in the old RWB network.

At some point, Earl realized that he'd said too much.

"You have to understand that no one has actually done anything. The only thing General Redmon did was transmit intelligence to others in the military who might be interested. Even then, they've only talked about what their response *might* be if some crisis occurs. There's nothing improper about that."

"What was their response? Who did you talk to?"

Earl just stared at me without answering.

"Does Redmon know you called me back?"

"No!" he blurted back emphatically. "And he's not to know!"

"How about the people in Atlanta? Did you talk to them?"

Earl looked confused. He didn't seem to know what I was talking about. Whoever was masterminding this was apparently keeping them in the dark about that part.

"General, you know he's crazy. Do you want to go down with him? This is your chance to get yourself out of this plot before it gets any worse."

He hesitated. "I called you back on this because I don't want any trouble."

For a second, I got the sense that he was ready to cooperate. Then he pulled back.

"I can't talk anymore." The screen went blank.

I LOOKED AT the empty vid-screen, trying to come to grips with what I'd just heard. One thing was clear: Eloni would have to deal with these characters. She'd have Redmon under even tighter surveillance than he already was. She'd round up all his sympathizers, if she had to.

But that didn't solve my problem. My guess was that Redmon didn't know any more about the real plot than I did. The same was probably true of Rufus Clay, the local gang members, and all the rest of them. Was I guessing? Maybe. But every instinct told me that they were all waiting for some unknown person or group to give them the signal to move. That signal would probably come in the form of an attack on the U.N.

And that was my department.

The thought made me sick. I had given up my military career two years ago. After what had happened, I'd vowed there was no way I was ever going back. But here I was.

I DIDN'T KNOW it at the time, but the operation in Baluchistan two years ago was to be my last as a U.S. Army officer. It began like all the others, in a no-nonsense, military transport. The men and women in the unit were sprawled out in their seats, trying to nap during the long flight. As senior officer, I had a small cubicle that allowed me to keep a light on and work without disturbing anyone. I found it impossible to sleep. I spent the whole flight checking and rechecking the orders as they came in. I was distrustful of plans—all of them. It was a constant guessing game to figure out where they would break down.

Baluchistan had been set up in the '20s by the United States as a buffer between Iran on the west, Pakistan on the east, and Afghanistan on the north. From the beginning it had been a disaster, degenerating from a puppet state, to a narco-state, and then to near anarchy. Ali Hamid and his brother had overthrown the Baluchi government in 2060, but they were ousted in the '70s after a popular uprising. The remnants of his loyalist army were concentrated along the Arabian Sea, mostly near Gwadar, the city where the Women for Peace leaders had held their press conference years earlier, before their ill-fated trip. According to U.N. Intelligence, several of Hamid's financial supporters were holed up with him, unable to get out before the fighting started.

Refugees were streaming out of the region, heading towards Pakistan in the east and Iran in the west. Both governments were threatening to intervene. The U.N. had ordered both governments to turn over temporary control of their military units to the U.N. and not interfere with the operation, but there had apparently been some compromises within the Council. The amended document placed a sixty-hour time limit on the transfer orders. I remember thinking that Madeleine wouldn't like that. We had less than forty-six hours to secure the region, or all hell might break loose.

Madeleine insisted that everyone follow the U.N. Rules of Engagement to the letter. The Threat-to-Peace indictment issued by a court in The Hague had cited Hamid's troops as aggressors and directed them to lay down their arms. Hamid was to be arrested and charged as a war criminal, along with his financial backer, Hakan Kolle, who was also suspected of soliciting the murder of the Women for Peace leaders. The Enforcement Order from the Council of Ministers had assigned a multinational task force the job of securing the area around the city. The main element of Hamid's troops had taken over a health complex in the middle of the city, and was holding the staff and patients hostage, threatening to kill them if anyone attacked. Our unit was given the job of capturing the leaders and freeing the hostages.

Control was everything. That was my mantra in those days. During the training sessions, I told them the goal was always to restore the peace. If troops opposed us, our job was to capture and disarm them. We always maintained our weapons in electric-arc position and only switched to deadly fire when we had no choice.

"We cannot afford the luxury of depersonalizing the enemy." I tried to let the words sink in during the training lectures. "When the Council sends us into the field, we represent all of the people, even the ones who may end up shooting at us. You've been chosen for this unit because you can use your head, exercise control, and not whip yourself into a frenzy."

THE PILOT SIGNALED that we were nearing the coast; she said she'd be activating the rotary descent unit in about ten minutes. I remember moving down the aisles, asking my officers to get their units ready. I got an affirmative response from all of them—none more enthusiastic than Raji, who gave me a smile and a thumbs-up.

Raji—I remember wondering at the time what the hell I was going to do with him.

I loved him dearly, but that didn't solve anything; it just made it worse. He wanted to sleep with me the night before we deployed. I tried everything I could to make him leave without hurting him, but nothing worked. He seemed desperate to be with me, so I finally gave up and told him to sleep on the couch. Since we were due to leave at 0500 the next morning, I had to try, at least, to get some rest.

Raji had spent the previous five weeks telling me how much he loved me and wanted to be with me. Once he had told me about his Lynn-Taksin condition, he seemed unburdened and unable to keep his feelings to himself. He came around often when I was off-duty. Truth is, I liked him, but fending him off had gotten to be tiresome.

He said he knew I loved him; he was sure of it. He said he could see it in the way I talked to him. Couldn't I see it too, he wanted to know? I did. The more I heard about his music and his dreams, his illness and his fears, the closer I felt to him. It had been awhile—maybe my entire life—since any man had gotten to me like that.

Why couldn't we be together, he asked? Was it the difference in rank? He said he'd resign his commission right then, if that's what it took. Don't do that, I said. Don't give up your career in the belief that something's going to happen between us.

Was it the age difference? Why should that matter? "I've read where your own Secretary of Defense has a lover fifteen years younger than her. That's even bigger than the difference between us." How did he know to pick that example? I thought. He didn't even know I *knew* Eloni. It was uncanny. "No, it's not that," I told him.

Was it his illness? Was that what was holding me back? "I'm not contagious," he said. "My prognosis is pretty good. Lynn-Taksin isn't hereditary, but even if it was I have a pre-disease sperm sample on deposit just in case. There's no worry about it being passed on to a future child." My god, I thought. This guy could really jump to conclusions! No, no, no, I told him. It wasn't that at all.

What was it then? I knew what Chloe would say: I liked Raji so much I had to run away from him. But that wasn't really true. This was something new. I loved him in a way I never thought I would experience. But it wasn't going to make him happy. I loved him like a little brother, and he wasn't looking for another big sister. But I couldn't make it something it wasn't. I loved him, but I didn't want to sleep with him.

DUST—I REMEMBER thinking that we hadn't planned for that. These were hard pellets, maybe more sand than dust, pelting at my goggles, getting down inside my collar. There was no mention of dust storms in the plan, but I thought that mistake might work to our advantage. Our equipment could operate in these conditions, while Hamid's fighters might have a problem. I figured we'd gotten lucky: the plan had broken down, but it had broken our way. The makeshift headquarters was sweltering, well above forty degrees Celsius. What was the roof made of, corrugated iron? Had we known it would be that hot when we chose it as the command post from the aerial surveillance? Of course, not. But the heat wasn't affecting our equipment. That was another lucky break.

The satellite was in synchronous orbit above the headquarters, and we had a connection with New York. Madeleine and her operations team appeared on the big screen, sitting around a conference table.

"When will you be ready?" Madeleine asked. She sounded nervous.

"Give us another forty-five minutes."

I prowled through the command post, looking over everyone's shoulder, trying to decide if things were going according to plan or not. Sergeant Rutledge had activated the electronic jamming: no vidphones or electronic signals of any sort could go in or out of the buildings being held by Hamid's forces. The high-amp speakers to the north and east of the buildings were already aiming the pre-planned surrender message at the buildings. They would be switched to the screeching, disabling noises the minute we started the assault. The white-light devices were in position. Rutledge said they'd placed three of them, but they had encountered heavy small-arms fire when they'd tried to complete the circle around the compound. I told him that would have to do. If the devices worked, those inside would be facing a blinding light that we could use as cover.

Rutledge said the hover cameras were in position over the clinic buildings. We'd spent hours going over the aerial surveillance, trying to find the best penetration points in the structure. Now we'd see whether or not the plan would work. If all went well, the cameras would give us a good view into the buildings. If not, there wasn't any good alternative. There were a few antiquated news-bots that had found their way into the combat zone, and they were snooping around sending pictures. Their images might be all right for newscasts broadcast around the world, but they weren't nearly good enough for our operation.

THE VID-SCREEN OVER the moving walkway on Lexington Avenue was following the news story along with the streaming images of the U.N. operation in Baluchistan. Jesse kept moving as he watched it, realizing it was too cold to stand in one place. He hadn't planned for the cold. He'd left his gloves in the apartment, so he had to stick his hands in the pocket of his topcoat to keep them warm. That was stupid; he couldn't afford to be stupid.

Commentators on the vid-screen were speculating that the operation might lead to the liberation of the hostages and the capture of former President Hamid.

This was nothing, the voices inside him said.

When everything goes up in flames, all of this will be forgotten.

He reached the side door of his apartment building and saw a strip of yellow tape over the handle. He ripped it away and opened the door. He was confronted immediately by a woman in a police uniform. The sight of her set him bristling.

"You can't come in here, sir."

"I live here." He made a step forward, and she put her hand up to restrain him.

"Don't you see the police tape over the door? That means 'do not enter.' We're gathering evidence about a robbery. You'll have to use the front door."

He raised his arm to brush her aside, as he tried to push forward.

The policewoman grabbed him and spun him around, pinning his arm up behind him. He struggled to resist, cursing himself for not being thirty years younger. She shoved him forward, ordering him to spread his legs and put his hands against the wall. She ran a pat-down search. A voice inside him screamed as she brushed by his balls.

She turned him around and forced him back towards the door.

"This is your lucky day. I'm not in the mood to arrest some old guy for resisting arrest. But if I see you around here again, I might just do it."

ONE HOVER CAMERA was in position over an air vent on the roof, and the other two were near elevated windows on opposite sides of the health clinic. Once they broke through the glass and started recording, we would only have a short time to gather information. I gave the command to activate. The first images were unsteady and twisting, dipping in and out of three dimensions. The sound was steadier than the pictures, but it broke into squawks every few seconds. The operators adjusted the remote controls, bringing the cameras into synch and steadying the quality. Suddenly, it all came together. The three cameras were working together, and we had triangulation. In front of us was a three-dimensional image of the room, filled with the cacophonous sounds of the hostages and hostage-takers.

I moved forward as close as possible to the image, trying to soak up every detail. The room was a sea of movement with people moving in every direction. Were the fighters, weapons, hostages all being marked on a grid? Were the rooms being plotted? One of the sergeants shouted back an affirmative to each of my questions. But by now, Hamid's soldiers had spotted the cameras and had begun firing at them.

"We've only got a minute or two," I shouted. "When they hit the cameras, our live scene will be gone."

A bullet exploded near one of the cameras. The next bullet hit the camera, and it went dead. The scene immediately flattened out to a two-dimensional tableau. Within seconds, the second camera was disabled. Shortly after that, the last one went dark.

"Okay, let's get a quick look at the recording. We've got to move fast. Now that they've seen us doing this, they'll start preparing for our attack."

The analysts detailed what they'd seen, with illumination points and overlays over each scene to match the rooms, weapons, hostages, and anything else they were able to observe. The hostage team said they'd accounted for all the doctors, nurses, and patients that they knew about. The head of the criminal team said she had seen Hamid come out from a side room and duck back when he saw the cameras. One thing that caught my eye, however, was one of the fighters as he came through the door, holding his pants with one hand and dragging a woman with the other. She appeared to have blood on her dress and was fighting to get away from him.

THE DUST WAS in my nostrils again. As we crawled across the street, it got worse. The white light prevented the fighters in the building from aiming at us, but nothing stopped them from firing blindly into the street. The disabling noise was partially blocked by my headset, but enough of it got through to pound on my brain and give me a raging headache. When we were within twenty meters of the building, the point man reached the door and placed the explosive charge. I got word through my headset that the units near the side doors were ready. I gave the signal to blast open the doors.

It was the moment I dreaded in any operation—the point where control threatened to give way to chaos. Tactical plans degenerated into a blur of movement, shouts, and weapons fire. It always came down to one-on-one, fighter eyeing fighter, making instant decisions in a haze of miscalculation. I didn't know whether our training would stand up against the onrush of animal instincts. I was trying to control a hundred mini-wars.

I remember rushing through the main room, trying to see everything at once, shouting orders though my gas mask. A group of fighters near the door dropped their weapons after two of them were hit with an electric arc blast that sent them sprawling. Near one of the side rooms, three of the fighters began shooting at our troops. The soldiers near them quickly switched to rifle fire, leaving two of them badly wounded and the other apparently dead on the floor. I found myself running from group to group, urging the hostage-recovery team to grab the hostages and get out the door as quickly as possible. Two squads headed to the back room where the leaders had been seen on the video, and they reappeared moments later, prodding Hamid, Kolle, and three others out of the building.

Then out of the corner of my eye, I spotted the man I had seen on the video, dragging the same woman he had been molesting before and pushing her into a back room. I saw cribs through the doorway, so I assumed the room was a nursery. Had that area been cleared yet? I wasn't sure. I made the quick decision to follow him, pushing my way thought the debris in the middle of the main room. I was beginning to realize what he was up to: there would be a rape charge waiting for him unless he got rid of the witness. I was determined to get to him first.

I stumbled over some chairs, righting myself as I got near the room. I was a couple of steps from the doorway when I heard a shot blasting from inside. I ran into the room in time to see the woman fall to the ground, as her shooter raced down the hallway, heading outside.

She was bleeding heavily from her chest. I knelt down beside her and reached into my first-aid packet for anything that might help.

I heard others rushing into the room behind me. Raji's voice was giving commands, directing others to check the closets and side doors. He rushed by me, heading towards the door that the shooter had taken.

"Be careful. He's armed, and he's a killer." But Raji was already out the door.

I tried mouth-to-mouth resuscitation on the woman, but it was useless. The life was seeping out of her. "*Mama, mama.*" I heard a child's voice behind me, and turned to see a little girl crying at the top of her lungs, reaching through the bars of the crib towards the woman in my arms. "*Mama, Mama.*" I knew the voice was coming from somewhere, but suddenly I wasn't sure where. "*Mama, Mama.*" Something was pounding in my head, but was it the child's voice or something from long ago? "*Mama, mama.*" How long could it last? A day? A week? A lifetime?

A shot rang out from the direction Raji had gone. I screamed and grabbed my weapon, forcing my way past the door and into a small alleyway. When I turned the corner, I was face to face with the man who had killed the woman. When he saw the weapon in my hand, he began lowering his own gun, hesitating slightly. He raised his free arm over his head in a gesture of surrender, but I kept my eye on the weapon. It seemed like he was getting ready—maybe—to release it and let it drop to the ground. Or, maybe not. Was he raising it again? Was he moving it towards me?

I looked to the ground. Raji was lying at his feet, not moving at all. Half of his face had been blown off.

His killer kept looking at me. From somewhere in the back of my mind, I could hear my own lecture. In this type of encounter, the proper procedure is to push the setting on your weapon from rifle fire to electric arc and prepare to disable your prisoner.

I heard my own lecturing voice, but somehow I didn't recognize it—or maybe I didn't believe it—or maybe I couldn't do it—or maybe I didn't care.

I raised my weapon in its rifle-fire position and shot him.

I RESIGNED MY commission in 2080, just two days after the end of the military operation in Gwadar. I couldn't do it anymore.

Raji. My grief about his death blanketed me like a thick fog, settling into my pores. I'd been living with loneliness for a long time. I suppose it took his death to make me realize that. He had gotten closer to me than anyone had in years.

I'm not sure what I did in the aftermath of that shooting. I know I went back to the room where the child had been screaming, but someone else was already looking after her. I got through the field memorial service that we held for Raji the next day. I remember speaking. As commander of the unit, it was expected of me. But I have no idea what I said. As soon as it was over, I submitted my resignation papers and left. I blamed myself for everything: I shouldn't have gotten so close to Raji; I should have held him back; I should have known he'd do something impulsive to impress me.

Pounding through my head was the most irrational thought of all: what I had done made everything worse. I couldn't shake the strong feeling that came over me—the feeling that I had cheapened Raji's life. I was unable to answer one simple question: what was going through my mind when I'd shot his killer? I tried to recreate the moment, but I couldn't. My brain had wrapped the brutality of it in a protective shield. But I'll never forget what I saw the moment after I shot him. There were two dead men lying there, and they had been reduced to the same level. With one bullet I had evened the score in a miserable, sick game. The death of a beautiful, loving young man had now been accounted for. One perverted killer had been received in payment.

Where would I go, I wondered? How far back would I have to go to start over? Jewel Murphy said my great-great-grandfather had come home from the Vietnam War a broken man. His son, Jack, my great-

grandfather, was a vicious man who returned from Iraq mentally disturbed, infecting everyone around him with violence and misery. He'd
created a perfect hating machine in his son, Jesse, my grandfather. And
then there was my father. Who was he? I would never know. But given
my history, he was probably as bad as the others. The proof of this
entire sad lineage was me: a woman prone to violence, who at that moment didn't seem much better than any of them.

I left as soon as I could, finding my way somehow to Europe. I
ended up in Italy in a little town on the eastern shore of *Lago di Garda*.
It was peaceful there. I knew no one. That's what I wanted. There was a
mountain across the lake, and I kept thinking that it looked like Mount
Tamalpais. It was larger than the mountain I remembered from my
childhood in California, but it had the same unmistakable contour of
a sleeping maiden. Would she ever wake up, I wondered, or would she
just continue to slumber? I probably went through more introspection
in those few days than at any point in my life.

How did everything end up the way it did? When I was in my early
twenties, the word among my friends was that it was the best time
in years for a young woman, maybe the best time ever. Women were
moving into places where they had never been before. I saw it with
Eloni and hundreds of others. The tragic fate of the Women for Peace
had changed attitudes and opened doors. I had decided I was going
to make the most of it. The new United Nations was going to need a
determined young woman like me.

That's what I had told myself, but as I sat there looking out over the
lake I wondered if that was really what I had done. Be honest, Julia:
your career choice may have been a fine one, but you were on a personal vendetta against the man who ruined your mother's life. Your
real life and passion was in your search for Jesse. It squeezed out everything else and left you numb to your own feelings. Did you really
think you'd find him? Would it make a difference if you did? Would it
bring back your mother?

All of that's over, I told myself. Go back into your memories and
search for the happiest moment. Find that spot where you were cud-

dled up with your mother reading stories. Savor it, and then move on with your life.

I WONDERED WHEN someone would find me; after a week or so, Madeleine finally did. As I approached the tiny *agriturismo* where I was staying, the *padrona,* an older woman with her gray hair in a bun, met me halfway up the path.

"*Signora, telefono.*" I followed her into the living room and picked up her voice-only phone. I'd never used such a device before; it must been at least fifty years old.

"Julia, how are you? I've been worried."

"I'm fine."

"*Where* are you?"

"In Italy."

"I figured out that much." Madeleine sounded more than a little annoyed. "Next time, could you find a place with a vid-phone so I can see you when I talk? I've forgotten how much I hate talking into one of these things."

"Everyone's been looking for you, do you know that?" Madeleine was now in her calm, reasonable voice. It was the one finely honed for persuasion.

"I didn't want to talk to anyone."

She brushed that off. "I talked to Eloni. She was surprised when she saw your resignation papers. She didn't even know you'd taken emergency leave." Madeleine paused, wanting to give me time to think about it, maybe feel guilty. "I even called California and ended up talking to your friend Chloe."

"The next time you talk to her, tell her the answer is 'yes.'"

"What are you talking about?"

"My friends always asked me if I thought I could kill somebody. At the time, I didn't know how to answer them. Now I know the answer is yes."

"Oh, stop being so dramatic!" The soothing Madeleine had been replaced by an exasperated one. That one was easier to deal with at the moment.

"I just want us to quit beating around the bush. You know I resigned because I shot and killed someone in direct violation of all your rules."

"Who said anything about my rules?"

"Well, then in violation of *my* rules."

"Let's step back for a second." Madeleine's soothing voice was back. "Do you know that the Council of Ministers passed a resolution congratulating your unit and praising your contributions to world peace? And Eloni tells me that she's going to recommend that Congress enact legislation providing a special decoration for everyone involved. Did you know about any of that?"

"That all sounds nice, but I know what I did."

"So do I, actually, I have it here in the report." I could hear Madeleine fumbling with her vid-screen. "I'll summarize it for you: it says the mission was carried off with exceptional professionalism due to, and here's a quote, 'the inspired leadership of Colonel Julia Moro.'" She read off bits and pieces of the report, emphasizing the best parts: "minimal casualties," "high-level captives," "valuable intelligence."

"The report goes on to say that some of the men who were captured have provided key information, which has led to several indictments."

"What does it say about the shooting?"

"It's right here: 'Colonel Moro should be commended for her courage in confronting a hostile fighter by the name of Takit Pervez, a man with a long criminal history, which included murder and rape. In this instance, Pervez had raped and killed one of the hostages and killed one of the rescue team. He was apprehended by Colonel Moro. As he was preparing to attack her, she was forced to use deadly fire in response.'"

"That's not what happened. Who wrote that?"

"Let's see, I have to scroll to the bottom. Here it is: It was signed by Master Sergeant William Rutledge. Are you saying that Sergeant Rutledge would lie to protect you?"

"Probably."

"Well, let me tell you what isn't in the report. Here's what I would have added: 'The courageous Colonel Moro was operating on no sleep for about forty-eight hours and under conditions that triggered blinding headaches during the operation. She was under severe pressure from New York to complete the operation quickly without any harm to the hostages. She put her own personal safety in jeopardy by trying to rescue a woman who was under attack, and in so doing she encountered a situation that triggered an understandable psychological reaction arising out of some tragic events from her own past. When she confronted the vicious killer, she had the shock of seeing him murder a fellow officer with whom she had a close relationship.' Is that a pretty good summary?"

"How do you know all those things?"

"It's my job to know things."

The air fell silent between us. I didn't know what was coming next. "Madeleine, what do you want?"

"I want you to come to New York and work for me."

That was the last thing I expected. "You can't be serious."

"I'm very serious. Our Security Director has resigned, and I want you to take the job. You're the only one I'm really considering at this point."

"I thought you were calling to tell me I'd been court-martialed. Now you say you want to reward me?"

"It's not a reward. It's a tough job. You're the right person for it; that's all."

"It's not that easy."

"Why isn't it easy to say yes?"

"Madeleine, you don't understand. I don't think I can trust myself in a life-and-death situation anymore. I have to rebuild my life in another direction."

"I thought you'd say that." Madeleine was in her accept-no-excuses mode. "So let me make it clear: this is a desk job. We won't be sending you out with a weapon in your hand. You'll be using your brain instead of that well-toned body of yours. Okay?"

She let that sink in. "And let me tell you something else: I would trust you with my life. I know that's not something you want to hear right now, but it's the truth."

I didn't know what to say.

"Will you at least think about it?"

THAT WAS TWO years ago; it scares me to think how lost I was. I needed help. I reached out anywhere I thought I could find it. I tried calling Paola, hoping to persuade her to come out of retirement for some counseling. But after a couple of hours on the vid-phone, she said she'd heard enough.

"Julia, this is really impossible. You're acting like a prosecutor, trying to convict yourself of something. You want me to buy into your guilt feelings, but I'm not going to do it. I can see from the look on your face that you've already punished yourself enough."

I finished the call more frustrated than ever. At the time I kept wondering why everyone was trying to reassure me. Did they think they were doing me a favor? Maybe I *needed* someone to tell me I was wrong, to make me feel guilty. Had that ever occurred to them? Maybe if someone else had done it, I would have stopped beating up on myself.

THE UNITED NATIONS job dangled in front of me for almost a month. I might have said no, if I'd had any other place to go. But I finally agreed. The day after I started, Madeleine insisted that I go with her to a cocktail reception hosted by the May 4th Foundation. I told her I hated that sort of thing. But she said Noah Fawkes' organization had put up a lot of money for the new U.N. building that was being constructed, and it would be awkward if I didn't attend. Besides, she said, it would be a good chance to meet some people that I'd be working with.

I found myself nursing a glass of wine and munching on crackers, just wandering around the edges of the crowd. Finally, Madeleine grabbed me.

"Come with me," she insisted. "I'll introduce you to some people."

I spent the next half-hour like the new puppy being shown around the play group. "Robert Luria, the head of the U.N. Economic Commission is dying to meet you," Madeleine said, "but right now he's talking to the new president of the Gates Foundation." Madeleine took me over to meet Fawkes, who was hosting the party. Madeleine then pivoted me once more and ushered me through the crowd, introducing me to a few elegantly dressed people with names that seemed vaguely familiar. Within minutes, she had me again by the elbow, moving me towards another group.

"There's the Secretary-General, and that tall man off to his right is his husband; he's the head curator at the Met."

Moments later we were talking to the President of the European Union and the leader of the Social Democratic bloc. As Madeleine eased me over to another group, I found a waiter, who loaded me up with a fresh glass of wine. I figured I was going to need it.

Madeleine was at my side again. "There's one of the family members of the Thirteen that I'd like you to meet."

I froze.

Even before she turned around, I knew who it was. Her dark, graying hair gleamed in the gallery lights. Our eyes met and held on to each other.

"Julia," Madeleine said, "I would like you to meet Dhanye Chandri."

For a second, I found it hard to talk.

"Dhanye."

"Do you two know each other?" Madeleine asked.

"Dhanye and I met once before," I fumbled. "Actually, we didn't really meet. We were just seated next to each other at a holo-conference many years ago."

"Really," Madeleine said. "Now, that's something I didn't know."

Dhanye's eyes grew suddenly sad. I had a twinge of alarm.

"We have a more recent connection, but I don't think Julia knows it."

Suddenly it hit me. The sadness began to spread.

"Raji was my brother."

I AWOKE IN the middle of the night. With the dedication ceremonies just three days away, I was finding it even more difficult to sleep. Dhanye was awake too. She was sitting at the window, staring into the night sky, looking beautiful.

"Are you okay?"

"I'm fine." She walked over and sat at my side. "The baby was moving around, and it woke me up." She patted her tummy, sending our unborn child a little reassurance.

"If it's restless," I laughed, "that's my fault. It's probably part of my genetic inheritance. That's what happens when you use an egg donor like me."

Dhanye moved up to the top of the bed, pushing me over a bit and fluffing up some pillows for herself. She kissed me on the forehead. "And just who else should I have used as a donor?"

"No one, I hope." I returned the kiss.

Dhanye snuggled in closer. "Maya called today while you were working, and we had a nice chat. I told her we were planning to be in California in October for the delivery of the baby. That made her happy."

"She was surprised to hear that Annabel is my gynecologist," Dhanye said. "She said she still thinks of her as a little kid playing with you in the garden."

"I sometimes think of her that way myself."

Dhanye let out a sigh and started rubbing my hand, finger by finger. "I was just thinking about how happy I am, despite everything. When you woke up a few minutes ago, I was thinking about Raji."

"I guess he's never too far from our thoughts."

"And he never will be," Dhanye's voice hovered somewhere between joy and sadness. "He's the father of our child, Julia. A little part of him will always be with us."

She slid down, pushing me towards the middle of the bed. We lay there, saying nothing. Our hands stayed quietly entwined.

"It makes me sad that I didn't know you or the family when he was alive."

"He wanted to accomplish something on his own," Dhanye said, "but he was afraid people would treat him differently if he used our grandmother's family name."

She rolled over to face me. "He never mentioned your name either, but he did say that he was in love with his commanding officer."

I gave out a groan. "Does that bother you?" I asked.

"No, of course not." She thought for a second. "I know it sounds strange, but in a way it makes me feel better."

Dhanye gave a little gasp and then shifted position. She pointed down to her tummy where the baby had just moved. "That's Raji's doing," she said quietly. "He must have known we were talking about him."

PART SIX

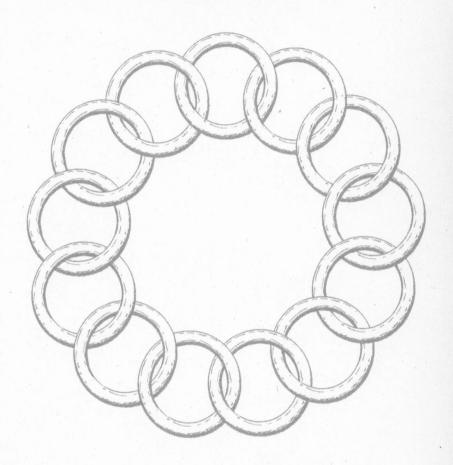

SATURDAY, MAY 2, 2082

NEW YORK CITY

JULIA

I WAS MISSING something, but I still didn't know what it was.

Saturday went by in a flurry of meetings. My staff went over the same information, the same contingency plans, the same everything. We found nothing new.

We went through files of past incidents, trying to find a pattern. Over the years there'd been many threatening calls to the old U.N. headquarters and to its offices in Geneva and Shanghai, but most of the threats had never panned out. But two relatively recent incidents seemed more serious. Five years ago a May 4th celebration in London was postponed when three bombs were discovered near the event. Information about the bombs was withheld to protect and aid the investigation, but the culprits were never found. Another incident occurred in Washington, D.C., but it wasn't clear whether it was an accident or intentional sabotage. The U.N. Liaison Office was gutted by fire. There were no obvious signs of arson, but the cause was never determined. Was there a pattern there? If so, I couldn't see it.

Everyone was just waiting. Rufus Clay, the Bergen County mob bosses, and god-only-knows who else were probably waiting for the money to arrive with their next set of terrorist instructions. Redmon and his cronies were waiting for the signal that the system had collapsed so they could make their move. And I was waiting too. It was like New Year's Eve, and we were all getting ready for the ball drop.

SOMETIME LATE SATURDAY afternoon an idea bubbled to the surface. It had probably been floating around in my memory before that, but my subconscious had good reasons for trying to bottle it up. Moise and Selva had invited us next door for dinner, but I convinced Dhanye to go without me. I said I needed to work. In fact, I needed to open an old, unpleasant video file. It was going to be bad enough for me to watch it; I didn't need to put Dhanye through it as well.

The use of Bible verses as a coding device: I thought I might have seen that before. I needed to be sure. I brought up the index of U.N. Criminal Justice records and scrolled back to 2055. I found the file I was looking for, labeled, "Julia Moro, age thirteen, hypno-scan." Could I watch it without driving myself over the edge? I was about to find out.

WHAT WAS SHE—what was I—thinking? The floating collage of scenes from the hypno-scan raced through my brain, competing with my own memory of the same events. Many of the scenes were blurry and confused like abstract paintings. Others were disturbingly clear, showing groups of men screaming, shaking weapons, and mouthing threats. The scenes from the hypno-scan pushed and jarred against the images in my own memory like pinpricks. Sometimes they canceled each other out, but more often they grew and fed off each other like overlapping, discordant waves.

This feverish thirteen-year-old—the one who was me, but not me—kept spilling out her memory and struggling with her emotions. I admired her powers of recall, but I feared for what she was going through. I was starting to fear for myself at the present moment as well, as I could feel the beginnings of a massive headache. I knew I had to get out of there soon. I raced through the images, looking for what I had come for, hoping this girl, this other-me, had seen what I thought she had. Finally, I found it.

At one point in the video, Rick—I'd forgotten how disgusting he looked—grabs a Bible. Someone asks why, and Rick says, "That's how we get our access code from Abraham. He sends it to us in Bible verses." What does he say next? I couldn't remember, but had this memory-girl heard it?

"He always uses that quote about Babylon from the Book of Revelation."

I SWITCHED OFF the video file and stared at the wall. It took a moment for my headache to turn around and go away. I looked around for help, but there was no one there but me.

This was going to get worse before it got better.

We were dealing with Abraham.

SUNDAY, MAY 3, 2082

NEW YORK CITY

JULIA

WHAT HAD HAPPENED to Abraham? After the destruction of the Ka-jakai Dam 2057, he had disappeared. There'd been no sign of him for twenty-five years.

By Sunday morning, I had my whole staff searching for any information we could find about him. Abraham's militia was apparently defeated by government troops after the destruction of the dam, and many of the militiamen were absorbed into that army. But what had happened to him? The Baluchistan government, admittedly not a very reliable source, claimed that Abraham's compound had been blown up and that he had escaped. In the twenty-five years since then, nothing had been uncovered to prove them wrong.

And that's where it sat. There were no fingerprints, DNA, brain scans, iris scans, or anything else available to identify Abraham. No one knew where he came from; there were no reliable physical descriptions of him. If he was still alive, most people thought he would be in his seventies. But like everything else, that was guesswork.

There were several psychological profiles of Abraham in the files. It seemed like a whole cottage industry had grown up composed of people trying to figure out what made him tick. But none of them were much help. Most said that Abraham was probably paranoid and a bit schizophrenic, but what violent sociopath *didn't* fit that description?

A few studies argued that the *Patria* network wasn't so much a movement as a criminal enterprise that Abraham had created out of his head, something he patched together by propaganda, computerized images, and appeals to male resentment. Experts pointed to the collapse of the network after he had disappeared as proof of this theory. But at least one study gave me pause: it said Abraham wasn't the type to ever bring his anger and hatred under control. He'd go underground for a while, maybe for years, but he'd be waiting for a chance to strike again. His one major dramatic gesture may have been a failure, but he'd be looking to do something else that would be even more spectacular.

I'd seen Abraham. If I'd had the stomach to go further through the video record of the hypno-scan, I could probably have seen him again. But I had the remnants of a headache to tell me that was a bad idea. Omar had people on his team looking at the entire hypno-scan in detail. They'd probably confirm what I remembered about him: most of his body was covered, and he had a computer-generated mask blocking out his face. The only things exposed during his tirade were his hands and some sort of band around his neck. But I knew they wouldn't find anything useful. They'd be watching a twenty-seven-year-old record of a computerized image, one that had been generated from my own hypnosis-induced memory. If that was all we had to go on, we were in trouble.

There was one report that might be helpful. Hamid and Kolle were still sitting in a detention facility at The Hague. In an effort to improve his plea-bargaining position, Kolle had signed an affidavit describing what had happened during his meeting with Abraham in 2057. I dug through his statement, trying to find something helpful. There wasn't much, but he did say he had paid Abraham a lot of money. He didn't come right out and say that he had hired him to kill the Women for

Peace leaders, but anyone could figure that out. He said he and Hamid had panicked when they realized Abraham might be planning to destroy the Kajakai Dam. That wasn't part of the deal. They decided to move in troops to stop him, but the dam blew up anyway during the fighting. Afterwards, Abraham apparently bribed a couple of government officials to help him escape.

What caught my attention was the money: Abraham had been paid two hundred million dollars to carry out the job. But that was just the last payment. He had received over three hundred million dollars in the preceding year alone for the *Patria* campaign of violence. Kolle said the two hundred million–dollar payment was embedded with an electronic marker that allowed them to trace it for several months. But the money finally became so commingled with other funds that they had lost track of it. Most of the money had started out, at least, in several New York banks. After that, the trail went cold.

Five hundred million dollars. I tried to imagine how much harm a man like Abraham could do with that sum of money. My imagination kept going and going.

MADELEINE WASN'T HAPPY being pulled out of the gala Sunday afternoon reception. The May 4th Foundation was entertaining the visiting heads of government, and she was expected to be at her charming best. But when I told her it was important, she came back to her office to hear what I had to say. I told her everything I knew.

"What should we do?" she asked when I was finished.

"I think you should consider postponing the celebration."

Her sigh sounded more like a groan. "That's out of the question. Most of the guests are already in town. This is the biggest event in the history of the U.N. It starts a whole year of celebrations. May 4th is May 4th—we can't move it to another date."

Madeleine didn't like the position we were in any better than I did.

"Think about it. What could I tell the Secretary-General, the Chairman of the Council, and all the rest of them?" She started enumerating the points with her fingers. "My security director has found some vague warnings going around in military circles. She had a hypnosis-enhanced memory showing that Abraham once used Bible verses, but we don't really know if he's alive or dead. Sure, there have been acts of violence in the city in the last few weeks, but the rest of it is just instinct and guesswork."

"They'd think I was crazy," Madeleine continued. "They'd say we should tighten up security for the event, but they wouldn't see any reason to cancel it."

"That's what I thought you'd you say, but I had to suggest it."

Madeleine fumed at me as I said it. She was afraid I was right.

I WALKED THE main floor of the building that evening, resisting the temptation to start poking around in the corners. I knew my staff had done all of that several times. Laria Kwon was there with Irene Castillo and her aide, talking about some last-minute changes to the tile work at the base of the statue. Fawkes was waiting to talk to her about how the wide angles of light from the chandelier would fall on her sculpture.

Laria excused herself from all of them when she saw me. She was an old friend of Dhanye's, and she was eager to say hello. I told her I had an awkward request. We needed to have one of our technicians get into the sculpture to check it for any problems.

She grinned. "Of course, I don't mind. I'll show them how to crawl inside."

"Also, Dhanye wants to know if you can come to dinner after the celebration."

"I'd love to do that," she said.

I wondered if any of us would be sitting down tomorrow night for a normal meal.

IT WAS NEARING 11:00 P.M. when my vid-screen showed a message from Antonio.

"Tonio, how are you? What's going on?"

Antonio was all seriousness. "I know you're busy. Dhanye told me you were working late. But I needed to tell you something. I just got a call from the Attorney General's office telling me that Rick's been found. He's being held near you in New York on Riker's Island. He was picked up two weeks ago for selling drugs to minors."

"My god, after all these years. Are they trying to extradite him to California?"

"Yes, but there's a twist they just called me about. He wants to see you."

"Why me?" I was caught off-guard by the news.

"He says he has information about what happened to Abraham. I'm not really sure what he's talking about. He says, and I'm quoting him here, 'Let me talk to that Julia girl. I have stuff the U.N. will want to hear.'"

"He's just a lowlife, Tonio. What could he possibly know?"

"I'm not sure. But when he disappeared from California about twenty-five years ago, we had pretty good intelligence that he had fled the country and joined up with the *Patria* guerillas in Central Asia. So there's a chance he might have some information."

"He'll want a deal on the California charges. Tell him that the prosecutor might follow your recommendation. The fact is, they'll go along with your judgment."

RIKER'S ISLAND HAD been New York's main jail facility for nearly two hundred years. It had been modernized several times, but it was still run down. It was past midnight by the time I got there, but Rick was in the interview room waiting for me. He was like a caricature of his former self: He had a sick, pasty look that was most pronounced in his jowls. There were random splotches on his skin. His eyes seemed to drift in different directions.

"Well," he muttered. "Look how Julia's grown up—nice ass, nice tits. Who the hell would have thought that little twerp I knew would end up like this?"

I let it go. I wasn't going to let him get under my skin.

"Do you have something to tell me, Rick?"

He wanted to negotiate. Was there something I could do about the charges? I said I'd put in a good word. He looked skeptical. I decided to press him.

"If you've got anything to tell me, now's the time. You and I both know that anything you have won't be worth shit after today. So either speak up, or I'm leaving."

"Hold on," Rick said nervously. He scratched at a scab on his cheek.

"Did you know that I was with the *Patria* guerillas after I got out of California?"

I nodded.

"It was great. We had women, all the dope we wanted . . . " He saw the look on my face. "Okay, okay, sit still. I'm getting to it."

I waited while he tried to wrap his vacant eyes around his memories.

"I was in his militia. For a while, I was one of Abraham's personal bodyguards. I got real close to him at times. He tried to keep his identity a secret, but we all knew who he was. I was right in the middle of things. I don't want to cause any more trouble for myself, but if you look at some of the pictures of those guys on top of that dam, you might find someone that looks like me."

I was startled by his admission, but I wasn't about to let it show. "This is all ancient history, Rick. If you've got something important to tell me, tell it."

"How about something since then?" he said. "Maybe, London a few years ago. There was a terrorist scare that shut down the celebration."

"That was in the press. Everyone knew that."

"But the press didn't mention the three bombs that were found." His eyes started to twitch as he said it. "Yeah, I can see you're finally thinking maybe I know something."

"Go on." I tried to keep an even voice. I wasn't going to let him know how excited I was, but I could feel my heart pounding.

"Okay, I'll tell you something else you don't know. After all the shit went down in Baluchistan, a bunch of us got out, including Abraham. And he took a hell of a lot of money with him; that fucker had money stashed away in banks around the world, lots of money. He made arrangements to keep in touch with us—you know, anonymous addresses, money drops. That's how I know about London. That was the last job I did for him." He caught himself. "I'm not sure what our deal is here, so—"

"—Why are you telling me this now? Has he contacted you to do something?"

"No, nothing like that," Rick sneered. "If he had, I'd be off doing it and getting rich rather than sitting in this shithole talking to you." He laughed at his own humor.

"I'll tell you what got me going. I saw a story on that vid-screen they keep running in here. They've got that goddamn thing going all day long, talking about the big celebration coming up for the U.N. tomorrow. They even had a picture of you with your name under it. I thought, Jesus, is that the same little pissant—no offense, doll—that I knew when she was a kid?"

"And then it finally hit me: if Abraham wanted to blow up that little celebration in London, he sure as hell wouldn't miss the opportunity to blow up this thing you have planned. I thought ahh . . . my little Julia, my sweet little Julia. She's probably shitting her pants right now trying to figure out how to stop him."

"So what are you giving me, other than a lot of talk?"

"What do you want?"

"For starters, how do you get in contact with him?"

"I don't," Rick said. "He always got in contact with me, same with the others."

I wanted the bank accounts; I wanted contact numbers; I wanted names.

"Whoa, hold on," Rick said. "I'm not sure if I can get you all that."

"When was the last time you saw him?"

Rick said he wasn't sure.

"There was an older guy, gray hair, beard, well-dressed. He was hanging around the edges of that celebration in London. I don't know if it was him or not. But I thought to myself: that might be what he'd look like twenty years later. But I haven't seen him—I mean *really* seen him—since the whole thing blew up in Baluchistan."

I sensed it slipping away. I needed something more from him.

"Tell me about him. What was he like? What were his habits?"

"Well, he's a crazy son of a bitch, I can tell you that. He was constantly making grandiose statements, quoting the Bible, you know, shit like that. He was an explosives nut. He was always experimenting with electrical devices, planning to blow things up. He had his whole compound wired; he could have sent it sky high, if he wanted to. He moved his guards around a lot, shifting assignments. Sometimes I'd be guarding him, and then I'd be moved around. He was paranoid about people getting near him."

"I need more, Rick. Does he have any scars or anything like that?"

"Shit, it's been a long time. Let me think. Yeah, yeah, I remember now. I remember thinking about that when I saw the old guy in London. I thought I wouldn't be able to really tell if it was him because his beard might be covering that scar. Abraham had a scar right here." Rick drew a line with his finger down his right cheek.

My body felt the excitement before my mind caught up with it: I'd seen that gesture before. Where? And then it clicked: Jewel Murphy. And then another piece clicked into place right behind it.

"He wore something around his neck, Rick, what was it?" I tried to keep the excitement out of my voice.

Rick looked confused, and then he remembered. "Oh yeah, I know what you're talking about." Then he stopped and looked at me. "But how did you know about that?"

"Don't worry about it, Rick. Just tell me what it was."

"Okay, okay. I remember he went into a fit once about something that had been ripped off his neck. He had some nice little piece of ass in his room—"

"Just tell me, Rick."

"Anyway, she must have ripped it off his neck and thrown it across the room. When he couldn't find it, he went into a rage and called in all the guards to pull everything apart. I'm the one who actually found it."

"What was it?"

"I don't know; it looked like some kind of war medal. There was a design on it. It seemed kind of crazy. I think it was something about Iraq."

I jumped out of my chair and ran towards the door.

"Hey, wait a minute," Rick said. "What about our deal?"

"You'll hear from me," I shouted back at him from the hallway.

Jesse is Abraham; Abraham is Jesse. Oh, my god.

MONDAY, MAY 4, 2082

NEW YORK CITY

JULIA

IT WAS DARK outside my office window. It was the time of night when anyone with any sense had gone home. Central Park was like a black forest hemmed in by the lights from the buildings on the other side of the park. The U.N. building was dark too. I'd called Avram and told him to have his team in the building by 5:00 A.M. But at the moment it was 3:20 A.M., and there was no one on my floor except Teki and me. He was doing a good job of fetching the documents and arranging the hookups I needed. But a robot doesn't provide much companionship at that time of night.

I'd called Dhanye about 1:30 A.M. and told her I'd be working all night. She listened quietly while I told her what I had found out from Rick.

I could see the tears forming in the corners of her eyes.

"I feel terrible about this," she said. "It's making you so sad."

"I don't have time to be sad. But when it's over, I'm planning to be really depressed."

"Please don't talk like that," Dhanye said. "Don't let it eat at you."

"You don't think I should be upset? I've just found out my grand-father not only killed *my* grandmother but *your* grandmother as well. That's not even counting all the others he's killed. Most people have him on their list of the world's worst murderers."

"Julia, that's not your fault."

"Violence goes back at least four generations in my family, and I'm not so sure I'm immune to it myself."

"What do you want me to say, that you're a terrible person?" The tears were flowing now. "I'm not going to do it. I love you, no matter what."

"I'm sorry. This whole thing has me rattled. I sometimes wonder what I'm passing along to our baby."

"Our baby is going to be raised in a nurturing environment. That will make all the difference. Please trust me. Trust *us*."

"Would it do any good if I asked you to skip the celebration to-morrow?"

"You know I can't do that. I'm giving the presentation on behalf of all of the families of the thirteen women. I'd be letting everyone down."

I nodded. I knew that would be the answer.

"Julia, I love you."

"I love you too."

She suddenly burst out, "Please be careful!"

IT ALL MATCHED: temper, movements, and misogyny—especially the misogyny: Abraham and Jesse were both real woman haters. The scar was crucial. Rick had used the same finger motion on the same cheek when describing Abraham's scar as Jewel had when describing Jesse's. And the medal. Could two people both be obsessed with the same medal from the same war? No, Jesse was Abraham, and Abraham was Jesse. Should I have figured it out sooner? Maybe, but I didn't have time to berate myself. I still had to find him, and I only had a few hours to do it. This morning's dedication ceremony was getting closer by the minute.

I tapped the desk impatiently, waiting for the identity program to complete its search of a worldwide network of computers. I'd stopped searching for Jesse almost two years earlier, right after resigning my army commission. It was an obsession, I'd told myself at the time. It was a symptom of a residual anger that was warping my life and shutting me off from others. But now I needed that computer program again—desperately.

I checked the locations I'd marked months ago for Jesse and compared them with what I knew about Abraham's movements. They matched. The fingerprints in the men's room of Victoria Station in London could easily have been left there by Abraham; the timing was right. Rick wasn't imagining things when he thought he saw him at the attempted bombing in Hyde Park. The DNA in the hotel elevator in Washington, D.C., also fit the time frame. He might very well have been in Washington when the fire broke out at the U.N. office. Clearly, it wasn't an accident; it was arson.

The light on the screen signaled that the update on the identity program was complete. I dove into the data, hoping to find something.

I found it. There was an investigation of a mugging in New York City almost two years prior. The data gathered at the scene of the crime included a complete set of Jesse's fingerprints. How did that happen? I wondered. I checked the location, and my nerves started to tingle: it was a large apartment house on Third Avenue, less than twenty blocks from the new U.N. building. I checked the clock: it was 4:58 A.M. I raced out the door.

THE DESK SERGEANT shook his head slowly and repeated what he had just said. "Ma'am, it's 5:20 A.M. I can't put my hands on the file you want right now. I told you that when you were on your vid-phone running over here."

"It's an emergency and—"

He put up his hands to stop me. "I see your credentials, and I'll take your word that it's important. But the report you're looking for isn't in our main database. It may have been in some extraneous notes that the officer wrote down. If it's in another file somewhere, there's an officer who can find it for you. But she isn't due until 8:00."

"Can you get her in here sooner?"

He got a sour look on his face.

"Please. It could be a matter of life and death."

He raised his hands defensively. "Okay. Okay."

As he made the call, I retreated to one of the benches near the counter. What next? My first impulse was to race down to the apartment building where the prints had been found. But what would I do then, run down the halls pounding on doors? As tantalizing as this information was, it could lead nowhere. I was sure we were dealing with Abraham, but that didn't tell me anything more about how the attack would occur.

I'd taken a look at the apartment building on a promotional vidscreen, and I wasn't happy with what I saw. It appeared to have many luxury apartments, but it wasn't a doorman-controlled building. It had three entrances and a few small businesses on the main floor and mezzanine. That meant that lots of people could have gone through the lobby. When Jesse left those prints on the wall, was he a tenant, a guest, a customer, or what? I hoped the police report would give me something more. In the meantime, I had to follow all the possibilities.

I CALLED AVRAM and told him what I knew. "We need to find as many names as we can of the tenants in the building," I said, "using reverse directories, tax records, anything. Find the management company. Call me the minute you have something."

The desk sergeant said he had reached Sergeant Alvarez and that she would try to make it down there by 6:45 A.M.

Fifteen minutes later Avram called back.

"Here's the story on the businesses in the building. There's an upscale convenience store run by a family from Nigeria. As far as I can see from the records, there's nobody involved with it that fits the profile we're looking for."

He described the other businesses on the main floor. One was a small payroll management company owned by a young couple from Guatemala. There was also a chain pharmacy on the corner that was undergoing renovation. There was a second-floor business that had gone bankrupt about six months prior; it was apparently an art dealership owned by two women. The building-management company was in Brooklyn, but nobody was in the office yet. The answering service just passed on messages. The people at the answering service didn't know anything about the building. They claimed they didn't even have an emergency number for the on-site building manager.

The information was frustrating. We knew a little bit more than we did before, but we were still nowhere. Jesse probably wasn't involved with any of those businesses, but he could have been a one-time customer or someone just passing through. My head was sending me noises; fatigue was knocking at the door, but I just had to fight through it. Minutes later, a woman identifying herself as Sergeant Alvarez walked into the precinct. I told her what I was looking for, and she nodded. "I'll see if I can find it."

Ten minutes later Sergeant Alvarez reappeared, holding a file in her hand. I scanned it quickly, hoping, hoping, hoping . . . Then I found something. I looked back to the cover to see who had written the report. "Is Sergeant Jody Kravitz available? It looks like she's the one who did the investigation and wrote the report."

Alvarez shook her head no. Kravitz had quit the force six months ago.

"Do you know anything about this paragraph?" I turned the folder over to show her what I meant.

While we were investigating the crime scene, an older white man broke through the police tape and attempted to walk through the site of our investigation. When I stopped him, he became belligerent and said that he lived in the building. He tried again to get past me, so I disabled him with an arm-hold and forced him to lean against the wall while I frisked him for weapons. Since he was clean, I let him go with a warning.

"Oh, that guy. Jody mentioned him later," Alvarez said. "I guess his prints showed up in the file with everything else."

"Did she get his name?"

"No, not unless it's in the report." Alvarez laughed. "She didn't really say much, only that he was an arrogant old bastard who tried to push her around. She said she was tempted to run him in just for being such a prick."

"SHOULD I MEET you at the building?" Avram asked.

"No, stay at the U.N. building; we need you on the scene." I was speaking in short gasps, trying to talk while running. The apartment building was still several blocks away.

Avram said he and his staff had reached the management company. There were forty residential tenants in the building. Thirty-three of them rented apartments under their own names; they were checking those names now, but so far none of them had any sort of criminal record. They'd found fingerprint records for about half of them, but none of them matched. None of them met the profile of the man we were looking for. But seven of the tenants were listed under corporate names, so the company didn't know who was really living there.

"Have you checked with the corporations?" I asked.

"We're doing that now," Avram said.

Five of them were big, public corporations that probably used the apartments for visitors. If Jesse was a guest in one of those apartments, I thought, we'd have a hell of a time finding him in a hurry. On the other hand, it was unlikely that he was living the life of a traveling corporate bureaucrat.

The last two apartments, numbers 431 and 527, were rented under the names of small corporations with no listed phone numbers.

"The management company seemed real nervous about those two," Avram said. "I got the feeling they were violating some city ordinance by not getting any personal information. But they said that both were good tenants that paid their rent on time. The tenant in #527 had been there at least five years."

I slowed down to catch my breath in front of the building.

"There's also an on-site manager in apartment 140. The management company thinks he'd know the names of the people in those apartments, but he wasn't there when they called him. I tried the number myself, and I got a video recording saying, 'I'm out with my little friends and will be back shortly.' I don't know what the hell that meant."

I told Avram I was going to try to get into those two apartments and asked him to send a police squad to the building. I raced into the lobby and headed for the elevator. It was computer operated, so it wouldn't move without an ID or a call-down from one of the apartments. I rang the manager's apartment at #140, but there was still no answer. I tried #431 and #527, but got no response from either one. When I checked the time, my heart leapt. The dedication ceremonies were starting in less than an hour; some of the guests would already be there.

I rang #427, picking the number closest to the apartment I wanted. The woman who picked up the call wanted to know who I was, and I made up a story that I didn't think anyone would believe. But the elevator started moving. At the fourth floor, I raced past the woman standing in the doorway of #427, and leaned on the bell outside #431.

"Is there something you want with those two boys?" the woman asked.

At that moment a young man answered the door wearing a towel around his waist. "Who are you?" he demanded.

"Who else lives here?"

"Who's there?" The voice came from a man in his fifties. He had stepped out of the bedroom wearing nothing but an open silk bathrobe, which he quickly tightened around himself. The young man at the door grew indignant; I made the quick decision to back away. I had to follow my instincts. This wasn't the apartment.

I RACED UP to apartment #527. There was no answer to the bell, and I thought of forcing the door. But as I tapped around it and checked the frame, I realized that it had been reinforced with metal. There was no way I could bust through a door like that without special equipment.

And if I was right about who lived in that apartment, the door might be booby-trapped.

I WAS SUDDENLY drained of energy, and my body demanded that I get off my feet. I slid down to the floor opposite the apartment door and just stared at it. Was the answer inside? Maybe. Maybe not. Certainly Abraham wasn't there at the moment. Is this how it will end, I wondered, with me staring at a door while the whole world goes to hell?

I had to think. I knew I was missing something important, something just beyond my grasp. I went back in my mind and started over. I raced through the whole security checklist: building sweeps, identity badges, security bubbles, flyovers, entrance security—all of it. Where was the mistake? When we had gone over the list a few days ago, we were convinced no one could get in. A ping of awareness—I repeated the idea: no one can get in. Abraham can't get in. Of course he can't.

He's already in.

I leapt to my feet and started racing towards the elevator. He's already in! The thought was screaming through my mind. What did the management company say about the tenant in #527? He'd been there at least five years. He'd been living here, just a few blocks away, plotting his next move, planning his revenge against a world that had refused to collapse after his last act of terror. Who? Who? Who had the easiest way to get in?

I banged several times on the elevator button, finally realizing that it wasn't responding. I looked for the stairwell and started racing down the stairs two at a time. I had an idea, and I matched it against some faces—that must be it! I reached Avram on his vid-phone, blurting out instructions as I ran down the stairs.

"I need you to check the contractors who worked on the Washington, D.C., building, the one that burned down, and match it with the current list. Hurry!"

By the time I reached the ground floor, Avram was back on the line. There was only one name on both lists; it was the one I thought it would be. I burst out of the stairway door and found myself in a tangle of leashes. Five dogs were trying to move in separate directions, each of them tugging on the man holding them.

"Be careful," he shouted. "Don't hurt my little friends. I'm the manager here."

I extricated myself from the tangle.

"Who's in #527?" I shouted at him.

"No one, now," he said. "Mr. Fawkes lives there, but he's at the U.N. Building."

RUN; RUN AND TALK.

"Madeleine, we don't have much time. You have to clear the building now."

"Where are you, Julia? What are you talking about? The ceremony has just started, and it's going beautifully. Dhanye's getting ready to speak."

"No, you have to get out of there. Noah Fawkes is Abraham, and he's in the building. You said you'd trust me with your life. Now's the time to do it."

RUN; RUN AND THINK.

How could we have missed it? He was rubbing our noses in it, daring us to catch him. The name: Noah—the man with the flood. The name: Fawkes—Guy Fawkes, the man who had tried to blow up the House of Parliament.

RUN; RUN AND TALK.

"Avram, you've got to find Noah Fawkes and stop him—no matter what," I gasped. "He's the one we want. I'm racing over there as fast as I can, but I may not get there in time."

"I'm looking at his whereabouts from his electronic badge," Avram said, "but it isn't moving or showing any feedback."

"He must have taken it off. He probably figured out a way to deactivate it. He could be anywhere in the building," I said. "Get everyone looking for him."

Run; run and talk.

"We need all the emergency and fire vehicles that you have available dispatched to the U.N. building immediately."

"Is there a fire going on right now? Are there casualties at the moment?"

"No, but there will be if you don't hurry."

"We can't—"

"Yes, you can! This is an official request. If it goes wrong, you can blame me."

Run; run and think.

An electrical contractor, the perfect cover: what could be better? Jewel said he liked to play with wires and explosive devices. Rick said he'd rigged his own compound with explosives. He'd been planning something like this for years. A big benefactor. Of course: get on the inside, schmooze with everyone. Wasn't the May 4th Foundation his idea? He had created a new persona, one that was old, gray, bearded, and distinguished. And rich. According to Kolle, he was worth at least five hundred million dollars. He knew no one would look at him too carefully.

I turned the corner on Fifth Avenue and ran for the building entrance. Guests were hurrying out the door. Madeleine would have been in the rotunda an hour or so earlier, greeting them and welcoming them to their seats, but now they were being unceremoniously ushered out. At that moment, a quartet of NYFD fire trucks appeared in front, and firefighters began pushing their way into the building, shoving aside the crowd of people. "Where's the fire?" people were asking. No one had seen a fire.

I squeezed my way through the crowd until I was able to get out of the main corridor and then on to a small stairway that led to the second floor. Once there, I was on a balcony that ringed the huge open space on the ground floor. I raced towards the back of the building, shouting into my vid-phone.

"Have you found him yet?"

"I think we know where he is," Avram replied. "Someone saw him a few minutes ago, heading up to the electrical room on the third floor."

"I'll meet you there."

I looked back over the edge of the balcony as I ran, trying to sense the progress of the evacuation. The fire warning was still ringing. Many had already been ushered through the doors, but there were still more people on the main floor. I couldn't tell how many. Keep moving, I exhorted them inwardly; please keep moving towards the door.

I reached the back stairway and was about to head up to the next floor, when I was rocked forward. A large explosion reverberated around the room, planting a hot gust of air against the back of my neck. As I turned, I saw the huge chandelier explode into flames. It detached itself from the ceiling and plummeted towards the floor, landing in a circle of fire nearly fifty meters in diameter. Flames spread in every direction. The only thing visible in the middle of the fire was Laria Kwon's huge bronze sculpture of the Thirteen, glowing in the flaming light.

I wanted badly to race down to the main floor to help with the rescue. Was anyone still under the chandelier when it had fallen? I wasn't sure. A few minutes earlier the political and cultural leaders of the world had been standing in that spot—writers and diplomats, spiritual leaders and legislators, presidents and poets—Madeleine—Dhanye.

I forced myself to move on. The firefighters were already on the main floor, spraying the fire with huge streams of water. The screams and cries had died down; the rescue teams were now in the building. There wasn't much I could do to help them. But there was something I could do up here.

By the time I reached the third floor, all of the main lighting was out. Was it a casualty of the electrical fire, or had Fawkes planned it that way? There were two small, dull glows from the lights over the emergency doors at either end of the hall, but the hallway was in shadows. The siren on the main floor had now been turned off. I could still hear the sounds of the firefighters downstairs as they struggled to get the blaze under control. I heard other sounds from the floors above: the security teams were going from room to room, yelling to each other as certain areas were cleared. But there was no noise at all on the third floor. If there was an alarm on this floor, it had been disabled; if there were people here, they'd left. I walked down the hall until I stood opposite the electrical control room. It looked quiet—too quiet.

"Where are you?" I asked softly into my vid-phone.

"We're all on the fourth and fifth floors," Avram said. "My teams say they've cleared everything below."

"I'm not so sure. Come down and meet me on the third floor."

I stepped through the opening into the electrical room, moving softly around the perimeter, waiting for Avram and the others. This was the place; I was sure of it. Once Fawkes had heard the fire alarm—once he knew that the timer on his fire bomb would be too late—he would have raced up here to throw the switch by hand.

I wanted to find him—Jesse—Abraham—Noah. But what would I do if I did? I wasn't sure. I was unarmed. It was a personal decision I'd made over a year ago, and it wouldn't do any good to debate the merits of it now. It was just a fact.

You little pussy.
You're afraid . . . you think it didn't work, and now you're hiding.
Do you think they won't find you?
There's someone out there right now, and she's coming to get you.

I scanned the darkened room, looking at the control panels and the counter that ran along the wall. Which one held the switch that he'd used to set the chandelier aflame and plummeting towards the floor? I was sure it was one of them. There was a small counter sitting in the middle of the room; it was an odd place for it. Then I realized that it fit into an opening in the larger counter around the perimeter. Had it just been pulled out? I looked closer at the wall behind the gap and saw why: there was the faint outline of a door in the wall.

A closet—of course. I remembered what Jewel Murphy had told me, and I knew this was where he would be hiding.

I inched backwards toward the door leading to the main hallway, keeping an eye on the closet door. There was a sudden noise. I froze. My foot had hit what sounded like a coffee cup that was lying on the floor, causing it to roll over until it hit the center table. In the darkened room, it sounded like a thunderclap.

The closet door burst open, and he suddenly emerged. As he walked slowly towards me, I retreated. He held a pistol pointed at my chest.

As I tried to fight back my fear, a question kept pushing at me: who was behind those eyes? It didn't seem to be Jesse, the tough-looking thug, or Abraham, the cocky guerilla leader. It wasn't even Noah, the aloof benefactor. There was something else there, something that had detached itself from any of his personalities. His hair was awry, and his facial movements were jumpy. He had the unsteady walk of an old man, but the lost look of a little boy. He twitched, reacting to imaginary sights and noises around him. Anger and fear seemed locked in a struggle inside his head. But none of that gave me any reason for hope: he was volatile, dangerous, and unhinged.

"It's over downstairs, you know that. The people all got away in time." As I said it, I hoped it was true. "You should lay down your weapon and come with me."

The look on his face got more agitated

"I'm unarmed. Are you going to shoot me?" I waited to see what his reaction would be. It was hard to read.

"You've killed a lot of people, but the only time you stood face to face and shot anyone was when you were a little boy and killed your mother. Isn't that right?"

That got through to him; I saw it in his facial movements. Would it make him more or less likely to shoot? I didn't know. I just had to keep talking.

"But you were just acting on impulse then, weren't you? You didn't actually plan to shoot her. With me, it would be different. You would have to look me in the eye and shoot me. That's different, isn't it?"

He moved towards me. I stepped back.

"When you did that as a little boy, you'd been psychologically abused."

His eyes glared again. I stepped back further.

"I know what happened. I've seen the reports. You were beaten up, locked up, and abused. I know your father used to taunt you."

"Shut up," he roared.

I stepped back a little further. He was at a breaking point.

"I've seen the videotape. Do you remember the camera, the one sitting over the crib? I saw what happened. You didn't really intend to kill my grandmother, did you?"

Grandmother? That got him. I could see it in his eyes; he suddenly wanted to know more. How did this woman know these things? Feed his curiosity, I told myself.

"You didn't know that was my grandmother, did you? And how about the girl in the crib? How about little Amy? Do you remember her? Did you ever think she would grow up and have a child?"

He was incredulous. He was debating whether to shoot me and end all this, but for the moment he hesitated. He wanted to know more.

"She did have a child. It was me. You're looking at your grand-daughter."

His arm holding the pistol made a sudden movement upward, like he was preparing to fire. Then it twitched; I could see fear and anger alternating in his eyes. He held his arm in mid-position and stared at me. Then he slowly started to lower it. Lower it more, I whispered to myself. Lower it. Then he stopped. Was he going to change his mind? Had he decided to fire?

There was a sharp crack.

He looked down at his chest in surprise. Blood was spurting in every direction. He dropped the gun, clasping himself as he fell to the floor. I raced forward and grabbed the gun, turning him over. He appeared to be dead.

AVRAM WAS STANDING in the doorway, his weapon in his outstretched hands in front of him. As he looked at me, he started shaking. Finally, he dropped the gun. I rushed over and put my arm around him.

"I've never killed anyone before," he said. "I didn't realize how awful it feels."

"You did what you had to do. He could have killed me."

"It feels terrible."

"I know that," I said. "Believe me, I know that."

We put in a call to the paramedics.

"We'll just have to leave him here. The others may need our help."

IT WAS OVER up here. What had happened downstairs?

EPILOGUE
SIX MONTHS LATER

OCTOBER, 2082

LARKSPUR, CALIFORNIA

THERE WERE circles within circles. Antonio and Lara asked me to be part of the innermost circle, and I said I would be honored to be there.

The breeze from Corte Madera Creek was blowing lightly. One wall of the community center had been opened up, allowing the circles of people to extend out into the garden in the warm evening air. Those in the outer circle formed a protective ring around the special plot of new flowers and vegetables that had been planted for the occasion. Inside, the lighting had been lowered so that the holographic images could appear in their own half-circle behind the others, allowing those who were far away to blend in with those who were there in person. Hovering behind them, illuminated against the inner walls, were the life-sized images of those who were there only in memory.

As was customary in their spiritual circle, the attendees wore plain white smocks. But some of them had added their own adornments. Rabbi Hershel from the Rebecca Meyer Center in New York, who was appearing in holographic form, had a light-colored Star of

David stitched on his smock. Several local attendees wore similar embroidered stars. Three of the members of the Green Gulch Monastery wore smocks with a symbolic saffron ribbing stitched around the top and the hem. Father John and Mother Margaret, co-pastors of the Conciliar Catholic Church in San Rafael, wore plain smocks with the soft outline of crosses stenciled across the chest.

My own smock had a special opening to accommodate the hungry mouth of the precious newborn who was sucking on my breast. The feeling was indescribable. Dhanye was standing next to Annabel in the circle behind me. They were both eyeing me with big smiles. I knew what they were thinking: how happy I must be that I'd taken their advice and joined the Co-Lactation Program with Dhanye.

The lights were lowered, and the soft sounds of a Bach Sonata filled the room and expanded out towards the water. Antonio and Lara invited members of the circles to hold hands. I had only one hand free, and I extended it to Li-Jin, who was holding the hand of her daughter, Deva, on the other side.

Those in the other circles joined hands as well: Annabel, Dhanye, Chloe, Flora, and Josh were in one group. Beyond them were Naomi, Paola, Bryan, Devon, and others from the community. Near the garden, a group of small children, who had formed their own circle, were asked to quiet down for a moment and join hands.

The holographic attendees were invited to participate as well, either by joining hands or simply standing quietly, if they were alone. I looked up and saw Madeleine in New York, who had reached out and was holding Avram's hand on one side and Omar's on the other. Indira and her husband were standing outside their home in Mumbai with their three children closed in tightly on either side of them. Moise and Selva were quietly holding hands in the garden outside our home in Tarrytown. Eloni was in Washington standing at her desk, smiling slightly. I couldn't be sure, but for the first time in all the years I'd known her, she seemed to have a tear in her eye.

Everyone felt the presence of the last circle. The images of those who were there in spirit floated over the wall, quietly illuminated in the soft light of the room, taking their rightful place in the life story we were there to celebrate. Lara had found a picture of Maya's mother, Rosa, in her mother's dresser; she had had it enhanced and placed next to the others. Next to it was the smiling face of Gabe, a man Maya often talked about but who had died before I was born.

There were others who were hovering on that wall, many of whom were part of my life story as well. My mother was there. Lara had decided to include a picture of her as a young teenager. Carlos was there too. We agreed that it had to be a picture in which his arm was wrapped around Maya. At my request, Raji had been added to the group. As the father of the child I was holding at that moment, he seemed to belong there. Maya had never known him. But if she had, she would have smothered him with love. I stifled a tear for a second, muttering a silent prayer to all of them.

The Women for Peace were there as well, in the fullness of life. Rasa was shown talking somewhere at a rally. Yoko was listening intently to somebody at a meeting. Rebecca, Magdalena, and Maria were shown on a panel, addressing a large gathering in Paris. Franca, Marta, and Gabriella were seen marching arm in arm through the streets of Buenos Aires, surrounded by a sea of marchers carrying placards. Wang-Li was serving in a food line, ladling out soup to an old man; Aayan was sitting on the floor, reading a story to group of children. Annette and Melinda were huddled over a table in a Colombian village, talking to several teenagers. Deva was sitting quietly, smiling at something—or perhaps someone—just beyond the camera.

Lara began.

"Whenever God opens her heart to the world and shares with us the life of an extraordinary person, we know we have been blessed.

"We're here to remember one who loved deeply and who was deeply loved in return. My mother made an extraordinary journey across the human heart and touched many, many people along the way.

"We ask the spirit of Maya—and of all those who have loved her and gone before her—to join us in this moment."

A FEW DAYS earlier, we had stood in the garden.

"Maya, would you like to walk down by the water?"

"Oh, I'd love that. You know the bench is still my favorite place to sit." She turned to Dhanye. "Julia and I used to go there when she was a little girl."

Maya moved slowly with her walker. I was alarmed at how frail she had become since the last time I'd seen her. But it was a warm, beautiful day, and I was determined not to let it bother me. We could take our time walking unless something happened to change things. And that something could happen at any minute: it was Dhanye's due date, and she could go into labor at a moment's notice.

"Maya, you know we're about due to have the baby," I told her.

"Look at you," Maya said, pointing at Dhanye's tummy. "Is it a girl or a boy?"

"We don't know," Dhanye said.

"You don't?" Maya seemed astonished.

"That was my decision, Maya. I think I want to be surprised."

Maya reached the bench and sat down. She gave a sigh of delight, as I moved her walker out of the way. "I'm so happy to be here."

"It's good for us to be here with you." We sat on the other bench facing her.

"Antonio told me about the wonderful thing you did. I haven't watched the news-screens very much in the last few months." She turned towards Dhanye. "Maybe I should ask you, because Julia's always too modest. Antonio says she saved the world leaders from being burned to death, is that true?"

"It is, Maya. We're all so proud of her."

Maya turned back. "And Julia, what do you say?"

"I think they're exaggerating a little bit."

Maya waved her hand and scoffed. "Oh, I knew you'd say that."

"Were you able to see any of the ceremony?" Dhanye asked.

"You mean the one in the park?"

"Yes. They moved Laria Kwon's sculpture out to the middle of

Central Park. We had a beautiful ceremony out there two weeks later, while the building was being repaired. Somehow it was even better outdoors."

"It was beautiful," Maya said. "I didn't realize it was you that was speaking until Lara pointed that out to me. It was very moving. Your grandmother and the others would be so proud of you."

MAYA FELT A *pain spreading through her head; it grabbed her before she realized what was happening. It was more intense than anything she had ever felt before, and for a moment she thought she couldn't bear it. But suddenly the pain gave way and was replaced by a bright light.*

At first, the light seemed to blind her, but somehow it changed and moved, letting her see more clearly. It gradually subsided, but it never went away completely. The light stayed with her, shimmering in many hues, bathing everything around her in a soft glow.

How wonderful!

Carlos, can you believe how wonderful this is?

That's our Julia with her beautiful Dhanye. She gave Carlos a soft pat on his leg, and he put his arm around her.

Deva, do you see what I'm seeing?

Yes. Isn't it extraordinary? I'm so happy to be here with you.

Our great-grandchild is about to be born. Can you believe how fortunate we are?

It's a moment I've always wanted to share with you.

They don't even know whether it's a girl or a boy.

But it doesn't make any difference, does it?

No, it really doesn't.

It's the most beautiful thing in the world.

I think this calls for one more kiss.

"JULIA?"

Dhanye sat down next to me and laid her head on my shoulder. I was so numb I found it hard to do more than just pat her on the leg

"Julia, it's beginning."

I hadn't moved since the emergency vehicles left. I'd probably been sitting there close to an hour, mostly just crying. Earlier, our little pathway by the water had been filled with people and equipment working furiously to save Maya's life. Doctors issued frantic orders over the vid-screen, which medical technicians rushed to carry out. But it was no use: I knew what had happened the minute I saw her slump over on the bench.

I just needed to sit there for a while. With Maya gone, a big piece of the ground that held me up was gone.

"Julia, I'm so sorry to do this to you now, but it's beginning."

I suddenly realized what she was saying. "Do you mean—"

"Yes, sweetheart," Dhanye said. "I'm beginning to have contractions." She was starting to get a little teary-eyed. "I know this couldn't happen at a worse time."

I stared at her for a second and then dropped my gaze. I was almost afraid to look at her. Dhanye must be so worried, I thought. Then something woke up inside me. I felt almost ashamed that I hadn't realized it all along. Dhanye wasn't worried about having the baby. She was worried about me.

How would I react? Would I be there for her, or would I be off chasing the ghosts from the past? I couldn't let myself be like that again. Suddenly, everything Maya had tried to teach me came rushing back: *There's someone out there who is going to love you deeply—you have to be ready with an open heart.*

I looked up and saw Dhanye's eyes. The love I could see at that moment was pouring through me.

"No, it's not the wrong time at all," I said. "This is a wonderful time for our baby to be born. If I know Maya, she probably wanted it this way."

I helped Dhanye from the bench. "Come with me, sweetheart. Something beautiful is about to happen."

ACKNOWLEDGMENTS

I owe thanks to a great many people who have encouraged me and worked with me in bringing *The Circle of Thirteen* to life.

Thanks to the team at Turner Publishing, including Mark Mandell, Laura Cusack, Lianna McMasters, Maxwell Roth, and Kym Whitley. A special thanks to Christina Roth, the editor who helped bring the book to completion; Diane Gedymin, who had the courage and vision to acquire the book; and Todd Bottorff, who I've decided is one of the smartest publishers in the business.

I owe thanks to a big group of people at Book Passage, our bookstore, for their help and enthusiasm. They include Calvin Crosby, Leslie Berkler, Luisa Smith, Sam Barry, and Kathryn Petrocelli (who also happens to be my daughter!). And a special thank you goes to Karen West, Book Passage events director, who kept me going on the book during a difficult period.

I received wonderful advice and support from Andy Ross, Carol Seajay, John Mutter, Jenn Risko, and Bridget Kinsella. Thanks also to Susan Griffin, who helped edit the book in its early stages, and to Elaine Markson, who gave the book an early push at a time when I needed it. And I also owe a huge debt of thanks to Carl Lennertz, who spent a great deal of time editing the book and giving me some wonderful publishing insight.

My agent, Lisa Gallagher, has been absolutely wonderful. If you have her as your agent (or friend), consider yourself lucky.

Finally, I can't say enough to thank my wife and muse, Elaine Petrocelli, who has believed in *The Circle of Thirteen* from the beginning. Without her love and inspiration, I would never have known that I could embark on such a journey.

William Petrocelli is co-owner, with his wife Elaine, of the Book Passage bookstores in Northern California. He is the author of *Low Profile: How to Avoid the Privacy Invaders* and *Sexual Harassment on the Job: What It Is and How to Stop It*. A former Deputy Attorney General and former poverty lawyer in Oakland, Petrocelli has been a long-time advocate for women's rights. *The Circle of Thirteen* is his first novel.